DESIRE LINE

Gee Williams

Gee Williams was born and brought up in North Wales and now lives in Cheshire with her husband. A widely-published poet and a dramatist as well as writer of fiction, her work has appeared in disparate places: from *The Sunday Times* to *The Pan Book of Horror*. Many of her scripts have been broadcast by BBC Radio 4. She has won both The Rhys Davies and The Book Pl@ce Contemporary Short Story Awards, was Poetry Review's New Poet, Summer '97, shortlisted for The Geoffrey Dearmer Award and (with Sol B. River) shortlisted for the Race in the Media Radio Drama Award 2001. Pure Gold Fiction Award 2008. Her first novel *Salvage* was shortlisted for the James Tait Black Memorial Fiction Prize 2008, her short story collections *Blood etc.* and *A Girl's Arm* were shortlisted for Wales Book of the Year in 2009 and 2013.

http://www.geewilliams.info/

DESIRE LINE

Gee Williams

Parthian, Cardigan SA43 1ED
www.parthianbooks.com
First published in 2015
© Gee Williams 2015
ISBN 978-1-910409-64-0
Editor: Susie Wild
Cover design by Robert Harries
Typeset by Elaine Sharples
Printed and bound by Gomer Press, Llandysul, Wales
Published with the financial support of the Welsh Books Council
British Library Cataloguing in Publication Data
A cataloguing record for this book is available from the British
Library.

For David

and in memory of my cousin Bel

I

Water

As I said to Alfred Hitchcock only yesterday, we'd had warnings.

Just down the coast for example, one February, the gulls found they weren't making progress through rain like a bath's overflow. Suddenly the high tidemark's out of date, the seawall's breached and nondescript village Towyn gets famous for a day. Plenty of images are around if you want the miserythrill of people dragging possessions in wheelie bins, parked cars sunk to the doorhandles, havoc by the containerload. Good browsing if you're the one behind the camera and not in front. After this hint, both we and our neighbour Prestatyn caught it in subsequent years and someone had a go at calculating what it would take to put our community in *real* danger. Answer? Depression over Iceland. Anticyclone beyond the Azores. Then onshore breezes at seventy-five knots should be enough to turn a spring tide hitting the north Wales coast into a surge, a two- to three- metre wave. It doesn't sound much. Except there's a saying around here – *never* buy a bungalow called Sea View. Which could be a line from one of your films, I tell AH. No answer.

Even so, it was the start of April, meaning a foul winter should be behind us.

I remember the night before it happened, a newish moon hung level with the roof ridges, ignored by most of Rhyl, myself included. With my background, I have to be alert to signs and

1

was wrong about this one. When I did go outside around eight into the small yard my kitchen opens onto (with my recycling because I'd cooked and can't rest till I've cleared away), my only thoughts were

1. that sharp crescent stuck in a neighbour's birch tree is *very* bright and

2. it could be one of 'A Hundred Lunar Aspects' by the great Japanese printmaker*—?

I hammered a tofu pouch flat and tried to pin down who. Unsuccessfully. (Yori? Could he be called Yori, like me?). Refused to stop and check. It would be the last time I saw that composition anyway— it was going to be the last time for a lot of things— but the eddies of air trapped between the walls were strong and cold and my other excuse is I was preoccupied talking to Tess. Her work station at Forward Rhyl is near mine so I'm constantly aware of her. After hours? We're into a different language, juicy as Italian. My throat constricts just vocalising her name, followed by the obvious male response. Perfect Tess-ss. A sea sound though she lives 'backaway' as she calls her patch of inland sprawl where Rhyl peters out. Whenever she smiles I think, who does she most look like just now? Sometimes it's the new Casino Pigalle presenter up on all the lightboards along the front, Cassie of the wannaplay fingers and the wantmynumber smile. But usually I stick to (star of *Unfaithfully Yours*, not one of the Master's) the stunning, tragic Linda Darnell. A brunette, she could never be first choice as a Hitchcock babe but she's a regular on my playlist that includes every classy film noir from the last century. From *The Maltese Falcon*, say, to *Chinatown* with, sandwiched between them, the Big Hitch's Catalogue.

---

*I was being reminded of Tsukioka Yoshitoshi. Like AH, his art trades on his eye for natural wonders – including attractive women – and an obsession with graphic violence. I'd recommend you start at 'Twenty-eight Famous Murders with Verse'.

Your loss, I tell him still bashing the tofu pouch and trying to avoid its drip. Should've given Linda a screen test, round about when *UY* was just made and Linda was twenty-five and flawless. Like Tess. But the wind was turning wicked, not that it registered with Tess of course, who was kidding me now, I wonder what you gonna do next? Because she knew. Work.

Work.

From its cramped quarters on the main drag, Forward Rhyl's just the latest under-funded renewal scheme to take a shot at this Victorian gem of a resort. *Many* failures lie in the past, stations along an unstoppable decline that got going c.1970 with the collapse of the Great British Seaside Holiday. Result? Everybody knows the playground song* from round about then, when the functional and the fancy went the same way as anything 'period', leaving us a beauty (the smooth arc of coast) with a scalded face. On Rhyl streets you could make a catalogue – everybody's got their own – of architectural atrocities. But I believe in the built environment. Why else return to my birthplace after years down in Oxford, then Bristol, both fine cities? Because of an obsession that can seem like fantasy but othertimes a credible plan, depending on my week, to Put Rhyl Back. It's worth doing. It was a fine location once. That's why I had all the pen-and-inks tacked up throughout the flat, postcards to myself from Rhyl Present snatched during 'leisure'. Usually drawings only suggest the volumes they hold but these, made using my Japanese father's technique, weren't bad. And grouped together, what most people find dismal become prompts. 'Frontage Of Lost Building, Sussex Street' or 'Pepperpot Lookout, East Parade' aren't relics. They're clues to our potential. Yes, I use the technology. But I'd worshipped it as a student long enough to know it saves time not mistakes – while

---

* Come, come to Sunny Rhyl/ The sea's half piss and the food's pigswill./ We got no pier, we got no cheer./ All we got is sand and beer.

a sketch from life gives ownership. Of this, for example, a derelict commercial block that looked to be eating the artisan's cottage stuck to one end. With my own drawings set out, right down to the smashed windows and the seahorse doorknocker (stolen next day after somebody saw me getting interested), I called up the pic from the database *WR/2042* of *Quay Street Area*, possibly our top eyesore. And that's up against major-league competition.

I shared the on-screen action with Tess as the warehouse is demolished and the cottage roof soars. Then I retile it before gentling the pitch five degrees to a vulture cloaking its prey. Excellent! The temptation was to rotate the whole site through a right angle, turn the Quay Street/West Parade corner and carry on towards the centre, making a new town for her as I went. Andrea Palladio and Christopher Wren would give an eye each for the power I had here on a scarred desk top in a Rhyl backwater.

—Oo, go on then, she conceded. It's bed for me anyhow. Just have a think what you're missing. (I obliged – forget the movie star, forget Cassie Pigalle of the pleaseupyourstake wink, Tess is three-dimensional and made of ivory, slim-shouldered, long-legged, hair the colour of bronze, a totally *Art Deco object*.) Bye Yori!

She must like my name as well, judging by how much she used it. Yori – another gift from my Japanese father. The closest in English is *highly-motivated* or maybe just *dutiful*? I prefer the first. And try to remember both when you hear the bad news about me.

I said I'd see her tomorrow— and here we go already with my first step over the charcoal line that marks Easy Street from Sinister. (Alfred Hitchcock likes nothing better, can't you see him over there in the corner licking his fat lips and rubbing his hands?)

Because I lied.

Chapter 1

Our event started towards midnight with a north-westerly thieving anything unstructural. Rhyl's flat and mainly lowrise, meaning not much would get in its way. Home being three rooms on the ground floor of a good brick house, all I could do was put my faith in the long-gone designer, an incomer called Thorp. Architect, inventor, engineer, his bizarre death alone (June 1914, from radiation sickness!) is worth a search. But at least he knew how things fitted together when he was alive. So lying on my back, able to trace the roof's flexion through each rafter all the way down to my own ceiling joists was fine by me. My earliest memories – I'd be three or four – were of the same sort of house, Rhyl's knee-deep in them. But this was at the Sorry End of town, the Quay Street end in fact, ROSEMONT in glazed terracotta above a rotten porch, Perspex taped into punched-out leaded glass. I learnt useful tips about buildings there, how you can put them on like a coat, feel out the seams as the slates get tested over your bedroom and the pendant on the landing sways—

I slid from under the quilt and sprinted upstairs to see if my landlord Libby Jenkinson who occupied the rest of the house was feeling nervy. A widow-more-than-once was how she introduced herself to me when I turned up to view, and Number 8 Gaiman Avenue is her only asset. 'I'm OK,' I could just about make out. She's an ex-smoker, her voice throaty, nearer a cough than speech. The next sentence didn't carry then she followed up with, 'I've known worse.' No point in shouting I bet she hadn't, that to me it was already starting to feel *pretty serious*. Either I was right or she was, but down in the hall again, with

5

my palms laid flat against an original front door, I could touch the growl.

Following Libby's brush-off, pride made me go back to bed. Several times I was tempted to shout up to her, Can we upgrade that to *more than pretty serious*? Actual damage was going on out there in a Force 7 – and rising. What was most vulnerable? The brain starts ticking them off, my Quay Street warehouse or that vandalised snookerhall right on the front? Another prime target would be the scaffolded hotel near multi-occupancy housing. Work stopped months ago and I'd sent alerts to Rhondda Jones at Borough about it but she hadn't even— when she should've at least— a surprise! I must've dozed off because suddenly I'm watching naked Tess cross a bedroom that's fantastically detailed, right from the architectural sketches pinned above her head down to the 'skull' in the walnut veneer of the wardrobe. Now— *now* she's indicating a constellation of small moles, my own recent discovery, she's just noticed across her left perfect breast— but dawn broke with Violent Storm Force 11. At first I resent how Tess is threatening to evaporate. Then I'm awake to an unbelievable racket even Libby wouldn't be claiming she'd known worse than.

Still groggy with afterimages, I opened the curtains. My single bed's lined up in a rectangular bay window so no effort. Parking's only allowed on the opposite side which means craning your neck gives nearly the whole avenue before curvature cuts off Number 57— and it's all present, so far, and empty how I like it. Built environment *good*, people *bad*. Without them the villas were ageless and reassuring, all in grey shades to my sense of vision since they faced north. More downstairs lights were on than usual though nothing much was up save flying bits and pieces— and this dull rolling noise from nowhere, from out of the air, it seemed, one of those non-mechanical dins that rises and falls with a beat you keep thinking you've mastered but haven't, and flatters you is about to run down anyway. Doesn't. And I might say *this is the moment*. I'm stalled at my window, tired but wired over setbacks out there in the town and then suddenly I get an intuition about deeper trouble, closer to home. I can even convince myself it happened. Yeah, Yori, you knew. Because a fitting to start this story would be right here. Right now.

Shiver.

Bring up music.

Yori's eyes narrow and he downs one pill and then a second that he's had concealed in his hand.

Cutaway to—

—but sorry to disappoint. I left my streetgazing to do stretches and lunges so the few kinks were soon out of a body in Grade A condition and if I couldn't stick with the rest of the routine, it was because my attention was on a regional bulletin we actually featured in for once. Through into the kitchen where I did take my morning meds but really I'd come in to zap soup while the power lasted. A degree under boiling's best for miso and since my father cooked for me in the early years and his flavours took root in my mouth, salt's my sugar which is why I always eat Japanese for choice and this wants just a drop of soy— I froze at the coastguard's update.

'It's breaking higher and higher up the seawall,' he bellowed like a sports commentator.

Another voice cut in with, 'the tide's still way off its peak. Across the River Clwyd, yes, we can get you that shot. Here it is! That's Beacon Point. You can see the dunes washing away.'

The Point's a bulbous nose of land that curls round and pokes into the rivermouth and is the harbour's only protection from where most weather came from. I couldn't not look. One local landmark that side of the town, the Blue Bridge, appeared on screen as usual a toy version of Sydney Harbour's. (Dorman

Lang built them both in the 1930s). Ours is in foam up to its belly now. The latticework once meant as homage to the next-door funfair is turquoise brash against a gutter ice sky, morning traffic at a crawl as Rhylites with jobs in better areas tried to get to them. But no one was risking the white footbridge just visible, edge of shot. Something to be grateful for.

Libby was stirring. She's very short but heavy. You know it. She came clomping down in her fleece suit, hair flat, blotched *mature* face with overnight creases. The smell of bed was on her that would've embarrassed me once— but I'm over it. 'What d'you reckon on the latest, love? Are we safe?' Then she was in. She lives to get inside. I maintain the place spotless and most of what's on show – a chesterfield with rows of dust-trap bellybuttons, a tub-chair I don't use, plus the unmatched items of wood furniture – are all her castoffs. I don't put her intrusions down to nostalgia. Libby's *never* described any rosy scenes from married life when she was able to spread out through the whole of Number 8. The opposite. One husband was 'always sodding off someplace', the next 'a bit of a whiner.'

'You mean from getting flooded? We're at least half a kilometre from, um—' Gaiman Avenue was uptown Rhyl in both senses. Hard as it is to believe this is where wealth used to holiday and its afterglow lingers in good houses along properly-laid roads. Hoping but not sure about the next bit I said, 'Yeah, should be safe enough.'

'There's good.' She scanned my walls but no new artwork was up for her to critic. She had to make do with wrinkling her nostrils at a soup breakfast. My theory is I was accepted as her tenant by getting mistaken for a Thai. Years ago she went to Bangkok on holiday using the first ex-husband's money, and fell in love with 'out there'. Which makes me an imposter – which of course I am. But further confessions would be out of place here. To be rid of her I gave up the last of my loaf.

Back in Rhyl mass departures were underway from both West and East Parades, also Sydenham Avenue, Marlborough, Osborne, Balmoral, Lake and North— and anywhere else in the beach vicinity. Most terraces actually fronting the sea were four storeys, some later apartment blocks more than that, but from the helicopter they seemed to have shrunk. It's hard to believe what you see when everything's familiar and yet a movie's showing. I was *That's the old Coliseum Theatre!* and *I walked across there yesterday.* Fascinated by a floating van about to hit the wall of BeltBusters I finally came to and got messaging the people from work that in theory I supervise. Unless contacted by Emergency Planning ♀ (and we all knew we wouldn't be since we were *not Borough*) they could take the day off ♂ I told them. Many systems were out already. Trying to speak to Tess would connect me with nothingness. And who else? Though this is my town, I'd been away for most of my twenty-nine years and back for less than a couple. There was nobody— which was fine, how I wanted it. I've edited down. The mutant growth of contacts made at university in Bristol – even at the time they felt like another person's – has been starved of updates. Particularly one ex-lover and fellow student, Kailash, now reduced to messaging from wherever her travels took her. It would make Libby mad with envy to see what she's sending. *Here's orchard road from floor 19 singapore savoy you SHIT! crappy where u r? hope you ☠ you* **ICON DELETED**! I get a glimpse, a nanosecond, of gleaming towers before the scene combusts. Still mad then, Kailash? I guess so. But it was for the best. You were a temptation, I admit, to a character like mine till Keep It Simple, I decided. Keep to the black outlines with space to fill in, life as a cleared site. A rented flat, a job, a movie library, some music. Tess, not up to Kailash's standard in many ways, understands this. And you're alive and well enough to insult me Kailash so stop whining like the second Mr Jenkinson. But I can't argue with **ICON DELETED**.

I don't reply.

Hindsight tells me someone I knew who'd left Rhyl, a man called Josh Meredith, deserved a tap. But riveted to here and now, I let the soup go straight to stomach untasted as the screen filled with action from Foryd Harbour, seaward of the bridge and the town's oldest feature. Now in jeopardy. The crumbling of Beacon Point's dunes and too much water in too tight a channel meant small moored boats were either disappearing upstream or already engulfed. The camera homed in on one, *The Cariad*. A slim pleasure craft that could take a sail, all elegant lines and minimal appendages on deck, I remembered seeing her at berth. Being primped by a surly owner whenever I took a walk that way. She was about to be turned to matchwood against the bridge piers though you almost expected a giant hand to reach down and fish her out. It didn't and her timbers splintered, shot up into the wind and fell across the tarmac to the sound of 'Wowee!' from the camera operator.

Those who had made it over the bridge wouldn't be coming back. At least it wasn't Tess's road in. Suddenly— *Yori?*

Tess! Where was she?

Where d'you think?

Spiky if she thought she was talking to her boss but jokey to a sexual partner. I said *OK,* instantly breathless, picturing her shiny-faced and definitely not in a fleece suit. Nude. Or in material her sparrow's frame would show through, it being her main attraction, that and the way she says I'm all toast-ty! as she does now. (She's more Welsh than you hear in town). Day off, eh? I wish we were— but her wish gets drowned out by Libby shouting, 'Fuckinghell!' above my head. Above her head the good grey slates must be grinding together like teeth. A dragon was touching down by the sound of it and about to swipe us with its tail—

So we got The Wave. But The Wave's not the thing. What it caused is the thing. And to be honest every meteorological blip on the earth's so well covered if you're watching them they'll blend. Towyn, that I described at the start, could easily be somewhere in France a decade on. It doesn't take many years to become a quiz question. 'Atlantic City or Rhyl? Ten seconds, team!' So not to make a drama of it, I survived. Obviously. But I want to say this. Don't credit any reports of panic. Buses loaded with families continued on inland. Exits blocked as entire fascia claddings and street furniture made landfall in the traffic and had to be dragged out. And Rhyl people stayed calm. Over fifteen hundred of them boarded vehicles of every sort and pulled back from the edge with their babies, gadgets and pet-carriers. See them. Not a work day anymore, a crowd had gathered on the promenade near the weak spot opposite Church Street, dead centre of our Victorian seafront. Through a gap between ruined shops and SuperWaterLazer, the esplanade was taking a pounding and cheers went up at every *Splat!* Until round eleven, forty minutes off high tide, when the sea broke in. It swept across the open expanse of the Events Arena and at one edge of this half-acre flat, pavers were loosened. As they lifted, the water became a tumbling trommel of brick and hard-core until the entire surface peeled back like orange skin. Round One to Water. Next came what Rhyl had wanted for decades. The hated ghost-hole of litter and tat, The Children's Village, derelict food concessions and rides, a perfect symbol of the That'll Do For Rhyl vernacular, was reduced to flinders. The Little People's Café raced Pirates' Den and a bright yellow roundabout to be mashed into a reef of wreckage three metres high and stretching right along the face of the old arcades.

A Wave hates everything, even its own. The Seaquarium's rear doors were stove in. At first the tubular viewing enclosures channelled a cataract straight through to spurt out the front entrance and, engineered against static pressure, the tunnels kept their integrity until flotsam arrived heavy and sharp enough to crack the toughened plastic. Then an entire marine collection, from sentient cuttlefish to blank-eyed dogfish, found itself heading inland.

Only SkyTower, our late-twentieth century 'attraction' bought from the city of Glasgow second-hand, stood. A 75-metre steel needle had a viewing cabin designed to go up and down like a doughnut on a stick, its sole claim to fame in Scotland being to make Diana, Princess of Wales, nauseous. Now looking a prime target. A corset of reinforcing rods gave rigidity but this was the Irish Sea at its base. Yet the needle stuck to its plinth on pilings sunk into the Triassic sandstone. Would they be enough? Eight bolts screwed into eight threaded sockets. Eight bolts each the height of a man. If you carried SkyTower's statistics in your head, suddenly it became too little, too human-scale. 'SkyTower's holding!' I remember shouting and punching the air. 'Lucky number 8!' While further east, evacuation of Waterhouse's magnificent Royal Alex Hospital continued. (But patients might as well have stayed put to watch the scrubby grass covered by a tide that failed to make it across the road. I guess few things can cheer up the sick more than the well-world sinking into turmoil.)

West was a different story. The gradient gave any break-in the extra oomph needed to sweep into Marine Lake and swell it to join the Clwyd where pure brine already lipped the embankment. Once the flood had found a level, one continuous sheet of water would comprise lake, river, estuary and sea. You could've got in your canoe at the Miniature Railway Museum (*UK's Oldest!*) and paddled to the Isle of Man. Or Iceland. A news crew captured the town again as the rest of the country salivated for lunch. It showed East Parade was still standing though gappy with a channel of floating timber and fibre-glass panels flowing down it. West Parade was virtually unrecognisable, subsumed in the new shore line. The helicopter hovered over what had once been a Lifeboat Station. Ha, ha! This image would become crass as it was reused during the day though presumably someone at a safe distance thought *neat!*

My account of the flood's suspiciously neat itself because most of the information's the post-happening kind. Yes, I was there, my updates coming from every media. 'This battered, once-popular north Welsh resort now braces itself for midday' – another editor smartattacked, reminding the audience where we were, what we were. But someone who worked for me – technically – a local man, Glenn Hughes, was out in it. He voice-overed the flight of Old Woolworths roof towards the Forward Rhyl office that employed us. (It missed, just.) That's Glenn for you. *His* house sat in the water's path yet with partner Alice Norman safe in Spain, he thought he'd cruise the prom. 'Look, *look* Yori. You gotta see this. It's Venus off the top of LoveSync— she's going past now. Loo-ok-k! There's her tits still moving in the water.'

'Get back. Glenn! They're saying—'

'Yeah, yeah. Bet you're nice'n'dry, lucky bugger. Hey, Yori! I am a camera!' He was on a rioter's high, no doubt about it. Before we broke I heard, 'Aw-w, this is disaster porn!'

Having just missed the seawall breach Glenn made it to Gaiman Avenue. For no reason. He wasn't invited. Nobody ever is. I can't afford to encourage interest. Rain was falling like gravel, souvenirs of our birthplace whizzed down the road at head height, but something must watch over the Glenn Hugheses of this world. Big compared to a half-Japanese, and wild-eyed and haired now, he looked like the Storm God himself on the doorstep.

Glenn's got at least fifteen years on me but now you'll picture older than he looks. Alice among other things keeps him in shape so you need to think of a big muscular body topped with one of those square, comic-book faces dictated by the subframe— brow ridges, nose, cheekbones and jaw, an Adam's apple like a corbel for the chin, all solid foundations for a rugby player, say, or a boxer not that I know if he was either. But straight from outside, his skin has post-match hyperflush. His electric-blue waterproofs dripped on my polished floor and a sudden twist round and he gives me a shower. The single other occasion he'd 'dropped in' had he taken off footwear without prompting? Too late. Collapsed onto a seat with *fuckme*, only then he leans forward and undoes his boots. He muttered, 'They say the surge'll knock out the whole of Kinmel.'

This was the opposite bank of the River Clwyd, a blight of cheap housing and ex-holiday camps. Rhyl's *barrio* it's been called. 'You sound pleased. Anyway I don't think so.'

''S'right!'

And then fury broke over me in its own wave. I've got a temper nobody knows about and kicking him would feel so good, Glenn sitting there in his pathetic too-young for him clothes (tight jeans, the sweatshirt covered in Indian script he couldn't understand) and putting on this *nadatodowithme* attitude, a spectator. I really hated him. 'Not bothering *you* though? You're—' I remembered too late the location of his own house.

He was paying more attention to his repulsive spongy boots. 'Tight-arse,' he said. 'Go on, shoot the messenger!'

(Honestly? He turned out totally correct— two thousand static caravans, their occupants fled not a moment too soon, were about to swarm inland. Models called Gallant and Rhino burst apart spilling mock-leather banquettes, dogbeds, broken toys, roller blinds and high-chairs across the fields. This ersatz material hasn't any patina of age to look forward to and makes unrottable garbage. As with nuclear waste all that could be done was burial).

The hot drink I couldn't not offer gave Glenn his second wind. I had a live stream on of teenagers in a water-fight along Vorderman Road but it wasn't enough for him. Dramas needed to be played out. A natural mimic, he did some woman's refusal to leave her bedsit only one street back from the front with falsetto cursing of rescuers from the *piano nobile* window. But the illogic of the damage was Glenn's main fix. In Abbey Street a trio of empty properties remained upright— with the just-completed clinic next door pulverised. He found that particularly hysterical. It was as if surrendering his home ('in the front door and out the back by I left, couldn't stop it— Alice'll have us well covered—') had freed him. Neighbours were sending him images of his street anyway. Why be there? he wanted to know. At first he checked them and then stopped even that and his cool wound me up all over again. 'She was talking of a bit of a change round anyroad and—' We were both hypnotised by the sight of a cancer-screening trailer (logo Take An Hour And Save Yourself Years) gliding along the prom like a big white barge, a movie director's dream. Glenn thought someone he recognised was in the next shot, changed his mind and then he fell asleep, mid-sentence. When I turned to ask about saplings on Stanmore Street put in all of six weeks ago, his head was thrown back, mouth agape, arms and legs splayed, Vitruvian Man dropped off his wheel and nothing at all godlike— but nor is he the clown I seem to have cast him as.

There's more to Glenn, I acknowledged, mopping round his steaming big feet. I should make an effort now and again not to want to hack him to death. You raise the *daito* above your head and bisect the target in a single downward swordstroke—

—but he's Rhyl-born like me and hasn't been tempted away

even though Alice Norman manages hostels in Malaga, meaning Glenn could idle in the Spanish sun. He chooses to stay and work. Like me. Yet The One Big we have in common, work, *is* the problem. Impossible to supervise in the office, he pretends to have a sly, undermining expertise about every past project. Maybe not pretends. He can pinpoint where Clear Skies Café was for example quicker than you can zoom in on the map *and* tell you the list of charity shops that occupied underneath. He has the only original photograph of Rhyl's subterranean Little Venice, all arches and frescoes*, something so unlikely even Rhyl people think it's a fiction. I've tried to trip him on minor details. No luck. But his sex life when Alice is home gets described daily— and drinking friends', the music group's and mine (invented, depraved). I'm his supervisor. I'm the one person he'll ever meet that values what Glenn has and to me, instead of generosity, he hands on his collection bit by bit. It's a power thing. And Rhyl's the great leveller.

I went next door and grated fierce radishes in my galley kitchen, making work the way you do when— I nearly said there's a death in the family. Stupid thing to think even at this point though you'll see what I mean, later on. Grating was better than doing nothing against the rock and roar. I could *feel* the punishment we were getting. While we wait for the flood to overtake us I'll explain how come. Child Yori up in his attic grew to love buildings by listening to them. I learned to identify even a downspout dribble as the housecreature's bleed and every creak as a knot in its spine. It left me with a mind that could reach out now to all that decorative plasterwork coming up in blisters, wrought iron being ripped away like fingernails and

---

*The Queen's Palace burned down in 1907 having stood at Rhyl's exact centre for only five years. It was a proto-Disneyworld. I'd have loved it. Apart from shops, restaurant, conservatory and waxworks, below its 2000-couples ballroom was a painted 'Imitation Venice' with a *canal* and some brought-from-Italy gondolas and real gondoliers poling them. A canal and boats— underneath.

the gable end's sigh as it fell on its knees. Once a glamour girl but finding she was unloved, Rhyl had stopped taking care of herself years ago. Self-harmed in fact. And finally she gets a slap in her only asset, the profile she's turned to the sea since 1800.

It was enough to break your heart if you had one (mine was never fully installed, according to Kailash). Instead I grated radishes. These were off an illegal day market, the junction of Vaughan and Bedford and were the dark round sort you can't usually get, with the bitterest blowback I've ever tasted. I worked them like a maniac till heaps of identical size and profile were lined up on the counter. Five centimetres high, five apart. Should've been calming. Wasn't enough. For distraction, there was only Glenn left— maybe a sketch? – no a caricature, big up the nose, inflate the cheeks to make Tess laugh—

—and then it registered. Highwater had come and gone. We were here. Yet because of what came after, I can't remember being relieved. I guess I was. On-screen rehashes looped through the swamp of Foryd Harbour, then a window shattering on Harkers Arcade, a girl being piggybacked by a grinning boy. The same family climbed into an orange inflatable but the strapline was detailing an explosion in the Scottish Parliament Complex now. *Injuries.* Suddenly there's an image switch to Enric Miralles' famous Edinburgh frontage. Three of his childish 'Think-Windows' made for the politicians to sit in are now stab wounds, ragged as Halloween pumpkins' eyes. *Much internal damage. Some deaths feared.*

So Rhyl had failed again by being not wrecked enough. The worst must be over?

Yeah.

Chapter 2

Things had slackened off to the odd heavy object getting rolled. A pigeon blundered against the window and was an after image by I reacted. The sky went from dark ash to paler like a stadium roof doing its trick. By the time I'd found fresh cups and come back we'd dipped from first to ninth most viewed news item. Two arguing women in formal wear replaced us, their strapline *This Slump! New Borrowing Figures*. Glenn dreamed on and I watched him in an idiot's belief that it was – even if you counted a couple from childhood – my grisliest Rhyl day so far.

Libby Jenkinson must have been in the starting blocks, weather-wise. She knocked to say she was going to her sister's on Rawson, the next street. 'Still blowing a gale,' I mentioned. 'You've known worse, though?'

For answer her tongue came out and she waggled its stud. 'I can't be here,' she croaked. 'I'm fed up. They're saying it'll go down now, the water. That's it for us.' Her dissatisfaction was showing in the set of a body wrapped up tight and cylindrical to the knees. The hair – a new olive oil shade, better really – was tucked under a hood. I'd never seen her leave home without full makeup and wasn't going to. The daisies beside her brown eyes were tattoos anyway but when she focused past me at unconscious Glenn, black brows shot up, questioning, to reveal glossy puce. She hadn't met him yet and I wasn't up for an introduction. Why bother? He wouldn't be here again I promised myself. 'See you two later,' she said and winked.

Our speech seemed to register with Glenn because his mumbling increased. There was drool. I needed Tess – if we could find a spider I'd stick it in his mouth. Shall we? Aw-w!

18

Why d'you have to be so clean, Yori? Never nothing yuck when you wan' it.

Otherwise, it had turned mysteriously quiet. Thorp's roof was settling back into place and *That's it for us?* Apparently. The light improved but stopped short of a proper mid-afternoon level and I lit my desk lamp and muted all news, bored if I'm honest. The day felt maimed. Who should I try connect with? My father, back in Kochi? No big consumer of world affairs, he probably hadn't heard about Rhyl. Or heard but thought, *Small moulis* compared to the savagery Japan endured regularly in assorted typhoons and tsunami and heat waves so was coping pretty well with any anxiety for an only son. It might be an embarrassment to have it even mentioned between us. There's no Japanese word for complain.

I try anyway. He's not listening.

Groans from Glenn. Scratching like something being sandpapered. I had to step over legs to go check again on the opposite terrace. It had given the storm the finger though Number 13's ashlar-dressings were still over-glossed in brutal black. An offense against stone. The drifts of rubbish strewn everywhere were colourful, with party hats in there and what looked like sweets but would turn out to be novelty condom packs. Handfuls of them were already being used as missiles, thrown around by Ram and Musa, the Turkish doctor's sons from Number 21, but even they looked half-hearted, the anticlimax getting to them. More depressing, at the back of the flat I found the snapped off birch turned intruder into the yard. Definitely the saddest injury to Gaiman Avenue, it made a giant's broom wedged against the rear exit and would need attacking with the late Mr Jenkinson's saw. No more walk-on part in 'A Hundred Lunar Aspects' for you. Otherwise we seemed to have lived up to Glenn's prediction of nice and dry. As for the rest—

I love it here. But the temptation was to pack up and not witness the worst, not be the co-heir of yet more trauma. My plotline had just been replaced by a jackass clip of Man Falls Into Own Wet Cement. Rhyl's saviour, is living undercover, relearning it while he buffs up his grand vision and a few modest projects come in! The decrepit Warren Road site is now embraced by a brushed steel structure nicknamed, not resentfully either, The Clam. Much photographed. New build, as calculated, is starting to defuse the hostile end of another soulless rat run. And then my paint scheme for East Parade's refurb (railings, seats, lamp standards and shelters in cool watery shades) has acted like a code word to release its charm. (So please note, I *have* done useful things.)

That was all yesterday.

At home, I work in an alcove at a desk and chair once Libby's husband's. I did the balancing trick on the chair's hind legs, back and back, a touch for insurance. Lifted the fingertip. Everyone likes to *say* they live simply but with my past I have to. So around me were enough personal items to fill a small bag. Next door, clothes would stuff another. Furniture and fittings all property of the owner— Get out, Yori! It was a lost cause when you returned— and *now*? The news presenter described 'a wave washing through the Victorian streets' which sounds pleasant, sounds refreshing. It meant filth from forgotten sumps was coating the promenade as it retreated. Not to mention the sewage. My money would be on a treacly cascade along Wellington Road right this minute.

Find a marker pen, tear a page from the sketchpad and attach to Glenn's chest, *Good-bye from Y. Have left.* (I'd never done it willingly before because as an eight-year-old I'd been dragged choking on my own snot into a waiting taxi.) And get going! – an easy option for someone with resources, someone like me. No trains? Hire a car. Travel straight inland then east across the

English border. As for Libby what about *Good luck from Y. Best of luck. Be lucky!* Whereas with Tess, who I'd have to consider once I was away clear, I mean would the whole thing work in a change of place—?

Without opening his eyes Glenn said, 'Got a drink?'

'Alcohol? No. Libby will have some when she comes in.'

The expression on his comic book face was cartoon-disgust. 'S'no good. Think I'll go see what's what.' Then he was getting into the waterproofs, searching the pockets, his big face coming alive. 'I'll bring us something if anywhere's cooking.'

He was coming back. How bad could this day get? 'I've already started preparation. There's plenty in.'

'I bet.' Glenn didn't classify my diet as food. 'Won't be long. You be here?'

'Where else?'

Soon as he'd gone, the curtains stopped bellying out and returned to the vertical like he'd taken a chunk of chaos with him. My tidy desktop lay undisturbed from last night closing *QuayStInfill* even though real Quay Street would probably be unrecognisable at this moment and the sketch that lay there out of date. My eyes surveyed a room whose wallpaper (Libby's choice) was covered by two years of aids to memory, uncountable man-hours of work capturing the very best of Rhyl— so *was* that it? Seemed to be. I took a breath. Down came a favourite, 'Tall Hooded Windows' (could've been lifted straight out of William Morris's Red House in Kent but belonged to Davies & Daughter, Contract Cleaners.) Next to go was 'Massive Boundary Stone.' It was to our doomed the 1870's Winter Gardens, the first opened in Britain with a skating rink, archery butts and zoo that bankrupted the founder. And of course 'Quay Street Cottage' went. Senseless because I'd no idea what had been smashed or how many records remained useful, only that sacrifice was a must. No balancing act involved. It was a decision I'd regret – that was the point. Pain. Pain is pleasure. Salt is sweet. Suck it up and smile. To prevent backsliding, the entire collection of a hundred plus gets shredded straight away and makes a tidy package wrapped in 'Greek Key Brickwork And High Baroque In Seabank Road'– took an entire weekend to complete.

To fill the vacuum I choose to put on Hitchcock's *The Trouble with Harry*. Its plush Vermont landscape, frame after frame artworks in themselves, is about as far from Rhyl as you can get. I enjoy the early shots taken using a dead man's POV, especially the feathered trees seen from between his feet. The killer kid with his toy gun. You know the boy is going to be a handicap to Shirley MacLaine's love life once the last reel finishes— but then, keeping an eye out for the director's walkthrough twenty minutes in, I manage to miss him as he strolls past a stationary limousine. Has *already* strolled past when I'm back from swallowing an extra something at the sink which seemed only sensible. I had to apologise to AH. Not amused. Top of my Ten Unremakeable Movies it might be but even *you* can't save this day from Rhyl's tendency to slob out. Talking of which, Glenn finally lurches in with the dusk and fills the room up. 'You don't wanna know!' he says just as wonderful Shirley's delivering her best line in the entire film about frosted glass.

A quick glance tells Glenn there'd been a change in here but not what, the pure lager breath having something to do with that. With all his gestures even bigger and contradicting himself, we get a repeat performance, throwing his ape's arms wide, piling on the impressions, his mouth ludicrously mobile. The hot news of a missing teenager plus two adults drowned in a camper van doesn't get the response he hopes for— the deaths were already stale, posted in the hope of keeping Rhyl's Wave going. I listen to descriptions of windfarm rotors lying on the beach, my newly-planted cherry trees washed out of their holes together with their guards, a baby Fiat car floating offshore like a plastic duck asking to be hooked. Glenn was at least an incident— and for a few hours the storm made addicts of us. 'And my place! Can't even get in there to look till tomorrow.' (This was yet another catastrophe though I didn't pick up on it right away.) 'I'll tell you what,' he took the tea I'd made as if ordered, switching suddenly to sober, 'it's had a fuckin' good go at us.'

And The Wave had one more surprise, an anonymous extra to the three dead, though unreported that first day. This person came inland with the main deluge before starting a tour, (a bit like a tripper!) of both East and West Parades. Passing the major attractions, then through good old Quay Street into Marine Lake, he/she stranded with the drainings on the riverbank. A greater mass of water, an extra pulse of ebbing tide, might have sent him/her back to sea and not become flotsam, incomplete and cradled by a portion of old cockle-dredge. Some limbs were missing and the front of the cranium had seen particular abuse which might or might not be important.

Things I learned pretty quickly *post* that I didn't know *pre*.

1. Every year 400-plus people drown in Britain and those are just the reported ones.

2. Any not recovered from the sea can be skeletonised in less than a couple of months, mainly by crabs.

3. After determining sex, race, age and height, plenty of teeth are your best hope of identity.

All of which means time went by before it – before *she* – got back her name. Sara Meredith. Forgotten by some but never by me.

Chapter 3

Nor by my father. Shame to the Japanese is a serious business. After our brief exchange that same week about Rhyl's hardly-world-class Wave, we ran out of words. Then once I convinced myself the impossible had happened, I let days lapse before revealing to him that she was here with us. Because Tomiko knew as much re: the crimes against Sara as I did, another good reason the ancient city of Kochi that lured him home several times, finally kept him. *No dishonour, Sato Tomiko.* If you always lacked enthusiasm for a son, you'd got alibis. My unplanned arrival was one, as well as Tomiko's age at not even nineteen. I've forgiven him because dragging along resentment is like tying a weight to your own foot. My father says so. It's our joke, his motto for every occasion. Tripping over for the seventh time. Finding a tiger is sharing your cave.

He's never invited me to visit Kochi. From Tomiko I get sandy skin, eyes with their secret lids, irises the colour of mahogany and little else. But there's a camera in his studio – he's an artist, a watercolourist though working just in inks now – and any time I want I drop in. I'm happy to watch him on the other side of the world, the flick of wrist and tetchy brushwork saying he hasn't caught what he's after. Again. Or I speak and get ignored which I'm well used to. My father's aged like a character in a long-running series. If I search out pictures (he and my mother on the beach, say, me in between balanced on a donkey) I'm amazed at his youth, the way people are with their favourite actors. But a scar, the first thing anyone would notice, Tomiko's had since before I was born. It blazes a comet trail across his forehead. He laughs, says, 'Another man's best work!' Lacking it, a bridgeless nose, workaday chin and just one slightly chipped incisor would've made for blandness. Wrong implication. This is a face fronting up real passion so that rusty scar, the Japanese *no* symbol of a dipped sword, big improvement. When we do talk I can compliment him with, 'You look well *otosan*.'

I should say something else about him. While I was growing up, Tomiko's major plus as a father were his stories. Not every night – do not count the skins of uncaught dogs! – but on nights when least expected. Winding me up, pretending he had to get away quickly, he'd then act out a glimpse of 'Old Nihon'. Our draughty first home boasted a live-in kitchen shared with other residents, a bathroom above and— one more flight— at its apex our own space, the converted loft you could see the sea from. The stairs were always lit because of a child's fear of the dark.

So here's Tomiko carrying the boy Yori in his arms, a small body padded out against Welsh midwinter.

'Goodnight Yori.'

His father's shadow leaping along the wall has raced them to the top. Now it seems anxious to get out of the room again. On this particular night the child pleaded, expecting a refusal which came. No more unskinned dogs though. His mother and Tomiko had argued over them, as they did over everything. 'There are not always fish under a willow tree,' he said in lieu. But he didn't leave.

'There was once,' he began, 'a fisherman whose fortune was low. It's winter – exactly like now – but fiercer. Big wind rages. He rowed out to fish and each time he's scared it will be last.' The bed rocked with the force of the breakers and then Tomiko was up and staggering around a room that had become a shifting deck. 'He wants to eat he must go. But the fish had left this part of the sea. Very small catches now.' An invisible sardine was chased across the bed cover and escaped overboard.

Yori shrieked with pleasure. 'And then when life can't get worse his net, most important thing, is fastened by stone on the bottom. He pulls and pulls – really hard work – and gets big hole right across. Useless!'

The net was held up and a hand poked through. Yori loved his father's voice which softened over the local dips and rises, unlike every voice heard, even his mother's and his own. Tomiko's English was at its very best during this period with fewer surplus vowels. Once back in the long silences of his Japanese studio it corroded.

'Useless,' Tomiko repeated. Use-less, the child parroted into the bedclothes.

'That night the fisherman walks up the beach. Snow falls. He was hungry and cold. He bumped into trees and rocks and even a horse because the snow was so thick – anyway at last he found home. And at his door a little fox! Beautiful and her eyes green – but the snow was covering her red coat and the fisherman saw the fox was hurt in the paw. Till then the fisherman thought nobody was more sad than him. But the fox was the most sad animal ever seen. So he shared his last piece of food. He called her Sister Fox – and when she went off into the dark he slept in his cold house not swept. His dream is foxes.

'We go fast now. Fisherman comes home next night. Still no fish. Very hungry! But big surprise! House is lit and warm and swept. Pot boils. Bath is ready. A beautiful lady puts down his dinner – no words, just dinner. He asks her many questions but she warns him off like this.' Tomiko made a shield of his hand. 'When he falls asleep she is making up the fire – when he is awake she is gone. Twice again is same. At last he can't wait any more – his tongue kicks in his mouth. He's got to get answer.

'She tells him she is from Fox People. Her people and ours cannot speak. Now she breaks the rule, she can never come

26

again. The fisherman cries salt. But in the morning, on his boat is a fine new net. Good luck comes too – he catches fish! One day the village matchmaker finds him a pretty wife to marry.'

His father told other stories but Fox People remained Yori's favourite.

It ends, 'Foxes and women are a lot the same. And if ever a woman is followed, a man must take care. If you're seen she turns into a fox and escapes. Never follow a woman when you have evil in your heart. The Fox People will punish you for rest of your life.'

Yet if you don't follow the woman when the opportunity comes along, you'll punish yourself for the rest of life. As his father says, 'The reverse also has a reverse side.' Which is why Yori followed Sara Meredith, wife of the same Josh Meredith he failed to contact the day The Wave came. She'd abandoned her car on a still-intact West Parade to ask directions.

He watches as she gets maybe a word in return and is left hesitant till a gull big as a turkey crashlands at her feet. Mad-eyed, the eagle-beak spattered like a blood-feeder, that gets her moving.

Sharing a slice of childhood is my way of establishing trust. Because façade's a term of abuse these days and getting behind one's meant to be a good thing. I don't know. There's my mainly Japanese (handsome) face, for instance. It's not very flat but not very light. The eyes are too deep-set to fool a true *nihonjin*. Of course I'm lean. Any flabby Japanese you think you see are Korean. I'm average height. My look's clean-shaven, easy for me, but to short circuit the minor issue of appearance, think a young Archie Kao. Usually I'm dressed down to dull, a lot of black, though the clothes are top quality which I got used to and you can never go back on something like that. But Rhyl's been made for outsiders, a real melting pot, so walking through these streets with the savvy of a native, you might take me for one of you. Wrong. Behind my façade are rooms you couldn't guess the function of, full of things you'd throw away. And they're not built for anyone's comfort, certainly not mine— but this is two stories. Sara that I followed the day she arrived is the main one. *So get off stage, Yori! Address always Chief Person in room.* And you can gauge Sara's importance by the fact that when her body washed up it made the town's troubles into nothing.

So, Sara's story. To start, there's her re-entry to Rhyl that could've been staged by Alfred Hitchcock himself. That caused a stir. How did she die? No—! Before that, who was she?

Who was she? I could begin She was the child of Professor Geoffrey Severing and Wife Number One that died when Sara was too young to remember. Her stepmother, Fleur, bucked the stereotype and was anything but wicked. Then as a young woman she met and married a man called Josh and *they* had a little girl and so on. Flash forward to the bones so polished they could be actually part of an old cockle-dredge. I shouldn't have started with The Wave I realise now. But backwards or forwards is a trick question anyway. I'm the teller and I don't get to decide. Biography was *her* flair – you may be the sort of person who doesn't need to be told that? – and the published work gives her independence beyond the grave (if she had one which she hasn't), meaning do a search if you like. From the verifiable facts this stands out. At the beginning of what everyone thought would be an academic career she wrote a book, *A First at Oxford*. It was about a woman who'd lived in eighteenth century England and had sort of dropped out of the records. Or at least was there in a low-key way but lucky Sara came across hers just as the Secret History concept became a craze. Characters weren't so much being rediscovered as reinvented and this one had everything going for it. Poor clever girl. Bad men. Sara's book was an immediate success. You'll find more tributes to it than it has pages.

'An effortless display of cleverness makes it almost too-readable,' *Guardian*.

'Pity the feminist icon. Her biographical fate is so often a grotesquely attenuated characterisation in the manner of advocacy for mediaeval sainthood. Meredith earns our gratitude for freeing Thomasina Swift from the plethora of sentiment surrounding that name: *why* is no longer severed from the *how* of her achieving the unfeasible.' *Pittsburgh Historical Review*.

My all-time favourite goes, 'Thoroughly absorbing, deeply humane… most impressive is the way she can use a sentence from a blathering Parliamentary speech – or even a statistic for Oxford rainfall – to put racing plates on her hobby horse…' *Sunday Independent*.

And for Sara it was life-changing. *Bestseller!* Like the name Tess, the word's enough to make the mouth water. In 341 pages – OK so I overestimated the tributes – Thomasina Swift goes from innkeeper's daughter to first female 'ever to keep a term at Oxford', which translates as managing to study at a university still ringfenced for aristo sons. Edition followed edition – then a huge printing to cash in on the *Tom Swift* film. But I have an original copy, the one with the awesome Pythian Press logo, the python drawn by Lucy Llewellyn, twisting along the spine and a dust jacket in mint condition. On the back the author is shy, proud, the eyes a challenge, her hair being swept away from her forehead in a move implying ready for action. She's very attractive, the chin down on her collar like that, a photographer's device to disguise the length of the face. Visible over one shoulder is Garden Quad, St Clement's College, Oxford (c.1765), it being the only survivor from Thomasina's era. The book is signed and dedicated, though not to me. Sara offers its new owners, G and F, her love but just the position of the rest of the inscription's revealing, '— may you have as much fun reading this as I had writing it' lies above the frontispiece Jane Austen quote, '*I was... dragged through numerous chapels, dusty libraries and greasy halls. I never was but once in Oxford in my life and I am sure I never wish to go there again.*'

She's saying, I don't care about snubbing Austen. Here's my view of Oxford. The great Jane's being called out by Sara Meredith, which makes what happened to her afterwards a real puzzle. Only a month ago on my way south by train, a fellow passenger was well into Sara, and I rehearsed one of those conversations you've no intention of starting.

'Yeah!' (All casual) 'I've got a signed first edition!'

'—?'

'Obviously not, it's to her parents.'

' —?'

'I think it's *very* good but then I would, wouldn't I?'

The woman's brows pinch up. My appearance makes connection with our topic hard to believe. I find it hard to believe. She's about to be spun a line, she thinks— and anyway the dialogue never happened. One thing Tomiko insists on is a Japanese *never* asks a stranger for information concerning self, family, education, place of origin, occupation and current level of prosperity. And never gives it. So I stayed silent— but I've butted in again. Trying to be dutiful— or maybe highly-motivated— leads you into it.

Actually this is three people's story. But what do you do if number three doesn't want to be heard?

OK. We need to start a long way from here. 'Sara married a man called Josh and they had a daughter—'

Named Eurwen, a Welsh name, a difficult name but to look

at her, you'd never guess she's going to cause the trouble we're all in. Every morning, from an anonymous saloon car, a tall rangy Mr Meredith delivered the child to the school door. Bradwardine's severe frontage disdains to broadcast it caters for Oxford's chosen next generation. But even here Mr Meredith was a presence as he moved through the mothers and childminders, his dark suit a male put-down of multi-coloured anarchy. While other children were chivvied or coddled he ran a hand over his daughter's chestnut curls letting her turn beneath, offering one sentence per day to exchange with the gatekeeper. Probably a bit wet for rounders? We're enjoying *The Hobbit*! When he walked away eyes other than the girl's followed him. The car might turn left in the direction of Carfax and the city centre but most often right, circling to Thames Valley Police Headquarters in Kidlington. Or at least it spent precious minutes trying to make for the seized carriageways that served Oxford as walls… and more than one mother speculated aloud that he must be so-o tempted to blast a way out with the siren.

Mr Meredith: the only rank he ever admitted to was parent. At three-fifteen a red-haired, thirtyish Mrs Meredith was waiting and she had a Christian name. 'Sara Meredith—she wrote that book!' '*She*'s the clever one— a Bradwardine girl herself!' 'Daughter of Geoffrey Severing – he was on *Newsnight* again over globalisation – or it might have been something else.'

This Sara chatted with the staff and joked, sometimes at her small replica's expense. Oftener the wit was directed at the well-groomed mothers. In faded denim her slight figure was easily shouldered aside by Human Resources mothers on flexi-time or Entrepreneur mothers with government-advisor haircuts. 'How do they do it? I can hardly manage to shop for food, never mind shoes. What amazing shoes!' Her intent was to provide an ear for pedagogic complaints, though *trying too hard* she sometimes admonished herself; the aspiration was for goodwill to be heaped on her child's head. Not that the child was ever in need of it, Eurwen, the daughter with the Welsh name, a difficult name, one that had come to school the first day written on a scrap of paper. ('Eurwen' – pronounced Ire as in Ireland and wen as in when!) Fragile, beautiful, green-eyed and blessed with a watchful father and amiable mother, sweeping the years ahead clear of slips, trips and falls. What could go wrong?

Afterwards, inevitably, Eurwen's heart-shaped face faded from school memory. But when refreshed on screen and under headlines, staff relived one special Christmas amongst themselves: the girl dressed as a fierce, miniature shepherd, hoisted laughing onto her father's broad shoulders while the woman she would become gazed up at her, a Quattrocento Madonna... *and Eurwen wouldn't play Mary... no way. Really wanted to play a sheep, d'you remember?* Now it was principal Renate Desmond's turn to send a note. 'All of us here at Bradwardine are thinking of you in this terrible time... and of Eurwen, of course. I can only imagine what you are going through. Staff and children alike... feel sure... are certain... think of the many happy incidents from Eurwen's years with us. Only yesterday we were talking of...'

Another memory: a flu outbreak had forced Mrs Desmond herself to take a lesson. Twenty heads bent over, ripe berries of tongue bulged from the sides of mouths. 'So,' she repeated, 'we've done the vowels. What I want you to do is write down all the words you know that don't have any vowels in.'

Circling behind Eurwen after a minute or so there in a neat, clear hand was the list: my, by, cry, fly, try, dry and beneath it the completely unexpected finale: Rhyl.

'Well done, Eurwen.' It let her favour the girl without guilt. 'You're the only one who's got it. But why Rhyl?' She didn't bother with the suggestion of a holiday, not there. 'A visit?'

Eurwen shook her flames of hair with characteristic energy. 'It was where my Daddy was born in!'

And seven years later the place from where Josh Meredith shouted down the phone, 'Sara, enough! Just go to bed. I'll talk to you in the morning,' before the line went dead.

Chapter 4

When her ex-husband rang off it seemed easier to slide down the kitchen wall and sit, legs inelegantly splayed, the handset nursed against her midriff. There was a sort of comfort in letting it dig into the knot of muscles... soon her wrist, never trustworthy since a fall on the Merton Street cobbles last winter, would start to quiver. But before this could happen her lids closed of their own volition and the room swam: at the back of her tongue was the taste of quinine. 'My name is Sara,' she startled herself by saying aloud, 'and I'm—'

Drunk. She put the phone to her ear again in case, somehow, Josh would be there to take back what he had just said. *Dolt!* At least it exposed her muddled state to scrutiny. *Get up!* She smoothed the trouser cotton to her hips and tried looking about. Obviously she had come in here with some intention that shock had dispatched; the kettle was cool to touch and apart from the white lozenge of missing plaster in the wall above it (old? new?) nothing suggested the untoward. A tad untidier perhaps... she traipsed into the hall and peered through the open study door. But *not that way* the still-functional part of her pleaded, *recent damage enough in there.* Only when she stumbled back upstairs to the sitting room did the empty vodka bottle offer an explanation: she had been down there looking for its twin. And it was late, or felt it, and she had to drive over two hundred miles now, right now...

...Waking crook-backed to find light beyond the shutters, Josh's news was debatable for only a moment. Then it was awful, cruel, hideous... horrendous. No, she lacked the word for its degree of badness. She shook herself like a wet dog and

34

agony through her temples provoked *Oh, sweet, suffering Lord!* as a string of yelps. Anyone watching (there was no one) would have seen her freeze up. Then blink and swallow. Time for a stock-take: head as expected and throat *and* lungs raw and dry as if she still smoked. But she had survived harsher bodily reproofs. Stomach… best not dwell on that. Just swallow again. The low-grade itchiness, a recent occurrence, was now more or less endemic inside yesterday's clothes. Eyesight was apparently functional. Tremors registered as medium to severe across her torso and into her limbs but she could stretch them, could stand up now, could scrape thoughts together… all of which she needed to do and do quickly since Eurwen, her fifteen-year-old daughter, had disappeared.

Some short time later she found she was outside, steadied against a car bonnet, oblivious to its grime soiling her blazer, the hastily stuffed tote bag clutched to her chest like a buoyancy aid. Now she stared dubiously at the silver VW that had sat in its allotted resident's parking space, unmoving for… she couldn't state how many months. 'Only two things to concern you, drive and reverse,' she heard her professor-father instructing. 'You will never want a manual shift again, believe me. Not that you'll use it… often.' This was his pact with the devil: giving her a new, safer car when he knew he should be taking away the keys to the battered old car and informing the authorities. *Not use it often…* a massive Pickfords pantechnicon rumbled into sight, already coming away from the city with its load and for a blessed moment the exit from Tackley Close was sealed, safe, bright-morninged, tranquil Tackley Close. She breathed its cool air heavy with Thames moisture, nutty garden scents and a mere hint of diesel. *This* Oxford enclave was not an early riser. A last look at her house, the adjoining half of which, the Peppers' half, was still swaddled in curtains, and she slipped into the driver's seat. To her astonishment, after its enforced hibernation the VW engine caught immediately and proved willing to edge out into the carriageway when asked. Taking a left at the corner, she was into Polstead Road almost without volition.

Mercifully it was devoid of other vehicles. Look, Eurwen! Lawrence of Arabia lived here… and in that house J.R.R. Tolkien got bored with marking exam scripts and began, 'In a hole in the ground there lived a…' Oxford had been her only home and she could always recite the roll call of its luminaries for comfort. Instead she tried a mantra of routes: make for the Woodstock first, leave via the Wolvercote Roundabout where the exit for Kidlington had once been Josh's. Keep going north and then west. After that she would need to… *just drive*, she ordered herself. Another voice said *don't* but she ignored it.

No arguments. *My* starting point's here, the first time Yori set eyes on Sara, a sunny afternoon, the last week in September.

In Rhyl. A strip of Welsh maritime wilderness began developing as a seaside resort in the eighteenth century and for the next hundred years or more it went pretty well so that the sound promised pleasure to the few and only later to the masses. But to Sara it's more like a curse. Because this is 2008 and we're a national joke. Rhyl – UK's First Shanty Town, a serious newspaper christened it. Rhyl – Twinned With Soweto! its graffiti read. Yet it's where she's fetched up and I recognise her instantly from photographs, film clips, the book jacket, etc— and for now all I want to do is watch hoping against hope she'll think *it's not that bad*. Beach-stuff to start, our major asset, five getting on six miles of it. I bet even she concedes *a fine stretch*. Screw up your eyes and you could think Bodega Bay where Tippi Hedren in *The Birds* asks us something along the lines of Have you ever seen so many gulls? But that's California. We'll need The Seaquarium for the only glimpse of blue, clean water.

Ours is one of those where the exhibits swim over and round the paying customers and the flick of the sharks keeps catching the eye. This being Rhyl though across the road on the main promenade – a choice location virtually anywhere else – there's the remains of a pushed-over, burnt-out building. Wooden props span the gap so the survivors either side can lean on each other's shoulders. Beneath them a couple are settled on plastic sheeting. He's terrible to look at with protruding eyes and a toad's skin. She is fortyish, near Sara Meredith's age, and has the face of Brigitte Bardot. But Bardot at seventy, lined and weary. The woman slides off her rubble heap and into the trippers along the front— and steps straight into the road as if the traffic will miraculously part. A silver hatchback with the sunroof open has to brake hard to avoid her and its driver's shocked expression can just be made out before the car accelerates away.

Two accidents and then nearly a third: heart hammering, Sara checked in the rear-view that the pedestrian had made it all the way across. Only then was she able to exhale and try to concentrate ahead...

Jittering neon and crude artwork combine, a linear carnival that almost overwhelms her thready vigilance. But away from the promenade's bold signage, she was offered hints of normal urbanity. Another turn and here were businesses selling soap and painkillers and food that had not been pre-fried. On real streets carrier bags replaced buckets and spades. Up one, down another... to the beach again not meaning to, heat building in the car. Finally she chose her mark and pulled in. That girl pushing a buggy looked a safe source for directions.

That *boy* mumbled *Av'nside* was across the river, the prospect she had turned the car from already once.

Over the bridge, then, this time to find yet more pubs

squaring up to each other, caravans almost to their walls... and *this* was where Eurwen had chosen, her father's home. Above, the sky was an immense and hurtful radience. Cowering and peering side to side, she was allowed one glimpse of a promontory sprinkled with birds before a messy boatyard obscured it. Avonside, her destination, was that line of pinkish, meanly-proportioned houses facing across a muddy inlet to open sea, and impossible to reconcile with Eurwen's description: 'Mum, it's gorgeous. There's the river and the harbour. On a clear day Dad says you see somewhere called The Fylde, that's a sort-of jutting out bit over in Lancashire. A naff name, isn't it? Who'd want to live on The Fy-ylde? But Dad says—'

She recognised his back before it was necessary to begin picking out numbers, Josh, caught off guard for once in his life, surprised in the act of opening his own front door. It had been how long? Her mind rebelled at the calculation as his tall figure swivelled loosely from the hips, youthfully. But the tanned forearm in torsion seemed older, veinier and strung with copper wires. The opportunity to see him as a new person came and went in a flash, then the familiar profile tilted at her and she almost moaned aloud. His deep, widely spaced eyes under thick brows slid off their current task. Suddenly the full face happened: symmetrical, handsome and affecting as ever. Grey lightened his hair, yet nothing could lift Josh's basic look, that of a man who would hang your pet spaniel in the orchard. His jaw jutted alarmingly... so much so she felt moisture spread through her scalp. Strength of maternal fear, her alibi, was going to be inadequate but... but Eurwen *could* be back. This very hour. Innards clenching, 'Josh!' she called as he spun on his heel, some sixth-sense alerting watched to watcher... and she knew by his expression. She got out only because he would be at her wound down window next.

'Oh. Right. *Brilliant!*' Her fumbling attempts with the key fob brought on, 'Just press the bloody thing, will you? It does it itself.'

'Yes. I'm... very tired.' At least she had parked with the unmutilated wing toward him.

They glared at each other across the car's snub nose. When she made no attempt to come closer he (too obviously) forced himself to moderate his tone, patting the air. 'Ok. Leave the roof. I'll come back and do it.' Then his fingers transformed into an *Inside!* gesture. The house had a nominal fence and no gate. She was ushered over flags skirting a green mat of lawn that was more sand than turf anyway.

'You haven't found her?'

'There's been nothing.' His expression hardened again. 'I mean, d'you think I wouldn't have called you straight away?'

'Nothing,' she repeated. 'I... if I'm honest, well, straight away? I don't know.'

He pulled her in after him and slammed the door. Tears were coming and she sanctioned them because at least their cause was irrefutable. But that moment of confusion on seeing Josh sprang from deep feeling stored elsewhere. Her secret censor hinted true maternal terror should be different, cleaner cut: if she were tenderised and plagued with nerves it was now partly for herself. What would happen next? Early in the relationship she had come to terms with the fact that her husband could be all that men are not meant to be any more, unrelenting, illiberal, combative and so long as nothing splashed back, she would not react... *no*, if she cared to strip off yet another layer, she would admit to being excited by it. Whereas a *mote* of his vexation landing on herself...

'Sara, don't!' Already close in a hall the size of a phone booth, suddenly his arms were around her, his body-heat seeping into hers, his sharp male aroma all-enveloping. 'Stop. I'm sorry – all right?' The pattern of stubble-growth along his collar-line filled her vision and was instantly known. For a moment she could almost believe he was about to kiss the top of her head... then he pulled away and steered her into the next room and into a seat. 'D'you want a drink?'

'A *drink*?'

'Coffee? Water?'

'You think it's my fault don't you? About Eurwen? Yes?' She put her forehead in her hands, trying to squeeze out the ache by hurting herself more and knowing exactly what she was up to and what the old Josh would do in response. But he walked away, kept her trapped in a childish attitude, wanting to break it... until a thrilling new fragrance told of his return. He was offering a heavy tumbler and she took it, took the tiniest sip she could manage: a blended malt but not too fiery or cheap. Took a gulp, groping with her tongue for its simple hit.

'How many?' he asked.

Once it had been *Why, for God's sake, Sara?* But, *How many?* stood in now.

'This is the first. As you might expect since I've just driven up from Oxford. A *dreadful* journey even before I got lost and...'

'So how many?'

'What difference does it make?' In an attempt at sangfroid she glanced around the small square room for the first time and raised her eyebrows. It was a shop-display. The walls were a flat cream, bare as sheeting. Two beige sofas, the faux-wood floor, a rug patterned on a migraine and the glass coffee table all appeared new or unused. As was the slim TV on a shelf. What the room lacked was a single recognisable artefact. Three years ago the entire contents of their lovingly assembled Tackley Close interior had been spurned, (wingback chairs, the restored peacock velvet *meridienne* that she had coveted to the edge of ridiculousness as perfect partner to eighteenth century Florentine lithographs: *good God, she had obsessed about losing a piece of furniture in an auction whereas now...)* Her heart was slipping in extra beats. She said, 'If you must know, I had just one.'

'That big, was it? Yeah? Bigger probably. Definitely. You'll be well over the limit... and I mean that's before what you started with. I *knew* last night on the bloody phone...' He reached for the glass but, rocking backward, she managed to preserve the contents. 'You shouldn't have come. It's so—' At least Josh was in control of his expletives still. Flinching from his obscenities was another of her frailties, one that would enrage him further. An early discovery: their shared language was not his first but an acquired one, solely for use with herself, her father and stepmother, even her friends. Obscenity-spouting Josh made milksops of student cursers. *No perhaps it shouldn't matter but it does.* 'Bloody stupid!' he ranted on. 'What if you'd killed somebody? You could've killed yourself.'

'As though you would care.'

'Care? Of course I'd care! You're Eurwen's mother.' His own words seemed to strike home, where hers could not, and woundingly so. 'I'm sorry. I'm not trying to... ah, I don't know what I'm doing. Sara, see me? I'm totally screwed with this... this...' Then refuting himself, 'It'll be all right,' he said. 'We'll find her. I promise.' A pause while she had to endure further critical examination. 'You look exhausted. You'd be better off lying down.'

'No.'

'Suit yourself!' Eyes hardened, he put distance between himself and her.

They seemed to have arrived at fully hatched aggression with the speed of a spillage. Surely it was permissible not to cosset oneself? Laudable even? But an important lesson to relearn was they had never found a safe way to disagree and an irate Josh was momentarily silhouetted against an arch beyond which the kitchen seemed spitefully white and reflective. Then he was gone.

The drink went down. She felt her head tip to one side, all the better for the sofa leather to salve her burning face. Every movement caused a friction-whisper to accompany her body's protests. *Eurwen!* The next instant she couldn't be sure if she had said it... this was a small oddity but becoming more frequent. *Eurwen!* Definitely only a thought this time, Eur as in Ireland, wen as in when...

Her eyelids drooped.

Discounting instances of infant naughtiness in public places, the first time her daughter had run away was at thirteen-and-a-half. Sara would qualify it further by appending, 'without warning' and occasionally by rounding Eurwen's age up to fourteen. Certainly they had not argued in preparation. In fact, perfectly amicable interchanges were happening right up until the afternoon Eurwen failed to materialise after school. Irritation... then sunshine beyond the windowpanes took on a sickly florescence as attempts to reach her daughter, or anyone else who had seen Eurwen during the day, proved futile. She was still on the phone to Fleur, her stepmother, demanding Geoffrey should be fetched, the police called, that Fleur should be there, *please, now*, when the text arrived: Hd2 b at Radle Pools Sty nite. C U 2moro Luv E

The Radley Pools Protest was against the dumping of power station ash beside the Thames into extinct gravel workings. But 'full of wildlife, Mum!' Surely she should be allowed to skip Friday English to join in? *No.* Eurwen by this stage in her education needed a book, any book, glued to the palm to make her read it. Of course, no. And it could easily turn into The Battle of Radley Pools, she had explained.

'Fine,' Eurwen had shrugged, though...

'Sara!'

But she was already made aware by Josh's tread. 'Do you know I was afraid it would be a police car bringing her home? Their telling me she'd done this or that thing and I'd have to sort it out, somehow,' she almost sobbed. 'Some misdemeanour. Then the disgrace of Fleur and Daddy thinking I was... and then... That's what worried me! As if... Now I'd give anything—'

He wouldn't follow her matted thought-chain. 'I told you on the phone.' *His* voice and not on the telephone was agitating in itself. His accent had eased to a mere cadence over time, was engaging. Strange that any trace detected in Eurwen's speech could act like wormwood. 'She's fifteen and a policeman's kid. Every way of finding her, we've got covered. Phone... switched off by the way. Friends she's made, interviewed. Taxi firms. You can rely on it. I've even told lies, you know? She came for the summer. We *allowed* her the last week off school. Had agreed she should have time with me.'

'Why say that? You've lied to the police. She's here without my permission. I thought you should never lie.'

'Grow up!'

She knew what was coming.

'Remember? Have you had a drink recently, *Doctor* Meredith? You say, No officer, nothing to drink, just an evening meet at my college. Worked, didn't it? Look, if we admit how she ran away from you first—'

'Don't say that. Don't you dare say that!'

'Christ, Sara!' His ran his knuckles along a chair back, keeping away. 'I said she's here on an *arranged* holiday. My daughter or not, if they get an inkling she's a regular runaway, mother drinks, father a no-show most of the time, it will matter to people looking for her. They'll tell you it doesn't and they might not admit it to themselves. Even so what they feel about her, whether she's worth being found'll make all the difference...' but unusually, Josh's *I know my own world* sense of assurance seemed to be eroding. 'It'll make all the… well, you get it.' He became a man wandered across a border without benefit of map or papers.

Close to tears again, she said, 'Her note, can I see, please?'

'I read it you last night.' But he fetched the folded sheet, pointing out the provenance: torn from the pad next to the phone.

Sorry Dad. Tell Mum sorry. I'm fine just need to be away for a bit and – I KNOW you'll be REALLY mad at me. See you both soon and everything will get sorted. Promise. Just in case you're thinking it I'm not off with some perv I met in a chatroom. As if! Please don't start looking for me or anything. Everything's good. And if poss don't tell Gramps and Fleur. I'll keep in touch. Home soon Love E

'Can you be certain she wrote this?'

'Aren't you?'

'Someone could have forced her to—'

'Read it again.' He closed his eyes as though the text were written on the inside of the lids. 'And if poss don't tell Gramps and Fleur? Nobody could get that right. How many times have you heard? Since she could talk!'

'But four days, Josh! And she hasn't been in touch, has she? Nor come home.'

Chapter 5

To try and get Eurwen back Sara was forced to return to the husband who'd left her— in a place she couldn't bear to think about. *It was where my Daddy was born in,* says one child. Another I remember screamed so loud put on a donkey it attracted an audience. I'll bet all families love their stories. But some families have legends and the Severings', not in order of merit, go like this:

1. Detective Constable Josh Meredith had been a perverse choice for the professor's daughter.

2. Absent or present, from an early age nobody could ever quite pin Eurwen down.

3. Sara's early genius was dimmed by Josh, by marriage, by Josh's profession, by Josh's cruelty, by despair over Josh, by Josh. And by Rhyl.

Like a town can be your enemy. I was born here with my façade I usually feel the need to add. And of course, Sara hated it. How do I know? I'm trustworthy, aren't I? – or was it dutiful? – and I have resources.

September 24th 2008

'Monday's child is fair of face, Tuesday's child is full of grace, Wednesday's child is full of woe...' The rhyme was throbbing through her brain next morning as she lay in the tiny second bedroom Eurwen had used, in Eurwen's sheets with the Coconut Ice scent still on them. Born on a Tuesday, *Grace* had been chosen for a baby that had been a perfect house guest for nine months but had almost demolished the edifice as she left. Grace was generally approved of. Charming, according to Fleur.

And as a virtue name it would always maintain its resonance: this was from her atheist father. Until Josh took one look and said, 'Eurwen— means white gold,' and in the feebleness that followed a prolonged unproductive labour followed by blessed oblivion, she was conquered. She had read that the giving of a name is the recipient's futurity, should never be done thoughtlessly... but precious as gold or full of grace, neither were contested for over a decade.

Was Eurwen eleven or twelve when the first tremors were felt? As her mother, she should remember. But somewhere deep inside Eurwen, a shutter slammed down that could never be prised free, so Sara thought in her blackest hours. The new school was an easy and obvious target: a fine school, the best, that she took against. But *her own choice*. Progression post-Bradwardine ought to have been smooth; schools competed for girls like Eurwen. 'Say where you want to go and you can go there.' Geoffrey Severing, holder of the Cunningham Chair in Economic History, would naturally be involved with the education of his only grandchild and, by then, Josh and she were in dangerous waters, therefore it was easier to... yet Eurwen had seemed happy. Until without warning school became a hated place.

'We'll find you another.'

'Not this school, Mum. *School*.' The cool-eyed, heavy-lidded stare's first outing: more chilling than the sentiment.

Next came reading. A scholar-grandfather, his wife the archivist and a writer for a mother all acted in concert to furnish a home atmosphere in which books held sacred primacy... but were now reclassified as instruments of torture. In 'Bookends', one poem amongst many Eurwen was studying, was *meant* to be studying, an unlettered father and poet son are forced apart by 'books, books, books,' the poet using the term as a malediction. And could have been written for Eurwen and herself. Sara reverted to it again and again, Tony Harrison's fourteen lines more often than not blurring before their faultless finale; how she had begun to love this merciless probing of the parent and child rift.

'Have you finished your Dickens?'

'Er...' No guilt in the eyes nor the uplifted corners of the mouth.

'Have you begun it? Opened it, even? Make a start. Please. You can't get much shorter than *A Christmas Carol*.'

'Yes you can. Nothing. That's shorter.'

'Eurwen!'

'It's rubbish. I don't believe in ghosts. Nor in all these stupid *men*. Who wants to read about them? I look at the page and I just see white rivers or snakes. No writing at all!' she finished as though claiming an achievement.

After books, speech itself offended and silence stood in. It was a year during which Sara asked what else is there to lose? Kept asking Fleur, what else can go wrong between us, what will she decide to take against next? And seeing Fleur's hopeless shake of the head. Time not Fleur answered her question: living at Tackley Close, the state of being home. Some imp had got inside her daughter's skin, was controlling her. It liked their house no more than did Josh, who had vacated it by now...

'You've my mobile number on your phone. Work number's next to the landline in the hall,' Josh called up the stairs.

The flimsy Avonside front door slammed and complete stillness followed. She was alone. In her husband's house. They were still married.

(*Why?* Geoffrey demanded, as did Fleur on occasion though without an accusatory tinge.) And positions reversed, would she have left Josh to spend a day in the present disordered Tackley Close? To find a letter on the desk, opening 'Since the final deadline for delivery of this revision is exactly two years ago, would it be helpful if we could arrange…?' and the bin beneath holding nothing but ashes. Upstairs would be a Smirnoff cap nestled beneath the French sleigh bed, whereas two rings *he* had once given lay safe inside her best kidskin gloves.

The thought propelled her from under-bedding warmth to check the room for any vestige of Eurwen. Why had she not done it last night? But she was in a box with few hiding places: she could afford to be thorough now. She felt into the furthest corners of the wardrobe's melamine shelves and shoe compartments and found a single blue cotton thread. From a garment she did not recognise… then into a sort of tallboy affair, even less of a challenge and empty save for her own things. Not so much as a hair-band or button; Eurwen had arrived 'with the clothes on her back', he said, as though a mother would not have known, and 'bought, well, the usual gear' with money he provided, jeans, T-shirts… underclothes, he presumed from the laundry hung around. Now 'the gear' had been efficiently removed. Or so she thought until, *ouch!* In the last corner of the last drawer something was sharp enough to pierce her fingertip. Out it came, a milky-pale stone the size of a pea in a spot of scarlet, its wrenched claw setting become a barb… She dropped back onto her haunches, wincing not at this feeble assault but because she knew it as her own, from a moonstone necklace. Much-treasured, she had passed it to Eurwen last Christmas after everything else suggested was greeted with eye rolling. And seeing her wear it had seemed more than adequate recompense when they dined with Geoffrey and Fleur. Melancholy threatened the small gathering in Pryorsfield's morning room but in the vast dining room it would have overwhelmed them. Yet Eurwen, conventionally clothed for once in satin, seemed to be in the mood to give herself as a gift. From the other side of Fleur's festive table Eurwen's square neckline and straying ringlets lent her the Regency look of a young lady's first engagement 'out'. And the moonstones captured the candles' flicker against the absolute whiteness of Eurwen's throat with her every quip or giggle. An enchantment.

Maybe Eurwen had only performed satisfaction though the trinket had seemed to please, shimmering with its own history. Because twenty years before, it was found on Sara's favourite market stall, a present to herself, an immature silly rejoinder to the 'good' Severing diamond bracelet and the family pearls, 'When would I wear them?' she wondered aloud to her housemate Polly, until a burglary solved the dilemma. But a week passed and the young policeman dropped by for the second visit: Josh, out of uniform this time and with her moonstones proffered in plastic. Finding him on the doorstep (and having been drawn to the idea of his reappearance on that exact spot in the days since the theft) still she managed to pass off her excitement as the liveliness that was never lacking in those days... Her necklace was simply there. Thank you! She accepted Josh had retrieved it, dealt with any impedimenta and delivered it to her outstretched palm...

At least there was hot water in his house... and a proper tub taking up most of the monochrome bathroom. Immersed to her shoulders, she whipped up bubbles and felt all angles as her limbs cut through the foam, nothing childlike but a forty-year-old woman who had lost weight again. She washed haphazardly with the fresh bar of soap he had put out till her own bag attracted her, its contents spewed on the slate floor like an accident victim's across tarmac... while the oversized white wall-tiles gave off an aseptic gleam reminiscent of things scientific, of laboratories, of mortuaries even. Against the heat, she shivered... and fingers tracked without being asked a line across her lower belly, the long scoop of a cutlass swipe and Eurwen's portal on the world. Over fifteen years it had changed not only by the good manners of its fading, falling back into the flesh as a redundant facility, but symbolically. An angry red failure slowly became a happy pink badge of achievement until... what? Just a nuisance, a blemish to consider when buying swimwear, alluded to by Eurwen if she forgot it, in their personal litany of, 'Don't you hate it? Don't you mind, Mum?' 'I didn't hate having you, so of course I don't mind. It gave me you.' A sing-song response hiding a truth deeper than tissue, deeper than any scalpel ever incised and, since last night, one proven bone-achingly basic. And yet somehow she had taken her eye off it to care about *Books, books, books... A Christmas Carol... Nothing for Christmas, Eurwen...? Many girls would love to... Why can't you always dress like this? Miss your Friday English class? Absolutely not.*

A paltry worry list.

She would go and find her! As a mother what could be more natural or who better? End the drinking, stay here of course... there would need to be an end to drinking here, and Josh, impressed by her sobriety, might fall back into an old habit himself.

Hope: another virtue name, another admission.

Everything was different on foot. On the far side of the river, Rhyl lay calm and mild under cloudless duck-egg blue. Accustomed to Oxford's curtain-walls, gatehouses, steeples and belfries, she was impressed again by this openness: only a spike or mast of some kind, very slim anyway, cut the sky at a distance. Traffic coming toward her was sparse. She crossed to lean on the iron railings: and to scan the dry sand ten feet below expecting activity not this vacancy, undefiled by feet. *Ah, the children were in school.* Suddenly the rails became bars, the sand pocked with pebbles... and she squeezed her lids shut and tried to reach out through her own inner landscape. If in town, where would Eurwen be at this moment? Doing what? A tingle that today she attributed to one particular abdominal area became a cramp, a sensation fired by *Eurwen!* as her flesh called to a piece of itself that had taken off. This was no conceit: numerous occasions supported the proposition. Eurwen, sickening at school with tonsillitis, had somehow kept her housebound ready for Renate Desmond's call. Further into the past, another instance of the same thing made it irrefutable, Eurwen, chasing an injured mongrel, criss-crossing the city... She had kept this secret from Josh, from her father, from everyone save Fleur, the incident that shamed and disturbed her, of Eurwen adrift. Through Worcester College pursued by and eluding a couple of porters, a seven-year-old had braved Walton Street's murderous traffic and made it to Tackley Close triumphant, with the stray animal in tow. All the while the wretched Frederika Hansen, in whose care she had been, from whose hand she had slipped, was literally wringing that hand with the other. But Sara found she was able to comfort the heap of Baltic self-laceration, 'Freddie, I'm sure she's on her way home this minute,' as Eurwen marched in, dragging the terrified dog on her little-girl's belt. 'Look, Mummy, he tried to bite me once on the arm and once on the leg but he doesn't mean it. He wishes he could bite the car what knocked him over.'

The pungency of its pelt was real enough to have Sara gripping the rust-pocked rail even now. Crazed yellow eyes rolled and flashed at her again, more hallucination than memory, the snap of teeth a pistol shot, the child's *shush-sh* so tender... Suddenly she felt able to *see* her daughter at will. They were a single entity. She had only to... only to... But her straining mind touched vacancy.

When she refocused it was still on the extraordinary. Directly across the road was the wreck of The Schooner Inn. This roofless, futurist construct of metal and broken glass stared blindly at the sea with more than a hint of the post-Apocalyptic and as reference point it stood out as the exact spot reached by the woman she had almost driven down yesterday: and now, coming this way, here she was again. There couldn't be two. Ignoring Sara, the woman took up station along the rail and a phone, shiny and new in contrast to her scurfy velvet jacket, was produced. 'It's Kim. I need, no-oo, hang-on, don't be like that. *Please!* '

Politeness dictated any listener should amble away now but this person's, Kim's, life was there, encapsulated in desperate appeal that managed to break into Sara's self-absorption. And when the speaker realised she was pleading with no one and started towards the town centre, Sara found herself following. Suddenly the sun was turned up and the brassy hair sizzled, making Kim an easy quarry. *Why?* she asked herself. *Because you have to go somewhere. Because it outbids going home*. In a few minutes they reached the base of the white needle. Much bigger than Sara's original estimate made from the bridge, this was the Sky Tower according to its peeling paint. Shabby huts, kiosks and parked cars surrounded it… so was this *thing* their objective? A cluster of bodies blocked her view enabling Kim to give another of her signature darts and disappear off Promenade. Sara almost missed the sudden break into a more densely populated… Queen Street. But here Kim checked, taking a second to rub the back of her neck and fondle the jacket's lapel. Decision made, she chose to enter of all places a little Italianate chapel sandwiched between shops. Sara had neither reason nor the nerve to follow but stood back to observe it from apex to street level… the carved grey stone was finely worked as was the modest campanile: someone once had cared very much that by nodding to Rome or Padua, it should give simple pleasure. And still did. Smout the Pawnbrokers offered Pay Day Advances emblazoned across three arched windows and behind them Kim's head bobbed and shoulders twitched as a dialogue progressed with the inner shadows. Lost in Hogarthian imaginings (shelves that groaned beneath tawdry items, the negotiation of ransoms), Kim caught her out. Straight from heated bargaining, the woman pivoted to stare at her.

Sara took a hasty step and kept on. There was an off-license.

She digs her hands into her pockets. Does the bit of necklace stay with her for luck, does she handle it? She's fresh to all this and any moment Eurwen could walk on stage, she thinks. I'll bet she sees that easy stride eating up the Promenade and then the light of recognition in the eyes. There she is! All you had to do was touch the charm.

I wish I could share the teasing payback all these early shots gave me – of a woman I'd heard everything about and up till now never met. To me she was magnetic and I lingered over them afterwards, Sara's screentest. Her smallness and occasional stillness gives cover in a sparse crowd. Unconscious of being important to anyone, she's playing a nobody! Gets knocked off-course by a blubbery woman half as big again as Libby Jenkinson but she doesn't retaliate. Forced into the gutter, her palm's raised – an apology as if in the wrong herself, misjudging the strength of Rhyl's currents. I've picked her up at the base of SkyTower only to lose her as a coach party's put down, then have her resurface, static and staring. She takes her bearings and makes for tidy, well-populated Queen Street and I tag along, high on the thrill of a successful stalk that even guilt can't spoil.

'Well?'

Josh refused to acknowledge the fraught one word when he came in at six. Dropping his tie and wallet on a clean bit of work surface, then a check of both trouser pockets all had to be done until finally he looked *at* her, abashed, (surely he could not be surprised to find her still there, cooking for them?) and managed, 'No.'

The steel platter of sugared citrus on the worktop awaiting the grill was a triumph, each peeled segment testifying to her steady hand, courtesy of wine. Sara stroked the Chianti's neck and then splashed a few ccs onto the pan of scarlet sauce. 'Have some of that if you like,' she could tell him, loftily. Her own glass was washed, dried and back in a cupboard.

'I won't. Might need to go out again.'

She fetched herself a glass, a different one for some reason, and made it ruby to the brim.

'Come and sit down,' he suggested.

'I'll need to—'

'Yeah.' Impatiently, he swept the bottle up himself but once next door, seated across from her, undid each shirt cuff slowly, fumbling even, setting her teeth on edge as the crumpled cotton was rolled to the elbow; a series of bruises were exposed beneath the tan.

'Always sporting a badge of your office,' she prompted.

'Nope. Helping somebody with their fence.'

'Your daughter is missing but you won't let that stand in the way of a good deed.' (Drink! Now! Don't say any more!) 'You had something to tell me?'

Josh, though, prevaricated, possibly the first time she had ever witnessed it. 'Did Eurwen mention what she's been up to... while she's been here?'

'What do you think? I've had long chatty letters?' There was no camouflaging the rawness. 'I've texted, I've emailed, trying to keep it light. When I rang her number often she wouldn't even answer. And you must have heard how she spoke to me on your phone. No. Yes. I'm getting on with some revision. All lies, I suppose?'

'If you think I was doing any better, I wasn't. She even tried the Miss Shouty-Pouty act. Realised that wouldn't work! You know Eurwen. It suited her, so then it's trying to keep me on side.' The smile he was tempting her with was almost reflected but she held back. 'That's something else she's been up to since she could talk.'

Though not with me, she refrained from saying, not for... how long? 'So what *has* she been doing?'

'Horse riding. Helping out at some stables. *Missed it*, she claimed. *Fine*, I said. She'd been when she stayed last year. To the same place. Decent enough people run it. They'd had their trailer nicked out of the yard is how I knew them... Upton... they're called.'

'A couple?'

'A man and his daughter.'

'Naturally.'

He was not going to rise: 'It's impressive, the way kids make this life for themselves you know nothing about. Took her less than a month up here...' In mid-June Eurwen's sudden manifestation had come as a shock. There she was, grinning on the front step, the bag already off her back, her hair wild and mobile as fronds in the tide: Eurwen, arrived. 'Anyway you— *we* agreed she could see out the summer with me, yeah? I fixed up the riding at the Uptons—'

'Uh-huh.'

'There's Megs, Megan Upton... the father's called Clive. She's nearer to Eurwen's age and I thought—'

'How near?'

'Twenties,' he said too quickly.

'And this woman, Megan,' she repeated the name on purpose, aiming for a show of neutrality, 'she has no idea where Eurwen's gone or—?'

He chopped her off. 'How could she? If she knew, she'd tell me. She's as worried as we are.'

'*Really?*'

'No, 'course not. Figure of speech.'

'Yes.' Play better than you are, Sara, don't be the Harpy that falls on his weakness the instant exposed. This internal advice (ignored on countless previous occasions) now came with a charm-like element. Do not step on the cracks! Do not look back! Touch that carven piece of wood every time you mount the stairs. Eurwen is missing and the torment will not be lifted until you, the guilty party, have rooted out whatever drove her away: in this case your entire self.

'Eurwen's changed.' Josh slumped back, his face bleak. 'I was still picturing—' a further drop of the shoulders and raised palms replaced 'a little girl.'

And she wasn't able to respond. Her anger simmering since that early, semi-drunken stagger out into Tackley Close with car keys held out like a weapon had been directed at Josh the deserter who, not content with this first treachery, had lost their daughter. But all it took was this bodily supplication on his part to turn every harsh judgement to vinegar in her throat. And yearning for Eurwen and love for her husband burst through her in a sob as their fierce acids combined. Finally, 'I know,' she whispered.

It was old news that Josh and Sara had split up. Unlikely as a couple, though not more unlikely than Tomiko and a girl in Rhyl producing me, Josh must've been mega-ineligible to his father-in-law. '*A policeman?*' You only had to meet Geoffrey Severing once or catch a recorded interview, to be impressed by his use of mock amazement in an argument. It was always followed up with scorn. Listen to yourself. Don't take my word. Also there's the dates. These two were married early the same year *A First* came out, Meredith replacing Severing on the cover with days to spare. He'll have tried to torpedo that at least! But to go back to what I did know – outstanding doctoral student, marriage to Josh, a bestseller, a daughter – I was now seeing the woman as different to my invented Sara. I've mentioned how much smaller than estimated but she seemed shrunk in other ways. Timid I wasn't expecting – very unSevering.

So right and wrong, Yori. Oxford Sara can still be genuine in her own world and then morph into this visitor jumping out of her skin at a car's backfire, trailing the woman Kim with a phony sense of purpose. But the first night she stayed with Josh counts against. A separated wife would check into a hotel, surely? Even around Rhyl there must've been some that weren't instantly repulsive – a decent farmhouse B&B 'backaways'. Research was meant to be her thing. Anywhere other than Avonside would impress a husband that *Sara's arrived*! She's an extra factor in their joint problem. Then my attitude changes. I flip – I'm for her. Being at least two people myself, I give her a contingency to draw on. Every build has its hitches. Cost of materials doubles. The virtual drawing looks like it means to stay that way. This woman's secretly expecting to see Eurwen. Half-drunk through the road accidents. Then another near miss down among the seaside kitsch, but with fear sobering the mix, she was looking forward to it all being whisked away the instant Josh's door opens and Eurwen dashes out to meet her—

Instead, she gets frost in more senses than one.

You have to sympathise. If Sara had been told what she calls autumn is actually another season, *higan*, the Japanese time for renewal, she might have come with a better attitude. Maybe got a better outcome. The leaves are gold, not gone. Fight depression! The temperature takes a dive? Quicken up! Here's a chance to sweep your mistakes out over the threshold. Even sins. For this year's *higan* my own house – flat – has been cleaned and all my wants printed on slips of rice paper. A shrine has been made ready. It's just a small thing in a corner, an arrangement that Libby, Glenn or Tess couldn't interpret anyway, if seen, a tumbler of fresh water, a wristwatch and book, a picture when the time comes, all meaningless to the uninformed. Now I can add an incomplete necklace, Eurwen's discard. The ritual also needs a handful of orange leaves easily got from the Borough's one intact greenhouse. Every leaf must be perfection, nothing sampled by insects and, trying for strict accuracy, I'll be saving each day's offerings for use at the very end. All this has to be on Tomiko's advice because Tomiko is still the only Japanese I know. Growing up in Rhyl meant continually catching sight of a wiry, fawn-skinned kid in the plate glass and thinking Hey, Yori! Another one!

Always me.

Staring at girls, pulling a devil's face behind my mother's back, always me. It taught an important lesson, the need to keep an eye on what Yori was up to— sorry, two lessons. Never expect to recognise your own image nor the things it does.

Chapter 6

Another day. Another evening. From halfway up the stairs, and with her blouse already in the process of unbuttoning, Sara called, 'What sort of restaurant?'

'The May Quay does food. At the end of the road... or we can walk in over the bridge if you like.'

She returned. 'Into *Rhyl?*'

'The May Quay it is then.'

'I won't bother to change.'

Josh's bottle of Becks disappeared in one.

The May Quay was the oversized, red-roofed mock cottage she had turned away from, driving into Avonside. It faced the road surrounded by vans and chalets in peeling pastels that blocked any possibility of a view even if the light had not been failing. Mud from the hidden harbour was pungent on the breeze in their faces though and by the time they reached the entrance Sara's teeth chattered. 'Weather's on the turn,' Josh conceded. Inside a wide choice of empty booths beckoned. She slid without friction across the port wine vinyl to the wall, a sensation of *mal de mer* giving yet another reason to request mineral water.

Josh snapped, 'Yeah, right.'

'It's what I'd like, please.'

Back with beer in a lettered goblet for himself: 'So what's the game now, Sara?' He was positioned directly across from her, interrogation style. 'How much have you had already?'

'Nothing.' She was recompensed by actual doubt in his eyes.

He leaned over and pinged her glass with a thumbnail. 'Good for you.'

'I am stopping, Josh. I've practically stopped. Don't— don't say anything.' She'd have put a finger to his lip but he seemed in a mood to slap it away. 'I must. Eurwen… for when she does return. It's what I have to do.' Music blared out from the back of the building causing her to jump, but the refrain was one she recognised from everywhere and throughout the summer, *You're the girl! You're the girl!* Eurwen's lips miming then, a third above, Eurwen's sweet harmonies…

Josh had no startle-reflex nor ever had had. He pushed a laminated menu in her direction. 'I'm for the steak sandwich.'

'Anything.'

To expect more from him was unrealistic though nothing prevented the desire for it: so this was what she had been looking forward to all the endless hours. Could it be only her second day? While they waited they discussed money: how much might Eurwen have hoarded. 'Credit cards, banks accounts— that's how you find adults, normally,' he instructed. 'She'll have cash. Thank you Geoffrey, thank you Fleur.'

There was no defence to this. Food arrived as did other diners who placed themselves annoyingly close. She murmured, 'I walked around, just hoping. I found the library. It isn't only money, is it? Once she'd have had to go there, if only to get access to… things. Now it's all on her Blackberry. I could have prevented that. I could have stopped Daddy and Fleur buying the wretched—' she broke off, hearing her own disloyalty.

'Don't beat yourself up. Like I said *that's* switched off. First thing we tried. She'll have got herself a cheap and cheerful replacement, a throwaway we can't trace.' Josh chewed. At each bite, shreds of bloody beef dropped back onto his plate.

In the next booth further meaty orders were being delivered; she could envisage an Eurwen melodrama concerning carnivorousness. How irritated she would have been. Once.

'She'll be amongst people we've never even heard of. That's frightening in itself. If you had some idea whom she might be with. At home I'd know her clique.'

'Would you?'

'I'd know her best friends are still the Fortuns. The Canadian girls? I've contacted their parents and Fleur has been to talk to them.'

A flicker of expectation in his leaning forward was extinguished as quickly: but it only heightened her desire to touch and comfort him. She shook her head. 'She hasn't answered their texts. Nothing dramatic; she's been slower to respond apparently and then… then, at the end of August, she stopped altogether.'

'Fleur should've checked their damn phones!'

'Oh, I'm sure that would have helped.' But secretly she agreed. 'If there were anything—'

'You're kidding yourself you know what she's up to in Oxford. We've neither of us got a direct line to Eurwen.' Even his extra Welsh pronunciation of her name, rolling the r to an unnecessary degree increased the toxicity of the words. 'So I'm doing what I can with what I got. Today I—' he broke off just as she heard someone walk across the bar behind her back, someone he recognised, plainly, from the look followed by a quick glance in her own direction. This was *the* woman whose shadow fell between them. Confident, she ignored him, and smiled at Sara with a pretty, tanned, unmade-up face that didn't keep laughter lines yet. Her T-shirt informed the world that its wearer Loves Loves Loves Miami *and* showed off large, high breasts whereas the faded jeans simply contoured muscular thighs. Taller than herself, Sara estimated, she was also broader but in a fit, strapping way. If dropped she might bounce.

'This is Meg Upton, Sara.' He glanced to the side, then away. 'Eurwen's mother.'

61

She said, 'Hello Megan,' just as Meg said, 'Oh, Mrs Meredith I'm—' and Josh said, 'Are you with somebody?'

All three were silent. Meg Upton broke the impasse. 'Just thought a couple of the girls might be in. I'm very sorry about what's happening with Eurwen, Mrs Meredith. I'm sure it'll be all right.'

'Are you? I wish I were.'

It was sufficiently hostile to get Josh involved. 'We've just got these. Are you eating?'

She shook her thick shoulder-length hair, acorn brown and very shiny, and released its herbal scent. One much-pierced ear was covered by the action and she re-exposed it.

'Please, join us for a drink,' Sara said. How much Meg didn't want to was in her fleeting expression but she sat, as far from Sara as the booth allowed. 'If there's anything you can tell me, I'd like to hear it.' Satisfied that her intentions were as stated Josh strolled over to the bar to order 'a glass of white and 'nother of them,' with Meg Upton's eyes fixed on him. 'You have been taking Eurwen riding?'

'Yes. She's very good.' The voice was as beautiful an alto as the expansive chest promised. How easy Josh must have found it to listen to: pitch perfect *and* indigenous.

'And who does she know here? I have to believe she's with people. But—?'

Another head-shake, a hankering look at the stalled Josh and then: 'Your husband's asked me that. I've no idea. She's been to our house a few times when we've had a crowd round… Josh's already gone into everything. He's spoken to the girls working for us. But if you want you can come over any time. Do it all again.'

'Perhaps I should.' *You're the girl! You're the girl/ behind the blinds.* Such a facile-seeming song at first… *You're the girl! You're the girl/ all out of dimes—*

Meg swallowed. 'That meal's getting cold,' she said. And then Josh was back.

She was running, past the chalets, then the drawn up caravans, past the shacks around the harbour and onto a road before she allowed herself time to think.

Completely dark now, what illumination there was came from the moon above speeding high cloud, disorientating to focus on for more than a moment. But at her level the breeze was just sufficient to make boats at their moorings restless as chained beasts. Surprisingly she found a trio of names came to her, though obscured: Olivia Jeanne, Merlin and of course, the Sarah II, all previously noticed. Presumably. Extraordinary the snippets the mind remembered and those it chose to forget... A distant blaze of neon denoted Rhyl proper with just a single car coming almost silently away from it. The footsteps suddenly behind her were much more significant. She didn't turn but speeded up. Even so the man's breathing became audible and then— 'Sara!' Josh's voice, of course. 'Sara for God's sake wait!'

She stopped.

'Who d'you think it was?' he demanded.

'I don't know,' she lied. 'Not you obviously. You and your friend seemed settled for the night.' She had stolen away on a pretend lavatory trip. 'Do go back.'

For answer he grasped her arm with a familiar nuance of action, that sliding of his palm over the elbow joint and reaching down and round to clamp onto the inner wrist. His intention was clear: to hustle her in the direction of his house. But first he must phone *her*. 'Megs, it's Josh. Yeah. Sara's not feeling too good. I'm taking her— Yeah. I will. I'll do that. Bye.' (Who is this stagecraft for? she wanted to ask. But speaking to the absent Meg seemed to calm him. Perhaps she was answered.) 'It's my fault, this. Let's get home. I'll tell you a few things about today.'

'No.'

'*Oh, for fucksake!*'

'I mean I don't want to go back to that place. That horrible house,' she added for good measure.

'Right! Come on then.' He swivelled them and halted though they had almost attained Avonside's entrance. They were opposite the first houses but stalled next to a wooden fence, its purpose apparently to keep back assorted weeds and a bit of Rhyl street art, stark black shapes unrecognisable in the poor illumination; in daylight they were a rotten rowing boat and a pair of oversized rusty metal spheres.

'I meant to ask you,' she said, 'why are these here? What are they exactly? Simply dumped… or emblematic in some way?'

He glanced at them as though installed in his absence. '*Fine!*' he said and marched her at the bridge, which now had a stream of cars crossing and none of them with drivers who gave a woman being dragged along by a much larger man a second glance. 'Marine Lake! That'd be nice wouldn't it?'

Sara found herself hurried over a waste area where she had turned the car, that first day in Rhyl. The only way to combat Josh's momentum would be to let herself sink to the ground. Undignified, it might also make him… too late! A shaggy hedge loomed up and they were through a gap: immediately the turf fell sharply away and she would have plunged headlong over an invisible impediment if not for his grip.

'What was that?'

'Train track.'

'We're on the tracks?'

'Miniature railway. Not in operation now.'

His feet knew the lie of the land. Ahead lay the lake, completely still and burnished pewter, very different from its normal face, nearly lovely in fact as the gloom transformed it into a natural feature. A golden beam leapt across the water from the far bank and was extinguished as quickly: a cry came from the same spot, harsh as a crow's. The hair on the back of her neck actually stood up. This was an abandoned place. The 'lake' she needed no reminding was a twenty-acre concrete construct, with an island bordered by kerbstones. She'd walked past it at noon... observed no one along its perimeter, bar a grotesque red-billed goose which seemed to prefer dry land, while the only floating objects were polystyrene cups. Now Josh almost towed her onto her face, so eager was he to get down to the edge and its well-trodden path. 'No!' she said. 'No. A man in a shop, yesterday... was talking...' her breath came painfully dry. 'He said to keep away. Especially at night.'

She may as well not have spoken. 'Here we are,' he said. Down by the water now: another brief flaring of light, directly opposite and in the direction Josh proposed, was like a warning.

'Stop it. I don't want to walk here. We could be attacked!'

'Oh Sara! D'you think so?'

They stumbled on. Her open sandals had soles thin enough to feel every sharp pebble of the path as though she had come here barefoot. 'How far is it around?'

'Far enough.'

It seemed they were to do the march in silence, all the time his pressure on her arm increasing. But as the lake shore curved away from the river they arrived at the trio of metal seats he had obviously been making for. Josh sat, changing his hold, turning it into an arm around her shoulder as though they were a courting couple, keeping her squeezed up against his furious heat and aware of his rapid respiration and the stored energy in his rigid frame. The gulls were still active... did they never rest? Dozens of them wheeling around the roof of some construct on the far side of the road where there should still be carousels and candyfloss sellers. 'Eurwen loved the funfair,' she said. The building blurred against sky dull as a blanket. 'You brought her here for your mother's birthday. She talked about the ride on the little train. How old would she have been?'

'Seventy. It was the year before she died.'

She felt the change in him.

'*Eurwen!* Nine… no, ten. Eleven?'

'You couldn't have expected me to come.' She tried to squirm around but he wouldn't allow it, nor could she free the trapped arm. '*We* were barely speaking. Can you imagine the four of us squeezed into Nora's house for a whole weekend? Don't make it my fault. You didn't want me to come.'

'No,' he said and pulled away and leaned forward, his head in his hands, giving her to understand she could get up and leave now and wouldn't be prevented.

But she didn't. 'These girls Meg Upton mentioned, you've checked on them?'

'Don't take anything from Megs calling them the girls. One's nearly thirty— she lives with a Neil Rix. He's older again. An ugly mug. And yes, of course I've bloody checked them out. First thing I did. He's gotta record.'

'For?'

'Relax. Criminal damage. Long time, now, student days. He smashed Boots the chemist's window. That's it. A protest. He got the conviction because he wouldn't accept a caution would be my guess. He's not had a mention since.'

'And what was this protest against?'

'Animals. You know, experimenting on animals.'

'*Eurwen.* Yes.' She experienced an overwhelming hatred for these strangers Josh described. They had formed part of Eurwen's world, might be with her at this moment and as if on cue, a siren sprang to life, on a mission to some *typical Rhyl* scenario. The official keening grew before being abruptly cut off. That they both connected the sound with their lost child was left unshared, a crime in itself, a father and mother split and Eurwen falling through the crack. So we ache and sit here, specimens of *Homo dolens* squirming under our separate glass domes. After five minutes or so she whispered, 'Josh. There's someone in the bushes.'

'What?'

That flash of light and the rasping half-word... it had been a human voice. Of course there were other people here. Hadn't she been warned? She pressed her face close to his. If they were being observed it could pass for a kiss. 'Someone's in there.'

Everything next came in double-time. He said nothing but as he jumped up she was almost sure a snatch of speech issued from a black mound of shrub that buttressed the hedge. Josh reached it and without a pause kicked out. His target must have been a couple of feet off the ground. There was a grunt... and then the branches seemed to explode in Josh's direction and her ability to distinguish his form against the background was gone. Nothing made sense to either vision or hearing; another noise that may have been Josh's had no words contained until an alien much louder voice shouted, 'Fucker!'

Even shapes were obscure: it could have been a man (Josh) caught in a tangle of living branches and trying to get loose. But the branches also possessed vocal cords and lungs and muttered, 'Right! Right you... fucker— you... right!' The combined creature, half-Josh, half something else lurched first toward the water's edge and then back from it like one single, huge inebriate.

Incomprehension left her static. What ought she do? Abandoning Josh was not an option and she did want to help, to protect him, she realised... but before anything practical came to mind, a second huge chunk of shade rushed out and launched itself at Josh's back. It had her screaming, 'Josh...

another one!' This extra being hesitated between them. For an instant the very air seemed to crackle and then Josh threw the thing he was wrestling with at it and after the impact, he came on instantly, kicking the nearest figure with a connection Sara heard as the sound of a clean-bowling on the University's Iffley Road ground. Very satisfying. Both fell. There was a howl, a string of obscenities... and the two figures on the floor separated. While one clambered to its feet the other stayed down, rolling and groaning. Now it seemed a real possibility that Josh might attack the standing man again, or be attacked himself. Was *she* in danger? The blood rushing through her ears and agony in the throat said so. She had never been so close to violence... and yet her fear was already lessening, changing... too quickly, she rationalised later. But then and there it was being overlaid by elation: because Josh will win! This told in the finishing-up, pushing off movement of his upper limbs and his barely-articulated dry *uh!* captive within the chest but pleasing for the maker. In any case he stepped away from both attackers and toward her. For an instant he actually seemed about to present them his back. She dodged to keep their whereabouts known, to maintain a line of sight for herself.

To the upright body Josh said, 'Run. Now!'

There was a moment's pause before it started off at a lopsided trot. From the other prostrate thing was only a low grumbling: 'You'll live,' Josh said. 'If you can walk, it's your lucky night. If not—'

The dropped sack heaved itself onto legs and followed the first into the shadows, while Josh stood with fists clenched, breathing hard. The Jacobean dumbshow had concluded.

'My God Josh!'

Several thumps of her heart passed before he muttered, 'I know that pair,' sotto voce. He came over and lowered himself onto the bench. 'The father's not even my age. He was the one

I didn't kick, right? The son's an even more evil little... bastard or will be.'

So very *quick*... and it was to be wound up, now, just like that? Only Josh's murderous aura confirmed anything had happened at all. Her head swam as, instinctively, she must have stepped up her respiration rate to match his. 'You *know* them? Who are they?'

Legs out in front of him, feet in heavy boots, he stared at the water. 'They were the Murcotts, father and son. Ike has been a professional nuisance since he got here. Manchester connections but real low rent. These two, they're the end of the line stuck out in Taffyland as they call it, which says it all. With Ryan it's knives and drugs mostly. Just pills.' A massive sigh. 'Too fucking dense to deal in anything you have to measure out and weigh, we reckon.'

'He may have had a knife.'

'Why d'you think I got that first kick in? If it's any good it tends to make you drop—'

'We could have walked away.'

'Yeah. We'd be sitting at home now, wouldn't we, if it wasn't for me?'

From the eastern edge of the lake an engine noise started, inadequately suppressed, powerful. Josh didn't move. 'Don't worry. That'll be the Murcotts found where they left their bike. Took 'em long enough.'

'A motorbike? They could come back this way.'

'They won't.'

The exultant surge of spirits at his victory seeped out of her as quickly as it had arrived. She was trembling, her knees refusing to lock. 'Please can we go?'

He shrugged and strolled off in the direction of the bridge leaving her to totter after.

These numerous crossings and recrossings were beyond

dismal, as was the thought that she would be doing it again tomorrow. Laughter and shouts, a dressing of hot grease to the air, and a diffuse hostility all seemed to combine and come drifting along from West Parade. Josh said, 'If you want to know about the Murcotts, how's this? Two old dears last summer, one of them has a little win on the bingo and they're making their way home into Wood Road,' he gestured over her head, '—made the mistake of stopping by the lake. She's knocked flat. He's chopped in the kidneys that hard one nearly ruptures. Everything they have on them's taken. His winnings. *Her wedding ring!* Wasn't worth buttons. They even took her bar of chocolate.'

'So were they found guilty?'

He laughed. 'Found guilty? Um— *no.*'

'But it was them?'

'Only they're stupid enough to take that ring. Probably ended up chucking it. So most likely them.'

'Only most likely?'

'What do you want me say, Sara? Yes? No? The prosecution's got no further evidence to offer in this case, M'lady.'

Eight hours later a sombre Josh drove away without reference to after dark alarums and excursions.

Her apology could not be put off. In the absence of writing paper, two sheets carefully cut from a notebook, a message in themselves, would suffice.

Thursday

Dear Daddy and Fleur

I'm very sorry if, last night, I seemed to be making little sense and, also, that I upset, you, Fleur. Of course I had no idea that you had rung several times already and left messages. I must have convinced myself the call would be some terrible news about Eurwen. That's why I grabbed the phone from Josh before he could explain. We had just that moment entered the house, having been for a walk and this being an alien place, please put it down to my feeling out of my element. Mea culpa. But I'd be dishonest if I do not say that every call is a disappointment because it isn't Eurwen, isn't her voice telling me she is coming home. You and Fleur have only ever loved me so I'll have to fall back on hoping you understand and aren't too hurt.

Thank you for trying with the Fortun sisters. As I explained, we've had no word. Josh is convinced she is with other people, probably people she's met whilst here. On occasions there have been phone calls from both a female and a male and Eurwen has been evasive about who these people were. The fact that they were one of each gender seems reassuring although I have no idea why. Josh has promised that he will take me to meet all her contacts that he now knows about. A woman called Megan is one I met within the last twenty-four hours. (Megan Upton is from the stables Eurwen has been haunting. Eurwen sent Fleur a picture postcard of it last month?) A couple who are deeply immersed in animal rights (yes, I know*, I see your expression!) have become friendly with her and she may have been drawn in. I'm sure with Josh's resources they can be found. This couple are not teenagers. Maybe they're sensible and can talk her into contacting her parents. I hope none of this is wishful thinking on my part. However Josh and I both agree it could be worse.*

Another thank you for sorting out home and Mrs Ali. The Peppers next door are very reliable and Hugo works from home remember so there will be someone about during the day. I'm sorry for confusion over the alarm. I must have done something to it as I was leaving. Poor Mrs Ali!

On the subject of clothes, Fleur, I didn't 'take nothing'. I <u>will</u> try to keep my phone charged in future and of course I'll pass on any developments. <u>Really</u> Daddy, sometimes… I can't know for how long, can I?

With my love to you both,

Sara

PS On the subject of that card, do you still have it? Could you put it into an envelope and send it here? I'm not exactly sure why but Josh thinks maybe something of use in it. Thank you, again.

And I was burning papers, Fleur. That's all. If Mrs Ali did what she was paid for they should have been cleared away.

Sheer exhaustion after the lake-side fracas had been responsible for what happened the moment she entered the hall and saw Josh pick up the phone. Eurwen! Not Eurwen! News of any denomination? Her parents at the other end became targets. Attempting to phrase an apology now, her face flushed… or *was* it all Mrs Ali's fault? Mrs Ali and the remains of that fire left cold and finished and yet still somehow *incomplete*, spewing from the study grate for Fleur to find.

Chapter 7

Forward Rhyl started life as a single open-plan room at the top of a turn-of-the-century building— with the promise of a move. By Wave Day it hadn't happened. Street level was unrecognisable on the Monday morning following, but our lookout was reached as usual by a sectional staircase bolted to the rear elevation. Because nobody said not to, we assembled at the bottom to make the climb. Our every recent improvement to Rhylites' quality of life lay under cubic metres of trash so the atmosphere wasn't buoyant. Glenn clutched his waterproof to his body to stop it becoming a sail. Omar, only with us a month, a tall good-looking Iranian who opted to be called Persian was already planning his escape, I decided. His normal five o'clock shadow look was a disguise in the making. He couldn't take his eyes off the Flintshire Foods vehicle buried to its cab in the side wall of the White Rose Shopping Centre on the opposite corner. A few courses of brick were intact above the hole, like an advertising stunt or something made for a film. *Everything* was unreal if you stopped to consider— but this was up close. And what had happened to the driver? Then someone somewhere decided to start a chain-saw up in the next street. Not reassuring. The noise gave us an extra buzz, an excuse to jump.

'I cannot believe nobody died,' Omar said in an accent I always link with the South of England and private schooling, word endings like knapped flints. 'Apart from the old couple.'

'Another went off the bridge as well. He was young.'

Omar pulled a face.

Low down in what had once been the ground floor of the Westminster Hotel, windows were slimy inside and out. But one storey up there's a picture of optimism. In a small kitchen a MultiCook was dumped in an armchair which had then been heaved onto a table, all unmarked. But having made it to our creepily unchanged office with its cramped work stations, dissatisfaction set in and we jostled each other to stare out.

'Cher-rist!' Even Glenn Hughes was lost for anything else.

It was a shambles. Familiar friends had gone and the absentees gave the sky extra volume. Only the grey-brown sea was intact and that was hitting a different beach. As we watched the tide inching in across our famous Golden Sands, Rhyl's Spring Festival could've just finished (we don't have one) or its refugee camp been overrun. The partygoers or inmates all fled, the spoilage everywhere. No one who hasn't witnessed it can understand. And the smell from the open window was a mixture of river mud, hydrocarbons, human waste, rotting fish— and the rest. Even now any one of them brings back that morning and the shock I thought I was ready for but wasn't. Both Old Woolworths and Clubbers further along had collapsed— no loss, architecturally, this gave an improved vantage point to spectate from. The sun came out and polished up the sluggish breakers and it only got worse. Now it was highlighting every oily pool and stripped-off sheet of corrugated iron. Fine for the clean-up though! A bulldozer fleet like giant dungbeetles had congregated at the base of SkyTower, probably because it was still there. Slowly they pushed portions of debris along a West Parade whose existence you had to take on trust because there wasn't a visible square metre of tarmac.

'Fuckin' 'ell,' Glenn said. If Tess had been standing next to him a baboon arm would've liked to snake across her shoulders. 'This has gotta be the worst acid I ever dropped. Bloody robber she is, that Rhondda Jones, Leisure Services. When somebody puts the town back I'll be straight up there for a refund.' He was dressed in the striped sweater and pants I'd laundered for him. Although his entire wardrobe, unfortunately, would be saved, everything on the ground floor of his home is gone. Why? I wanted to know. Why not get what you could? Why all that walking around Rhyl, all that I-am-a-camera, asking to get yourself killed? Why are you at my house?

Nobody spoke. Next he tried, 'The first thing'll happen, we'll get a new name. My money's on Backward Rhyl.'

'It could've been worse.'

'*Puh!*' A blob of saliva shot from between two rows of big teeth. 'Worse? Even for Rhyl— *worse?*'

But it could, if the flood had reached the hospital, if it'd come in darkness— when even in daytime it did *this*. Still, I'd made my choice balanced on a wooden chair and Glenn wasn't going to tip me over by acting like he's not involved. I'll never understand him and the only way to deal with someone like that, someone who won't defend the side you're both on, is you don't just stick to your guns. You give them covering fire. 'A lot's repairable and most of what isn't was waiting for the wreckers anyway. And at least there were only three deaths,' I said.

Our mystery dead person was still a footnote to any media mentions of us. Not even a gender had been released. (I was living in a lull – didn't know it). Glenn Hughes occupying my sofa, that was bother. He'd stayed. The night of the storm it felt OK to shelter the deluged-out. These things have instant payback. A third of the town is underwater and you have a loud, pink refugee in your house – the upset's nearly gratifying. But next morning and the next, to have him pebbledashing the mirror, removing his yesterday's sweatshirt, bag of sweets and finally dirty socks before finding a seat— he was like a tomcat spraying its new home. I hate cats. Only the second night he picked up an image from my desk and wants to know, 'Who's this then, Yori?' and when I answer 'My mother', it's grinning and, 'Still about is she?' like there was a chance for him.

'Alive, yes. She moved away. After my father went back to Japan.' Not quite true but near enough.

Libby's ground floor wasn't designed for even a single man. Its sitting room I slept in, dining room I lived in and the shower room was a step outside the back door to an open porch for access— like the admired Muroa house in Tokyo but not meant. Also there was Tess. For the last few months on Fridays I cooked us a meal while she pretended to be interested. '*Yakisaba*— means fried noodles,' I'd say tasting, holding up a sample I longed to see her eat. 'The pieces of fish are marinated tilapia. The little cakes are called *mochi* – white ones plain, green ones coloured with seaweed.'

Well I bet nobody'd guess to taste them! is what she always said, which is fine, and afterwards we'd have dependable sex during which her face stays smooth, as do the generous lips you want to dance your fingers over. Tess-ss.

What she didn't know was I remembered her from school. A little girl with twigs for arms, always on the edge of things, poor-looking, trying to be invisible. I saw her though. And – me that bit *older* – I'd speak to her. She was too shy. I got *yes, no, I dunno*. But like the town's reward for coming back, here she was again, grown to a perfect Linda Darnell, not-shy, standing naked on Fridays – smaller breasts though – some Saturdays, an Art Deco statue in ivory and bronze. Impossible, now. Well, stopped. My private Hollywood star couldn't appear. Tess's home was off-limits as well, due to crowding because her backstory was filled out with a feckless parent and, worse, brothers. Of course away from wrecked Rhyl I could have rented us another flat. Or bought a house for Tess who'd grown up deprived and whose mother and half-brothers were always in scrapes over money and semi-illegalities, an entire house for Tess to ogle and touch the surfaces of— part of me saw it happening. A cottage in the hills, properly done up by English weekenders where I'd point out the garden through an original, five plank door— What d'you think, huh? But that needed the Yori Tess knew to explain how he was able to do it. A major reboot. Time consuming.

So instead of Tess, 'Hiya!' from Glenn Hughes in the mornings, and, 'race yer to the crapper!'

Only a couple of weeks and I found out all of his tastes without asking. I gave up trying to eat well, work at home, keep tidy, watch movies with proper attention, and, a continuing project, listen out for the things that made J.S. Bach Top Composer. What do you do when you find a tiger sharing your cave? Wear stripes. Even catching me talking to Tomiko would have Glenn joining in. I'm not recording here what with. Tomiko and I never referred to it afterwards. As I lugged the salvaged pieces of Glenn's life back to his drying out semi in Bank Street I smelled the river under all that detergent and kept quiet. The original quarry tiles had come out pretty well thanks to me, the new skirting boards showing only a slight warp already. 'It'll be better in your own home again,' I said. But it's a case of live here, Glenn or I might have to kill you too. Except it couldn't be 'too', because I wasn't counting my first victim back then. 'As for the present, the poster I mean, there wasn't any need. And you're right, you shouldn't let Alice see it till you've got more things in.'

At least Alice wouldn't be coming home a widow and how close a call was that? Before he stumped off to check upstairs he surprised me with, 'Any time I can do something back, I will you know, for putting me up,' which turned out to be a promise he kept. In return for houseroom, Glenn would go on to give me *three* presents over the summer. The poster I already had. An annoying mug from Spain followed and would end up my favourite— once I'd handed it on. (I'll explain another time.) As for Glenn's third favour, that changed everything.

But happy enough to eat an aubergine sideways, hot enough

to boil a kettle on my navel, lucky enough to pick seven winning numbers on Casino Pigalle, I took the beach road home, the pretty way, not. I wanted to wallow in disaster and index its huge opportunities. They could make my revamp of good old Quay Street before The Wave more of a scab-pick— so attend to the plum sites, I told myself, now you get to see them and now actually moving from one to the next was possible. They were spread out in a chain from Foryd Harbour along two point five kilometres to Rhyl's untouched Edwardian east. All the way you have the sea on your left. On the right there was action and colour and amazing structures and people coming back to fill them, landscaping, sudden vistas, new and old, though all still in my head. An empty blue sky's thrown over the lot, making one of those days you lay down in the memory, warm, hardly a breath of wind so of course you treat yourself to a twenty-minute walk along Rhyl's ultimate desire line that has just, to use another technical planning term, had *the crap* rubbed off it.

With Glenn further behind at every pace and my plans branching fractal-like, I wish I'd stayed out the rest of the day. Back home Libby Jenkinson and her younger sister – I could tell you her name but not relevant – were sunbathing strapless on the front crazy paving. Flesh bulged above Libby's tight top the way excess sealant does. The sister was starved in comparison though sharing Libby's other traits of loud and over friendly. They were drinking from cans and shuffling away from the shade with chairs attached, giggling between themselves, girly and non-threatening. And when, 'What you done now?' Libby wanted to know, it was still laughing and aiming her cider at me, slopping it. The sister tutted over the waste. 'There's been somebody here for you. You've gotta contact the police— oo-o! He left a proper letter I had to sign one of them things for. It's sitting on the stairs.'

News of Sara was inside.

Chapter 8

Writing and reflection through writing had often allowed her to recoup what alcohol stole. A journal can be used to document and, in some fashion, constrain *extremis*... also to record small successes: cheap homilies, both, from an expensive therapist after Josh left. Absolutely, Dr Tilney... Tilson? Buying the notebook in the little general store in Sussex Street on a meandering walk this morning, had served as alibi for a Smirnoff purchase. In Oxford she was expert at entering run-of-the-mill booze merchants intent on something very specific, 'a 2001 Meursault for my father? He's very particular about his Burgundy.' Usually a safe choice to be thwarted in, then swayed by the special offer on spirits, a sop to the retailer becomes almost a pleasantry. But as the afternoon came on she redrafted her letter to Fleur and lacking anything else, opened the book to find it a useless diary, its year unplanned and nine months of blankness already in the past. As a memory test she tried filling in names and addresses of acquaintances, though telephone numbers escaped her save Pryorsfield's, the Severings' family home. Then, scoring through the printed date, she wrote 'September 23rd. 12.05 am. Josh rang' and recent events came easily at first. But a few sentences into 24th 'I'd read, after discovering I was pregnant, that in the giving of a name lies much of the receiver's futurity—' she fetched the Smirnoff. Stopping cannot mean stopped, she told the absent Dr Tilston, or perhaps it was Josh she explained to. You cannot stop as though pulling the communication cord. It causes damage, is not recommended. Experts agree. (Somewhere there would be an expert who agreed). With drink, no, with a certain dosage of drink, everything matters intensely. Another, and nothing does. Each day the hands shake a little more or less. Estimate well and there lies the key to contentment: now try and fit to the lock.

Sara was never going to fit the key into that lock, not here. Or now.

I own a poster of past Rhyl. Not a famous one, not the Jackson Burton you might have seen if you call up 'Rhyl', with children on sand like icing sugar, the Pavilion behind them— or better, Douglas Lionel Mays' Punch and Judy audience that fetched a record at auction recently. Mine is a bit of an embarrassment, hangs above the veg rack and was gifted me by Glenn Hughes. I suspect he made it himself, it's his sort of thing and he's forgotten admitting to that little fakery business he ran twenty years ago in vintage ephemera. He's done a passable ageing job on my piece, graduated the fade and then put it in an old-fashioned tube. Added damage to the top right corner just where you might grab hold to take it down— all, so one day he can say 'Y'know that poster I gave you that time—?' Bars of printed text prop up sepia roundels of vanished views. The Belvoir Hotel is fancy as a wedding cake, the elegant East Parade fountain hasn't been broken up yet, and parked under the pier are a convoy of horse-drawn wheeled sheds to bathe from. And so on. Central is a head-and-shoulders portrait of John Sisson, First Developer, the Father of Rhyl. Each morning I read, 'Indisposed and Delicate as I am, I do not believe there is another place so good in the country... having visited the South of France, Spain and Mexico... I prefer the atmosphere of Rhyl to any of them.' A pity the writer's holiday was taken (as it admits) in 1848.

At 6 a.m. and ready for another day on Project Sara I don't let it bother me. Like a lot of projects this one's mutated as it goes along but I need to say it started harmlessly. I was very attracted by her better qualities, like her respect for parents, love for Eurwen, who I knew from personal experience wasn't an easy love, and doing good work. OK, she was a forty-year-old semi-famous woman and I was a younger half-Japanese but I kidded myself if we'd met *in ideal circumstances* we'd have got on. Am I wrong to?

Showered, I walk naked and chicken-skinned back into to my three-metre-long kitchen which contains a sink, shelving, a basic MultiCook and not much else, so reminding me of student days. Access is via a sliding door. A finger of yellow light poking through says Success Is Waiting! But the signals are everywhere. For example the alloy runners of the door into the living room are grit-free and move with the silkiness of the recently installed, something I can't usually get to happen even by rigorous cleaning. Tea scent is filling the kitchen but I repeat the action. Each time the panel of board vanishes noiselessly, leaving a crisp cutout in the wall through which Sara's shrine is on view. Along a tarnished silver chain, her moonstones, one detached, catch the sun.

September 27th

Two calls this morning, the first from Geoffrey: 'You'll ring often from now on? But I feel I should I speak to—?' her father tormented her with a short intermission. Sara conjured him into being: the silver hair, raffishly curled to collar length but also neat and gleaming against a fresh Viyella shirt... now pinching the high bridge of his nose as forensic eyes focused two hundred miles to his north. 'No? I'll bide my time then. For the present.' Their conversation finished with the professor softened as much as a man wrestling a huge annoyance could soften and Sara felt the nails in her palms gradually relent.

A decent interval while Fleur made sure he was study-bound,

then the excessive precision of her: 'It is just me, darling!' came as much more welcome. 'I'll send the postcard at once. But I thought you may be in want of reading matter? Something you can't get there to help pass the time?'

'I'm not in hospital, Fleur.'

'Of course not. But what about work, then? Something that could perhaps—'

'No. Really.'

Fleur gave up. It left Sara wishing she had prolonged the conversation instead of this lapse into vacancy, staring out at the river, a glass of orange juice cradled to her breastbone. No drink today, yet, hence the slight *crawliness* across the back and shoulders, as though a colony of small beetles continually searched for a way out of her clothes. She shuddered. Since Josh left, very early, she had gone through his room. This was perfectly permissible: as she'd begun to dress in a white bra and cotton briefs picked from the tallboy drawer, she realised her own pathetically few belongings had already been searched. The two items of underwear were neatly lined up together whereas her distinct memory was of throwing the briefs in on top of her only sweater. Her small empty vanity case had *just* budged from the wall. *I've stopped*, she had announced to him in absolute sincerity… and he had looked for her hidden supply at the first opportunity.

The master suite: half the size of their three-windowed room in Tackley Close it accommodated a double divan (just) and his and hers wardrobes connected by a white melamine counter. Josh's laptop, removed from the living room on the day of her arrival, sat where a woman's brushes, combs and creams might be laid out but weren't. Connected up in an amateurish way (in a hurry?) cables trailed to the carpet and out of sight. She sat down on the end of the bed from where it was perfectly usable… and opened it. His emails were password protected as expected. A complete waste of time but she entered *Eurwen* then *Rosemary*, Josh's long dead twin... *Megan?* and experienced joy when that one failed. She was no adept (Geoffrey or Eurwen often having to extract her from a state of techno-paralysis) and giving up, she tried other easy, familiar routes, Microsoft Word, Adobe Reader and found an oddity in the absence of any stored documents, in fact cyber-rooms bare as Avonside's actual ones. Everything she presumed had been deleted and was beyond her powers to track or recall, making the back of her neck prickle at Josh's surveillance from afar. Just on the point of shutting the machine down she thought to click on My Pictures. *Accessible.* A dozen images, and from the first Meg Upton jumped out. Yes, she was significant... that had been apparent... so not even a pretence of shock, please. Yet her heart's flutter transmitted itself to her fingers, mis-keying and the resultant frustrated sob, more painful than it justified. When the thumbnail was enlarged all it revealed was a bigger restaurant scenario with an empty chair pulled away from the vacated table setting. A slinkily dressed Meg leaned towards the photographer, the blemish-free throat and upper slopes of breast on display... the sexual fantasy this one photograph engendered in her mind was surprisingly crude. It was of the woman naked across Josh's loins, the slow rhythm of intercourse stolen straight from a lesson in equitation... *a seamless transition of pace is what you're aiming for, dear, into a rising trot that comes directly from the animal's movement...* She actually giggled.

And then, Do *not* cry! It doesn't matter. Or shouldn't. Or not very much. She could almost believe *that* (or she could in a while, once she returned with something stronger in the glass). Even if Meg had been left on show as Josh's spiteful joke, it mustn't matter. Because the vodka's smooth hand caressed her brow and would soon enter the chambers of her heart. And because all of the remaining images were Eurwen.

The series began in the backyard of Josh's mother's house; Nora Meredith clasped the hand of a white-frocked fairy, though a wicked fairy blowing bubbles straight into her grandmother's benign face. Funfair settings followed, the Ferris Wheel and the well-remembered shot (what would she be, nine, ten, possibly less?) of Eurwen's dangerously oblique silhouette as she leaned out... unfamiliar beach scenes... an aquarium visit. In the final frame Eurwen was attending some sort of outdoor event and still blissfully happy. Craning forward, trying to read her daughter's expression gave no further clues. Eurwen remained a willow-limbed, wild-haired enigma beneath the tattered bunting, as did the figure in a droopy-eared dog suit that postured at her side. For backdrop, a group of beer-swilling males. But coming straight towards the observer with one arm outstretched... *yes*. The shoddy jacket and the brittle thatch meant only one person: Kim.

Eurwen in alien company induced... bafflement? Anxiety, for sure. But jealousy was the most potent effect, stronger even than Meg could inspire and beyond control. The bed felt both her fists. She had never been so rebuffed by any other subject: Eurwen, undocumented, uncategorised, slipping away out of the *present* and leaving her literally clueless. What she did know was her daughter should not be portioned out to these strangers, eaten away at, transformed into someone she couldn't touch.

She closed the laptop and attempted to reposition it. From her bag next door another big splash of vodka joined the juice. But while she considered further moves she was drawn back up to her perch, Josh's bed, the only place in the house from which the river was visible... a mouthful from the glass, held stinging deliciously on the palate then let surge down, refreshed her numerous dry channels while her attention wandered over the view. That Eurwen thought gorgeous... slowly some optical illusion softened its divisions and caused the murky Clwyd to appear as though about level with Josh's larch-lap fence. Impossible, of course: it was just the tide at full, covering up the mud and at slack water by the looks of it. Call Josh? How might that progress? You didn't trust me. I took it as carte blanche to snoop through *your* private world and found... we're married, after all, separated but married in everyone's eyes except our own. A couple who had made a daughter... the words recalled a lecture from Fleur. A couple joined in a quest to retrieve that daughter, couldn't afford petty disputes, couldn't behave like tin-pot, nineteenth century kingdoms, bankrupting themselves on parades and bullets.

Long-focused on the water during this debate, her individual ideas circled like swallows until they lit upon a bright yellow item in the water, bobbing off the far bank. She watched its regular roll action, suggestive less of an object about to float free than of something contained and trying to get out. And she thought *Genie*. Its prison a plastic drum of industrial detergent instead of a lamp, consider finding it... and the release! Golden skin swelling with spite, the pigtail slick with the dregs, spitting bubbles bigger than a little girl could blow, it bats aside branches, squelches ashore, threatening and malevolent. Silt has dried to putty on its muscular calves with the heat of frustration... she took a long wanton gulp at the glass... but she was its mistress.

Three wishes. The first was no problem. 'I want my daughter Eurwen to be found by her father Joshua Meredith absolutely safe and well this second.'

Weasel words in the small print, though, were instantly apparent. Josh could, *this second*, come across a safe and well Eurwen only to have her disappear, worse, have her dash into the traffic before his eyes. Her own doing, a stupid waste of a wish... Get the first one wrong, nothing else could put it back together. Get the first right and there would be nothing else to wish for.

'If you restore her I'll give up the others. I don't need to be happy or have my husband love me again. I won't ask for the big one only a genie can give, to be able to drink as normal people do, sharing a glass of wine with neighbours. Or alone. If I've seen the swans flying north to Godstow across the face of a Hunter's Moon and I hear Eurwen, she's above me... awful music... but she calls down over it Coming now! and a brandy is all that's needed to reacquaint me with gladness, I won't ask for that.' But her head throbbed as the thoughts bounced around: *Evensong at St Peter's with Fleur... the altar is the white, green and gold of myrtle, solidago and Shasta daisy and Eurwen helped...! back to Pryorsfield...* 'Ah, Sara Althea and how has the week treated you?' *Geoffrey murmurs...* 'there's a sherry ready-poured through there...'

I won't ask that.

Two wishes returned completely unused, so *Give her back*, she begged.

Around three the phone rang. He had her! 'Josh?'

'No. It's Meg Upton.' In the background the rattle of a horse bridle just dropped, bit and buckles impacting on concrete. 'I wanted to catch you on your own. I know Josh is doing everything he can but... look I've been thinking.'

Don't antagonise the genie whatever else you do. 'Oh yes? What?'

'There's a group around here Eurwen's met. I'm not saying nothing against them but—'

'My God, what do you mean a group? Are you talking about some sort of cult, is that it?'

'No. The opposite really.'

'The opposite of a cult?'

'These are the sort of people won't speak to Josh. But just

you and me, say. They might talk to us. You're her mum, that's gotta count hasn't it? They've all got mums.'

'Where do I begin?'

'That's why I'm ringing. They're having a— there'll be something tomorrow night.'

'How do you know this?'

'Jay and Neil, they're going. Josh mentioned them, probably?' She waited a moment before deciding to add. 'It's on our land, actually. Dad let's them have it now and then— in return for, you know.'

'For what?'

'Work, what else?'

'So, will it be all right? For us to turn up at this event, uninvited?'

Meg laughed. 'Yes. It'll be all right. Come over here, 'bout ten.'

'I'm not sure what to tell Josh. It's a Saturday, I've just realised. So… but going out at that time—'

'Up to you, isn't it?'

September 28th

She would not have found it, even during the day. She would not have found it sober. By the time Josh gave in, they were huddled and chilled, needing the street lamp next to his car to see each other for a final round of sniping… then Josh's deliberately slow movements to climb in beside her switched over to manic once the engine caught.

The pavements were already filled with the half-drunk and half-dressed. A thick knot of young men unwound onto the road feeling safe in their numbers though a glance at Josh's expression would have disabused them. He swerved but came within inches, not braking, hand on the horn. They yelled and cat-called in the car's wake, gestured impotently.

'Josh!'

'It's just a couple of miles. Have you got your phone? I'm thinking now—' he did take his foot off the pedal for an instant to let a female party cross their T, 'that maybe I'll park up in Green Fields. If Clive's about I'll have an hour with him, then ring you to see.'

'To see what?'

'What I can come and do. Or if you're ready to pack it in… as a no-hoper, which it will be.'

'Your friend said she will bring me home. There isn't any point in your staying.'

'Not your call is it?'

The dashboard clock said *10:19*. By 10:30 they were into a dark lane with only the distant bypass lights to show tall hedges. A pair of five-barred gates opened up suddenly to the left and the headlights sent a pale bird fluttering panic-stricken into their path. For what felt like only the second time since leaving Avonside they braked. Josh manoeuvred the big saloon onto a square of concrete and cut the engine. 'Come on then.'

She pulled the borrowed coat across her body as armour before getting out.

Security lights flicked on to reveal a courtyard enclosed by low structures in the manner of a *villa rustica*. But the occupants were shifting silhouettes, their shadows giant knights from the chessboard and an iron stamp the only sound. The spiciness of horse was a perfume that overpowered salt this far inland. Sara was about to speak when a blast of sound hit her from only a foot away, so terrifying she was back behind the car without having made a decision to move. The klaxon continued and then, bizarrely, seemed to draw breath before finishing with a strangled moan. Josh laughed.

'It's Crook,' he said. 'Best burglar alarm ever invented.' The donkey's cartoon ears took shape as her senses recovered. Its muzzle split horizontally, the top hinged up showing a set of teeth. Josh reached out to rub the outsized, woolly head.

'He can break into anywhere there's food— and don't believe in work, do you? Chucked every kid off when he was on the beach. This way.' As he disappeared into the dark beneath the arch, a horse snickered its welcome.

The Uptons' house was unsightly and extensive. Numerous lit rectangles let into the weather-boarded front produced glare sufficient to make concrete containers on either side of the steps into marble funerary vessels. Curtains inside the hall were flung open and Meg could be seen struggling with the door lock.

'You got here.' In jeans again, the thick sweater obscured any tendency to embonpoint Sara's imagination furnished. 'At least it's dry.' Meg may have been speaking to Sara but her eyes were on Josh. Each expecting the other to reply, they following her silently into a room which, despite its barn-like proportions, was overly hot. A scaled-up version of Josh's home was how it struck Sara: showroom-type furniture filled some of the carpeted floor space but the walls were bare, the exception being provided by the most enormous television she had ever seen hanging above an empty fireplace and watched by Clive Upton... she guessed. Caught lounging across three sofa seats, he killed the sound, slid bare feet into a pair of moccasins and got awkwardly upright. A thin brown arm shot out in an offer to shake.

'Mrs Meredith. How's it going?' He was no taller than his daughter and certainly weighed less, with a ribcage that jutted through the tight denim shirt: a neat old/young man whose darting glance came from a leathery face. The hand was leathery too. 'Josh. Meg said you might tag along— No news, eh?' His voice, though primed for it by Josh, still came as a reminder of home to Sara. The Pangbourne Valley was in every rolling syllable. Josh had described 'a jump-jockey not too shabby in his day but going nowhere— met a Welsh girl at Bangor Races and stayed. He's made more up here than he ever would of as head lad. Owns half of Rhyl, now, I sometimes think. Into everything.'

Clive Upton subsided again, rubbing his hip. ''Scuse me, won't you? It's true what they say. It's not the falling off what does it, it's the hitting the ground.'

'Yes. I rode as a child.' For some reason she added, 'Elderly spinsters ran the Pony Club in those days...' but when Clive Upton countered with a comment about how very good a rider Eurwen was, she felt a fool. 'Yes. Yes she is. Thank-you.'

'She'll turn up.' This was completely disinterested in tone, though considered. 'She's been round here a bit this summer. Got a good head on her shoulders. Kids these days, they know it all, huh, Meg?'

Emotionless, mantis-like: seated beside his own too-solid daughter yet he ignored her as he spoke her name. *These people...* Sara felt an inner pressure building, felt it tighten deep in her chest. Any moment her impatience could become too powerful and unruly. In the blink of an eye she seemed to stand outside the person trapped in a superheated room ranged against a trio of enemies, and wondered which one of them she would go for first. Josh because he deserved it, Meg because she desired to, the father because there was least to lose by it? Those unused wishes were about to come in handy. And then one was granted without her having to ask: Clive Upton struggling unexpectedly to his feet and limping over to an almost vacant set of shelves, pouring a generous measure from a decanter into four glasses. His small hands gathered them in like the reins of a double bridle, expertly, without looking. 'This'll keep the cold away.' He passed them around.

'Josh isn't coming with us,' Meg said.

'They think I'll cramp their style.'

'Well have one anyway,' Clive Upton said.

'I'm driving.'

'Your loss.' He put the extra drink onto one of the small tables coupled to each sofa end. Sara accepted hers and sat beside it chatting to Clive but watching Josh and Meg act a pair of acquaintances in a play by Rattigan, measured space between them. On the TV screen a woman's desperate features were captured in close-up.

'It's an oldie,' Clive motioned. They all turned giving Sara opportunity for a mouthful of Scotch. 'Have you seen it, *The Fly*, Sara? No? This scientist turns into a fly. Starts loving the smell of raw flesh. Stupid, eh? You think you're not going to bother, you know, load of balls? But when you lot're gone, I'll probably stick with.'

She drained her glass and placed it down softly as if made of eggshell. 'I don't watch much television.'

'But you wrote for the tele, didn't you?'

'I wrote a book and the BBC dramatised it and then it became a film.'

'Yeah, I thought Meg said you did.'

'Someone else was responsible for the script. It's quite a specialised art, adapting a book. My book in this case but any book really—'

His expression was one of mock horror. 'Can they do that? Take your story like that?'

Still holding his gaze, her hand reached back and found Josh's drink. 'They don't take it. You sell them limited rights.'

'That's OK then. It's like renting? I do a bit of that. That I can get. Or breeding? It's like you own the stallion and you make the other side pay to have the mare covered. Yeah, Josh? No foal, no bloody fee. Yeah?'

Meg Upton said, 'I think we should get going if you're ready Sara. We'll be off now Dad.' And to Josh, 'I'll bring Sara home.'

Josh said, 'Sara?'

'Mm... what?'

'Am I coming with you?'

She shook her head. 'Meg said not,' she added with a hypocrite's relish.

'*Fine*. See you Clive.' Josh was through the door before even Meg could make a move. 'Thanks for the drink.'

'What bloody drink?' Clive Upton laughed at his retreating back and then must have noticed two empty glasses.

Chapter 9

'I'm sorry about Dad,' Meg said. The screech of Josh's departure was dying on the crisp air as they walked along the rear of her father's property and away from the road. Ahead of them appeared to be featureless even under a risen moon. Only the smudged rim of the treeline gave Sara's brain something to focus on. It was *noticeably* cold after the Upton's hothouse and without the Scotch, she would have been at the teeth chattering stage already. She had no idea of direction but a noticeable breeze, straight off the sea in Avonside, was now chilling her left shoulder. Suddenly she smelled smoke.

'You have nothing to apologise for.'

'Since we lost Mum he can be a bit sharp. And the hips don't help. He needs 'least one replacing but he won't—'

'Where exactly are we going?'

'It's after you get through the windbreak. Straight ahead of us now. I'll get my torch out. You're all right. It's good underfoot.'

'I'm fine.'

'It's a field, that's all it is. There's a back entrance into the lane Dad let's them use. He won't have people he doesn't know in the yard. He's racing, see. They're security-mad in racing.'

With her night sight returned Sara saw before them an open grassy area crossed by a built-up causeway the width of a vehicle and standing a foot above the level of the turf. The spice-scent of horse was stronger than ever and she was aware of kicking nuggets of dung over the side or squashing them flat as though walking on ripe fruit. Easy progress... but she found a reluctance to get any closer to the trees ahead and her flesh inside Josh's padded jacket began to prickle. She wanted desperately to be on the other side of the copse and to learn whatever she could from whoever was there, yet going on was another matter. Was it in the trees... or beyond, the thing she feared? She stopped. After a moment Meg noticed and came back.

'Is there a better way?'

'To find out Eurwen, you mean?'

'No... no. Is there a way that maybe doesn't go through *there*.'

'Well—'

'I've always disliked woods at night.' This was untrue. She had grown up in a house surrounded by woodland and never had a problem until this moment and here. So not the dark and not trees— so why did her throat threaten seizure and dampness start in her clothes... her hair?

'Um-m—' if exasperated, Meg did a good job of hiding it, 'It'll be OK really. It's not a proper wood. It's just a shelter belt for the grazing. The path goes straight in and out again. No need to be scared.'

'I understand.' She was faced with blankness solid as a wall and as they had closed with it, a terrible void beckoned. Her mind labelled it *deeper than black*. Which was impossible. Blinking rapidly introduced a shower of brilliant speckles, hallucinatory, of course, yet this *nothing* suddenly housed wraiths, throwing off bright droplets as a fur pelt throws off water.

'Sara?'

She feared she was about to turn and run. Then as quickly as the panic had arrived, the sense of things emerged. 'It's a fire,' she told Meg. 'I can see sparks from a fire... and people.'

'Well, yeah.'

Her fingers caressed the bottle nestled in a pocket. 'Do you want a…' of course Meg didn't want a drink. No one could ever be relied on to want a drink. Only she wanted a drink every waking hour of every day. 'Just give me a moment.' She drank deep and, 'Freezing,' she explained. 'And I'm nervous. I need to find out everything I can. But I don't like having to ask strangers about her. D'you understand?'

'Bit awkward, I suppose.'

'Usually it's… my research, I mean, it's documentary in the main. From archives and libraries. That's how I do my work. Not from people. We should have brought Josh.'

'No, we shouldn't. You'll see.'

She attempted restraint before allowing herself one extra swallow.

'Come on,' Meg said.

An arm thrust itself through hers. *The wife and the mistress walked arm in arm*, ran through her mind though not who nor where. From absolute shadow the backbeat of the music reached out or maybe it was her blood drumming… she couldn't do this… she could not… and then they were across the divide into a world of sound and smell and movement and illumination as flames leapt and smoke and sparks headed for the treetops above an encampment of tents and vehicles scattered in a rough crescent with the horns stretching into the field. At the centre of the open area a massive bonfire of logs crackled while straw bales were being disentangled, sliced and fed in by a couple of genderless figures who prodded the red heart of it with sticks, as though the inferno needed any encouragement. They approached them. Meg scanned faces before discounting the duo… while Sara narrowly avoided stepping on the outstretched paws of a dog and felt the full force of what it was basking in. 'Will you know everybody here?'

'Prob'ly not,' Meg said cheerfully.

The real action was further off; a flimsy domed structure had been erected and beside it a generator to power coloured lights and a sound stage with a drab-clad, dreadlocked giantess presiding. In this semi-open amplified music, though mind-numbing, was just bearable and Sara appreciated Clive Upton's arrangement. Overspill from the scene might filter away across the land to any neighbours in the vicinity but fail to reach Green Fields itself and disturb the equine occupants.

Maybe fifty figures were up and dancing. Despite membership of a host that was rhythmically in sync, most moved in a solitary, self-absorbed way: no looking, no touching. A boy, a stripling, naked to the waist, baggy jeans clinging on precariously, circled the dancers. He was juggling with fire, ignoring both dancers and music with his gestures, and was ignored in his turn. But the bright passage of the fire-sticks was compelling, as was the thought of the flame sweeping across childlike arms, that pathetic concave chest, the seared flesh left in its wake… Between the main event and the blaze proper, small huddled groups of non-dancers sat on blankets or in entrances to tents, drinking and smoking. What she had thought the scent of burning straw was in fact a fug of skunk.

As if reading her thoughts, 'D'you… you know, like a smoke?' Meg said.

'Not for a long time, not since undergraduate days. You?'

'No… well. But you see what I meant about Josh? It wouldn't work would it?'

'I'm amazed your father allows this.'

'He's been known to come down… if he's in the mood. If the hips let him. It's a great painkiller.'

Sara tried to scrutinise her more closely, tried to see beyond the benign simplicity of responses: this woman was intimate with Josh, with Eurwen. But for a second time Meg as if aware moved off. 'Come on then.'

'Who do we speak to?'

'That's the thing, nobody just now. Come and warm up and we'll see what happens, huh?'

There were intact bales spread in twos and threes around the fire. Someone had constructed a sofa with a back and arms but that was already occupied by a pair of skinny, intertwined bodies, fully clothed, booted but linked at the groin and moving in slow tempo. They were near enough to bathe in the glow; occasional shooting sparks fell on them, unacknowledged. Meg chose a spot as far as possible from the coupling and sighed at the heat. Fire-juggler apart, everyone else seemed to be sliding down into a slower form of being, in time to the music whose rhythm was a faltering pulse and whose words were so languorous they melted into each other without boundaries or meaning. Perversely Sara came alert, the vodka and whisky and adrenalin an unholy alliance. 'We just sit here all night do we?'

'It's cold. Don't worry, they'll come to us.'

'I see.' Behind her back one of the lovers gave a sustained rasping moan. 'You and Josh... are you seeing each other?' Almost she gestured behind her but thought better of it. 'If people still do that, do they? Date?'

'I'm into him, of course. Why not? But mainly it's been with Eurwen when I've seen him. We had a gymkhana here and a bit of a party afterwards he came to.'

'Lovely. It's not my business. We *are* separated. Who here might Eurwen have—?'

'You're sorry you let him go aren't you?'

For the dozenth time she found herself challenged by Meg Upton's candour. *I didn't drop his lead on a country walk!* came to the tip of her tongue but fate intervened by means of a slim, female figure's wandering over. The trailed fragments of what had been several skirts, tattered and worn one on top of the other dragged heavily in the dampness... *an inconvenience of skirts?* In a swirl, she sat down next to Sara and Meg grabbed at the chance: 'If you stay I'll do a quick once round. See who I can see.'

When she had gone the woman said very softly as though it was a secret to be kept from the lovers, 'I've seen you in town.'

Sara almost leapt. Fire was the kindest illumination, especially as the woman was in profile, seeming to address the foundry-like heat. Nevertheless Sara recognised the owner of the ruined face as the one she'd almost knocked down that first day... and since followed. Kind had she said? Kinder than kind: when she turned to Sara now she seemed to reference beauty. And she had been near Eurwen, perhaps on this very spot and not long ago. The desire just to touch the woman was intense.

Kim said, 'So who're you?'

'I'm nobody.' She tried for a self-deprecating note, false even to her own ears. 'My name's Sara. I'm staying... for a while.'

'Thought you hadn't been round much.'

Laughter rose from the direction Meg had disappeared and immediately Sara imagined her out there not on a mission as promised but sharing gossip, enjoying her freedom. A search for Eurwen had never been the intention; rather she, her mother, was the butt of some joke. Josh would be in on it, had colluded.

'Hey,' Kim whispered. 'Got anything?'

'I'm sorry? Oh... I have got this.' She found the bottle, could virtually feel its level without looking and handed it over. Distaste at having to share was disposed of by Kim's downing most of the contents and, at Sara's shake of the head, finishing the dregs.

'Ta. You're all right. I'm Kim. Sara, yeah?'

'Actually I'm here looking for my daughter.'

Kim nodded as though this was something suspected and now verified and ran her tongue around the interior of the bottle cap before tossing it away. The bottle was also dropped and it took effort for Sara not to protest... a cheap, sweetish odour was coming from Kim's clothes as they warmed and steam began to rise from their ragged edges and you could see the vodka doing its work of relaxation. Kim seemed to blur from the inside out. In a rush of fellow-feeling that just pre-empted resentment, 'Her name's Eurwen,' Sara said. 'She's not quite sixteen. Red hair. Very pretty and talks... well like me, in an Oxford... shire accent.' She added details. Too many: Kim yawned. 'Have you seen her? She's been in Rhyl since the end of June and it's a small place.'

'Yeah. Yeah, I might have done.'

'*Recently?*'

'Dunno. Red hair. Yeah. But you don't always, like, clock who you're seeing and when—not me anyhow.'

'But where was it, the very last time you saw her? You're certain it was Eurwen? Please, if you can remember—'

'Wel-ll.'

Suddenly Meg was there. 'Sara, I think you should come and talk to someone.'

Eyes fixed on the prize, she said, 'This is Kim. She thinks—'

'Yeah, hi-ya Kim.'

Kim was on her feet, stepping on the skirts, swearing... now in a complete tangle of skirts, so for a moment she could easily have gone into the fire. Her leaning forward may have been part of a genuine loss of balance but then her face came close to Sara's, shielded from Meg's line of sight. 'See you tomorra by the bridge, 'bout eleven,' she whispered.

When Sara made to go after her she found an arm out, barring the way. 'Don't! Please— that woman's seen Eurwen!' She tried to push Meg off, turning one way then the other in frustration but still losing track of the departed Kim and, a sudden breeze maliciously in her face, the tears sprung from saying Eurwen's name became streaks of ice, 'She *has* seen her.'

'Sara! That's just Kim for you. She'll tell you anything, if only for a bit of attention. You have to know what she's like. She hasn't see Eurwen. Or if she had she'd never remember next morning. Kim's lit up most of the time. But never quite bright enough, get it? You need to be careful with—'

'She's at your party or whatever you call it. On your land!'

'It's not like that. Come on.'

There were more vehicles arriving and the crush around the sound stage had definitely grown. Dreadlocks were everywhere framing pasty faces. Scanning for novel clothes, new heads, there were too many androgynous bodies and with hanging on them either strata of clothing, like Kim's, or not nearly enough, like the fire-juggling boy. A selection of over-sized felt hats topped off some of the girls: pantomime-wear. Under any one of which Eurwen could be lurking. But was not.

And yet... and yet. For a split second she heard Eurwen's voice, only in her head but true and clear, clearer than clear. 'No,' it was saying, 'no, *no*.'

Anticipating a faint, Sara gripped the empty bottle in her pocket and staggered against Meg.

'Sara?'

'It's all right. I thought that... that... for a moment.' But Eurwen had no other messages.

'Over here, then.'

Meg pushed their passage through, though it was getting harder. Something in the atmosphere was definitely evolving, the dance more purposeful, fuelled by a fresh sound that seemed to fill the field at ground level and swell higher than the treetops. What baffled was that the rhythm had not quickened, yet from faces close enough to be read, this new pulse, its focus internal, was strong enough to burst organs. Heads flicked in violent negatives, hands clawed the air... at the decks the woman crouched and loomed up again, weaving and flexing, even her own shadow failing to keep pace. Now she grinned, mouthing lyrics that were stale but turned potent to one listener: *...gabbing on threads that are well beyond dark/ You don't know who you're rumouring/ He bites like he barks/ You think you're playing him girl/ You think so, you think so/ But it's you that's the mark/ You're the girl, you're the girl/ found dead in the park.*

'Dear God,' Sara said.

But if Meg heard, it signified nothing. 'Are you coming or what?'

They dodged the action, making for the far hedge where, in grid pattern, most of the bigger vehicles had been parked with the darkness between like black pits. Meg's object was a high-sided van, pale, possibly *yellow* but streaked with overlaid designs. Its side shutter was rolled almost down but not quite and it was this attracted Sara's attention until an entity jumped from the driver's seat, slamming the door. A boy... another woman? The latter, though muffled up. She was less than Sara's height, was smoking and the kindled end as she inhaled showed up a sharp, pixieish face, not unfriendly: as to generation, her own or Eurwen's...? Indeterminate.

'Hiya!' Her voice was sing-song. The smoke was offered to them both in turn. ' Megs? No?' She turned back to Sara. 'You're Eurwen's mum, yeah?'

Meg said. 'Jay, poor old Kim's been spinning her a line. Tell her, will you?'

'No one has been spinning me a line!' Sara heard it come out loud and brusque but too late. 'If *you* know anything about my daughter, I'd like to hear.'

'Can we move it away, d'you reckon? Neil's in the back trying to chill. He's just done a twelve-hour shift. Give it a rest, huh?'

'I'm sorry.'

'She's upset,' Meg explained.

The woman, Jay, exhaled with the slowness of a yogi. In her pockets Sara's very fingernails ached.

'Neil and me, we got this rescue down backaways—' she gestured vaguely into the darkness. 'We get a lot of abuse cases. Eurwen asked him if she could come over, just to hang, be with the animals. She's got a way with them. We got this old staffie come in, nobody else could get near him, first. Some scrote had—'

'When was the last time you saw her?'

'—painted him. And, like, it's his poor coat's on fire with the reaction.'

'Yes, but Eurwen. This is very important. *Please*! When?'

Jay shrugged. 'Sorry... not sure when. She did tell Neil she oughta be going back by now but wasn't gonna.'

'What day was this? What actual day?'

'Like I said, nada.'

'I'll talk to Neil, then.'

'You'll have to let him have his kip first. And he'll only tell you same as me—'

Meg cut in. 'We'll catch you both later. Thanks anyway. It'll be a cold one, huh? Come on Sara. Let's go find—'

She let herself be herded in the direction of the bonfire again, but once out of earshot, could not contain her outrage, found she was shaking with it. 'If you don't do something I'm going to go back and I intend to pull Neil or whatever his real name is out of that grocer's van. I will get to the bottom of what happened between him and Eurwen. And you and your friends can try to stop me! Or I'll phone Josh to come here with half of the North Wales Police and let them get it out of him. Which he will do. Eurwen's his daughter. You are *nothing* in comparison, believe me. You are! I am as well!'

'Shush! Calm down. We're not missing anything. We'll talk to Neil. Or you can if you like. But not now— he'll have come off shift. And Josh'll just make it worse. That's why it's you and me. Neil and Jay are good people but when Neil gets his act together, they'll be selling legal highs. D'you understand?'

'No.'

'OK. Whatever. They'll have their skunk with them as well. They won't get caught with that, they're old hands. Most of the other stuff's not... illegal. But—' she seemed confused herself as though unused to considering the concept of illicitness. 'You don't need to say anything to Josh.'

'I'm meant not to react? I'm supposed to stay calm when you tell me Eurwen's involved with people like these?'

'Yes,' Meg said. 'Come on. We'll go get a coffee.'

At the lighted back of an old Land Rover someone else was dealing, but in bottled water, chocolate in unfamiliar wrappers and scalding coffee that could have been made from ground acorns. Certainly it had nothing to counteract the— would it be five spirit measures she felt stifling her will? Meekly she went with Meg as near to the fire as she could get though now besieged by a replacement crowd and Kim was nowhere. Jay appeared carrying steaming cups, saw them, and veered off... Sara closed her eyes, counted fifty and opened them again looking straight up. Gradually the cold, glittering constellations were discernable. It was the sort of sky that swung over the Boar's Hill of her childhood, for spotting meteorites in and waiting for the next, making wishes, all the while feeling her singularity, the experience of discrete selfhood as Sara Severing painfully *there* on the cool of the lawn. Only a daub of grey in the west threatened the perfect arch of it now. Then the stars came alive or some of them did, clustering and rising in families, adding more to their number all the time, moving up and yet remaining in sight. 'Good God!' she tried to will away the hallucination, and clutching at Meg's arm.

'They're just sky lanterns. You never seen them before?'

'Lanterns. I... Yes. I suppose I have.'

'Candles. They're in balloons, you know? The girls said they'd got a load dirt-cheap. That's all they are.'

In Vauxhall Gardens servants light a thousand lamps at a signal of a sudden to banish the shade. Thomasina Swift, sixteen, up from the country to London with her lover, saw the spectacle once. *Like night in Heaven but with kissing and sweetmeats!* she had written guilelessly to a Betsy Clark, her less fortunate, more virtuous friend.

'Just lanterns,' Sara repeated. Yet divine. The word liberated, letting her fasten onto Thomasina as her spirits rose. The Peerless Girl, never abashed, never fearful was herself a sort of stimulant. Did she trust in anything? No! Here was the Thomasina that had enthralled a subsequent age, musing on life, playing God off against the Devil? There were rumours: among them that an Oxford education had spurred on innate inquisitiveness and edged her towards dangerous ground. Atheism, Magick. But correspondence destroyed by the husband meant it wiser not to take a view. And Thomasina put faith in learning, at least, and had believed in that...

Eurwen was with her next as though by Thomasina's agency. Eurwen is saying Rubbish! All rubbish! yet the barb is blunted now, the desire to wrap Eurwen in her arms intense, to whisper that even if this is all there is, no hope, no meaning, no ultimate Saviour, the indifference of space over us and the cold earth waiting, even if the lanterns are a cheap trick designed to make us cry, still they offer a glimpse of night in heaven. Of kissing and sweetmeats before we fade.

When she came to, she saw amongst her fellow stargazers an addition; a new man had arrived and taken up station on the other side of the fire. An Oriental. Alone, apparently, since he'd claimed sole occupancy of the ragged bale vacated by the lovers. She stole another look at unremarkable features. There were smooth planes to the brow and cheeks that provided no haven for shadows, and yet it was not a calm face and, more arresting still, he was observing her. As an interesting object. Or maybe a misjudgement, catching him in a moment of abstraction? She peeked, peeked again, shivered though more irritated than troubled, feeling a touch curious as to what he saw. *Nothing sexual.* A thin pale woman in garments bulky enough to erase gender. And he was young, judging by the vigour of his physique. The legs in the inevitable jeans were thrown out towards the warmth and all his weight rested on widely braced arms, with the neck being thrust forward out of a dark fleece zipped to the chin. Not a position to maintain for long. He kept it though. Flames blazed up between them and still he did not flinch, making her suspect this was not imagination, this was more than a random act and she herself had been singled out. He *meant* to speak but was failing to and she was just about to rectify the situation when the single word Oriental came back to stop her mouth. Was it quite proper... ever? ...any more? Oxford's *School of Oriental Studies* operated blamelessly in Pusey Lane and Geoffrey spoke of *the Oriental perspective on world trade* without embarrassment or fear of correction... but a sudden loss of confidence over that singular person (masculine) usage meant she never did summon up the will to meet his unblinking stare.

After some little time she was conscious of his getting to his feet and drifting away and felt only respite.

Sara's lost to me the instant Josh wrenches his car off the main route out of town. Nobody could've followed without being noticed and Josh was even more vigilant than most, driving fast on narrow lanes built up across marshland— some of which had an unlit drop of a metre on either side to drainage ditches— and enjoying scaring his passenger though he'd never admit to it. I'm forced to go ahead to the parked vehicles cringing at the thought of the tricks being played on Sara and not just by firelight. It won't be pleasant. Strangers and familiars come together in an empty field, doing nothing but dance against the cold, watch the juggler and have sex till they fall into a stupor— she'll be baffled and never more aware that she's off her patch.

Where the hawthorn's at its tallest, a battered Ford transit has just drawn up. The female driver slides out and opens the side shutter-door. Two men emerge, loiter, staring around before one shrugs and they disappear, leaving her to roll herself a smoke on the vehicle's wing. And all the while it's obvious she's listening to or answering a third passenger through the cab's open window. After a long slow drag she offers it inside. Then the leisurely tempo is interrupted as something in the distance registers, something that alarms her— she scrambles back up and the glowing tip is rested out of sight. You would need to be very close to see another body slide over the seat and be swallowed by the van's interior. The driver hesitates – it becomes a farce – she jumps back down and runs around to the shutter door. Stuck wide open! She struggles in vain. (The voice from within must be desperate now). At the last frantic attempt down it comes. She runs back around and takes up position— just savouring a lungful. See?

As Meg walks into view with Sara.

Three women, pinned to the field while the talk goes round, Meg the taller, the youngest but definitely in control, Jay Rix, the locks flicking out at every head shake, not openly hostile but the attitude disrespectful. This is the sort of scene you can watch with sound muted and still be in no doubt what's happening. At one point Sara stares into the vehicle's inner darkness. She shivers and makes a pleading sign— then her hand goes to the shutter door and I imagine Rix holding her breath.

And it's over. Meg and Sara are gone.

Rix is left pressed against the Ford's bonnet. Her shoulders start to heave with laughing.

Chapter 10

September 29th

Her first thought was not of defeat but *Kim knows where my daughter is*. In the bathroom mirror her eyes may be curds under marshmallow lids but they were registering optimism. At least until she went downstairs. Josh had returned from a run, sweat-stained, flecked with mud, exuding male scent strong enough to fill the room. 'I've been down that way but sticking to our side of the river. You can see them all still there. Clive Upton wants his head examined! The fire's still smouldering. Apart from the bloody dogs, nothing else is moving. Have this.'

Sara took the cup and noticed suddenly her wrist's lack of a watch. Had she been wearing it last night? In fact when was the last time she saw it at all? One more example of myriad tiny absences. She thought of them as holes, literally holes in the brain: perhaps they were what ached now. 'I have to go out.'

'You're going to meet this nutter, are you? I'll come.'

This was a continuation of a previous argument, begun after midnight. That Meg's offer had brought scant return from Jay and nothing from a sullen Neil Rix when cornered, in fact that Meg gave every sign of regretting her invitation, had overnight begun to count against Josh. Whereas contact with Kim was a point for her and, though it didn't bear scrutiny because based on a glimpse of photographs she didn't intend to own up to, still, she felt out ahead and empowered. She took a deep breath. 'No.'

'Ha! Of course bloody no.'

When she came down a second time he surveyed her up and down. Burst into laughter. 'Well done, Sara!'

107

The creased blouse, the soot-speckled chinos and the jacket thrown over her arm with an embellishment of straw to its sleeve all provoked mockery. 'At least this woman won't think she's tapped into money, not you looking like that. In disguise, eh?'

She searched for her Marc Jacobs tote so he shouldn't see it first (Josh was not above rifling it) or the tears welling at his sarcasm.

'What's her second name?'

'Tighe.' Meg had known. At least that was one thing she had remembered to ask.

He shook his head, finding a new way to undermine her: with despair. 'Right… OK… So after you meet her where do you think you'll be going?'

'I could…' she had no plan, 'er, suggest we…'

'So what you do is *this*. You tell her you'll take her for a coffee. For breakfast if she'll go for it. Give people food and drink, 'specially this type. She won't be getting a lot of treats. So you buy her what she wants, someplace grotty she'll feel comfortable. But try to make sure you choose the venue. Got it?'

'Yes.'

'Don't tell her about yourself or about Eurwen. Nothing. *No facts*! It's like going to a fortune teller. Give them anything, they'll try feeding it back to you like it was theirs. So watch that. Get her to talk. She'll ramble on. They always do, go off on a tangent, and what you do is pick up any word or phrase that you can use to get them back on track.'

'Yes.'

'She might want to bend your ear, say, about the rough time she's had as a kid. So you look like you're understanding, you make all the right noises, and then you come in with *I know*! And if that was *Eurwen* I could see a reason for her going off but it isn't. So when...? Then you get back to who and what and where? Quick as you like.'

'Yes.' But everything he had said was seeping away through one of those voids that seemed less like pinpricks this morning. Bullet holes?

Kim Tighe. What Meg couldn't know was the spelling. *Tighe* offered itself.

She was afraid of Kim Tighe: the seasoned air of a Rhyl morning woke her to this. Either the woman herself was intimidating, or she would give information about Eurwen that knocked every other fear for six.

Stalled traffic on the bridge connected to raised voices and a bare-chested man leaning from his car window; a proper view of the meeting place was impossible until Sara was almost upon the first flight of stone steps down to the beach where a thin figure hung on the railings. An orange beanie might have hidden her identity except for the strands of hair whipping around a face turned to the sea. It was Kim though tinted glasses hid the eyes. Leggings emphasised her emaciation to the extent that her knees jutted pathetically and the fisherman's jumper that swamped her upper body, gaped at the neck. Closer now, Sara could identify the tattoo above Kim's protruding collar-bone as a crude, plain-ink Gordian Knot and felt queasy at the injury to such fragile skin. 'Hello... Kim. I wasn't sure you'd come.'

'I don't sleep much, me.'

Hot fat was already scenting the breeze. Sick and sicker... her empty stomach wanted to roll up like a touched caterpillar. 'Why don't we go for a coffee? I'd love one.'

Kim sniffed. 'Got any fags?'

'I haven't I'm sorry. I'll buy you a pack from where we go... How about breakfast?'

'If we try up the Clear I can maybe bum a couple off Harv.'

'No, really. Let me buy you some.'

'I don't need fucking charity!' The change of tone stung like a slap. 'I'm off now.' Come or not, Kim's body language said. In fact she seemed anxious to end their encounter before it had hardly begun, judging by the speed of departure.

Sequential lights and mind-bludgeoning tunes were operating to the empty arcades they passed but visitors were already on the streets. Sara contented herself with keeping up with a target that bobbed and weaved through the strollers so nimbly she was convinced it was some sort of test. If she demurred or lost Kim, the chance was forfeit. And for a woman as sick as she looked she could certainly move. Stopped, about to cross yet another junction, Sara managed to chip in, 'I don't know about you but this time in the morning I feel like death. I drink.'

'Who doesn't? We're there, anyhow.' Kim turned and pointed above her head. Clear Skies Café was over a junk-shop by the looks of its window's assorted objects. FOURWAYS, whatever that meant, was painted across the glass. A steep flight of stairs had sharp metal edges… Kim was up them with the lightness of a shore bird and pushing on the solid door at the top. Sara followed. The upper interior was much dimmer than expected and fuller, a space only the size of a double bedroom holding a half dozen battered Formica tables and most of them were filled with people who had turned to stare.

'Hiya Kim,' someone out of sight called. Sara searched for the voice and found a hatch in the far end of the room with a man's upper body and shaven head blocking it.

'Harv! I'm gasping.' Kim threaded through the tables. The door's hitting Sara in the back was the hint she needed and someone's laugh at her expense seemed to restart the hubbub. Kim kept her waiting until she had her cigarette, had it lit, only then did she drag two chairs to the counter and motion Sara to sit, her attention transferred now to the person providing the treats. As it would always be, Sara thought.

Harvey would have been unremarkable were it not for thick black swirls of tattooing that licked up out of his T-shirt against the chalky neck like a high collar and his brows, nose and lower lip that were pierced with steel. Younger than she had first estimated, a tough-looking thirty, perhaps, but with a confident demeanour of fifty. The slight cast in one eye made it difficult to decide which of them he was concentrating on or expected to speak next.

'This is Sara,' Kim said.

'You all right?'

'Well—'

Harvey gave an abrupt nod that reminded her of Josh.

'She's OK aren't you Sara? Couple of coffees, Har-*vey*.' When Kim drew deeply on the cigarette her cheeks flattened along the gum line in rictus as though smoking were an ordeal. To Harvey's suggestion of toast Kim snapped, 'Not got'ny cake?'

Sara waited until Harvey disappeared although privacy was not an option, the tables jostling each other. 'Am I here to talk to him or you?'

'Oo-oo! Please yerself.'

'I don't wish to be rude. Is this a place you've seen my daughter? Or are we to meet someone else?'

'Just hold on. I can't think till I've finished the first fag.'

Two squashed jam-filled Swiss role slices were put down between them. 'You not got chocolate?' Kim wanted to know. 'This'll do then.'

'Let me pay.' Sara had her bag off her shoulder. 'There's nothing else, no? Then how much?' Her next question was going to be about a red-haired girl. But she could *not* find her purse. Fingers searching the recesses of tissues and unidentifiable bits touched only coins, a couple of pounds which she offered and had accepted.

'The last of the big spenders,' Kim said. She drank most of the steaming cup in one go. The room was heating up, unsurprisingly with the number of bodies packed into it but when the door opened again and a teenager backed in pulling a child's buggy with her, somehow the space managed to absorb them. Sara's rapid scan of the clientele told that most were young, several with wriggling toddlers attached, the exception being at the next table where two old men in woollen overcoats had wedged themselves into the corner. Apart from a rota of puffing and coughing they were dumb and vacant-eyed beneath the notice THIS IS A NO SMOKING AREA IT IS AN OFFENCE TO SMOKE HERE PENALTY FOR NON-COMPLIANCE £200.

Swiftly, Kim's cigarette was down to the filter tip. 'It's council, see? Harv's some sort of, I dunno, worker for them. He runs it like a centre. The library's another place you can go but not on a Sunday natch. And they'll be down on you like a ton of shit if you light up.' There were no ashtrays and with conscious good timing she leaned down and stubbed the cigarette out on the wooden sole of a sandal that looked too big and heavy for her skeletal feet.

'If you want more…?' Sara remembered just in time.

But no need for nicety. 'Ta. Harv. Harv! How much you charging for—?' she rattled an imaginary packet at the hatch.

'Three-eighty.'

'Fucking robber! Give us one.'

A black packet came flying in her direction and she caught it. 'This one's payin'.'

Sara handed over a five pound note from the discovered purse, her bag's contents spread out between them, lipstick, comb, reader's tickets for specialist manuscript collections she no longer made use of. An invitation to an August book launch 'Garden Quad, St Clement's College, 7pm' lay next to the dog-eared card with her own contact details… how long since had she needed to offer one to any new acquaintance?

Kim folded and unfolded the five pound note without passing it on immediately. 'They're knock-off, sort of. You couldn't afford to smoke if you had to pay the tax'n everything, y'know, could you?'

'You said you'd seen my daughter.'

'Yeah. Redhead like you? She's the spit of you.'

'It *is* Eurwen.'

'Yeah, that's right. But not your height.'

'She's going to be taller—'

'I don't think I know 'er other name, she never said.'

'It's Meredith.'

'Could be.'

She was unwrapping the new cigarettes but kept the note between her fingers making the operation difficult. Then it had to stop as Sara grabbed both her hands and said, 'If you've really seen her, where and when? Please. I'm her mother. I only want to make sure she's safe. I only want to… find her. To talk to her. *Please.*'

'Let me get another fag out will you? How come you lost touch? You, was it?'

'Yes… I suppose so.'

'Where d'you live, then?'

'Do you mean when we lost touch? Um, down… south.'

'I thought you sounded London. Straightaway, last night, London I nailed you. So you've come all the way up here to find 'er?'

'Yes.'

'God, you're putting the work in, I'll give you that. Or you're feeling well-guilty.' Kim scratched the crown of her head through the wool of the hat and finally, she took off the huge glasses to reveal swollen eyelids and crusted lashes fringing blue irises. But inspiration came bubbling up behind them. 'Y' boyfriend was it?'

'I don't have a boyfriend.' Two could play at this. 'There's been no one since her father left us.'

'Oo-oo, Sister Sara!' Kim hooted. But it was a good answer, another test passed. The cigarettes open, Kim chose to eat cake, raspberry jam settling into the corner of her mouth. She nibbled another morsel, delicate as a duchess. 'Your Eurwen, she's close with that Meg, yeah?'

'Yes.'

'I'm surprised she don't know where she is.'

'She doesn't. So, Kim, when did *you* last see her?'

'Meg? Last night. You were there.'

'You know that I mean Eurwen.'

But a cigarette became a necessity now: getting it out, tapping it, getting a light from one of the old men. 'Ta, much!' When she blew her first exhalation away from Sara the smile was condescending. 'Might be best if... when we meet up next, I just told her you was here, looking.'

'Don't you dare do that!' Everyone in the tight space seemed to turn, to fix on her, though a moment before a child uttering wordless shrieks remained unattended.

'And don't you fucking shout at me!' Kim responded. 'Who d'you think you are? '

She jumped to her feet and shoved and wriggled her way to the door and was gone. Sara was about to set off in pursuit when, 'Oi! Sara!' a voice said.

It was Harvey. One big raw hand was thrust through the hatch, close enough to catch her sleeve if it wanted to. 'Money, love. What d'you think I am? A fag factory?'

By the time Sara was at pavement-level, Kim was nowhere

though pedestrians were few and the length of the street visible in both directions. To return was an option and demand to know from Harvey – with accompanying bribes or threats – where Kim might be found. But it was not, not really.

Sara's rooted there, dazed, a passenger come up from the Tube into the wrong street. Surely she can't be afraid of losing her way in Rhyl? A step into the road and SkyTower rears over the roofline, its cabin near the apex, a landmark. But she cranes in the opposite direction for— Hat Woman, I name her. If I were superstitious I'd label her Sara's unlucky charm. Here she is at her own game. Having attached herself to Sara, with their business obviously unfinished, she runs out. A woman of that age playing hide and seek! And winning. Sara's certainly the loser. Instead of home, she makes for town and it swallows her up. On the plus side by a trick of the light Rhyl looks almost inviting today. Not exactly picturesque, but the effect makes her linger in front of battered, ornate shopfronts with their reminders of a past allure – a bit like Hat Woman.

I wish I could tell her, Drift along while you can. Focus on the family coming towards you. That clumping boy and his mother, behind is the father, bobbing and twitching his way through the foot traffic like a fighter. A little girl shelters among them. Blonde and smiley, her stubby fingers are grasping for anything within reach, a display of apples, a revolving barber's sign. She even gropes for the black fur of a giant dog. Their general shabbiness says they're out of funds and luck. But they're laughing. The father gives the son a playful push. The mother seems going to intervene but they settle it with a grin as the child begins a war dance, wants to be hoisted level with their faces. Choose them and share the pleasure, I encourage her. You haven't got long.

Does she, doesn't she? She puts a hand out and it's to the

nearest wall and to hold herself up. Then a small thing happens. One second she's drag-footed, the next she stares into a shop window and heads inside. Back out again almost as quickly, it's with a small wrapped package— so small it could fit into her shoulder bag and the transfer's half-complete when she steps back against the shop doorway and shakes out a silk scarf by its corners. It balloons from her hands in the breeze, making a passer-by side-step as the material turns into a live thing, look, it's trying to escape and soar up and away from the woman that grips the tassels. The scarf's design of turquoise and peacock blue with silver edges will blaze out in this strong sun like stained glass. And I know who this is for because I know those colours and who'll always choose them given the chance. So a welcome home gift, a connection with the missing even though Eurwen's never touched it. Sara has picked by instinct. Easy for her and more like slipping into another self than remembering a fact. Outside time, mother and daughter are one and the blue-green silk goes slithering round the neck, drawing the girl to the grown version of herself who stands holding both ends. In a drowner's grip. I decide to let her go for now— with the fiction running through her head of everything healed and Eurwen's slotted back into a remake of their old life.

Sara's Sundays are a work-day for me. I thread through West Rhyl's loiterers and pass the abandoned fairground site, its furthest point— where my own head should be full of what to do with it, for it. Once it was a tourist town's powerhouse—

—but Sara and Eurwen have unbalanced my mood. You're wrong Kailash, I must have a heart or which organ is registering Pain of Regret now? In this place especially where past and present are like cut and paste. What's gone? Brash flower beds and the Golden Horses carousel, helter-skelter, rowing boats, hot dogs, palm-readers, minature golf, ice-cream, *Strike It Lucky!* and Rhyl rock. And the Ferris Wheel brooding above the shabby roundabouts right up till the moment the last pound coin was extracted from the last punter. I know, thanks to a photograph of Eurwen, craning out from her cradle at its summit, not scared, in fact a picture of relish. As background that great symbol of human fortune, the Big Dipper, is about to descend. Listen carefully and you can make out how halfway down the metal carriage will morph into an old rickety Water Chute boat that caused Rhyl's first ever funfair death, long before a certain famous murderer got a job on the Dodgems and made his play for the screaming girls—

Long before I'd meet Sara here.

When a sudden impact comes from the direction of the river and the bridge, I turn my back on the desolation and clamber up the embankment for a sight of the water or the traffic or anything but this. Over in what's left of the harbour I think I can recognise a familiar character, a retired seaman called William Jones at work. He's repairing, he tells me, a fishing dory. There'll be the usual bits of metal, wood, ropes and sheeting about, mainly gash stuff waiting for someone to summon up the effort to shift it. But round William Jones it's ship-shape (not that I can see from here but I've been up close) with everything to hand. If I had time I'd go over to watch. I've become a bit obsessed actually. A dory is an exotic craft to be holed and sunk in the estuary mud— then salvaged with enormous effort according to Jones. He made a good story of finding the half-buried craft thirty metres upstream. How he hosed the hull out at low tide and attached empty barrels he calls camels, working always against the clock to fix them way down and float it off. But worth it. When he finishes and fits this last piece, this *strake*, then the bow and stern will both rise well above the line of the *gunwale* in a characteristic shape that's elegant *and* practical. I know all the nautical stuff thanks to William Jones who's made impressive progress since I got him the off-cuts he needed. Still struggling with his workplace, though, the silt sucking at the waders every turn. I'd like the rest of the morning on that hull with him, do something productive instead of this self-pitying idleness. Irony's only one of the concepts I never mastered – my education got going late, there are big gaps – but it might be operating now. Just when I've the tools assembled for Project Sara, personal weakness gets in the way and I could leave her be, easily jump ship. Switch horses. My hands are feeling the metal of the plane and spoke-shave, and the give of the grain to its blade as the teak I gave William Jones surrenders another red curl.

My face imagines the breath of wind that has bellied out a blue-green square of silk.

Chapter 11

October 3rd

Since she ran away, Sara found she noticed Eurwen more: how the hooded-eyed expression had become habitual, her default setting. How the lips... *God!* she could draw and colour the mouth, wider than her own, a pure shade of peach and slightly open when she is unaware of being observed. Ready to mock though or more likely, to contest... But this spiteful, perfunctory summing up is halted in its tracks. Sara 'sees' herself arrested in treachery, for that is what it is, and, thunder-struck, stalls halfway across the room in which she was making for... who knows, anyway? *Of course* this isn't the sum total of her daughter. What of Eurwen's instant return to humour after yet more of their 'words'? No sulking! And the gift of time given with such a good heart to *Gramps Geoffrey and Frau Fleur*, Eurwen's own inventions, new characters that she managed to coax out of an elderly couple and sustain through play. To personalities Sara treated as complete and fixed, Eurwen proffered the chance for surprising themselves and they had taken it up with gratitude.

And what of Eurwen's preternatural feel for the sufferings of the voiceless and her passion to defend them? And its corollary, her absence of self-love?

Sara sinks down into a chair, palms pressed to her eyes, hiding, sobbing.

Lack of resolve was a physical burden as she moved around Josh's house later the same day, nearly convinced that in the next room Eurwen was wrenching a comb through the unruly mane... pulling on the boots she seemed to want to live in, summer and winter. Always on the threshold of departure she could still be clutched at, not quite out of reach. Yet.

Everything Sara wrote down re: Eurwen would be in the present tense from now on. I know because I've got her personal effects however risky that might be (for me I mean). So for example I can read off, 'October 3rd. Very late or early. Through the wall I strain to hear Josh turn in bed, to receive 'the comfortable words' of his proximity at least in a silent house. Even the little clock he has lent me in lieu of my watch barely ticks but still counts out my errors... for example a conviction at each waking up I need to weather just a day, one more day that will bring us close. Tomorrow we'll hold each other: touch, smell, listen to, see... tomorrow. Whereas in fact time is not the problem, time is a construct and means nothing. The *place* is at fault. Eurwen is here in the minute that begins *now*, my minute that I'm wishing away. But elsewhere.'

October 4th

Those beetles were back, crawling across her chest and into the valley of the breasts, so lifelike you expected to see the silk twitch and a pair of black antennae emerge from between buttons, the shiny carapace pushing after them, a squeeze... But she'd had no drink for five days which was a working week for some. This morning, soon after Josh's departure, a huge Red Cross-type parcel seemingly for the intellectually deprived was delivered. From dependable Fleur. She carried it into the living room and sat on the rug, tearing at the brown tape with her nails... and found books. A brace of paperbacks, Blackwell's labels still attached, were Ian McEwan's *On Chesil Beach* and William Boyd's *Restless*. She scanned their covers. Oxford novels... naturally... poor Fleur. The home connection should have made them welcome, so why did she fling both away and watch their flight across the room as if a scorpion lurked in the pages? And when they came to rest, did the grimace they'd provoked remain? She shook her head, knowing too well.

An entire layer of journals to remove next. October's edition of *The Historical Review* was flaunting 'Catholic Loyalism in Early Stuart England': but where was the woman who cared? It and the rest went the way of modern fiction, leaving a single slim clothed-in-drab monograph. *The Ladies' Persistence*. Irritably, she flicked through... hardly persistent... a paltry ninety pages. According to the flyleaf, 'it catalogued for the first time the achievements of the Kensington Circle, four genteel Edwardian wives to powerful men intent on improving the lot of vulnerable young girls in London's East End...'

Surely a mis-choice for the pursuer of her own runaway daughter... and from Fleur who was so precise in her classifications usually. But the author turned out to be Apolline Reith. Of course. And only a month launched (Garden Quad, 7pm St Clement's College, Drinks and Savouries) by the same diligent toiler in the field they had shared. Sad surpassed, outsoared friend Polly... once. She let her eye cherry-pick the half-dozen scholarly puffs filling out the unadorned cover until it closed on, 'Here is a quartet of interwoven women's lives, undramatic yet well worth the recovery...'

But no Thomasina Swift amongst them. (How punishable is a smile Polly if you never see it?) *No Thomasina Swift.* In the protracted period of abstraction this caused her, she almost missed the picture postcard of a donkey, identifiable as Crook, standing foursquare in the Uptons' yard; on his underside Eurwen's handwritten line, more telling to Sara than twelve volumes of Gibbon, than the whole of Herodotus, ran, *just lush... super time... soon see u!* before it blurred.

Still Fleur had not finished with her. Thick A4 envelopes

padded out the bottom of the box, justifying its weight. Attached was the inevitable letter.

Darling,

Just a few necessaries. I think of you every day and I hope this distraction can be useful. If not, then humour me and let me pretend.

Would it help if I came? You've only to say, darling. No, you've only to hint and I'll be there. Geoffrey and I talk of little else. Your father is very concerned. I also but I believe that Josh will be doing all the necessary things. He's a good man who loves his daughter very much. Try to keep that thought uppermost.

Eurwen is intelligent and mature beyond her age. When I think of you at fifteen! You were a fey little creature. But from the note she left she had a plan and somewhere she was making for. In many respects she's quite an extraordinary girl, as were you but in a very different way.

I promise not to plague you with calls. Are you able to check emails? I know it would give Geoffrey peace of mind to let you have a sentence or two and be sure of getting one in return.

My intention was to gather and send your current working material for when or if you felt able, you understand? I can find nothing. You appear to have had a very recent and thorough clear-out. So I enclose a nice fresh photocopy of 'A First' taken from the draft you showed us. You will have a disk or whatever but I know how deeply you are wedded to the word on the page!

It's such a familiar world and our dear Lady Quarrie the choicest of companions.

With my very best love
Fleur

Was she *wedded* to the word on the page? Fleur would not

intend the rebuke, but...? Like an automaton she straightened her spine, pushed off from the floor and left the room. When she returned and resumed her position she was running the back of one hand, coarsely, across her mouth not caring if the glass held in it dripped a final drop. An open bottle of Stoli was placed down next with greater care.

The photocopy of *A First* divided between envelopes, being too much for a singleton, her Peerless Girl though the book made no such claim. The story was fable already, if only from Virginia Woolf's catty, eighteen-hundred-word essay, 'Who?' which she made sure to acknowledge, here in Chapter 1: '... tiresomely exquisite, abnormally calculating girl. I suspect the taste she brought to Heystrete would have caused her lord to blush, the acquisitions made in her occupancy, ripe fodder for its lumber rooms. Yet the past is unserviceable in attempting to assess her life. She is the first potato pulled from the pease field; though no more savoury to a refined palate, the future is hers.'

Woolf was accurate in this if nothing else. Thomasina was certainly destined to be Sara's future as sole subject, a book, a play and a film, as they used to say in a game played at Pryorsfield Christmases... all there, even the earliest synopsis, written at Geoffrey's suggestion and delivered by him to Pythian Press's old office in the Euston Road she had loved visiting.

Thomasina Swift was born at Heystrete Newton, 30 miles from Bristol in 1758, the daughter of an innkeeper. At fifteen, she became mistress of Louis Quarrie, heir to Heystrete Hall, a spoiled young man. Sent up to Oxford he continued the affair and, having boasted in drink about the accomplishments of his lady, bet John Cane and the Hon Spencer Goodridge fifty guineas each Thomasina could keep a term there, passing for a student.

At the start of Michaelmas, Louis Quarrie reappeared with

his young cousin, Tom Swift. (He bore the cost of the adventure. His account book shows expenditure of 10s for a greatcoat, 4/9d for a plain cloth coat, also two waistcoats, a dozen muslin cravats plus stockings, breeches and shirts and a hat all bought for his 'cozin'). The pair took rooms in Longwall Street. It was not a completely successful ploy. To Cane, who had left the University early, Louis describes having 'thrash'd an insulent fellow in The High who calt my good cousin Tom Swift a molly'.

Tom attended lectures in classics, philosophy and divinity and came to the attention of Dr George Buller, (1719-1788). A classicist, he was Louis Quarrie's tutor and despite humble origins, a much-feared character in the University. No one's fool, yet Buller encouraged Tom Swift's studies. The curmudgeonly don had fallen under Thomasina's spell and the masquerade was sustained. Tom Swift kept 'his' term at Oxford and returned to The King's Arms, at Heystrete with 100 guineas in 'his' pocket.

When Sir Philip Quarrie's horse threw its rider at the Heystrete Newton crossroads, the twenty-two-year-old heir was suddenly Sir Louis, with an income of £8,000 and only a pious mother cluttering up his Hall. Thomasina and he married before the harvest was in and she became celebrated as a charmer and wit. Invitations to Heystrete were sought by statesmen, artists and philosophers for the next four decades. The poet Robert Southey had to be thrown bodily down the main stairs at Heystrete by Sir Louis for 'versifying to my wife and therefor causing much anoyance'. Though her beauty dimmed, she remained, as William Lyle Bowles was moved to write in a fit of hot blood and bathos, 'the wonder of her sex, our age, and this blessed County of Wilts,' the peerless Thomasina.

An impressive thickness of paper, grown out of that couple of hastily written sheets, forced itself down onto her thighs. Each envelope had been enumerated and headings and pagination added. You could believe an actual revision was about to get underway! Yes? No? When I'm drinking I'm not working and when I'm working I'm not drinking, a pithy and presumably sober other writer once said. How long had the fool lasted after double usage of a word immeasurably potent? See! That ba-ba-ba-bum of the pulse resulted from merely thinking it... now Fleur's shocked face flashed up. She would have recognised the scattered ashes from both bin and grate as the putative new edition, notes and letters and, who knew? The leads unfollowed, even where the references had been tracked and indexed. But no final draft: attenuated preparation, a type of scholarly foreplay, had proved that pithy sometime-drunk's adage. *She* had not been working. Had not worked for years. How could she? How dare she?

Her glass was empty again. Reply to Fleur, she counselled herself. Or at least speak to Fleur before... you... before you get... She did neither. But when she answered her phone, 'I'm up at the Clear,' Kim said without preamble, 'and don't take forever!' She complied.

Kim's Lycra still bagged at the knees yet everything else about her had altered subtly. Movements were smoother and more controlled. The wide eyes shone despite pinpoint pupils. To Sara's anodyne 'How are you?', Kim catalogued her regime with a sort of bravado, ending in the teatime Rhyl Hotshot: diazepam and codeine phosphate needing to be injected 'to get down'. Why not a Coldshot? Sara wanted to ask but substituted, 'I'm ignorant when it comes to drugs.' It was what Kim would expect. 'Hence so worried about Eurwen.'

Kim simpered over the top of her mug. 'I was a bit of cow the other time. This kid of yours—'

'Eurwen.'

'I know. Well, I'll tell you this for free.' She leaned in closer. Her pointed little chin was sore-looking today as though she had been rubbing at the clustered whiteheads stuck like mites into the flesh. 'I reckon she don't want to be found.'

Sara had to lace fingers beneath the table so as not to slap her. 'How can you know that?'

'Som'dy would be seeing her. That lot at the stables, for one.'

Coffee gathered in Sara's throat ready to be fully regurgitated. Harvey's afternoon blend had a fugitive aftertaste of fish but Kim happily knocked back a couple of pills with hers. Then her phone buzzed and she read the text with a pursed mouth.

'Please Kim— if you can think of anything—'

She held up a hand for quiet. 'I've thought of something, as it happens. But— na, never mind. You won't want to.'

'Anything.'

'All right. Well, maybe.'

Trying to maintain a conversation with Kim was like a steeple chase, one difficult fence cleared revealed the next. Her touchiness was infectious, tempting Sara into a surface narrative, playing her game... because it was *her* game. 'Maybe sounds hopeful.' The woman seemed appeased or at least not about to quash the overture. Relief bloomed before she wondered what was coming or even what category of proposition it might consist of.

Kim's face was tight with self-importance. 'I read the cards. That's it. I'm bloody good as it happens. Ask anybody— never wrong.'

The rattle of crockery and a range of cleaning up sounds filled the background as the café prepared to shut. Without warning the hatch crashed down behind Sara's back but Kim didn't so much as blink and, without sunglasses, the blue unguarded eyes were even more disarming.

'I see.'

126

'Na-a! Forget it.'

'I've never met anyone who was... adept at that... type of thing.'

'Like I said let's bin it.'

A steeple chase, maybe, but not lost, not yet. A steeple chase, a sine wave: having dipped at the ludicrous offer, now it began its ascent on an assemblage of possibilities. Sara could feel the effort involved in mentally plumping up the heap. 'Really, what I meant was—' Her own first day's foray into Rhyl must be weighed: *With my mind I will touch my child,* she rebuked herself. But what of the myriad cultures where divination was accepted, from classical times to... no, *no!* predating the classical, three thousand years earlier in Ancient Sumaria whose every city hid an entrance to the nether world of knowledge and power. What were the rules that gave access? *Do not wear fresh clothes to find it; do not treat your kin in the familial way?* She had known the entire list... and in the Egypt of the Old Kingdom priests and scorpion charmers tried to foretell disasters, protect houses and give assurance to women in childbirth, who would then survive. That day, crossing the bridge, reaching out to Eurwen *she had awaited a response;* maybe the one and only excuse for flirting with the Inexplicable was that it could prove we are more than cloven tissue? If only you had faith... As the actual world seemed to spin off and leave her free-floating, there it was. Faith. 'Yes. I think we should try,' she heard herself respond. The one thing she must not do now, for Eurwen's sake, was to play the sceptic. 'Why not?'

Kim's focus was on the room. To the backs of heads she said. 'It takes a lot out of me. I don't do it for a laugh, you know. I have to charge.'

'I see.'

'Takes years of studying. Like being a vet or something, isn't it?'

'That's fine.'

'OK. We'll do it then.' Kim got to her feet.

'So where do you practise your... your skill? Here?'

'I'll come to the house, won't I? Could be tomorrow— or the next. Depends. But you'll have to be in on your own.'

'Yes.' Sara had no idea what Josh would be doing on any particular day, where he was likely to be. 'I will be,' she promised, surprised at the steadiness of her voice when her nervous system was telling her it was shot to pieces. 'Yes... I can arrange that. Whenever suits.'

October 5th

Until then, do something. How about information gathering, where once she had excelled? The real Thomasina had to be painstakingly resurrected from the sort of dross the landed families of England waded in: sermons by second sons, orders for 'black furniture' to smarten up the Norfolk Trotters, amateur treatise on the cultivation of the apricot, and bills for tablecloths, sulphur paste, lemons and lump sugar that somehow survived linen, horses and orchards. When at home she might call a friend she had left who was *not* Polly Reith... But there would be no stain of *mañana* on today. Her latest brush with Kim had the effect of a stimulant. In research, for instance, at the third or maybe the thirtieth look at some scribbled note, a door springs open. From near-defeat you are offered the prospect of Canaan, though for her it always took the form of an intricate walled Italian town *a la Bellini*. So rather than self-laceration, let us, she reasoned, label dealings with addict-cum-charlatan Kim as one of those long slogs against the gradient, the stones sliding under the feet, the terracotta roofs as far above as ever. And for what? There's the rub. Maybe nothing or maybe precious, squirreled away booty, as had been brought her, carton after battered carton, that amazing day. And not to a mediaeval scriptorium on a sun-baked Tuscan hilltop, but to Heystrete Hall and its Comptroller's chilly den.

The house had been nearing the end of a big sleep. In a month they would admit the year's first injurious light and even more damaging push of bodies. Carpets and rugs were being groomed, rosewood and ormolu tables unclothed and distorting glass in the runs of bookcases must sparkle again for Easter visitors... which was why a vacant slice of desk space had to been found for her elsewhere, a too-small space that the reeking mass of papers, newly ripped from beneath a water tank, soon filled. In the distance the volunteer workforce prattled and jested while a dozen vacuum cleaners droned and in front of her lay an afternoon of sneezing and shivering and cursing as the fan heater set in motion anything not anchored down. But nothing would ever be sweeter: suddenly, between smudged thumb and forefinger, she held a poet's lost lyric to Heystrete's chatelaine*. They signalled a vein of pure Thomasina had been broken into and was hers for the processing, this biographer's sole claim to status: an accident of maintenance.

Amongst Fleur's photocopied pages the poem lay, safely embedded in her own text.

---

* The poem SM refers to – and misquotes – is now in the Heystrete Collection on loan to the Bodleian Library, Oxford.

DONNA PRIMA
The timbre of thy speech so mild,
Youth's dew illumes thy cheek.
Yet putting me thus from thy side
Has caused my heart to break.

So art thou famed – 'tis just my Tom –
Prima of Oxenford?
But, sweet, that mind, so burnished keen
Hath pricked me like a sword.
                    Robert Southey (1774-1843)

In putting me thus from her side/ Has caused my heart to break,
Southey whimpered.

Was there such a thing as a broken heart? Probably not. Or
last week she had been at risk of accepting the condition but
was this week more secure. However steep the incline, I shall
find you, she told Eurwen. Determined to accomplish *something*
she sat with (yes, more helpful than a drink) the phone in hand.
Polly Reith will be unlocking her rooms in Garden Quad about
now for another day of industrious existence… and Josh is gone
to his. 'Mr Upton? It's Sara Meredith. I hope it's a good time?'

'As any. Na-a- up since five. Racing hours.'

'I hoped, well… you mentioned you would ask about
Eurwen?'

'Did I?'

Why the unhelpful tone… or the belligerence? Without Josh
as witness he was not going to waste his politeness on her, it
said. 'It's your rental properties that are of interest. You might
consider any new tenancies? Even if the name were different,
Eurwen's description would stand out to someone. To whoever
manages them?'

'Bit of a long shot.'

'But they sometimes win, Mr Upton, don't they?'

'Fair enough.' The snap though belied the words: Clive
Upton, body of an insect, head of a man. Or vice versa? 'I'll
have to get back to you.'

Meg's mobile went straight to voicemail. '…so if you could
let me have a contact number for Jay and Neil? Other questions
have occurred. Could you get back to me? Please.' All perfectly
true; since that night she'd become convinced they knew more
than they were saying. Jay, wary as a coney, Neil with that show
of rubbing sleep from his eyes when he came from the van's
interior though the smell of the fire was already on him. And
Meg herself, she knew things: the whole of Rhyl did because,

oh yes, it was a small place. If anyone else told her that she would tear her own hair.

For the hundredth time she called Eurwen. *It has not been possible...*

Chapter 12

The ailing and unemployed are cruising with ice-creams through Bad Luck on Sea, stalked by gulls. Not that they mind. Air this clear gives a Technicolor zing to everything fake or real. That could be a distance shot from— I was going to say *The Birds*, again. Honestly? Rhyl's nothing like Bodega Bay but then neither is Bodega Bay. Hitchcock built it on the Universal Studio lot. That's the film business where even real isn't enough to convince. The actual Californian fishing village couldn't match up to his auteur's vision and now the actual BB trades on illusion – advertises itself as Home of That Movie! – and tries not to disappoint the cinemabuff tourist.

At least there's a bit of recovered energy in the way Sara's moving today. Her head strains forward of her shoulders. The SunCentre, ugliest construct in town, is her likely destination, a sheaf of leaflets clasped in her free hand. Very purposeful. Catching her in close-up where she'll need to cross, the face, though unmarked by Josh yet, is almost haggard. Then a fresh reflection off the sea remakes her. She's my Sara again.

This is the evening she'll give Josh the postcard of Crook. He'll take one glance and throw it down while he prods Fleur's box with a toe.

'Another edition is… overdue. Fleur thinks I should try to get on with something.'

'Work? *You?*' (She could only guess at who that day and other than herself had put the cruelty into him.) 'Yeah, go to it! Just what the world needs, more bloody Thomasina,' he said and left them together.

Sara at twenty-one, busy on a thesis, had two things happen to her in the same week. First came the 'discovery' of Thomasina Swift.

The second? A house she shared with others in Cherwell Street, equidistant from St Clement's College and Magdalen Bridge and in those days not the best part of Oxford but certainly not the worst, had the side door forced and every room tossed. It would emerge that Polly's cheque book, Damon's money and hashish, and her own jewellery had been stolen. Petulant and shaken, she called for Fleur, who set out from Boar's Hill but only after having summoned the police. Fleur and PC Josh Meredith arrived virtually together. He stood back— and then darkened the entrance, tall and in uniform, his eyes showing private amusement at female flurry, she thought. 'The lock they broke's pretty vintage. This on the front's no better. Not exactly secure is it? You've done everything bar hang a Please Rob Us sign up.' The voice was *very* Welsh then and she knew no one Welsh.

Her annoyance was tempered, interestingly, by a wish not to be in this ancient sweater nor the cycle-oiled trousers. She was aware of their stains with heightened senses: filthy streaks on the inside of both calves and an oily smell that would be associated with loss forever after. Working Class Fascist was how she categorised Josh and, at twenty-one, she was infallible. He was the type who would alter as though by hidden switch if he had found them both cashmere-suited and kitten-heeled; whereas here she was... and Fleur had arrived in gardening garb. But Fleur laughed. 'Absolutely! That's telling us, Sara.' Fleur's genuine laughter, another indelible memory. *A week passed... he arrived out of uniform and with her moonstone necklace in a plastic evidence bag... she took it.*

'You've actually caught them!' was about the most offensive thing she could think of to say.

''Fraid not. This was handed in. Chucked, I guess. Once they looked at it properly.'

'*Thank-you.*'

'Not the crown jewels, is it?'

'It is to me.'

'Why I brought it round.'

Eurwen loved *this* history at least. As a little girl she would beg to hear it told, correcting Sara if the smallest detail were omitted. '*No-o!* You couldn't get it out of the policeman's bag thingy and he had to take it back and... and *then* he gave it you Mummy and you said—'

'Thank you for troubling.'

Her impulse to mock had evaporated. His jeans looked almost new and had creases ironed into them. The polo shirt's first outing? Certainly. But did she believe she had the upper hand with him, ever? Arguably in that final second as he lingered with a touch of a smile that never did find the eyes. 'Would you like coffee, since you've been kind enough to come here... um...?'

'Josh,' he said.

From the date Josh walked out of Tackley Close, Geoffrey Severing's unspoken rule was never to mention him by name: it was possible to refer to him by position. When Eurwen won an essay competition, the professor enquired, 'Will the other proud parent be at the prize-giving?' The need to ask this sort of question again was unnecessary, it being the final accolade of her school career. Then there was the fall from the pony that necessitated an overnight in the Radcliffe. 'And is Eurwen's father intending to visit?'

With Fleur it was very different, all built on that solid plinth of their first meeting: Josh dry, reassuring, handsome, Fleur placid, stoical, a no-nonsense, Well, that's telling *us*! as she took to him.

So from Fleur came a gentle, 'So it really is over?'

'Apparently. He intends to leave Oxford.'

'Don't be flippant, darling. You know better.'

'Do you think we should go with him? Eurwen and me to that awful place?'

'No... no. But a married couple who have a child can't make decisions for themselves *and* that child based on a postcode.'

'So what do you suggest?'

A liquid shine in her eyes now: 'Oh Sara, I'm not *suggesting*. I'm reminding you of something you know. That two clever people, caring for each other as you do still, can find common ground.' Fleur's voice, so soothing and humane, almost does it. 'He's never cared for us, you know—' small deprecating shrug, 'but for Eurwen and... and *you*. There's always a way with enough good will. You could, for instance... I'm giving an example, here, you could—' but Geoffrey Severing strode into the Pryorsfield's kitchen, home from a cancelled something or other. Incensed, to judge by the meticulous way he sorted the contents of his pocket and then by the curtness of his explanation. So Fleur's solution remained unshared.

As did her own admission that she loved Josh more than he could ever love her. This man who hissed, 'When was the last time you did any work?'

And why must he take a wad of flyers and crumple them in front of her face to make his point? She had chosen an image of Eurwen at the aquarium, copper hair against the blue glow like tendrils in the tide but he barely gave it a look. He grabbed at the pile, insensible to Sara's own backstory of failure, the locations where she had hoped to display them barred or about to be, so many closed on this brilliant clear day. *Out of season, love.*

When, for goodness' sake, is Rhyl's season? How short can it be? she had wanted to demand of people who were blameless and harmless. Now about half a dozen rejected Eurwens were being turned into waste paper just for emphasis. Small wonder it went rapidly askew. She shouted, 'Don't do that! That's Eurwen's face you're destroying. Can't you see?'

'Oh wonderful! First it's some crackhead you're putting your trust in, now it's– what? What are we into now, Sara? Voodoo, is it?'

'Don't be ridiculous,' she said, shaken by how close to a hit he had come.

'Me?'

His voice turned foreign in anger. From that one sound, if heard in isolation somehow, she would not have been able to recognise the man she had lived with for years. But further destruction of Eurwen's image stopped. Though he was claiming to be above superstition the rest of the pictures were thrown down with contempt but intact. Those big hands ran across his scalp and he changed from the intimidating figure in possession of the centre of the room to a normal Josh looking down at his wife through sickness at their joint loss... but if he expected her to smooth things over he was going to be disappointed. So much for the morning's energy; her frustrated trudge around town was weighing on muscles, bones, every chamber of the heart like the first salvos of a virus. *Feel some of it, Josh. Small wonder I needed that drink...*

Suddenly, he relaxed. He dropped onto the sofa beside her, sending it backwards on its castors and stretched out an arm revealing the dark sweat rings in the fabric beneath. 'Couldn't you have told me what you were up to?' he said.

'You may have stopped me. There would have been some excellent reason for not doing it.'

'There would've been— because *there is one*.'

'What harm can it do?'

'We said we'd handle it quietly. *You* agreed that first night here that we'd let the lads look for her. That's how we know she's not turned up hurt or… injured. Not been in an accident. Teenage boys run away and walk the streets. Girls run to other people's houses. Always. She'll be sixteen next month and she's gone off of her own accord to a friend.'

A tiny part of her craved for him to carry on with this scenario, to be carried away with it, but it was a part growing weaker day by day. 'That's not true!'

'Ah— what do you know?'

And then it shrivelled up entirely. 'Of course I know. Do you want me to prove it to you? Because I'm able, at this moment.' Suddenly he was looking straight through her, which should have been a warning, while he watched his own internal metamorphosis, Reason lost to Rage. She did not care, plunged on with, 'This is the way to prove that you and 'the lads' are less than effective. Pretty inept, in fact. Eurwen! Eurwen— come in here, will you darling? *Eurwen*!'

A moment of silence is followed by another, unbearable one: no parent is permitted to call up a missing child's fetch for the purpose of argument. Sara turned towards him, self-aghast, and in Josh's eyes the woman he had loved was so debased, he mistook it for triumph. The open hand that came from rest on the sofa was so quick. It snapped her head around and sent the body after, sprawling onto her knees and onto the floor. Another second and, 'Shit,' Josh said.

She cradled the point of impact, not able to look up, feeling him kneel, trap her forearms in his arms and pull her against him, the back of her head in his hands. She knew the instant he began to cry, the strain sending tremors through his ribcage long before it burst out in, 'I'm such a shit, Sara.' Her hair turned moist. Somehow they settled onto the floor, the rug's roughness under the cheek that was on fire… and they clasped each other in the same instant, the ten years' practise producing the old configurations. That place on his upper thigh where her knee naturally found its rest, his big flat collar bone used as pillow for her brow, the slight minute adjustments jointly accomplished to a state where the body becomes master, quenching speech. So often, in the past, the last words said: *yes-s... I ... promise.* Her tears were smeared away by his hands and still dampening his fingers as they moved over her. *And so do I!* A chimera of sensation came next, all imagery at the forefront and its hindquarters a neural pulse. Love. Someone... could it possibly be her? ...was in the throes of a piercing love for Josh that struggled and threshed and squeezed but like all monstrosities might be yet short lived.

He cried properly now, she dry-eyed, holding him. The day carried on outside the window and people and cars passed and dogs barked as in the distance an express train hooted. Every single night she had been under Josh's roof here in this rabbit hutch of a house she must have heard it. For the first time now she *heard* it above the gulls' shriek.

They lay: either one might have slept such was the need for physical and mental numbness but neither did. When they disengaged, finally, and sat up it was a shock to find the light still there, the evening not yet fully in and the pictures of Eurwen scattered beneath them, hardly creased, hardly changed.

But nothing is healed so effortlessly in an ex-marriage. During the final year they had been becalmed in this blessed place time after time, coming across love like a remaindered favourite, handling it, reading aloud its best lines. And those days were from a wounded marriage, not one deceased. Once up and not touching and sitting with coffee the sight of him slouched across from her stirred something like hatred. A slug of liquor might have dampened it... His exhaustion, the plum puffiness of the under-eye soft fruit, wasn't it all his own doing? He had lost

Eurwen and not brought her back. She said, 'I think we need to get something out in the open Josh... the reason for all this secrecy. You must see I can't go along with it.' He opened his mouth but she overrode him. 'It would be wrong to Eurwen. That's what I feel today. Now.'

'That's what you feel today, is it?' No need to wonder how good Josh was at his job. Gently confiding to begin: Just need to check... fact-finding, nothing serious... followed by the hardening up of accent and raising of volume. 'Well everything has to change, doesn't it? Because that's what Sara says? Handy to get a regular bloody update on that score. Otherwise how would I know where WE WERE BLOODY WELL AT!'

'We're nowhere! How long have I been in this pit of a place, a fortnight? What would you be thinking if this were another case, Josh, some other woman's child missing for *over* a fortnight? No! Don't say it. And don't get angry, pretending you can't help it... if I were that other woman you'd be oh, so patient... oh, so understanding. Because taking your frustration out on the victims is one of the things you learn never to do. A policeman told me that a long time ago, Josh.'

He glared. 'Right.'

'Keeping this to ourselves *may* have seemed prudent. But not now. What if Eurwen had still been close by when I arrived? Staying away one day then another day, just to see what happened... daring herself to leave it a little longer?'

'This isn't doing any good—'

'No.' She tried the glowing cheek again and found the skin unbroken but tender. It was enough to keep him silent. 'What if that first week Eurwen had seen herself plastered over every shop window? On the front page of every local newspaper, on television? She could be sitting here with us now.'

He shook his head. She was not tempted to stop. 'I can't say for certain – and you're not able to gainsay it. But it isn't just bad judgement I'm holding against you. You wanted to keep everything secret because you couldn't stand the shame.' Was he following? *Let me spell it out for you, Josh.* 'How you had no more control over your own daughter... I don't mean control, I mean no more understanding of, no greater ability to intervene in her life, than all those pathetic people you're meant to police. Think of it on the news at six o'clock and again at ten every weekday and once on Sunday, Eurwen's face. Letting the world into the secret of how *your* family's broken, just as the others are, the ones you used to call your best customers. The ones that are... everywhere,' she finished weakly.

Josh's phone gurgled. All through his taking it out and glancing down she fully expected him to snub the caller by click... instead of answering it with a normal, 'Hello Meg.' And then to listen and reply, 'Yes... yes. I can. OK.' And to get up and walk out.

It was midnight. Her legs numb, head aching, the empty tumbler warm in her grip: Josh called and for a moment she was back in Tackley Close.

'I'm sorry,' he said. 'I'm sorry.'

With a tongue made of felt she lisped out, 'It doesn't... matter.'

'Still...' He paused to let her speak if she wished, then, 'I'll stay here tonight. There's somebody I need to see first thing— Neil Rix. Meg got your message so I'll follow up. You'll be all right?'

'Of course. But that Neil person... with the dreadful skin, he pretended he had been asleep but he hadn't. He smelled of smoke! He'd been out already. He was with a Chinese man... perhaps. I've just thought that: they *were* together. Like a conspiracy. And he was avoiding me but he was watching.'

'You sound all in,' he tried diplomatically.

'I am. What time are you coming back?'

'I'll go to work from here, first thing. I need to get out early, so makes more sense. I won't wake you and— it's closer than—'

Freud's Kettle, she thought but feared to say. 'Of course. So when will you be home?'

''Bout five— if nothing comes up. I'll call if it does. Straightaway.'

'Goodbye.'

'Sara?'

'Yes?' She tried not to breathe, waiting, giving him time and space... in the Uptons' house, in the hall probably with a figure just on the other side of the door. 'I'm still here, Josh,' she said.

Chapter 13

She has been whacked in the face. By an open hand. Sara's one
for fine distinctions but the distinction's pretty coarse if it's your
face and Josh's hand. I'd worshipped the man once. Learning
he'd struck her was a bit of a blow to me— OK, inappropriate.
The wordplay comes from Tomiko again. Once he nearly killed
himself clinging to a young coastal pine in a typhoon, the rain
hard enough to wash it out of the ground and the quake alarm
sounding— mistakenly, as it happens, but he couldn't be sure
of that. All to capture a riot of weather and somehow get it onto
paper. Now straight to camera he tells me this, 'Stinking wind
near my end, near gone today,' and let out a fart that must've
filled his studio. And laughed. People don't understand the
Japanese laugh. 'People' includes Yori.

Yori doesn't laugh when he finds what Josh did. He may be
going to the bad but he's not that far gone. Shame isn't funny
and someone has to feel it if Josh won't. Managing to keep close
today there are plenty of Sara sightings in his town but they
embarrass him as well, as though entire Rhyl had decided to
join in the bad behaviour. Sullen expressions everywhere or the
sort of scowls that go with Whocaresafuck? Then one
disgusting gesture behind her back. He feels like whispering in
Sara's ear *migi ni magatte kudasai*. But she wouldn't please turn
to the right, would she? Always to the left— which is the side
of her face Josh will naturally strike as a right-handed man. It's
a shock when Yori sees himself about to reach out the moment
her back's safely to him. He doesn't try to detain her of course.
Even though running through his head is No good! That place
you're making for's closed. You're wasting time. Come with me.

I'll tell you things if you come of your own accord. It can't be any worse than home with a missing daughter and a husband present. If you knew me – but I'm nothing. I'm not two people, I'm less than the one you've stared straight at late at night – surprised him watching you. Do you remember? But your senses were primed for a familiar face. Eurwen's is what you craved so you're not likely to linger over a stranger's, a not-very-round and not-very-pale *Oriental's* without even a scar to give distinction. So don't. Won't stop me heckling you now. Look again! Just say something! You can see he wants to talk. And it's your only chance. You'll hate what you hear about Eurwen because he won't lie and— and yet it *could* save your life. Which he wants to. (Wretched Yori wants him to.) Has never stopped wanting to ever since. *This* is it. The exact point things hinge on— if you're the great AH it's the frame to pause at, pump up an eerie Franz Waxman score. Just touch on the pairing-off dancers who drift away before you let the lens slide over an empty bottle clutched in a woman's fist, the cords of tension in the young man's neck— and have the audience on the edge of their seats.

And all it would've taken to stop the plot was a line of dialogue across a roaring fire— or is it dying down, being abandoned? I do know there were lanterns, and the smell of smoke and skunk, and you— unapproachable.

Fade to black.

Then days later she'd been hit and nobody would think it's unconnected with her vanishing. When Sara's father, the great Professor Geoffrey Severing, made the discovery— well, his response is documented elsewhere. Almost any reference to The Mystery of Sara Meredith includes quotes the reporters or serious writers felt legally safe to include. How unjust is history? I'll bet less than a handful of people ever considered the after-effects of a 'party' on a freezing autumn night in a horseshitty field back in 2008. But that blow of Josh's would turn Sara walking out on him into a suspicious death though minus a body. That single blow seemed to put Josh in the frame with me.

I imagine a fine network of cracks from Josh's punch – sorry, open hand – spreading through her brittle glaze. And having softened her up, Sara was ready for Kim Tighe.

October 7th
Kim would not be on time.

Yet again Sara adjusted the low table placed parallel to the fireplace, then stood where she could also keep an eye on the road. Soft grey drizzle was still falling: perhaps it would take for Kim to cancel. Outside the Clear Skies she had said, 'I'll give you the address', and Kim was suddenly close enough to make her flinch (the unwashed hair about to touch her lips) whispering, 'I already know it.'

At around twelve, making coffee to wash down Nurofen, the boiling water slopped over the worktop but miraculously missed her exposed inner arm then her feet... a good omen? *Omen!* Geoffrey Severing's collection of taboo words included omen. *Spirituality* was another, and *logical* when used in any non-mathematical sense. The weight of his judgement would ordinarily be enough to make it a pariah to her own brain and tongue... But a father was someone who seemed to be receding from her daily existence. It came as a shock to be conjuring him up now like the dead, silver hair, just a suggestion of roundness to the shoulders as he stooped unnecessarily beneath lower ceilings than he was used to in Tackley Close: *only two things to concern you about this car, drive and reverse.* That he lived was a sudden relief, that Fleur the good stepmother lived also added warmth. They existed! It was midday and a weekday, so he was in his dark-panelled study, the stained glass throwing patterns across the desktop where photographs of Fleur and Eurwen and herself were the sanctioned clutter. The newest Apple Mac might otherwise have sat in solitary perfection, utile *and* art object...

When the bell finally announced Kim's arrival, paranoia kept her cowering out of sight at first. What if this were just some sort of... what? A charade was the least frightening option. Maybe rough hangers-on were ready to spring into the house, on the attack the moment Kim gained entry. What if—?

The smile she managed for a Kim alone on the threshold was of reprieve. 'Come in. I thought you may not be able to find the house. I was about to call.'

Kim glinted with moisture and brought in the sea. 'Said twelve, didn't I?' She stepped past Sara, looking around, curious and openly disappointed at the smallness and bareness. Her old jacket was sloughed off; underneath she had dressed for business in a navy skirt so thin it outlined her leg bones at every movement, and a giant black T-shirt displaying DON'T ASK WHY with the rest of the slogan obscured by a mannish waistcoat. Minus beads, sunglasses, dangling earrings, she looked less unwholesome too, even about the hair. There was something touching in it all, the dark clothes' ripple making a downed bird of her. From the drawstring bag she took a plain wooden box and put it on the coffee table. 'We're on our own, yeah?' and when Sara nodded, she added. 'You need to sit across from here not at the side.' Josh's bruise, spreading as it matured from Sara's jawbone up to the corner of an eye, a massive stigmata that she expected to have to explain away, Kim didn't notice. They sat.

'I wondered if you would want something of my daughter's?' Sara had ready the little moonstone pea. It rolled to rest on the table top.

Kim barely gave it a glance. 'Yeah, well— can't do no harm.'

Then an odd gesture: she stretched out her index finger as though to touch, and at the last moment pulled back. 'Leave it there. I might— no... it'll be all right, there.' The box was placed in front of Sara. Out came a pack of playing cards, oversized, childish somehow. They were new.

Sara's panic rose again at this newness. The cards were part of the hoax, an acquired prop, whereas true skill should depend on weathered apparatus, shoddiness even. She watched as Kim squared up and tidied a deck the size of a brick, only the reverse of the top card visible, with its mundane patterning. 'This is the Tarot,' Kim intoned. 'It's not a laugh, OK? It's a proper thing I do. If you can't get your head round that— if you can't give it respect, we may's well not bother.'

'Yes. I understand.'

She seemed satisfied. 'Also, there has to be a charge— it's like I said, if I don't charge, the value's not in it? Y'see?'

'That's perfectly acceptable.'

'So what I'm saying is— it's like got to be a lot, 'cos if it isn't, it means nothing, right?'

'How much?'

'OK, well— it's got to be like, a hundred, hasn't it?'

An involuntary spasm of annoyance at this delay appeared in Sara's face and she saw its being read. 'I would need to check how much I have in the house. There's a possibility I don't have that amount in cash.'

'I'll wait then.' Kim leaned back from the table and stared out of the window.

Upstairs, with her head suddenly light, she thought if I allow myself to sit down anywhere in this bedroom, think, react rationally, I won't be able to keep it from Kim. Even if I decide to proceed. To find the beautiful matching purse she upended the beautiful scarlet tote onto the unmade bed: three twenties and a ten. Coins clinked in a jacket pocket... but nothing like enough. *Do you take plastic, Kim? How would a good, old fashioned cheque suit… Perhaps I could owe you? We will go straight to the cashpoint, immediately after this, I promise.* Clutching what she had, she descended. (If she were in her father's house now, Pryorsfield, she would have touched the carven Pryor newel post for luck). But there by the phone was Josh's address book and Josh's voice in her head from better days: Money in here if you ever… for emergencies…

Had she noticed any when she'd searched for Clive Upton's number? But twin fifty pound notes were folded and tucked into the inner cover.

'Come on then,' Kim said.

First Kim shuffled with hands smaller than Eurwen's, smaller even than Sara's own.

Sara was ordered to cut. 'Can I ask—?'

'Shush-sh.' It was as if to an infant. With a practised movement, Kim reformed the pack. 'Now you've got to say what you're hoping the cards'll tell you. *Don't* ask no questions. Say what you'd like to know *if* the cards wanna give it up.'

Sara swallowed down panic, her morning's alcohol intake too feebly diffused to be registering. 'I want to know—' She began again, speaking slowly and precisely as if the cards were hard of hearing, 'Would like to be told whether— no! *That* my daughter— Eurwen— is safe.' Desperate now, she scanned Kim's face for signs of approval, disapproval. There was neither.

The first card was turned up. Kim said, 'The Emperor.'

Sara must crane her neck for a view of the bearded man seated on a throne.

Kim gave a cynical smile and rotated it. 'No surprises there, then.'

'Why? What do you mean?'

'Never mind. It just tells you there's a man at work, like in a male power thing going on. But where's not, huh? Let's see what he's up against.' A second card was laid down. 'The Ten of Pentangles.' It showed a slender girl with white hounds at her feet. *A girl*. The pentangles hung like bubbles about her in their golden circles. In the background, through a bridge's arch, stood a sandy-coloured tower.

'It's Eurwen!'

'Could be.'

'Everything to do with her is there. You can't know. I promise you, it is.' But this was offensive and she blundered on, 'I'm sorry! Sorry. Yes, you were saying...? What does the Ten of Pentangles represent?'

Kim shrugged. 'It *might* be 'bout things getting sorted... Like getting out of a bad sitch. You find the way that suits. And then just hang on in. Yeah, that's it.'

'So she's... finding herself? Is that all?' Contempt wrestled with frustration which straggled despair. Yet on the very cusp of disbelief, her hunger was for more. Evil *omens* couldn't sway the prepared mind (she clung to an image of her father here)... in fact, unsettling news should be expected, almost comic. Clichéd! Kim piling on the agony to command attention. And hadn't comfortable assurances from Josh been offered with as little basis? It will be fine. Trust *me*. 'So how does the Emperor interfere?'

'Perhaps it's like... him doing the sorting.'

'But he isn't a *dangerous* influence? There's nothing there to suggest it will lead her to harm?'

A slightest shake of head: 'We'll do three cards today. I don't think we should do more than that. All right?'

'I have no idea... If that's your advice.' She tried to hold herself in check, tried to take a slow breath against a pounding pulse. Kim, of course, intended to reveal what was to be the last card with extra slowness and recognising the cheap drama of it couldn't shore up her own waning control. The shivers and the beetle-crawliness returned and that ache in the back of the throat and numerous other bodily alarm calls if she deigned to listen. These were mere background chatter though in comparison to a totally novel sense of intellectual vertigo. Suddenly the air between Kim and herself was charged... and she believed. She *believed*. Knowing nothing of Tarot nor wanting to, stored fragments of data, phrases from somewhere, now suggested she was about to face Death on a Pale Horse... or The Hanged Man. Either could turn up. So when a voice said, 'Judgement,' her heart filled with joy. But it was not a good card. She could tell by Kim's pursed lips and the hand that came up to them, preventing speech. 'Let me see! *What is it?*' Firstly her eye was drawn to the central angel, a boy/man blowing a trumpet from which a red and white flag hung, a confusing emblem... definitely an angel, though, against a background of jagged mountain peaks. But the foreground was gruesome as a scene from Bosch. From their graves figures were being summoned by the Call, a naked father and mother with a child, a *girl* child, all displayed at the point of rising, their skins ghastly as befitted three corpses. 'Oh God,' she could hear herself say, 'Ohgodohgod. Not dead. No-o.'

Chapter 14

Into Forward Rhyl even earlier than usual after a chill-no-jacket ten-minute ride. The sky's cloudless, the sea free of its usual chop and letting the sand bars of Rhyl Flats show mauve as beds of underwater heather. Survivors out at the wind farm seem to poke through it, barely creaking round. Daylight's crossed England and the rivers Mersey and Dee and now it's caught up with snail-like, stupid Rhyl. Needless to say workstations are all unoccupied when I walk in. I wander straight past them to look down on a mega truck, parallel parked to our building, engine running, come to take away temporary barriers. Or those that have not been already stolen. A patch of new tarmac spills out from under the truck's wheels like an oil slick. No one's loading, no one's even standing around and gulls have settled on its cab. When a dull thud echoes from inland there isn't a single bird bothers to lift off. They don't even complain.

PalmWalk is my prize for being in early. The new route. Just a path in one sense, but one that'll stitch together the entire broken beachfront since The Wave, one that will let me do what years of picking and patching never could, use all that energy for a purpose. I bring my plan alive and run yet one simulation, gathering perspectives – here's out across a populated beach, the next is down the Water Street intersection then down Abbey Street – ahead is a glimpse of river now. Honestly? I'm struggling with it, convinced there's a best line of sight at some spot, probably where the line-walker rises that extra half-metre and the distant prominence of Great Orme rears up. Can't find it yet. Has to be past SkyTower. You don't want both in. What does it matter? Tess asked when I showed it first, not expecting help – she's technically untrained.

The two things shouldn't crowd each other, I say. A progression that's designed to surprise – *and give you a buzz, Tess!* – should actually work.

—Well nothing else round here does.

I repeat some things don't connect. Sara, for example, can't have trusted in Kim's 'talent'. Where was the scholar in her? You only had to look at this shell of a person to ask yourself how likely is it? Tomiko's craziest sayings make more sense. And respect for Sara isn't easy to maintain after Kim Tighe— I'm distracted by that woman now, seen running away from Avonside with money in her pocket, fear in her wake, wearing black and totally right too, Kim Tighe, a variable overhead even Josh couldn't cover. If Kim Tighe hadn't latched on things might have ended differently—

—Outside there's a commotion. In fact what sounds like a fully ripe rumble's in progress. A car hoots. An extra loud, aggressive 'Yeah-h-h!' is the response. But by the time I'm across to the window again the truck's being driven off. Empty. Vehicles pass underneath and a few pedestrians, old, young, in-betweens who've witnessed *something*, drift away and keep going. It's nearly eight now and maybe a handful have jobs to be at while the rest are just out, sea-gazing, waiting for events like this one, any happenings. Whatever it was happened. That I've missed and they caught. Most of them will still be boarded in cramped, makeshift accommodation. A recent news story was about a family preferring to camp in St Thomas's vestry – what's a vestry? the reporter joked to camera – instead of the badminton court they'd been given space in.

Twinned with Soweto, it made me think.

Rhyl isn't ever properly awake till past midday not till, to quote Libby, the streets are aired. But it's given itself a shake, rubbed its private parts and yawned— which is virtually what Glenn Hughes is doing when he comes in. He nods and starts unpacking a rucksack. He's wearing an open-neck shirt, mauve against Celt-pink flesh. The jeans are the latest cut. I get a wicked grin, obviously to do with the small wrapped object he drops in front of my screen which I've blanked anyway.

'Either your Casino numbers have come up or Alice Norman's home.'

'Gottit.' Glenn's smile is crafty. 'This is for you. She told me 'bout them last time she was over. I said to get you one— for putting me up.'

I handle a squat cylinder, heavier than expected at around 400 grams. No rattle. 'You bought me the poster.' Giving in, I peel away paper and padding to free a white earthenware mug. The curved handle's poorly proportioned against height and circumference. Drinking from it won't be comfortable.

'Turn it round.'

On the other side is a pair of silver blobs contained by black ovals. Eyes. Cartoon eyes. No, the more you looked at them real *eyes*. 'Thank-you.'

'Don't thank me yet. Move about a bit and watch!'

Glenn flattens himself against the window ledge and clears a space leaving no option but to do as I'm told. As I stand the mug's eyes – which seem to be fixed on my face – are raised as well.

'Good, innit? They follow you. Come on – come on! Over here – see? Still fixed on you.'

'Movement sensitive—'

'Not just that. Keep watching.' In his enthusiasm, he edges me sideways. Loyally the mug's eyes strain to the corners of their black surrounds. 'Dip round behind the cabinets – here, come on! Surprise it from the other direction.'

This is humiliating. I'm being asked to outwit a piece of

ceramic. But, I do as instructed and arrive back to see the mug's eyes flick across and hone in on me.

'Yes.'

'Ah-h! Wait for this now.' Glenn promenades across the room. The effect is meant to be casual but closer to camp. 'Keep watching!' he whispers as though the mug might overhear. An obstructed view makes the pupils seem troubled. 'It's all in the molecules— d'you want to know how—?'

'No.' I run a fingertip over. The black eyeball is just detectible by touch. Oddly, I'm not willing to poke the silver pupils. 'I'll work it out. Thank Alice for me. It's a good present.'

'Yours for life. If you pass it on to somebody else, well-ll:' He shook his head.

'Well what?'

'Just *don't do it*. So the salesman warned. Bad pow! You'll be sorry— or *they* will more like.' He laughs nastily and then turns thoughtful. 'Y'know while Alice is in Spain I miss her like buggery but when she does shift herself and turn up, it takes getting used it. Can't sleep with her in the bed. She's still there of course. Gerroff! I told her, it's a work day. Now I wish I was back with Alice.' He shrugs— a happy riddle, a *koan*, to himself.

I recall Alice's wiry woman's physique and then her aggressive look. Alice was once a psychiatric nurse. At our Christmas party she explained architects were responsible for most social problems, her proof being one of her hostels had recently subsided down a Spanish cliff. 'Alice Norman's one in a million,' I say. 'But how d'you rate Alfred Hitchcock?'

'What?'

'The world's greatest storyteller. Everything is black and white.'

That gets him to shuffle off. 'I only worry about you 'cos somebody should.' His baritone breaks out from his cubicle with a blast from *Peter Grimes*. I know a lot more about his musical taste now than I did pre Wave. Rarely any Bach but surprisingly varied thanks to choir membership. Yet he's been singing this stuff for days now – many days.. '*May he restrain our tongues from strife/ And shield from anger's din our life/ And guard with watchful care our eyes/ From earth's absorbing vanitie-es!*'

Even the mug's panicky. Glenn's rehearsing for a concert in aid of the flood victims and he's given me the story. Only in Wales would they be practising bits from a child abuse opera with a megastorm and multiple drownings to cheer people up. 'Earth's absorbing vanities?'

'That's it.'

'Not exactly catchy.'

'Sounds better in force. If a couple of dozen of you are belting it out, yeah? We've had no complaints so far.'

'Is the rest of the chorus your size?'

'Bigger. And younger, some of them.'

'That'll help.'

'*Oh hang at open doors the net, the cork/ While squalid sea-dames at the mending work—*'

'Can you call sea-dames squalid in public?'

'Nobody'll know what they are.'

'I don't know what they are.'

''S'how we get away with it. "*Whoever's guilty gets the rap./ The Borough keeps its standard up-p!*"'

'I didn't know it was a comedy.'

'That's the only joke. Too deep?'

I shrug.

Sara has her puzzles, her *koans* as well. She wants to and needs to find Kim Tighe after the Tarot reading, after Kim's taken her money and fled. But she can't. I can though.

So watch out, Kim Tighe.

Chapter 15

An innovation, two in fact: a besuited Josh announced he was off to the County Court in Mold to give evidence in an Actual Bodily Harm prosecution (not his own) and several vodkas later, a person called to save Sara's soul. Sara was dumbfounded by the woman's being there at all, as well as by the pinched face under a grey bob and billowy summer dress worn with an anorak. The instant they made eye-contact, her visitor took the opportunity to demand, 'Are you ever afraid for the future? Do you know someone in distress? Have you thought how many problems in this world could be solved if we only listened to Our Lord Jesus Christ?'

Sara shook her head gently and as gently closed the door. From behind the living room blinds she watched the caller pass by the parked VW, oblivious to its potential for griming her skirt and bare legs... rather shapely, smooth legs that made her glance down at her own downy ankles poking out from the chinos, remembering buying a razor her first week but never using it... Further along Avonside, the evangelist was able to up her rate as older houses clustered even closer, lacking fenced gardens. Most seemed empty and unresponsive. Each merited an insert through its letter box. Where she did get an answer, it was of seconds' duration... a step forward, a step back as though joined to each door's movement by string. Such a display of fortitude: Sara felt her own eyes prickle with it. After every rebuff, the woman's shoulders were squared and she adjusted the angle of the chin for the next, resetting hope. At the road's curve she vanished, a flap of fabric the last token of oddly assembled parts. But sneaking back to the hall now it was safe, Sara found no digest of sacred texts lying there for her, nor any personalised free gift of succour. Apparently she'd had her chance with the Lord, this augmented version of Professor Geoffrey Severing, rigorous, benevolent, even more irascible (had He not once cursed a fig tree?) and *disappointed with her.*

But if you do know something, Jesus, Saviour, Father, Counsellor… Smug Sadist, I can still be yours. So, please, please, whereisshewhereisshewhereisshe?

A refill necessitated a lurch towards the kitchen, to the vodka she had hidden in a new place, a gap between the wall and the refrigerator. The tumbler's wide mouth was not enough. She spilled a measure at least but with the rest of the glass safely drunk, she and Jesus scrambled back onto better terms somehow. If Your Emissary had been less ridiculous, she told Him as she wiped down the worktop, discovering a peculiar satisfaction in unstickied whiteness under the matching trinity of Sugar, Tea, Coffee, and if only, *Sire*, the woman's expression could have been less pained, I might… but already the actual look in the woman's eyes was dissolving, followed by the mouth, the entire face and the shape of the hair. Only some dress fabric hung on, a thicket of patterns and movements and botanic uncertainty… and after the next glassful, knocked back in one standing at the sink (who knew when Josh might barge in?) her confusion worsened… the anorak had been *fur-trimmed* like her old Bachelor of Arts gown with its silly hood which, to Eurwen's disgust, sported white rabbit. White rabbits and rabbit holes and sunny Oxford afternoons and adored children: the muddle incited the desire to throw herself upon the mercy of the Professor, to feel the reassurance of his love. All my sins and failings have been visited upon Eurwen, Daddy, she will say. Mea culpa… mea culpa… but elsewhere in the house a radio was playing and she thought to turn it off before she rang Geoffrey, whose hearing was not as acute as it once had been, and she did go as far as the next room in her search, the while rehearsing, 'I have a confession to make, Daddy, a terrible confession that should have been... could have been... made years ago. No, no. Not drinking, we can't mention the drinking, can we? Such a small falling off anyway, I think. As will you. When you... when I... once I tell you what I did....'

She opened her eyes and Josh was there.

'What are you sitting in the dark for?'

'Listening to the radio.' Her head throbbed. No wonder she'd had to turn it down... turn it off.

His case *had* gone well: he burst out into genuine laughter. 'I don't have a radio 'cept in the car.' There was friendly tap to her upper arm as she looked about to rise from the sofa, 'Stay put,' he said and clicked on the light.

He was able to look at her now and the bruise was an old friend. 'I stopped in to talk to this Neil again. Clive's signed him up for odd-jobs. They live hand to mouth this lot, glad of anything. Gives you a bit of leverage,' he trailed off.

'And?' was all she could trust herself to say.

'I got the same as you did at first. Don't know. Haven't heard from her! But,' he bared his teeth, 'just as I was packing it in I came back at him with, Look, you're no kid yourself. This is a young girl we're talking about. She acts big. She's not. She shouldn't be on the loose on her own. Her mother's frantic.'

'Thank-you.'

'Anyway,' Josh was speaking but also summing her up, police-style, every swallow and blink added to the total, 'are you taking this in? Sara! He said she wasn't on her own.'

'What?' Fully awake now she found her tongue when two second's thought would have suggested *leave it lost*, 'Oh God, Josh, so who is it now? These people Eurwen knows, they're all older. You said it. Twentysomethings.' Apart from speaking more loudly than the small living room warranted she felt quite lucid and was sure that he fielded her reference. 'And thirtysomethings. She ought to be with girls her own age like Henriette and... not those Uptons. Who is she with? And what were you thinking of?'

Josh should not be accepting this. Josh should be calling her hysterical and insisting Meg was a decent person. What she did not want to hear was, 'Not arguing. But Neil mentioned a *boy*. He'd asked Eurwen why she wanted to stay in Rhyl when she could go back to a city. Eurwen said the boys in Oxford were *beyond totally lame* which sounds like her. But *here* there was a nice one.'

'A boy,' she repeated stupidly.

Eurwen had met a boy. A boy she could hypnotise just by talking and dazzle by walking into any scene. A suggestion or two about her past – she didn't even have to lie – and she had him writing a new story in his head, this innocent or idiot, about the Little Fox that didn't leave, that broke the rules and stayed. For him. That's Eurwen for you.

Big surprise, Sara? (So what did you think *your* Thomasina was trading on? Her Latin and Greek and a quick way with numbers behind the father's bar?) At fifteen, Eurwen was taller than her mother already, a lot more beautiful though that seemed to matter less to her than to other people. To me. A woman— she thought. She'd pass for twenty if she wanted to and she wanted to. She was an irresistible force and I should know. But then there's a fog of sex everywhere. What else lights the fuse? Watch Hitchcock's people blundering round in it, falling over symbols of it— and violence, of course, all the violence you get over sex because attraction means death for AH. He was an outstandingly ugly man that assaulted actresses for a living. By hand was favourite. In Hitchcock Heaven, a fragile woman's being perpetually stalked and however often you tag along it's to the same car-crash finish. I've binged on three, four movies end to end then got out there and lingered over the entire VistaVision openness of the coast. It tends to lead the eye, crying out for a good director and, more often than not, I see it as *he* does, with the horizon suddenly cut by an attacker. At hip height for the male and his victim by her waist. They sway and grapple. A dance. Her perfect spine bows dangerously, enough to snap it you think. If Bodega Bay served better than anywhere, I'm a fool for Bodega Bay, then Rhyl's got its big sky and empty sand. And gulls. Tippy Hedron is always wanting to know if we've ever seen so many birds?

Yes, I have Tippy.

Watch her, you really should. I did while I went through that packet from the Coroner's clerk a second and third time, with my hands gone shaky like I'd forgotten my meds and Libby and sister scraped chairs out on the flags after the last sun.

Chapter 16

October the what? The effort to get to her feet and check on the exact date was not worth it. Sara transferred the pen to the line beneath.

Days had passed since Kim's show, the sham, the worse than sham, the con-trick according to Josh. Sham was preferable: it guaranteed Eurwen was not in danger, Eurwen was not dead. Sara found she could manage to repress emotions connected with the Tarot results by labelling them counterfeit. Still Kim tormented her; now with her uselessness, now with the possibility, fast becoming a certainty, that Kim would know the boy. It was a small town and she knew everyone, knew instantly that Sara didn't fit, that Clive Upton was deep and crooked, that Josh was a detective—

—Or would pretend to know because this Kim, who was she? Information from a doubtful source could prove more mischievous than ignorance. Consider John Cane's assertion that Thomasina (she who had lost him his wager) was none other than Orlando Tansley. Not a girl, not *her* peerless girl, but an effeminate wastrel and swindler hung at Newgate's Debtor's Door, the year preceding the slander. How conveniently! Because he existed, Tansley, one of three unfortunates in *View of an execution before the Debtor's Door of Newgate*, the famous 1809 engraving by Fisher Nuttall. But no record of any Oxford connection has ever come to light nor any Tansley accomplishments bar criminality. So entirely preposterous, yet the fiction dogged Thomasina and was one of the first things Sara set out to dispel. A lack of corroborating facts must always require *Quo bono?* being asked. In Thomasina's case, John

160

Cane... or now *Cunning, parasitical, every-cruel-tag-Josh-could-attach-to-her Kim Tighe*. Kim benefited, she reasoned, not materially (it was natural for Sara to discount a small sum) but in melodrama and the chance to star... which she has stupidly provided. Self-disgust broke out more powerfully than ever. Why begin to analyse now in excusatory mode, a woman she despised? So it seemed. After fear came fear's fishy aftertaste, humiliation; she had been made a fool of and it was with gritted teeth she set herself to record the next incident.

Out again with the Eurwen leaflets she was high on hope, courtesy of the day's opening shots of vodka: *Excuse me... this is Eurwen Meredith. Have you seen her?* No one refused. They said *nope, don-think-so, sorry love*. Two teenagers laughed in earshot, a young man whose earthy smell registered just too late to have her veering away, muttered incoherent sentences to himself rather than her. But no one refused. At the crossing of a side road she spotted a cluster of middle-aged women, the Holy Grail. When she called out they changed course; their small, dumpy leader, straining coat belted tightly though it was mild, said, 'What's up?'

'It's my daughter.'

An Eurwen was passed from hand to hand: 'Na-a, you save your papers love.'

Haven't, no. What about you, Shirl...? Oh, it's a sod when they do that... She'll turn up. I'll bet she does. Luvly mum like you! For a few seconds before moving off they stood and enclosed her in their half circle, a female bastion. Then she was aware that, subtly, without meaning to, they freed themselves from her distress and she was grateful they hadn't extended the conversation to become tedious, sickly. Instead, without needing reference to any etiquette, they had done just enough. She felt very tired. The midday turned drear above and cooler below and a tumbledown wall on the corner of Westbourne Road was something to make for, her face welcoming the onset of drizzle as excuse to give up. Her ankles ached from hard slow walking and a hollowness in her chest warned she would need drink the instant she was inside Josh's house, well before thought or speech... or anything.

And suddenly there was Kim. Kim was smiling at her from a billboard.

She blinked and looked again. The collapsed wall she perched on seemed to be in defence of some sort of builders yard though no bigger than a suburban garden. A padlocked, tumbled-down shack at the far end was the sole indication of business premises. The predominant usage was as dumping ground for the extinct funfair only a street away. Remains of grotesque mechanical arms, other obscure contraptions and a cup-and-saucer roundabout with deep vessels into which toddlers could be strapped, all were stacked or spread. And propped jauntily against a giant cup was the billboard advertising Palace of Pleasure, a painted blonde in a red bikini reclining on her elbow, one leg bent while the other pointed skywards in an ecstatic stab of flesh. Kim's calves and thighs were scrofulous with weather but the familiar smirk remained or a girlish version of it. 'I was painted once, me, could of bin a model,' she had bragged. Pitiable now, the idealised Kim... cushioned in scrap.

Fireworks! A crack and whoosh returned her to Westbourne Road. She pulled up her collar and made for the bridge, a rattle of shots following her out of town.

But fireworks were going off every evening as soon as the light faded. 'A whole bloody month of this!' was Josh's response. On consideration, Rhyl did have an especially rowdy feel as she had walked it, as though Carnival were just around the corner, something to look forward to, a relief from yearlong Lent. But the hard-eyed children begging at the back of the Queens

Market, their hideous Guy slumped like corpse, did not look safe to try Eurwen's picture on.

'You didn't give them anything?' Josh wanted to know.

'Of course not,' she lied. Guido Fawkes lay racked and broken at their feet... one of them had worn a death's head mask and could have been a girl behind it. Another's thin boyish face was daubed livid. Bonfire Night, All Hallows' Eve, the Druidic *Samhain* and the Romans' *Feralia* seemed blended, a brew to salve every lack and loss. Or just something to anticipate for this bunch of wild uncared for children that would come to no harm. As she focused on the eggs she was cooking and their yielding to heat, she was about to say more... maybe a mild disagreement with his attitude? But sirens sounded back across the river and his phone went off as the first golden solids caught at the spatula.

Hours later a burnt scent still filled the downstairs rooms. When he returned it was left to Josh to clear away the aborted meal. From the kitchen he shouted: 'Just kids having fun out on the game reserve.'

Without even Polly Reith's pamphlet open as prop he had surprised her staring at a blank television and inert long enough for one curled leg to crumple when she jumped up. She wore jeans still, though was half-ready for bed in a pyjama top, an intimacy interrupted or thought better of. Yet she had waited up, sobered by the suspicion he had gone to *her*. Then his expression as she staggered caused something to snap. 'The game reserve. That's what you call it?' she asked, supporting herself in the arch.

'Cher-rist Sara! The state of you.' His hair had grown in the time she'd been here and needed a trim, needed to be brushed impatiently out of his eyes. He pushed past. 'I'm getting a shower!'...and there it was, now it didn't matter, the time and date on the kitchen wall. Five to ten on October 25th. The Feast of Crispian, she mouthed. This day in 1415 Welsh longbowmen turned back the French knights' charge and won The Field of Agincourt for King Henry V.

Quickly she went and gathered her new, warmer clothes. That she owned the wool thing she was about to get into was a novelty, also this jacket with its nylon whisper. But both pulled on easily enough and she made it outside while the water was still thundering in the pipes overhead.

It's the vodka – that's what she should have realised. When she thinks she sees danger, she's looking in the wrong place. Alcohol makes her imagine the children are squinting through slitted lids as she edges past them – and just visible, gleaming like citrines, are their rodent teeth.

Night had taken over the streets: it was their time, what they were best at. Sara made for the lemonade glow. At the front door of an arcade a mini roundabout-ride was being watched by two teenage girls. 'Na, don't know 'er. You, Col? Na, me neither.' The tot that belonged to them shrieked with fear as he circled on his plastic pony to *Ghost Riders in the Sky*. Beyond this vivid little drama, acres of chortling gaming machines stood unused.

'He's not really enjoying it, is he?' Sara said.

Eurwen's picture could not do what slight criticism managed instantly. 'He wanted to go on,' the tall one answered, looking her in the eye. Squaring up.

'It'll stop in a minute,' the other explained. Small, more placatory, her nails combed through shockingly bright hair, not Eurwen's colour but a chemical carmine. 'It's rubbish. And you don't get long.'

The story of Rhyl. Sara retreated into a collision with a heavy-set man. He, at least, examined the picture, frowning an already deeply-creased brow to signal effort. 'Na— sorry. Oi—

Colleen! Get that babby 'ome. It's too bloody late to be in 'ere with him.' To Sara he said, 'You look wrecked, love.'

'I'm... very anxious.'

'Step into the office a minute. What made you come in 'ere looking? Plays the slots, does she?'

'No. I'm not sure.' Trailing behind him, she noticed the trodden down heels of his shoes and the holed socks. His office was tiny: a desk, a chair both piled with paper, walls covered in imitation wood onto which he pinned Eurwen's picture next to a calendar. October featured a spotted puppy in a bed of autumn leaves. 'I'll ask around— that's all I can do, yeah?'

'Thank-you.' A bed of leaves. When had October come, or gone?

He gave her a long speculative look. 'Wait a sec.' The desk drawer opened. Down, out of sight, she heard the bottle cap unscrewed and when he passed the mug across it was near-half full. She would never have taken him for a Drambuie-man. 'You'll be glad of that. Give it an hour and it'll be brass monkeys out there. Get it down you.'

'Yes.' Sweet... sticky as myrrh. 'Thank-you again.' Her feet dragged as though in the man's old shoes, fingers made contact with the freezing glass of the outside door a split second before her eyes told her they would. The cold was something to embrace not shrink from, though, now eased into that best of all drink-induced states, physically armoured, but mentally diamond hard, more lucid than she had felt in days... *On the blue, number twenty-two-oo!* came an amplified voice from further along the Promenade.

Waiting out the traffic to cross to The Sky Tower, each vehicle added to the surrounding brilliance. And once at the structure's foot as though the spot were designated for that very purpose, she saw *everything*... and it was stunning. Her eyes swam and, rather than spoil the effect it was intensified to an almost unbearable degree, ripples of dazzling energy. Overhead may be a no-colour but down here vibrancy and pattern became a cipher and its message hugely benevolent: pleasure and forgetting. Tears ran the separate lights each softly against each until she lost the knowledge that these elements were mundane through pure visual sorcery. Part of her held onto the daytime map with its blots, that burnt-out hotel and an abandoned site she knew intimately, glimpsed through shuttering, overrun with growing weeds but still unclean; it could never revert to natural because trash lay waiting for the frost, for a chance to bloom again in naked squalor. But this night real Rhyl stepped forward, a small enamelled *resort*, tendering two centuries of *panem et circenses*. Ah-h! *You're the girl!* thumping from bars and basements, Eurwen had heard it, seen it, exactly this with the ears and eyes Sara had given her, not minding the cold, breathing out, '*Stun-ning!*' as a wisp of silk.

I *understand*, Eurwen. Complete comprehension at last. This existential joy has eluded me always… but for you? Your luck has turned and the coins are raining down in a silver shower. *Stunning, huh Mum?*

Eurwen had first run *to* Rhyl. And she was here still: the certainty urged Sara to her feet. At any moment around the next corner *she* would be; Eurwen no longer avoiding, not needing her *spa-c-ce*, instead lingering to be caught up… just as the last time they had walked through Oxford's covered market and Sara had taken her arm.

OK, now they'll we're think gay! and you're the fem, Mum! But Eurwen had not pulled away. That slim freckled forearm, sinewy with lugging buckets and pony fodder, was strong enough to fend her off in a single flick. Instead the latent life let itself be trapped by a mother's elbow and could be pressed under the heart.

'A scarf, what about that scarf? I see they are wearing them tied so that—'

'Put it in the charity box, Mum. The drawers are full of scarves.'

Her first week she had been told to 'Keep off the Lakeside after dark.'

Josh was laughing. She told it to Josh and he'd laughed into ugly new lines and nearly killed a… a *Murcott*, still laughing. But all was quiet enough. She didn't intend to go as far as they had done then. The first seat would be best, close to the road and safe yet with a… *nice view* (she had to suppress her own snigger), a rather *lovely aspect*. This did force her to laugh aloud. Every light in the town must come down here eventually, settling on the surface to provide a spectacle to buffet the senses. And not lonely at all: people passed behind her, people who had no idea she was there, whose conversations could be eavesdropped on, a donated sentence or two, a homily from each.

'I'm not doing that for nobody, not me— I told him fuckin' straight.'

'So next week she's in again and they say they'll have another go but they tell the family straight they're not giving much for her chances. Hardly worth bothering. So no she says.'

Finally: 'Won't come back here… well I don't think so anyroad. Got better things to do.'

Nothing after this though she waited. But there had to be a last reveller to walk home with a decisive summing up. Someone had rebelled at last: good for him or her. Or was gone away from Rhyl already… or had rejected one last try, having exhausted the very dregs of optimism: such a relief. It was enough to make her sigh and snuggle down into her alien clothes, letting peace and the smoothness of the scene filter through her veins until it combated the cold, drove off the need for a next thing, whether action or event, movement or speech. Finally, even those *particular* thoughts were quietened that had plagued her like moths fast inside a lamp. Her phone chirruped and the temptation was to pitch it out there and enjoy the splash, throw it as far as she could. Instead, 'Hello?'

'Sara! Where are you?'

'I'm here. Watching the water. Josh.'

'Where the fuck's here?'

'Here. Josh, listen... listen. It's very... polished... and peaceful.' The alliteration was a trap and caught her tongue. 'Pestil... pest-il-lent Murcotts... nowhere to be seen! Anyway I think you made it all up, about... wanting trouble when they... all wedding rings and... bars of chocolate. *You* came looking... Yes?' But it seemed an age ago. 'Now no one's here at all. Won't come back. Got better things to do. Never much of a chance anyway. Remember?' Ought he to remember?

'Eh? Yeah, yeah... 'course I do. Why don't we keep talking, huh? Sara! Hey, *Sara!* Describe to me how you feel.'

Strangely she couldn't think of anything significant. 'I'm very... calm. I know that.' Out from the blackness a duo of light blades came slithering towards her, eating up the ripples like live things.

'OK. What else? *What else Sara?*'

'And tired.' She would have tried to continue if only to please him but now a series of novel sounds, scrapes and crunches and then some dry thing snapping, distracted her. Maybe not that close, going away in fact... or were they coming closer?

'Tired? Are you? Sit down then. You just sit there. Don't move!'

'Really, really tired. I'm so-o sorry Josh. I can't find an answer... to tell you. I have to go.'

'Sara!'

When the dark figure loomed at her back if she were aware,

it went unremarked by Sara, giddy but determined, dragging her reluctant body upright and forward. There was neither lip nor discernible edge to the lake or none her toes could detect in the new cheap shoes beginning to rub.

II

Shade

The List's always being maintained by somebody so it can look like the people on it are still active centuries later, works in progress.

The Vanished. We love them better than The Here.

Welsh chieftain Owain Glyndwr and minor league writer Ambrose Bierce are never coming back nor lunatic Lord Lucan, yet they've plugged into a way of staying famous. Go with plenty of style and a lack of witnesses and you join the tribe of the mythic. That's your payback the world over. In France, for instance, they worship vaporised intellectuals and favourite is Louis Le Prince who not only beat the Lumière brothers to inventing motion pictures by years but was way ahead of all the other competitors, including Thomas Edison. Yet guess who went on to patent the process? This leaves Le Prince's small-but-massive achievement as a frustration. Watch his few frames of loaded wagons crossing an urban bridge. *Please.* Only the second film ever made— but blink and you miss it. A restless-footed man squeezing an accordion will be Le Prince's next subject and if he'd stayed around somebody could've asked about that. Of all things to record on silent film why choose a performer on a *really difficult* musical instrument? Is it a joke? The first ever prediction of the talkies? A Gallic metaphor? We'll never know. Both these clips play as if on a time machine because remember they're the second and third glimpses *ever* of the past. But best of all is Le Prince's first attempt. A dead

171

woman walks in an English garden. She's his relative and in just over a week, and before the film is seen by anyone outside the family, she'll die. Of natural causes. I've watched it over and over and every time an odd thing strikes me – she steps *backwards* out of shot. No obvious reason for it. But in that instant the camera becomes predator and this solid woman upholstered in clothes, nineteenth-century style, seems to deflate. Like she has a premonition and is sneaking away, avoiding notice. Just as the figure behind the lens will soon do. September 16th 1890 Le Prince boarded a train for Paris and never got off and wherever he went, the secrets of the world's first cinematographer went with him.

Alfred Hitchcock, you made use of every one of these motifs but never provided a solution for Le Prince. What a movie that would've been!

My own subject Sara Meredith, (b. Sara Althea Severing, 1968, Oxford, England) was an historian who arrived in a certain seaside town and never left. She featured among the UK's missing for nearly three decades and for most of them also on the wheressara? site, hosted from the Virgin Islands by an American named Charity Weiksner. All the known facts about Sara were here, plus Sara tributes, Sara theories and every nervy interview Sara ever gave— have a look, see if you agree she'd rather be anywhere else. And of course Sara sightings. These go right back to her disappearance in 2008. The best (May 9th 2010) has her coming from 'a Eucharist service', a Sara-like shape on some tourist snap of Salisbury Cathedral. One illegible line entered in their Intercession Book, same day, was 'almost certainly by Sara'. Another year she popped up in Florence, among crowds leaving the Uffizi as the light fades. It's billed as, 'Our only vid but fully checked out!' (Who by?) Yet you have to give credit. Sara was known to love the city. The recent authentication of *St Francis Tended by Doves* as by Bellini had brought his fans flocking and made it extra smart as choice of venue for a faker. But a believer of Charity Weiksner herself, among others – I'd guest into the wheressara? community from time to time. Just out of curiosity, just in case. I wasn't tempted to clue them my identity. I preferred to enjoy in private a following that seemed to swell – and swell. *Sara really was a work in progress.* Female students from Munich to Manila added courses of brick. Abused, low-status women testified to turning their lives around under Thomasina Swift's banner. Sightings dried up and the tributes substituted. Frequent updates and moderating meant crazies with this lost one in their cellars got hustled out of Saraville automatically.

The day her body was identified the site went down.

Here's a lighter note to finish up. Only in Britain would The Missing Top Ten include a horse. When national characteristics come into play a bay colt easily takes the lead, our equivalent of Louis Le Prince. Shergar won the 1981 English Derby by a record ten lengths. Then he was kidnapped by the IRA from his stable and a perfect animal's never seen again. My mother never had much interest in history but when I was a child she did tell me Shergar's story.

Chapter 17

Three weeks after she came ashore, and less than twenty-four hours since I found her ghost waiting in Gaiman Avenue, I've fled Rhyl. Or it looks like it and I'm content with that for now. The instant Sara Meredith was known to be deceased, I'd merited a personal visit from the authorities. Unpleasant, even if you manage to be out. Having organised leave of absence – suspicious otherwise – from a Forward Rhyl not far off deceased itself, I'm tucked into a seat aboard the Sealink morning ferry out of Holyhead to Dublin with someone else's drinks containers already rolling round my feet. Just passed Salt Island's conical 1821 lighthouse (probably the second oldest in Wales), the good/bad/ugliness of a failing seaport at the tip of nowhere is behind us. We're aimed into a big swell under a roof of boiling cloud, though aimed sounded too positive. Hopping is more like. The *Stena Coole Park* was Dublin-bound in a series of ungainly, mistimed splats. Even spray hitting the curved glass failed every pattern test. Up to eye-level, then barely above the sealing strip then it was washing the whole pane as though we'd dived. I hate planes— and boats almost as much. I should've been doing this in summer at least when strong light gave the surface proper edges, made shapes and fins for a half-Japanese to sketch and keep his attention off any messages routed direct from belly to brain. The ALL-NEW ANTI-SICKNESS DRUG!! TRANKIJEN!!! sold me in the port cafeteria, as replacement for my effective discontinued brand, didn't work for me. Nor did shutting my eyes. Nor did trying not to think about who I'm going to meet.

Like Trankijen, this journey wasn't what it seemed for me.

For a start mine isn't a random flight but a familiar one, being the *n*th time I've taken a train and then boarded a boat (the testing bit) before picking a car up for the four-hour slog north west to Josh Meredith's home. In Co. Mayo now. I've known him, *thought* I've known him, known *of* him, and tried to get to know him, in that order, throughout my life. And usually the trip's something to look forward to because we don't meet often enough. Also – I may as well own up – because my destination is Westport. Laid out by Cassels and the great James Wyatt it's a masterpiece and that rarity in Ireland, a model town. Each return tells me something new about developing a coastal site for habitation, how any vista should include a glimpse of water, a bridge or at least one mountain, so adding value to the other elements. There are streets in Westport that are pure planner's erotica—

—such as this, inviting South Mall. Trees along it *and* with a river diving under in a grey stone channel. I've come in via the N5 for speed but am cruising now through the pocket, busy centre. Small-scale shops and numerous bars and offices and houses are spruce in multi-colours and new combinations of strawberry and cream, silver and jade. (Always cheerful as they can make it— also *wrong* today.) The Jester is one building I can pick out straight away, being a public bar inset into a pair of villas that lord it over the street. Lemon and lime livery is being finished off on the pub frontage half— redoing your property is, as Josh says, the local obsession. Something to be proud of OMP. Respect to Westport.

Reluctantly I follow the CARROWBAUN sign to where Westport will thin out and already I can feel my anxiety rising another notch. Just to be perverse, the heavy cloud I've travelled under suddenly splits and late-afternoon sun catches the fresh grass along verges that replace pavement here – and makes me notice the samey white coats on many newer homes. So the house I'm after really stands out in cobalt blue. It definitely isn't new – the front was rendered when Westport was first Georgian-ised but low eaves give away a cottage past, that and opening straight onto the road. I've always admired Josh's choice of solid and workmanlike. But this year – the Year of Rhyl's Great Wave, the Year of Sara's Comeback – I park and knock, different moods fighting it out inside me. Impatience to get what I've come for over and done with looked like winning.

He was quick with the door. 'Hello, Josh.' I hadn't noticed the chill till bowing my head gets me a cold hand on the back of the neck. At this last moment it occurred to me I usually had a gift – Welsh cakes or the sticky fudge he liked and couldn't get in Ireland – and today I was here worse than empty-handed.

'Yori! Get in!' He backed into a hallway wide enough for only one not-fat person at a time but beyond there was a flicker in the gloom and I smelled the familiar wood smoke. The room he lived in had a fire lit, something Josh did every day apart from the summer months, at five. 'You on your own?' he said over his shoulder. 'What about bringing a girl here sometime? I know that girl from uni wasn't – in the end – but there's another, yeah? Bound to be.'

'That project might be on hold.'

He laughed.

A couple of grown men in a space less than twenty square metres, we were awkward. He did raise an arm as if about to— but the gesture fizzled out. At least, 'You're looking fit,' he could say.

'Yes.' He wasn't. His hair was still thick enough to stand cropping, the scalp barely visible, and he was dressed as ever in wrinkle-free khaki pants and a half-zip tan baselayer open at the neck. There were sports-shoes showing bare feet through. He was a figure from my past and loomed over me just as he used to, sinewy and spare. Pretty good so far. Except time had riddled him, unchecked, like a disease. Much worse than I remembered. I had the weird notion I was back home after one of those faster than light trips they're saying now will work, you're still young and then you find everyone else is ancient. 'I'm here, anyway.'

My feelings finally hit the floor seeing the wreck of him and knowing I was about to do more harm. As if Sara between us and Furwen between us wasn't enough. And I have his complete attention and he certainly has mine so I note the weather-beaten skin with masses of tiny haemorrhages across his cheeks and chin and, deep in their sockets, his eyes, dull as a photograph's. Nothing would ever change for the better behind there, they said. I'd meant to deliver my message straight out so the rest of the stay could be spent in its wake, sticking with him while the surface calmed— now the idea only brought my seasickness back and I stayed dumb. Driven away by the fire and still not saying my piece, I couldn't find a right position. Over by the window or lean against the wall? Wanting to keep to the promise I'd made myself – Don't make a production of it! – my fingers went up to a spot on my forehead where my father's scar ran. I must remind Josh Meredith of another young Japanese that came to his door once. 'Are you busy?' I asked.

'Na-a. Don't know the meaning of the word. Up the mountain the other day— no, yesterday. When I should've been tackling the garden. Old slacker, that's me.' His accent remains strong against the pull of Connemara. He points to a Windsor chair. 'Sit.'

I can't.

One thing I could start with is the fate of the Avonside property we once shared. Had he seen the pictures? Beyond repair post-flooding, it's scheduled for demolition. Would he care? I couldn't make a guess and to put off giving even this information, I scan around as you do in two minds, catching up with Josh's way of life, or as much as the room displayed. Against the blank wall the first thing stands out is Josh's framed letter of commendation from Thames Valley Police. I knew it virtually by heart... *the assailant in Littlemore, South Oxford who threatened an elderly cashier with a baseball bat and what appeared to be a handgun* – it had been a replica gun which he had no way of knowing – *but as a result of the courage and professionalism of Officer Meredith a successful arrest was made whilst the safety of other members of the public was never compromised.* He'd been very young with everything to lose and, stuck in a sort of policeman's hostel, he'd not even met his future wife yet. A brave man – just being beneath Josh's roof once made my chest swell with pride. I never said though and should've.

Imaginary conversations, always easiest. On the mantelpiece was the polished chunk of driftwood resembling a lizard we'd unearthed together, pulled free of sand and mud and carried home, filthier than the trophy ourselves. Meg screaming in mock horror — then laughter from my mother, who happened to be there. Suddenly Josh's room seemed even more crowded and I ran a finger along the lizard's head, anticipating its spines. 'I remember finding this—' but that'd be the year I left Rhyl so we were in danger of wandering into quicksand again. Most of our joint memories were pretty raw. Hence not only no screen in here but no images up— and *wooden* chairs with the sofa pushed back to show the cracked flagged floor as though this was a cell. Just three books propped together on an otherwise empty window ledge were – I'd no need to check – *Chambers Concise English Dictionary*, a dog-eared *Pocket Guide to the Trails of Mayo and Galway* and *A First At Oxford*, an identical hardback copy to mine. But unsigned. He'd bought it on eBay for £140 the year Sara went rather than ask his father-in-law for a copy. I picked Sara's one and only book up like a visual aid. Bleached cover. Inside pristine. The seller's courtesy bookmark *Trinders, Chetwynd Cottage, Hay-on-Wye, UK, Dealers in Rare Editions, Manuscripts etc* lurked at the start. 'Sorry to give no warning—'

His expression lacked energy not intelligence. 'You're welcome any time. You know that.' The tone verged on suspicious and the eyes narrowed. Josh the detective. 'Spit it out, then. Eurwen, is it?'

'No. Not her.' Of course that's what he'd be afraid of. Bad news of Eurwen. Was there any other sort? I started again. 'It's something else, some— thing. A shock. Yesterday I got a message from the Coroner's clerk in Rhuddlan that they've identified a body.' No sign yet he expected what was coming. 'Well, part of one. They've found pieces of a skeleton that washed ashore on The Wave then got left. They haven't even started the clear-up in a lot of places so it could've just lain there but a man was down by the water and thought he recognised a human skull. It's taken a couple of weeks to identify because things are really disorganised. But they're sure. It's Sara.'

Not a blink. His mouth, a firm line once, was slashed with vertical wrinkles now. And stayed shut. He took it in and then his shoulders jerked up and fell back like somebody stabbed. But it's the complete freezing of the Josh mask I'll remember for a long time. '*Sara?*'– like he'd forgotten how to say her name, a barely known person's or a foreign word he lacked confidence with, Glenn Hughes attempting *Sayonara*. Then, 'Why tell you?' came out hardly audible.

Because you're my grandfather? Because I'm her grandson?

I said nothing. He would've realised it didn't matter as he asked.

'Right—' Comprehension was rushing in fast. 'Part of a skeleton? Yes.' He raised a hand like a claw. But you could see the levels of understanding gone through while he glared at me and then, craning forward, it felt like *into* me. 'Sara!'

Never at my best with Josh I stepped away, rattled. He'd always had this capacity, my grandfather, without knowing it to remind you what some men are *really* like. Sudden. Button-activated. Men other than Tomiko, I mean, or Geoffrey Severing, for that matter so it's not race or age, it's men *like Josh*. No use blaming the dead alone when considering Eurwen's personality. Look at the other parent. I'd seen him punch a door in Avonside so hard it warped out of true never to close again. Now he jumped the gap between us with all the old speed and wrenched the book off me. He clasped it to his chest. A low moan escaped through his clenched jaws, a long base note it must've hurt to make. With his face still rigid he circled the chairs and then extended it to knock against the sofa with his knee – an irritated retreat towards the fire – to the window again, like a beast pacing its cage. I became just another obstacle to avoid. The keening continued. Got louder. Something was building behind *his* façade, that was for sure. Louder again. Speech was impossible even if I could come up with a single sentence.

So what did you expect Yori?

Laps and laps of the room. Still loud but maybe not louder. A good sign?

While I was debating whether to go and find the bottle of spirits he kept in a kitchen cupboard and one glass – and I've never wanted to be able to join a man in a drink so much – the moan just stopped with him facing away. He let out a noisy sigh. I waited. He'd demand every detail of the notification, I'd convinced myself. Which was why ready inside the jacket I'd hung up lay the hard copy describing the finding, the identity solving and then the pathologist's first thoughts, such as they were. Basically it was a list of things that couldn't be determined. But 'Yeah, well,' Josh said, 'everybody knew she must be dead.' He came and knelt down in front of the fire, seeming to realise what he had hold of, the book with Sara's black and white portrait uppermost. I'd often examined it myself, Sara at her best, the possibilities still all there in a face being swept of masses of hair known to be copper.

They stared at each other, Josh and the wife who'd walked out nearly three decades ago, although that woman had been forty and the hair less amazing by then— like the possibilities. Then he seemed to examine the book for condition, pondering, a potential purchaser, and ran a fingertip down the sinuous Pythian Press logo.

Another moment and Josh began to dismantle *A First*.

The frontispiece is easy— the glue and stitching aren't any real match for him. Then he finds he can tear out thicker and thicker sections at a time and post wads of paper into spaces between smouldering logs till they flare up. I've never seen a book destroyed before. It's shocking— especially this book. But all I do is watch. Rip, feed. Rip, rip, feed. Soon Josh is puffing and wrestles with the thing. The point comes when he gets worse at it, tearing pages in half rather than removing them properly. A thick, well-made book— but he sticks to it until only the cover remains. The dust jacket is crumpled into a ball and he almost bowls it in. The binding breaks with a crack and the end boards are thrust on either side of the blaze so that for a few seconds they contain ashes with the blue and green flames of the inks running through them. Then the colours burn off and there go the last flakes of Sara's work. He gives a satisfied *huh!*

Still breathing heavily, 'So you've told *her*,' he said as though we'd just agreed it. 'You've told Eurwen?'

I went for the overdue alcohol and found a nearly full bottle of Bushmills— and went again to boil the kettle, giving him time, I pretended, and lurked in Josh's kitchen which would strike anybody as surprisingly sleek after the low wonky living room. The MultiCook shone, the steel table gleamed, also the stools pushed under— though the unopened blister pack of Alecer next to the sink was out of date. I put it away. On the counter top a lone ripe banana sat in a glazed platter, itself new-looking, a bit holiday present-ish, maybe a bit Meg Upton? They'd come to Ireland as a couple not long after Eurwen and I left his house, and had managed to stay like that for a while. A fresh start even if a late one for Josh. What went wrong wasn't a subject my grandfather was ever going to discuss. But the cheap pottery looked North African— and Meg had always craved the sun. It *could* be her choice and I scraped a bit of relief up from that. Someone other than me was out there sharing responsibility.

I came back and he'd stayed down. The fabric pulled tight over his protruding vertebrae was depressing— enough to make me want to put my hand out to feel for some muscle, a token of the old vigour. I sat on the nearest seat instead, actually afraid for him. He was seventy-five years of age and looked every one of them, stooped and passive. The hearth seemed mesmerising through the amber contents of his glass— until he tipped it down.

'I'm very sorry, Josh.'

'Something else?'

'Something—?' I was up again to get him a refill.

'To say.'

'Only it's confirmed. It *is* her. They couldn't have done it without—' what should I choose here? What wouldn't give extra pain? Emeritus Professor Geoffrey Severing, M.A. (Oxon), D.Phil, F.R.S.Hist.S., O.B.E? 'Without Geoffrey,' I said. Geoffrey being Geoffrey, he and Fleur had archived his daughter in numerous databases, nothing left to chance. I waited for a reaction to the hated name but there wasn't one. 'Before he died he filled a safety deposit box with—'

'Medical records, images of course, DNA from her hairbrush,

from him and Eurwen— and from a woman called Charity
Weiksner.'

'Yes, she's—'

'The half-sister. That year he had in Chicago, the old bastard!'
Josh finished for us, his face ruddy. 'Christ, what a family! They
made her how she was. She was— she was really—' he gave up
on that. 'His first wife, Sara's mother, she killed herself with
pills, you know?'

'Now I do.'

'We'd have been all right, otherwise. I reckon. Me and her.'

I said nothing. Whenever I'd tried to picture them together I
failed, a good reason to stop. *No one* ever talked about Sara,
not the way a normal family would, trying to mix love and
respect for her memory with a hurt that never got any less—
nice stories, funny ones, the sad. Then as years passed maybe
even the odd negative one to make her seem real. A vital
Severing constituent left one day and never returned. From
where? What was happening with her now? They must all have
had their theories. But till three weeks ago who could choose a
tense to speak in? Sara was or is? It was beyond even Fleur, the
family commentator, negotiator and general smoother out. I
came to realise Geoffrey Severing *thought* about not much else,
though. He carried on playing himself the way public persons
do. Upgraded his technology. Met other old professors in The
Lamb and Flag on St Giles. He still published on his pet subject,
how the Industrial Revolution had failed at delivering civil
progress to keep up with the technology. It kept him in demand
till his death at ninety. But talking up Social Luddism (*his*
phrase) or pottering in Pryorsfield's garden, say, or listening to
Fleur's arthriticy Prelude in C on the piano or even to me, his
mind raced round the same tight circuit, exhausted between
hope, grief and loathing his son-in-law.

Get Josh outside.

'Let's move, should we?'

Incredibly, he did. Down the narrow passage and out— no coat. I snatched mine.

Early evening. Westport would be at its best with the doors standing open to the street and laughter and music spilling out, as genial and different from Rhyl pubs as you could find. We could handle Westport. I said to Josh, 'I see they've done up your place, The Jester—' I knew he went for company more than drink, so no disrespect here, 'in a new strip since last summer. It's—' But he jerked his head and turned the opposite way. And we were off from the front door and aimed straight at a painful low brightness heaped with cloud, avoiding a woman coming towards us who seemed to know Josh and would've stopped given the chance, not speaking to each other though the tension was eating into us, our feet never in step, his stride too long for me.

If you've come out and you've just swallowed a coal, there are worse walks than Josh's choice. A few minutes' march along a straight quiet road of guest houses and tattered palm trees – ruburbia covers vast tracks of Mayo – and you could taste salt. We were into the 'golf palaces' as Josh called them, stuccoed, sprawling, risen up from acres of velvet turf. I thought I could guess our route, a circuit of Roman Island, actually connected to the mainland and semi-spoilt by industry, then out onto a man-made promontory called The Point and worth it for the view. But he slanted away, into an alley between walls, two homes' curtilage, down a little nuisance right of way (for the property owners) I'd never noticed on past visits. I had to drop in behind, stonework gave out to hedge and I lost track of how far this corridor was taking us, trapped in a deep rut under huge skies, cowed and a bit resentful— that would be me. And Josh—?

Finally we came out onto lumpy ground covered in gorse

taller than me, already in flower. Just visible through it, shingle and black weed stretched along an inlet.

The marvel of Clew Bay! Josh had blocked me ahead and it had come suddenly as a wide dazzle. 'The quick way, see?' He inhaled with effort as I came alongside. A sheen of moisture slicked his face, neck, arms and not a healthy one— but my attention was shifting. How not? This is a spectacular sight. Like nowhere else. Formed by glaciers and changing sea levels, smooth fragments of Co Mayo, too many to count, were spread out through a shallow stretch of open sea. Mist faint as one brushstroke is laid across them— I'd been here in other seasons and conditions but never seen this perfect composition in sepia, white and greige. Every other pigment was leached out by the dying sun as I looked for and found Clare Island out there, the sleeping woman with her draped skirts, surrounded by her smaller sisters, said to be one for every day of the year. And all in black mourning, back-lit. On land, away south, Croagh Patrick's bare pyramid loomed, a child's drawing of a holy mountain. Its pilgrim path showed as a chalk line still. Yet there's not a human figure in any direction so the whole panorama, tide included, seems in suspended animation. Apart from ourselves. Josh doesn't pause, won't slow even to take in this wonder or maybe he can't, because going forward is what's holding him together while he decides to— to what?

There's our foot-crunch, the chest-wheeze (from Josh, something new) and the stupid complaint of a bobbing raft of geese. Josh ploughs on. Me after. We were doing seventy-nine steps per minute, I calculated instead of thinking of something useful. Sudden silence— we'd stepped off shingle onto a concrete slipway. 'Um, Tomiko—,' I said, 'We spoke yesterday and he wants me to tell you he hopes you're in excellent health.'

'Does he? I'm all right. He's OK himself, is he?'

The slipway dived straight out, but twenty metres short of

actual water an upturned hull of a blue boat was something to make for. For Josh to make for. 'I haven't informed him or anyone else about Sara so far. Not before you. When he knows— no, he won't be OK. He'll think he should be here to say it himself. He'll be full of shame.'

Josh said, 'Now that's a word you don't hear every day,' and breakers we couldn't even see clawed away at however many islands whispering shame, shame, shame.

We were at the boat. Tiny, up close— the type of thing used to get out to a real boat, it was holed in the bow, needles of fibre-glass around a wound still sharp. Not drawn up then, washed up. 'What can I do?'

'Nothing. You've come here, soon as you could. *That's* something and you've done it. She's dead. Always had to be, didn't she?' Harsh— but the final two words lodged in his throat. That's that, the tone said. He retreated. The slipway was getting fainter by the second and I thought I'd take one last eyeful. Many islets I knew by silhouette had already winked out. Even so, what a shot! You'd wait a week, a month, then miss that line of birds cutting across in precise formation, a single wingspan above the flat water, the gap unwavering. Since I could live anywhere, why not live here? I never would, though. Do what? Where was the work? 'Sara must have been—' but I was talking to nobody because Josh was for home, going strong.

When he noticed I'd caught him up, 'More shelduck than mallards out there this morning,' he said, making another mention of Sara awkward and almost grubby coming from me. He tapped my upper arm, our first touch. 'Come on back. I've got some stuff there for you.'

In any other circumstances it would've been funny, Josh coming down the narrow stairs carrying a fancy red leather woman's holdall – I think they were called tote bags – with rounded corners and a bright metal initials plate and zips, all top quality. It got dropped between us on the flagged floor and unzipped too easily though there was dust on the surface. The rose-watered silk interior was in fine condition where it showed. But the bag was almost full. 'Take your pick,' he told me, rocking back on his heels, gesturing at his dead wife's possessions like a street trader. Sara's stuff.

What had I expected? Second time of asking, Yori. Not these objects sealed in plastic jackets, opaque with age. I tipped one out onto my hand. A gold watch, more decorative than useful, the bracelet small enough for a child's wrist though able to expand. In another identical bag I felt more hard edges, a necklace this time of jointed sections, pearly beads set in crude silver leaf-shapes strung along a chain. A detached bit was trapped inside, stuck in a corner. 'This is broken. Both hers?'

'She's dead, you say. You don't own things once you're dead.' As an afterthought he added, 'That's something I learned in the police,' making it come across extra callous.

After her jewellery were the photographs in bunches, held with elastic bands like decks of cards. Dozens of them. A hundred maybe. I can't resist a real image, a single untampered-with freeze-frame – especially when it's Eurwen, my own mother. I get sidetracked and pick out Eurwen Happy – a young girl, chestnut hair streaming behind her in the wind, the sky faded almost to nothing and a fairground wheel filling it. But this Rhyl scene's not the norm. Spreading the deck on the flags shows me most are of Sara's world. With Fleur, Sara leans on a terrace balustrade, tiny Eurwen in between, brilliant head part-obscured by Fleur's skirt. An older Eurwen in school uniform hams it up on the Ashmolean Museum steps with a classmate I was on the edge of recognising. Straight black brows – small mouth – a severe razor-cut framing the blunt very regular face – 'Henriette Fortun,' Josh provided for me. She was – is! – Canadian but he made it Anglo, the aitch sounded and the name grating. Obviously he still blamed Eurwen's friend for a lot that's gone on. I kept my eyes down and jettisoned the pair in favour of Eurwen and Sara arm in arm, not quite of a height, coming out of the crowded entrance to Oxford's covered market and into the High. Everyone passing seems to be in smart summer clothes as though fresh from Eights Week or college cricket. Sara wears a pale blue blouse and well-cut trousers— and Eurwen stands out in ripped denims and a slogan-bearing T. But 'We're good right now,' the identical smiles are telling whoever's snapping them. Reading my mind Josh said, 'Not one of mine. She brought that when, she, you know— she— it was the only one she carried with her. Must've been her favourite. You have them. There's copies stored and I mean no one else,' he meant my mother, 'will want photographs.'

'How did you get hold of so many?'

'Fleur.'

First to the smallholding he and Meg bought I'd never seen – not allowed to visit by then – and to Sligo town after they parted and finally to the cobalt blue house, he'd lugged along all this, whatever this was. Evidence of bad conscience would be Gramps Geoffrey's definition. There was a period after that first heart attack when he emerged from the John Radcliffe Cardiac Unit as a model of Professor Severing, hair trimmed and combed, all the outer layers lifelike, *but*— He sat at his desk for hours idling, waiting for the power to be hooked up. And Fleur took me aside. 'Please consider, Yori, that being ill doesn't come easily. He has had no practice. He may express concerns— ' you could see behind her worried look the decision to leave this open-ended. Fleur needn't have bothered. (He never did to me and then later, by reclaiming some of his lost ground health-wise, made it less likely). But I knew from then on Geoffrey thought Josh was guilty of something. Of course I'd always wondered about this missing grandmother. Now I was alert for clues. Officer Meredith, a DI to the end, retired from the police early and left for Ireland – tarnished as far as a teenage Yori was concerned – with Meg but without an invitation to Pryorsfield before he went. Still Geoffrey never spoke, except to say *What sort of man gives up at fifty?*

I notice the quiet now. Nothing was ever on in the background to simulate company in Josh's home. I couldn't remember him watching TV or playing music, though plenty of rows with Eurwen when I was small about its volume. Go through this in the morning, I thought. I'd already dismissed her necklace as worthless, making me a bad grandson— and paranoia said *everything* contained in here was some kind of test. Josh was just too eager.

Who had killed Sara? Me, I always thought. I wasn't playing games with you, acting a part. I did it. Pregnant Eurwen ran off rather than face her mother, meaning incomplete, unnamed Yori was haunting Sara from the moment she stepped down onto West Parade. (If a Bogey Man *really* got turned up by Kim Tighe and the Tarot, guess who?) Then Sara goes missing herself— forget the 'missing' element because like Josh said we all knew she was dead. Had to be. Her bones returning was unexpected but their storyline couldn't be tucked away in here since Josh had had this *stuff* all the long years. Hadn't he? For good manners' sake I pulled out the A4 manila envelopes that came next, bulging at the seams, threatening to split. I looked at dog-eared pages all crossed with ink or pencil notes. Sara's. This, I guessed, was how books got written when they were actually *written*, surplus materials hanging around once the job was complete and they should've been removed from site. The great thick wodges of paper were too unappealing to tackle. As was the diary rammed down there with them, embossed 2008. I hadn't even been born then.

'She wrote a lot down,' Josh said.

'I thought Geoffrey gave everything to her college, the research?' For the book you've just cremated, I didn't have to say.

When he tried to smooth his forehead with both hands deep runnels reformed. 'I don't know 'bout that. This is what she left.' He settled on his haunches, grunting, aggrieved at somebody. But the clenched fists covered in age spots lacked a target.

At the base of the bag apart from three yellowed paperback books, were its last secrets— orphan sheets of doodles, unreadable scribbles but also printed off lists. Courses in Animal Husbandry in Southern England would be for Eurwen, and Psychotherapists and Addiction Treatment Centres in North Wales would not, surely? The business card of Private Enquiry Agent with contact numbers were also intriguing. 'Regent Private Investigations, Rhyl' offered Process Serving, Vehicle Tracking, Photographic Evidence Generation and Missing Persons. I surprised myself by itching to know how they figured and dropped the card before Josh caught on. Then there was spare stationery and unused envelopes, and at the very bottom a few letters on a proper writing pad, never torn out. It gave up a name and address I knew. *Darling Fleur*, someone had made a start and carried on for two sides. 'She wrote to Fleur while she was at your house? So how long was she actually there for?' No response from Josh. Family history maintained that Eurwen had gone to be with her father one summer, her parents having separated, and then 'played up a bit'. So Sara's first trip to Rhyl to bring her home was meant to be brief. But Eurwen didn't intend to be brought home, as I knew from my birthdate. And something tragic had happened. Obviously. Or uncanny, depending on how you looked at it. Anyway an intelligent successful woman, a forty-year-old mother with a daughter of fifteen, had walked out of existence— and left no note.

I tidied up some loose pages I had hold of. On the point of putting them down I thought, one piece, one piece won't kill you. It's what he's wanting.

Dear Dad

On TV it says Mum might have had an accident looking for me or maybe lost her memory! This is stupid Dad. I told you there's nothing wrong. You should have made her understand. If she's been hurt I'll get the blame from you. And from her and Gramps Geoffrey and Fleur. Why couldn't she just stay in Oxford? When Mum turns up say I'm sorry. I can't come back yet. Wait a bit please both of you. Please.

I've got this friend he's really nice and on his own and missing his family in Japan so I'm all he's got. He needs me more than you and Mum. Don't get mad. And don't blame him because every day he wants to come and explain it all and I said no. Only now Mum has run off or something which is just stupid. I don't want you to be sad or Mum. I'm not that bad person you all think. Why didn't you sort things out with Mum? And when he comes can you just be cool with Tomiko – he's really scared. I'll call you tonight. Tomiko says he wants to but I don't know.

x Eurwen

Mother and daughter's hands seemed identical. Both needed effort. I reread parts but even after I was sure of the sense, there were still problems with it. Then all it took was a question too far from me and— another first— Josh cried. In a dry, grating way, trying not to but at least without the howling and destruction this time. He kept his eyes covered, wishing probably that I wasn't there. I've never been close-up to a crying

man before. Redness and moisture and the spasms of throat and
lips you see in the very young are the same when grown-ups let
themselves go, making unsightly babies of them— of him, so I
couldn't stand to see. Age must come like a sneak thief to men
like Josh and carry off their reserves. As it had Geoffrey's but
with different results. He never cried.

Ravenous myself by now, I gave Josh a bottle of Harp from
the cool store instead of another whiskey while I went and filled
sandwiches out of vacuum packs of meat slices and added
mustard from a tube. We made a grim picnic of it, silently
chewing our share of the food like we were each eating alone,
him mechanically, gagging on the crusts because he hadn't left
beer for the end. There was even something dry and *papery*
about the cough. It had me regretting the fudge all over again
and that sent me back to his attempts at kindness in the past
that couldn't be wiped out by a frightened boy obsessed over a
shattered door. I hadn't any comfort to offer but it was
important to keep thinking of him as a responsible, decent man,
to admire Officer Meredith's *courage and professionalism*. A
good man, my grandfather. Yet his years were passing uselessly
in Westport and you only had to look to be reminded how hard.
'Can I get anything else?'

'Na. You know where the bed is— if you've about had it,
which I know I have. What's the time?' Raising his chin's an
extreme effort. He's made of lead. 'God! It's only ten. Seems
more like midnight— but go up if you like. Take it— with you.'

The brass poker gleamed, the letter commending bravery
wasn't readable in the shadows and Josh lowered himself into
a chair with an oldie's *urh-h!*

What a release to leave the lot.

Opposite Josh's bedroom the L-shaped guestroom was fitted
tight into the eaves with a narrow skylight for a window and a

single divan positioned under it. One cupboard only provided, always cracked open to prevent mustiness. Accessed from the landing, an old-style shower stall, lavatory and basin took up the perfect square cut out of this space. I emptied my overdue bladder and got a cold wash without disturbing Josh's possessions with my WeberKit that holds razor, toothbrush, clippers, scissors and my supply of ▲ all in a box the size of wallet. It's a complicated design puzzle and I'm the sort of person who couldn't help stop and admire – even at a totally wrong time – as I toyed with an extra pill before replacing all the contents. If people were this easy to put back together then Big success, Yori! Instead of no-use Yori, who went and lay down naked under the skylight, the visible few stars a reminder of Tess. Despite everything I still expected to sleep. Japanese can sleep anywhere, hence their trains according to Tomiko used for bedroom extensions. But each time I drifted off I was aboard *Stena Coole Park* again, plunging to the bottom of the Irish Sea with it. The pink meat sandwiches were not that well stowed and the thought of my return trip to Holyhead grew unbearable, the way trivia does if you add in plenty of other troubles. Being a murderer. Sara coming back. Josh. And having to contact Eurwen— and Tomiko. Josh. In a sweat I jolted awake yet again, staring at the same constellation till I gave up and I set myself a task. How do you mould the recent hours into any sort of shape? Obviously Sara's death had been a body blow to the one downstairs but was he really *in mourning*? Did he have any right to be?

Sara's story always used to end with *me* killing her by getting conceived.

Unless—?

Only *another* murderer could understand how involved this got me. OK— so Josh was doing Man in Love now even though he'd left this particular love well before he became a widower and anyway no other couple was ever *that* badly suited. Eurwen and Tomiko only managed a close second even though they once— but couples aren't that simple. Love finds out your crazes and cracks as I know, Kailash. How about this then? My grandparents' attraction fermented to top strength during the years she was alone in Oxford while he withdrew to Rhyl. And here's a stunner to them both, it burst out of the bottle when Sara arrived on the Avonside doorstep. They had *stayed in love.* For the first time ever Tomiko had got it completely right— *Forget who you love? Easier remember who you haven't met!* So they couldn't just play house waiting for Eurwen, couldn't just eat and sleep and bathe and keep the place tidy, could they?

Until he—

And then she—?

And then he—?

Geoffrey's speculations were pretty dark. His own wife hadn't joined him in them, judging by the collection of photographs given to Josh. A gift like that goes to the innocent not the guilty, not if I knew Fleur. She never believed he'd hurt Sara. Josh did though. Look at the state of him— I recognised it because I'd been cast in the part of Killer all my life and I'm an **ICON DELETED**. But with Josh everything was complicated. He was tough as corundum and I'd felled him by asking, 'You couldn't sort it between you, you and her?'

If the reverse has a reverse side what was on Josh's? What had he done?

Tomiko used to tell the story 'Burning Girl'*. It was a very sad one. And unique in always finishing with an unexpected twist, as though a box of endings were stored in his head. So the hero might be *choja* (undeserving-lucky) and he and the girl of the title survive, just, and their son grows up a good man.

---

*I've moved it. Probably a mistake. Probably a bigger mistake not to take it out altogether. Its a story that makes Tomiko look bad.

Othertimes they both died. Sometimes only *he* died and she married a *daimyo* (a lord). And this last was *Tomiko's favourite*.

Maybe Josh's too if he ever heard all the options.

Personally I preferred a punchline I could anticipate like 'Good luck comes too – he catches fish! – and one day the village matchmaker finds him a pretty bride—' except bride probably wasn't in Tomiko's vocabulary. Girl, then. Woman. Wife. I flipped onto my back for about the tenth time, instantly uncomfortable again in Josh's spare bed that had been ready made up though only I slept in it as far as I knew. Never Eurwen. I'd questioned Josh, Why didn't Eurwen want her mother's watch or her mother's necklace? More tears were the result. Should've persisted though. By tomorrow the armour would be back in place and I'd missed my chance with this stranger that made animal-type cries of pain. We'd always struggled, even when Tomiko left and it should've been easier for him—

A knock and, 'You awake?' and he was in the doorway, fully-dressed, sleeves rolled to the elbows. He must have woken in his chair and needed to come and check I was actually in the house and not a nightmare. Now he stood there swaying.

'What?' I said.

'She—' Josh looked ready to overbalance in more ways than one. 'She came for Eurwen, that's all she did.'

'I think I knew, yes.'

'It was only normal and right and I didn't give her credit. I treated her like— ah, fuck me, fuck fucking me! Everything was messed-up. Eurwen was acting out— she'd gone off, yeah? You'll have heard all this, yeah? I was onto her, though! I was all bloody over it. I'd have rooted her out. She was with her mates, girls always are. I knew that. Boys'll live on the streets but with girls it's a mate. But oh, no-o! Sara had to come and find her. Can't trust me!' (I thought of the enquiry agents and had to agree). 'But any mother would do the same. They would! You're not meant to die for it.'

'No.'

'She shouldn't have died. It was wicked, you understand?'

'Of course.'

'No you don't. My fault.'

'OK.' I expected him to carry on, get it off his chest at long last. Starting with Eurwen. *She* ran away first. Everybody glossed over that fact afterwards. The humiliation alone must've stung for a father and a policeman and it's from *his* house she went! Then all the things he'll have tried straight away don't work. Sara is suddenly there! – He was wheezing horribly. *Go on*, I willed him. But by staying dumb he gave me time to do some tipping of my own. Against. The wheeze just invited me to worry— was self-neglect. He still had enough oxygen to say she'd killed herself if she had or provide an alternative if not. *Go on!* But we're not a talking family. Lack of encouragement from me let a moment like a pinchpoint slink off and then it was gone. He seemed to shrink into his own outline before pulling the door shut so hard it jumped in the frame, wouldn't have been a surprise to hear the handle clunk onto the floor, Avonside all over again. And that was it, a teaser, a ninety-second trailer for a movie not yet out.

I cringe at my unconcern. I'd apologise to Josh if he could let me. Back then the choice I made was to flick the light on and instead of going after him, tug Sara's case out. Both plastic bags got emptied onto the bedcover. *Had Eurwen not wanted her mother's necklace— or watch?* A proper examination of said watch held directly under the bulb showed the gold to be very yellow, meaning pure. Spidery Arabic numerals were embossed on an oval mother-of-pearl dial and for inscription there was just a maker's name, Girard-Perregaux. It was splendid and very much hers, something I could just see on her small wrist and when I wound the miniature wheel, the tick in my ear was like a reward. Next up was Sara's necklace, a silver chain meant to be hung with seven milky stones, not opals and now six. (OK, not splendid— I'd been right— but pretty-ish.) Luckily number seven's keeper remained attached and open just enough to make a repair simple. Position the elements, close the ring— why hadn't anyone done it? I set to. But my fingers weren't strong enough. I realised it first attempt and still can't give up, changing my grip, getting puncture wounds in the process from neighbouring leaf shapes that were sharper than they looked. Every time I started to apply pressure the ring wriggled out of my grip. First I laughed at myself – so much for loving things, Yori, so much easier than people. Then swearing, each attack more ham-fisted than the last, it took a while before admitting defeat. I dropped it in favour of the rest of *the stuff* and rummaged not caring what else got damaged and who they'd been precious to, pictures, writings, novels— and I pulled out the diary. Actually it was an organiser as well (Fleur had kept one) big and heavy as a vintage softback. Inside, instead of Sara's own details, she'd written *Please return to Professor G. W. & Dr F. Severing, Pryorsfield, Boars Hill, Oxford* with a postcode and phone numbers for both as though they were still there.

Every page after this was covered, not just the diary part where printed dates from January 1st 2008 (Bank Holiday, England & Wales) had been crossed through and overwritten, but the coloured section dividers as well and the blank A to Z of names, all readable as in her letter to Fleur if you were willing to skip bits.

September 23rd

Please understand, darling, that when we are together again, I mean to be completely honest. That has been part of our problem, my keeping too much to myself. How last night went, for instance: it would be easy to feign that the following never happened, to convince myself, and then you, I behaved differently, but I do not intend to.

It was nearly midnight when your father rang and told me, gently as he could I have to say. I shouted cruel things back at him which I regret very much now. He said, 'That's it', as though I could turn myself off at command. But I'm so hurt and scared for you and the stupid wrist that I broke is aching and I am on my own in the kitchen with the floor tilting under me. I remember sliding down the wall and just staring around. In here for a reason, Josh's second sentence, the one after 'Sara, it's me', had wiped the tape. Back up in the sitting room an empty vodka bottle on its side solved the enigma. I had been looking for its twin. Then I woke on the sofa still and the news he had delivered was debatable for only a moment. My daughter has run away, again. I was someone with two hundred miles to drive. I must pull myself together and <u>get going</u>.

The first accident was victimless. I misjudged a left turn whilst still in Oxford, just trying to join the Banbury Road. The VW bucked and the bumper scraped on a post or something. Oddly the incident put heart into me or the adrenaline surge woke me up at last. With vigilance, I made it safely to the motorway and at one stage my confidence grew to the extent that I was able to negotiate the whole business of services and buying petrol. Then came a second accident, on real roads again when somewhere in Cheshire I met an agricultural machine. The noise of our contact was horrendous but stopping did not occur to me. Only when I had to pull up at a filthy public lavatory, I thought to check the damage since I was out. There were several lacerations and paint missing in a new deep gully across both front and back doors. The car seemed to have escaped the clutches of some giant beast.

Because Rhyl is approached through suburbs the sole warning of coastline is via increased luminosity ahead. Suddenly I am on the Promenade. One side it is all tall houses, on the other cast iron railings painted a vile orange and acres of sand; the sea is almost an afterthought out on the horizon. What I ought do is stop, attempt to get my bearings but the urge to cruise, scanning the crowd, proved irresistible. Teenage girls were everywhere, redheads, even, cavorting, laughing, bodies miming their inner lives. None were you. Victorian terraces gave way to shabby hotels... outside one of which a family waited, two young women, an older woman, twin toddlers and an obese man on crutches... all so dishevelled, exhausted. They stared at the slowed car and then a child was hoisted onto a hip as the matriarch stepped towards the kerb, her hand reaching out. I felt bathed in their disappointment as I accelerated away in the direction of the arcades. The crude monsters painted across their length seemed fitting to my mood. A pair of plaster caryatids held their own severed heads. You understand? I could feel for no one save myself... then the zone became single-storey burger-bars and rock sellers, before soaring up to a giant pub plastered with inducements: Double Vodka and Red Bull Buy One Get One Free! I ought to be seeing Ocean Park now, a Ferris wheel and a Big Dipper, both of which you had mentioned. There was a photograph: your hair is a red blur as you're caught rocking in a jazzy cradle. But instead of a fairground, I find an artist's impression of a block of flats on a giant billboard.

I parked and for the first time since leaving Tackley Close, checked my watch. Where had nearly eight hours gone? And where was the rest of this town? Ahead the road turned into a steel bridge over a wide inlet edged with trees that seemed to say, 'This is it, this is as far as it goes.' I turned the car on a *piece of wasteland with a wonderful sea view... and prepared to do it all again. Rhyl had failed. I should have been discouraged but the reverse was true: messy, hectic, it was also small. If you arrive on a mission and that mission is to find somebody, then <u>small is good</u>.*

Really desperate for sleep, climbing into bed again I dropped the journal and somehow the necklace and wristwatch went flying across the boards, much heavier sounding than they ought to be and more of them. But next door Josh wasn't asleep anyway. Drawers are opened and rammed shut. Through the fibrewood wall that cuts the bathroom out I hear him enter— and throw up repeatedly. Then there's the sort of groan that forces you to see him sinking down, shattered.

I kill the light. The wrong time ticks by on Sara's watch somewhere.

So she drank. For me with an attitude that's part draw and part disgust (basically like many Japanese I can't do alcohol) this stood out. Why did she? Why would someone like her need to—? No one had mentioned it and, Rhyl-schooled, I could think of a lot more charming faults – Sara *drank*. And she's here, somehow. (In the dark I could be instantly home). Good weather will mean the attractions are open. The arcades rattle and blare at her. Inside the Seaquarium the water's clear as a tropical lagoon. It's one of those where fish swim over and around the paying customers and the flick of the sharks keeps catching the eye. But this being Rhyl, across the road on the main Promenade will be a burnt-out building in a crumbling terrace. Props bridge the gap so the survivors can lean on each other's shoulders—

— I'd expect to dream about Sara, or those closer to me. Not this familiar sight that's been popping up since I was dragged away aged eight. Here's the town. But from above, as a map of blue sea, yellow sand and the built up quadrant showing as crisscross streets. Melting tarmac and grey slate roofs in white heat. Non-existent shadows mean midday and height of the season— what Rhyl's made for. I take it in, identify familiar landmarks, the attractions, the church, *the pubs*— but here's the difference, black specks are swarming past my shoes like ants, thousands of them. Except they're human holiday makers in the sort of numbers we used to get once and all buzzing round with the dynamics I bet I could calculate down to the last footfall. And I'm a giant! Do what you want, Yori. Stride over the river and sort out the Foryd. Sweep Quay Street with one swipe. Only I'm a statue, have to be. A small movement will crush hoards and though I could grab SkyTower and reposition it like a tent peg or drain Marine Lake with my cupped hands, I'm trapped. And out at sea the rumble of thunder is heading my way—

Chapter 18

Up and active before me Josh, with a face extra raw from a bad shave, was in clean clothes and clunking plates in the kitchen. While I'd skipped my stretches and lunges altogether. He acknowledged my (ironic) salute by nodding, no hint of a man about to unburden himself as he butchered the soda bread. I thought I detected changes in the way he held himself though, the last twenty-four hours showing like new ailments piled on. Then he nudged a jar along the tabletop to slide and stop directly level with me, a familiar trick and one he hadn't done since I grew up.

'D'you want something frying?'

I took the toasted oval from the flat of his outstretched hand. 'This is enough.'

'You still don't have butter.' It wasn't a question. 'Just jam without bits. Dig in!'

He always used me as cover for his own sweet tooth. Come on Yori, don't cry. (*His* eyes were particularly bloodshot this morning, I noticed). Your mam doesn't mean it! We'll get ice-cream. With a Flake in? Megs doesn't want one so we can have hers.

'How's Meg?' Naming Sara's replacement was something I instantly regretted.

But, 'She's fine,' he said. 'The driving ponies are all the thing now. Keeping her busy. She was here— Christmas, yeah, she dropped in.' He cuts more bread, letting the thin slices peel from the loaf, before stacking them much as I'd tidied papers last night. Crumbs get swept up and thrown through the open door. But he hasn't properly looked at me once. Back when we were grandfather and grandson we reached a sort of accommodation, despite everything being wrong and difficult and abnormal. Eurwen wouldn't act the daughter or the mother. Tomiko went home leaving the gap to be filled by Josh— whose own wife had vanished into Rhyl thin air. Most of the time he must have wished all our roles switched around with child-again Eurwen, wife Sara, Yori, un-created, but he hid that as he shined my shoes, walked the tideline looking for anything interesting to a small boy, made toast and jam when my mother forgot. Domestic Grandfather is a lot more pitiable than stricken Arsonist Grandfather.

He joined me at the table, not eating. 'Go on. Apple-and-sloe!' he encouraged. I detested marmalade, he knew and few things connect or repel us the way food does. Planted into an Oxford Thick-Cut-taking household, I decided it was a practical joke being played by grown-ups. Frank Cooper's? Brown jelly with gristle! Time after time and meaning no harm, Fleur or Geoffrey offering, Marmalade, Yori?

It's gross!

Then a simple no, thank-you will suffice.

But that was an age ago. I said, 'Sara just turned up— did she? She wanted to get Eurwen home to Oxford and away from Tomiko. Away from Rhyl.'

'What? We-ll.' Don't bother me it implied. 'What you're doing back there's a mystery. You've got your whole life ahead of you. You want to get out. You want to—' he shrugged. 'It's done for.' His mug of coffee was for staring at as well, too much effort to drink. And he wasn't putting it on. I could tell by those eyes he kept rubbing he'd had no sleep as I'd been busy not crushing ants in Drift Park.

'But Sara can't have liked the idea.' Josh drew back the corners of his mouth baring his good teeth. It didn't stop me. 'Eurwen ran off instead of facing her. Must've been something behind that— maybe a poor Japanese?' The word just hung. He gave no sign of receiving it. In a couple more seconds it was plain he wasn't going to rise and I didn't try another shot because self-disgust had come on. I'd never picked a fight with Josh. Now, the day after bringing news of Sara's death, here I was. Wealth and family and occupation and place of origin should've been left alone. Or started on *and finished*, as it had been at Pryorsfield that day Fleur and Geoffrey responded to my father's bow from across the world with their own unused, creaky versions. Too deep from Fleur, about right from Geoffrey (who always was stiff as the oak Pryor carved on his own staircase), both translated as 'respect'.

Probably my new notion was juvenile. Too late.

'You don't know what you're on about,' he said, quite quietly so I missed what was grinding away underneath. 'A Japanese? Sara wasn't like that.'

'OK.'

'*Yes*, OK!'

'Do you want to tell me about her, then?'

'No I fucking don't! Christ— what a fucking stupid thing to say! I'm meant to describe the best bits of her, am I? You'll have had that from His Lordship anyway. Yeah? By the bellyful. All those years stuck in his bloody castle, him making out like I was the serf that nabbed the princess and then couldn't wait to bring her down. Fine, you keep thinking that. Fine by me. Or d'you want the well-she-was-no-saint herself version? You and me we sit here and share all the— the— what she put me though and I get to feel better? Well you can just fuck that.' His blotched face was now almost unrecognisable as my grandfather's. 'Because from the first time I saw her I— I—' but it wouldn't come out, the word and he shook his head in frustration. 'And till the day she died I'd have licked the dogshit off her shoes.'

My breakfast rose up in my throat. 'Yes.' Safer than nothing.

'Yeah, so fuck that,' he repeated.

Yeah, *kuso* that, Josh.

The plan had been to stay the weekend and my big concern how to fill two whole days. Despite *kuso* that, I could've stayed. Once I took an Early Delft dish into an Oxford garden and reduced to powder with a stone— but it was the exception. I've had long practice at holding my anger in and any small job the cobalt blue house needed— we usually shared one while I'm here— would've seen us through. That picket gate visible from the stool I'm on, was ours, and the stain would take a recoat. Since I was a child Josh and I'd done things together, dragged a lizard home, tried to fix a door. My arrival yesterday flashed into my head, the blue paint fragments in the rainwater runnel along the front wall. *The render's friable as Stilton cheese— there'll be patches to the north side worth checking on.* At the same time, rapid retreat was tempting. This decision I'll want to go back and do differently but I record it as a just a change of mind. No thought. I said I needed to be off. Josh nodded. I said, a not-planned visit after all, blah-blah, and he grunted. Wiped the table. I said, work, etc, Forward Rhyl under threat, and you can imagine what it's like with the clear-up. Later in the year maybe? More my normal time—

Not to be taking off in a huff, I walked Josh's strip of grass with him. Hardly a garden, I stumbled on the rocks in the 'lawn' and pried loose hangnails of varnish on our gate and commented on his apple tree, very ancient and gnarled, silver with lichen and fresh into blossom. *Should've pruned the bugger at the back end, too late now.* We looked up in unison. I thought the open hand shape reaching for the sky was much better for the neglect. 'You can do them after the fruit's set.'

'Can you? I might, yeah.'

Upstairs I packed my belongings, pretty sure Josh wanted me gone. If I couldn't bring the ferry booking forward – I put myself on standby – a bed in Dublin would be preferable. I get things wrong about people and this was. But loose objects out of Sara's case and all her papers get pressed into my pack with the unworn clothes. The beautiful red tote bag gets left on the bed. Then when I'm ready for off, he has to come out with me, ghastly in the face, not unfriendly, almost as if he's seeing me for the first time since crashing my room. He made a bit of a thing about the smallness of the hire car, with surveys of it from different angles. 'They're good, these, though. Don't often see you behind the wheel.'

'No other way this time.'

He nodded up at the thickening cloud cover already turning the cobalt blue house navy. 'Watch how you go.'

'I'm meant to say they'll adjourn the inquest. That's from the coroner's clerk so reliable. You'll know about how it gets done, better than me. Expect to be called when it starts properly. That's the last message I got anyway.' He nodded. 'Her name's J. Preece— it's all in the report I've left you or you can speak to her if you like. Beforehand. I wish I could—' I was repeating myself, just prolonging the ordeal. Still I got back out of the car and we stood staring along the route we'd walked. Then a woman, I swear it was the same one as yesterday, same shopping bag, appeared in the distance and she hurried things along. He capped my shoulder using his palm, I said OK, yes, right then— and he'd stepped inside. We haven't been together since.

It's easy to travel hopefully when containing a free omelette, which I'll be offered later. As I explained at the start of Sara's story, the order of events isn't mine.

Driving across Ireland able to actually look at things now Josh wasn't threatening at journey's end, I registered the downslide. Decay may be softer here than Rhyl's but the road hadn't been repaired since a year ago and plenty more indications of This Slump lay scattered along it. A centuries-old wayside cottage had finally stove in, a housing estate begun and abandoned now had scrubby trees running through, stitching it to a nearby copse. The little hedged pasture on the N59 into Galway town I always look out for was dotted with even more fused tractors and heaps of ironmongery.

The rain came, of course – then a downpour turned the world outside the windscreen to murk. But nothing slowed the heavy traffic out of Athlone town. On-coming vehicles made a bathescape of my car. It (one of the electric Artell 400s picked up at Dún Laoghaire) began to stutter. Listening to Morten Zeuthen's cello doing a lively *Suite No 1 in G major*, a Fleur favourite, I managed to miss my cue. Before I can remedy this I'm across the first fixed section of the Portumna bridge over a pocked-zinc Shannon river and being hurried onto the swing-to section by thuggish traffic. The voice of the Artell is female and wheedling. It overrides the cello to suggest I go back.

'No!' Searching for left turns, I try the second one and immediately have to swerve to miss a cart being pulled by a donkey and a pony yoked together. At the reins a pretty girl is maybe going to smile before rain smears her away. *The driving ponies are all the thing now.* I hold on to her image until the map comes on, command mode again. I outwit it shouting, 'New!' Pause. 'N7 to Dublin', and get pointed in the direction of Toomyvara. The kilometres should've slipped by now but the Artell's an urban device, constantly threatening to buck at reverse cambers and needs supervision. Just as well. I learned to drive in Oxford but never used it much in Bristol nor Rhyl so the succession of ribbon settlements keep me sharp. Ireland, an UWE lecturer told us in all seriousness, is the one country in Europe that lacks a vernacular architecture. I'm just starting to pull this to pieces with him six years too late when a sign saying Borris-in-Ossory, comes up—

It's the name on the eye, the half-pattern in sound *and* letters, does it for me.

I pulled in next to a tiny grey church with a pencil tower— can't count it as vernacular, unfortunately, Anglo-Victorian— and tried to see about. Wet. Wet didn't come close. Rain was falling, yes, but also water was oozing out of the earth as well, every drain a spout. And floating on top, is Borris, a compact little town with bad-design streetlights spoiling an eighteenth century roofline. Between parked cars and vans only a single figure moved— in the opposite direction. The place could've been abandoned. I stayed put to start on the tea Josh had provided me with and thinking of him, I scalded my tongue and spat out all the pent-up obscenities— at a burnt tongue, at poor performance (mine) and Josh not satisfying my curiosity. Josh and Yori *the man* could, at long last, have sent the boy clutching a driftwood lizard to bed. But Josh had given a big fat zero. *Kuso!* it's not like it's Charity Weiksner got her claws in you, this is *me*, come in person, your grandson, because Eurwen would refuse, so I didn't bother even asking—

—nowhere convenient to put a cup down, of course. When I accidently touched the RedLips icon, thicker and more succulent-looking than in older model cars, not an improvement, the Artell purrs, 'Place. Borris-in-Ossory.'

Ads first. For Casino Pigale which you can't escape. Hello Beautiful Linda. Then Rudd's Bait and Tackle Merchants were the locals and a Teach Your Baby to Swim School. 'Ten babies needed for class to commence.' Finally, 'this small township lies in County Laois.' I lean back in my seat and close my eyes, ignoring the show '—with a castle' for a small place Borris has a stack of history 'but— *blah-blah-blah* —by Oliver Cromwell. Only a shattered shell remains. In 1798 the Kavanagh family built – *blah-blah* – but was destroyed by fire. To the south-east beside the Dublin road—' at least I was on the Dublin road '—

once stood the chapel. The walls were taken down over a century ago as a result of which so it's claimed terrible misfortunes came about. Even having a job at the mill on this site caused bad luck. It certainly brought the owners mis—'

'Stop!'

Josh had said *nothing to do* and I'd taken it for advice. After Sara, he meant, there'd been nothing left. Him, notorious and a laughing stock with love of birthplace and pride in work both ripped out. Eurwen he could hardly bear to look at. (Me as well I guess). But careful not to show it and we left anyway. He tried a new home here in Ireland— that subsided. And for what looked like the next solitary decade, he'd co-habited with Sara, her images, her voice, *her stuff*. Sitting across from him night after night in that other Windsor chair, I'll bet Sara made Megan, Eurwen and me unreal by comparison. Over the homely woodsmoke, did he catch her scent? Whatever perfume she wore, he'll know it instantly, look around. Every creak in old timbers would be her step. So far I hadn't asked to see the bones— and there and then I decided not to. I've no religion, despite Tomiko and Fleur trying their separate prospectuses on me. Tomiko's beliefs were automatic as sneezing. Who'd go for it unless forced? And Fleur— those Sunday morning services were temporary relief for an ache even Alecer couldn't fix. Her church is a mix of gold leaf over gesso, difficult language, flowers, ultramarine pigment, tiled geometry and vague promises. Don't forget the choral singing, made by Bach for a world that didn't even use the steam pump. Still—

—I'd have a go at rebuilding that chapel, Borris-in-Ossory if I was you. See if your luck changed. There's always something to do. For a start I described the Artell's minor faults to the rental franchise back at Dún Laoghaire and – here's that free omelette I mentioned – was offered enough credit by a motherly woman called Tammie to pay for my meal on the late ferry.

After that, I hunched up in a window seat again. My fellow passengers are mainly Traveller families or one huge family. They're on their way to a wedding and discuss it at volume, incessantly, using a word I don't recognise that sounds like *bar*. 'The dress is bar dear, from Manchester it's been got. The hotel's bar dear too and they made them pay for everything first. It's bar cruel to do that 'cos of who we are'. Though it's been much calmer than the voyage out so far, the ship gives a sudden single leap. Something in the depths is trying to shake us off— I regret the free eggs. My seatmate's a stringy man past my age though not by that much and ruddy *and incredibly wrinkly*. I've chosen him deliberately for his shifty, can't-see-you manner because I can attract attention from both sexes, a side-effect of young-Archie-Kao looks. Traveller Man turns out to be a poor bet, in charge of at least four children near us but dozing after the boat's major lurch. The children become devils, rioting up and down our aisle, constantly coming close to check on him before they screech away again.

Chat with Tess? In this noise it would end Aw-w, tell us tomorrow. G'ni-ight! I start on Glenn Hughes' multiple messages. 1. An expected funding rejection of some modest reconstruction around the paddling pool on 'technical grounds' – I don't bother getting to the end. 2. Beardie Bloke!!! – a face has formed in black mould on Glenn's lounge wall. Like who, do I think? Michelangelo, the Imam of Leicester's Grand Mosque or the late Brad Pitt? 61% of his contacts have already voted for the Imam but don't let that influence— 3. Property in Butterton Road given way this a.m. and he's streaming views of the wreckage. The final image is of the interior pre-collapse including a close up of a listed floor. Edwardian pine never meant to be seen under a drawing room carpet, has been exposed and the boards painted in every shade, then over-decorated with various motifs. Zooming in reveals zebra stripes abutting polka dots up against a fake shagreen section. No two alike. A worn area from the door to the marble fireplace is well captured, showing how it has aged nicely. Zoom out and it reassembles into a Navajo rug, a turn of the century oddity someone had the vision to preserve— till now. I love it and couldn't feel more furious at the loss had it been mine.

Then I try to find one thing in London, Tokyo, Oxford, Kochi, Bristol of interest. Fail. In Singapore Kailash has finally shut up. I wish I was decent enough to tell her, Be Happy! Instead fall back on Tureck's version of *The Well-Tempered Clavier, Prelude and Fugue 2 in C minor*, a three and a half minute sound ladder that ought to help anyone claw their way out of a hole. JSB's not up to a contest with the shrieking horrors, who seem to've multiplied and I give in and let a Mexican company pitch Chromyle™ to me, *a new coating full of potential and your practice's next project could be first tryout in your arena!* Seductive stuff. They let me wrap a building in it, pop it neatly onto the site, tip it south to catch the sun and I want to be home. And for some reason I'm drawn back to the lost painted floor. Though can't be, it's familiar – blue next to fawn, then yellow dots on grey, *never* step on black and white zebra stripes! I fall back on Yeah, but any child would play that game if they'd lived there, run across it everyday counting colours in a lost Rhyl— screams are good for blunting memory and I lose the thread. *These* children are smart. *Now* they go quiet, hanging round in case money or food is coming out of my pack. A book gets rid.

I open Sara's diary at random.

Josh broke off as I heard someone approaching from across the bar at my back. That it was someone he recognised was obvious from his expression followed by a quick checking glance in my direction. It was the woman. Confidently she ignored him and smiled, staring me in the eye. She has a round attractive face with just a suggestion of laughter lines. Her Love Miami T-shirt emphasises large, high breasts while faded jeans are contouring very muscular thighs. Taller than I am and wider in a strapping, fit way, she might bounce if dropped—

Chapter 19

Just out of the station in the early hours what I took to be a dog turned into a rusty feral streak as it crossed the lighted patch and dived through a gap. With the wind coming from the south all the gardens beyond Vale Road were giving off green scents and I was lapping up Rhyl's improved mood— you could feel the subsoil shrink and the bloom of salt flaking from timber so tomorrow maybe workers tracing The Wave into our innards, hacking back, would find sound brickwork. Somewhere. Out there. Two years ago, when I'd come back, one of the first things I started to do was take walks through the old streets at night trying to pick out what I did remember from the completely strange, till my brain put the map together. The whole town was held in my head, a long curved waterfront and the blunt built triangle, exactly as in my Westport dream. Snuffling like a fox myself, suddenly charged up, I couldn't help making a detour into empty untouched Brighton Road then Bath Street with its clean-cut architecture in tall terraces. And at the far end there it was, the sea—

—and 'She drowned', I'd wanted to say to Josh and get agreement. It'll be just a case of finding the right spot, toppling over and giving up. Result? Loss of self, whatever that felt like. But I hadn't dared. (I should be calling Eurwen now, having a real conversation not a made-up one.) *Nothing* isn't acceptable, grandfather. I'm here intending to walk the length of sea-meets-land, for instance, while I reshoot the whole film of you and her. She was hard-going and a drunk, jealous when sober but— *but,* I tell him, you don't look out at the moving acres of *that* and only bother about the rubbish the tide leaves. You loved her. You killed her— or I did. *You're* sorry? Me too and – and this is a bit macabre – I'm also worrying about the thing with the molecules that made up Julius Caesar's last breath. Maybe you know it? A lesson in numbers, well probability really, and Geoffrey's favourite tale. I bet Sara'd been taught once how, inhale and you've a molecule of the ex-dictator's dying gasp in your lungs. Right now. Statistically. Those are the odds and better than Casino Pigalle ever offers. And it'll work for anything, air, water, anything,* which means the normal sized waves breaking down there against the concrete each have a taste of my dead ancestor.

See that, Josh? (I'm speeding us forward.) There's the rancid remains of Seaquarium, where you took Eurwen as a little girl. She loved it but 'wanted to let all the fish go'. Then those stretches of cleared ground let you see SkyTower ahead, still here! The skirt of huts is the clean-up crew's rest area, floodlit to prevent vandalism. I jog on but then have the urge to halt and lean out on a bit of surviving cast iron and smack my lips on brine. Another wave, Josh! Another grain of Sara just made landfall. And why not? Tomiko's hand is what I recorded Quay Street with before it washed away. Part of me's still in Westport with you as right here, right now, my brain sprouts plans for a vacant lot that even in Sara's time was taboo.

My feet have brought us to Rhyl's black hole. And even Josh has run out on me. I'm on my own.

The board fence put up after The Wave has already been breached with lollipop-shaped holes hacked out. I stop at one, listening against Rhyl's wet white noise. We *must* be a ghost town like they claim— there's not so much as a rattle. The only

---

*Honestly? I'm wrong. It doesn't— only works for air. Next morning I realised my mistake. Volume of Atmosphere v Volume of Sea? No contest. Geoffrey would have expected better from me, even tired and distracted and Trankijenned. Me not him.

drop-ins tonight apart from gulls are oldies, asleep in their beds but riding the Waltzers, young and reckless again. The Ferris Wheel Sara expected was already scrap by she gets here, gone the way of the first wooden Roller Coaster you could hear halfway to Llandudno— and the rest. Britain's oldest funfair had boasted every rickety ride you could want and every thrill, every promised beauty, every sleazy side-show and freak-show and their hangers on. Wonderful. Human life in miniature. This is a place you can't make, it has to grow, Glenn Hughes will tell you, Ocean Beach, a Pleasureland for a world short on it. Rich kids, poor kids, teenaged lovers, couples so vintage they remembered bathing machines still used as changing huts or thought they did. One size fits all. Then we let run through our fingers. Thirty years on and they've tried their best with gradients in dual planes to lake, river and beach, the finest empty lot in Wales. And every scheme crashed.

I'm scared of the dark and there's not even passing traffic this end of town, the bridge still shut. I'm scared of Nothingness. Started early with Tomiko. He had his alibis, so OK, but missing *Kochi* he filled the dark with *onyudos* and *kashas* and *satoris* and every other subspecies of monster. 'Pear Tree Spectre', that was a good one, eh Yori? And don't forget dear old 'Cobra-Demon That Eats Boy's Ears' and how it had you pissing the bed. Right up till I step inside I pretend I'm going to turn and walk off fast instead of stooping through into the void, feeling my way. *Why?* Yori's not saying. Above it's black overcast, underfoot *very* spongy ground. Deprived of one sense you have to rely on others. I 'see' by memory and nose and lack of echo the vast space stretching ahead, heaped with debris. Further on, across a deserted Wellington Road and beyond there's plenty more of the same, till your imagination takes a startled plunge into Marine Lake (one plan I'd heard was to use spoil to fill it in) and throughout, the overwhelming reek is from pulverised buildings, brought in over the last couple of weeks and spread a metre thick, caustic as lye. I blink with it and teeter forward— then I do brush an object, a good solid flat something, maybe a chunk of Victorian stonework. I clutch on till the shooting stars in my eyes finish. You're meant to clap three times to the *kami* of any location to get on its good side. I managed once and then had to pee, legs spread just where I was— another insult to all the discounted, conned, defrauded and poor that loved the rides.

And now Josh had left me, suddenly Sara's here, jostled along with them.

Links. Outlines. Patterns. Sound. Tightness round the heart. 'Sara's here' didn't pop up in words. On the rubbish-stench and the ammonia of my own piss, an extra Big Bad wafted up, a certainty. (Not that I believe in ghosts. Or half of me doesn't. But try telling it to your teeth, Yori! Hear the clicking? That's fright music.) *Sara's here.* Part of her always was and what's left has come home with you, Yori. Before the water made bones of her there was a woman chasing the child who loved the Wheel who became the girl coaxing ducks off the lake with bread – as sketched by a young Japanese that taught her, 'Three clap-hands to the *kami!*' Because if you came to Rhyl you came here.* Then all you had to do was wait.

At 3 a.m., late spring in Rhyl, 2040, about where Sara ran aground I sat on a pile of trash and called Eurwen and even though a warm wind still blew from the south, I shivered. When I say we hadn't spoken in years it implies somebody's mistake. A fall out plus brooding results in a final flare-up. Then you get the weight tied to a foot, hers or mine. Wrong. Never over-generous with words, Eurwen's muteness came on gradually.

Having dropped me off with *her* grandparents, Geoffrey and Fleur – thanks to bunching up of the generations they probably

*Appendix A

216

seemed like mine as well – Eurwen roamed. OK. She couldn't live with us so didn't. It was almost a relief. And thanks to Fleur I had a lot more communication with a vaguely-familiar Japanese man on the other side of the world than my own mother for the next two decades.

It did me no credit revisiting this as an adult. I got punished. Eurwen made me wait. Then VoiceOnly should've meant a soft reintroduction, neither of us needing to overact. Apologies for waking her first. Not asleep, she corrected. Dead air was her background while the gulls would be pinpointing my location. I finished my story and could feel her thinking hard. I tried a round up with, 'It is her. I've been to see Josh— that's why it's late. Just back from Ireland. It seemed right to tell him first. Maybe you don't think so?'

'Mm.'

'But I didn't wake you, at least?'

True to form, she ignored questions. 'I knew it would be a shock when— no, *if* we did finally know. But it seems unbelievable. Yet I'd decided she was dead. She may have gone but she wouldn't have *stayed* gone,' she clarified. 'So it's astonishing *and* half-expected both together. You didn't know her.'

'No.'

'And what did *he* have to say? And how did he—' she was able to answer herself at least. 'Badly, of course.' But her tone had already given the game away. Another ear was listening. I knew whose.

I said, 'I could come and see you.'

'You should. Yes. Not now though. I'm about to move.'

Goodbye Eurwen. Never really lost, always there if you kept looking. She actually sounded very close for once.

Chapter 19

Libby Jenkinson in a black and sulphur one-piece was at my door next morning like some mad wasp. I was wearing just pants. It earned me a loud coarse whistle, Glenn Hughes style. Why've I let myself got fond of her? Why haven't I moved? Do I think this is what *I* deserve? Before she can start on about so what happened to your holiday etc I get in, 'Back late— no bread. Never have butter.' Usually it didn't stop her asking.

Her weekend make-up threatened to shatter. 'Got my own, so—' she gave me the finger, 'to you Yori. It must be a laugh a minute down them council offices.'

'Forward Rhyl isn't run by—'

'Right.' She walked straight ahead, pushing past. Libby has no embarrassment setting. Her little bright eyes darted round my living room that had been her dining room. Not that I could ever see a table set with china and the candles lit. Across the yard was an outhouse with Mr Jenkinson's tools laid out on a homemade bench and a mechanism in bits that he'd been fixing and wrappers from chocolate bars he seemed to have lived on. I still didn't know his first name. 'God you're massive tidy,' she said, a Tess line. Something else was brewing, I could tell. 'Oo-oo, hang on what's this then?' She was over at the desk that had been shielded from the door. When I didn't answer she chose Sara's little watch to paw, giving the necklace only a brief poke. 'Lady pressies? I hope they're not for the one came last night— no night before last, I mean.'

'*Who?*'

'I dunno.'

'A woman?'

Libby thought for a moment, puckering her mouth for me to notice it. It took another dry look before she convinced herself the question was genuine. 'A she. Never seen her before.'

'Wanting what?'

'I wasn't going down there, was I?' Exasperated, though that should've been me, Libby pushed at her fringe with fat fingers. All the heavy rings clinked, the Jenkinson's and pre-Jenkinson's. 'It was well late and she's banging on the front door. I didn't like the look of it to be honest— I just opened the window and asked what's up and she kept knocking. *Ru-ude!*'

'And definitely not a person you know?'

'*No.* Head covered. Ignored *me!* So I shouted you weren't here and she went off.'

'But she walked like a woman?' I tried.

'Ah-huh.' Libby's attention was usually short but she stayed with it 'Prob'ly bladdered,' – while she took another inventory of my possessions. 'What happened to all your pictures you took down?'

I shrugged. 'I'm doing better ones.'

'They weren't that bad. I'll have to go'n buy milk then. Anyhow, good to see you back, love,' she finished, leaving me puzzled by both my late visitor and Libby's out-of-the-blue swerve into niceness. Like someone had propelled her there.

Or scared her.

Speak to Tomiko? Also try to contact Josh and check on his mental state, though Josh often cut himself off from every form of messaging and now was bound to be one of those times. Talking to Tess – much better. The Casino Pigalle lightboards were back up so I told her how I'd walked from the station in the early hours past three Linda Darnells – all *you!* – bodies hairless as geishas, nude apart from their flickering numbers, all with the same invite, Hi Yori! Wanna play me? I've only played CP the once to shut Glenn up but that's all it takes. Now every board in the entire world can go Hi Yori! Wanna—? No, I told it, I'd rather play Tess.

Thought you'd be longer in Ireland, Tess prodded me. You could-of come round. But she liked it I'd rather play Tess, I could tell. It got me out of trouble. Never happened with Kailash that way. (Stupidly I have the odd flicker of regret over Kailash just because of that sort of thing, not being able to get out of a fix easily, never measuring up. I crave salt.)

Tomiko, then. He exists nine hours ahead and I'm lucky. My father's basic model Japanese face with the marked forehead materialises looking straight at me, his visible upper body this morning, his evening, in a smudged shirt. 'I'm very sad for,' came the response to what I had to tell him, outdoing Sara's husband and daughter. 'A sharp knife in here. She is dead.'

'*Yes*. No doubt.'

'A good woman—'

'But you never met her!'

'She was your grandmother. *A good woman*,' he said.

'Of course.' I thought I understood though it would turn out I hadn't. In my defence I hadn't read more than a page or two of the journal, remember. It was still in my pack in the bedroom. His reaction seemed pretty genuine after Josh's and I let it go.

'When did she die? When—' struggling now, '—actual day?'

'Why does it matter?' Particularising the date must be a Japanese thing, I guessed. 'They're not sure. Soon after she left the house, Josh's I mean. I mean, where else could she go? In Rhyl. What they *can* tell probably isn't enough to decide cause of death— so they're not saying how long they think she's been dead, just a long time. Nothing about any injuries— it's a skeleton. Thirty years in the water! I bet all the changes happen fast and early on. Then less and less once—' Talking to him was the first time I'd thought about what I was saying. The flesh. Gone. Sara, quick and clever and maybe a good woman as

Tomiko said, and more important than any of it, Eurwen's reflection. Younger than Eurwen *but the flesh gone*—

—first the white freckled skin gets peeled back from her arms like Grace Kelly's elbow-length gloves, then the face starts to flow into soft focus, into nobody's, and that's even before the crabs get under her ribs. Break in at any time, I felt like saying to the screen. 'You'll find the story's everywhere because of who she was. Still very interesting to a lot of people.' Tomiko nodded extra respect. 'Dr Sara Meredith and this town, they think it's a meekfreak combo. Like some Royal caught in the kebab queue.' Nothing. 'Students from Bristol I haven't seen since I left have started messaging.' Tomiko wasn't intending to join them. 'And Charity Weiksner's right in there as family spokesperson. They're making do with what they can get. Have you caught any of this? Or her?' Tomiko indicated no on all counts. To be honest Geoffrey's other daughter was ageing well. Olive-skinned and intelligent and mannish— very Geoffrey apart from the colouring. We'd had no further contact once Fleur died and I found I didn't appreciate her staking a claim, (which she could only do because Josh and Eurwen were yet to be tracked down). Now it was all that My Tragic Sister stuff— 'Oh and I've got a bunch of Sara's possessions he gave me, left in the house after she went. Most were. So what do *you* think happened? Because, you know, something doesn't add up.'

Tomiko examined his garment's streaks and blotches. He'd been kneeling over his work like a floor scrubber but Japanese must be the best-made people with never any sign of cramp in him despite days hunched like this and in his hemisphere it was near the end of his shift. When he jumped back up the paper came with him only to be crumpled and thrown out of shot. The hand picked out a fresh ink stick from somewhere. 'Bamboo thicket—' he said, then a couple of words I missed that might've been English and to me or Japanese, to himself, and then, 'snake', he finished.

'OK.' This was a new one. We exchanged a few more sentences, me smiling to cover my ignorance and anticipating Tomiko's explanation but the ink stick poised mid-air, the bamboo-thing and the snake caused enough of a mix-up for him to disconnect before I was ready. Of course, as far as he's concerned he *has* explained what happened— many times over. He told it as a story.

One version of 'Burning Girl' goes, 'There was an artist who travelled to another country. When he came to a certain place, the lodgings were cheap and he stayed. Though the town wasn't handsome, the mountains behind and the shore made up for it. But the young man had no friends and wanted his home. One day he was sketching by the harbour and a beautiful girl asked to see his work. She had red hair. It lit a fire even icy eyes couldn't put out. But he had been taught to be respectful of women and the last he saw of her was throwing crumbs to the birds. That night the young man dreamed he was sitting with his paints and brushes when the girl walked toward him out of the water. Her skin was white as bird feathers. She touched his forehead and he cried out, branded.

'Each day he waited. Sometimes she came. His own home faded, too faint to pain him. Finally, they ran away from the father's anger and the mother's sadness to be together. But a dishonourable life can't stay happy. The artist begged to go to her parents and make peace. What else could they do? 'Nothing' and 'Later' she answered. And Nothing stayed Nothing but Later turned into Too Late.'

I'll stop there because it was *Nothing to do* finally sent Tomiko back to Japan. And cats.

When I was born the three of us went off to Rosemont to live with Jay and Neil— again. Neil of the toad skin who worked in a paint factory, who painted floors with the leftovers and who dealt in *anything*. Eurwen's chosen refuge. Tomiko got work at the local college and despite their differences my parents were 'happy enough'. Then came the day Tomiko walked up the tiled path and found four-year-old Yori sitting on the doorstep. There's me, pleased with life, eating cat-food out of a dish and their disagreement started over Eurwen's negligence. She'd been trying to feed a stray tabby and hadn't noticed my interest in the bait, or even my whereabouts. She did explain, laughing – she always laughed when *she* told the story – that cats are fussy eaters. They don't eat rubbish. 'Now if it had been *dog* food—!' Though it took a while, the end was with Tomiko leaving.

But I had my own problems. I could boast that back from Ireland and walking round in the early hours with Josh like a weight tied to my foot, I saw it all. I bet in future an old Yori will be saying, 'Faced with the ruins of Rhyl— that's how it started, Sara's story. She'd been *here* of all places.' I find what would become a favourite bit and let my eyes skim over,

On the landward side Victoriana gave way to shabby hotels. Someone had a keen sense of irony: Westminster Towers, The Chatsworth, Buckingham House... outside which a family waited... hoisted a child onto the hip and stepped toward the kerb meeting my look with her own... a severed head.... zombie-zone segued into single-storey burger-bars... according to Eurwen should lead to the fair...

Instead, backed onto the most extensive area of dereliction yet, there is a lone, rotting pub, a shipwreck cruelly named The Schooner. It remains plastered with its own doomed attempts at survival and these inducements to become thriftily unconscious, (Double Vodka and Red Bull Buy One Get One Free!) for some reason are what caused me to pull over.

I don't have trouble slotting in behind Sara's eyes even if what she's seeing had either been swept away, (the Chatsworth and The Schooner for example) or evolved into— how could I break it to her? In the case of vampires and ghouls on the billboards, into a lot *lot* worse. Un-describable. Unimaginable by Sara. Rhyl makes money where it can now. If, with all her own troubles, she ever bothered to speculate, did she think our prospects were *bright?* What's that grandmother? It's thirty years on and the soft sheen along our famous front isn't just reflections off the sea? Not any more. Rhyl's slick moving-pavement filled with soft-spoken visitors, all in paid work, is the wonder of the coastline. And those personalised helicopters dropping down beside the Lake are piloted by sleek, clean Rhylites cured of their colds, anger, unwanted pregnancies and all bad habits. Yeah, absolutely. Or sadly, no, grandmother. There's a limit to what A can do. We've got better bones and teeth and skin with fewer wrinkles. But it can't fix the stray cat problem in Kinmel Bay post-Wave. Nor the poor families that Sara had been struck by as she drove in and every day after, groups that were female-strong, haunting the burger-bars, then left without transport. Only the olde-worlde alcohol ads she describes (they come across evil as Hitchcock's smoking villains) place Sara's writing firmly in its time.

Anyway I got going on her story not by interrogating the dead but the living. When I threatened Tomiko, 'I want to find out about her. We'll leave it till tomorrow, if you like,' he flinched. Then counter-attacked, 'Work well.' Nice closing line. I had every intention of working well. Better than well. So watch out. After I'd drunk tea and eaten vacuum-packed oatcakes bought on the ferry, I stowed away the surplus clothes then searched for Eurwen's letter – *Dear Dad on TV it says Mum's in Rhyl* – and I called Tomiko again and got him. He hadn't budged. I read the whole thing aloud. He pretended his attention was down on the paper but the ink stick between his fingers didn't twitch. I said, 'Did Sara know about me?'

Something rare happened— he shook his head.

'Never?'

'No.'

'When you— *hang on!* Josh smacked you. I mean you come from Eurwen with this letter and he hits you? Just because of who you are?'

'Eurwen is very young.' He still won't look to camera. 'More young than—' He needs to explain it to the floor. 'And fathers different. Then.'

Jay's radio had started broadcasting 'Fears are growing for Oxford writer Sara Meredith and today an appeal goes out for her daughter Eurwen to—' Of course Rhyl's Romeo and Juliet had been with Jay and Neil Rix all along but the sudden fuss sends Tomiko straight to Josh. The instant Eurwen's letter is understood, the carrier is attacked by yes, a pretty different sort of father. I'm surprised he was let off lightly with a head injury that gets stitched by a police surgeon. Hence the scar and no complaint ever made. Tomiko checked here to give me a grin that was like all his grins, not self-mocking, not bleak or cynical but as seen – satisfied. Apparently he had an unusually thick skull, he bragged. I don't know if he meant for a Japanese or for anybody but it was probably the God of Luck's only part in the entire episode. And that included them making me. 'He look for Sara then, baby not mattering. Not much. Everybody look. Eurwen is on TV asking. The professor and wife there. Important people. Everybody.'

'Got that. But—'

'So *work!*' For the second time this Sunday morning, Tomiko explodes into a shoal of carp and swims off.

It was good advice because my non-working self is trash. I took an afternoon recce of a town where nothing is being fixed or moved or set aside to be saved. I wasn't the only ICON DELETED round here. Someone had dumped an unsorted mass of broken ceramics, shredded plastic, sodden lath-and-plaster and household waste straight off the seawall. A huge pile – a small truckload – which in half an hour the tide will be distributing up and down the beach. Seething I call Borough before I move on as far as Blue Bridge— and it produces my first ever conversation with William Jones. He's a disabled, Welsh old man I've never spoken to before but I know him by sight. It's a small place. He said '*Bore da*', which I could manage to return with *a chi,* my Welsh and Japanese running about neck and neck. After testing out my origin – Butterton Road area, Rhyl gets me a long stare— he gave his name and pointed to the boat he'd salvaged. 'It's 'bout twice as knackered as I am,' he says, rasping a square stubbly chin with fingers that are all callus. The boat, maybe five metres long and high sided, is tipped awkwardly in the mud below us and plastered with gunge. Like it's been shot and threshed around. It's not a patch on *The Cariad,* also down there but broken-backed and destined to be written off for insurance. But William Jones' treasure was simply and superbly constructed once, even I could tell that. 'Clinker-built of teak,' he agrees. 'In Portugal,' he says, 'for certain, though how it's here is— well, guess if you like.' He shrugs. The bridge shut, William Jones can lean on the metalwork without cars whizzing past behind him and shifts his weight from crooked aching leg to aching leg. I keep my back turned also because upriver Avonside is in sight, the houses with gaping sockets and open mouths, waiting for the bulldozers. Fast, ragged cirrus is throwing shadows across the estuary and you keep wanting to look up for the big carrion birds passing over. Down with us is virtually still and we talk, we follow the tenders out to the windfarm by eye and it ends with him making a pitch for the wood he needs— for free. 'Just offcuts! Nothing to you is it? I've seen you round, some sort of manager, eh? You've got the access to things—'

He sucks in wind-burned cheeks that remind me of Josh's. All these old men, they're like a committee overseeing me and for some reason I allow it. Even Glenn Hughes however old he is, a good example— if Omar, polite and a better employee had turned up on Wave Day he'd never have got in, let alone moved in. This William Jones is clever and only spoke for what he'll get out of me but I promise his *couple of lengths* if they're there to be found because his failing legs in thigh boots are grimy to the knees, drying as we stand. He's only just struggled up from the harbourside, from a project that's hopeless unless I help. I mean, *teak?* And he's already tried, he laughs. 'But there's bugger-all pickings left. And I'm the best bloody picker there is.'

Suddenly a wild idea – he's Sara's finder! 'There were bones washed up.'

He's about to tap his screen and write me off but shakes his head, stares into the river channel, serious again, 'Heard they found some poor woman from years back. She was lovely too. Pity.'

I understand why I'll provide him with teak even if I have to buy it myself. 'I wouldn't want to fall in there.'

'Na, she'll have gone in the sea! Otherwise tide'll bring you straight back to Foryd.'

'Drowned in the sea? Not the river or lake—?'

'I didn't say drowned, did I?' The sentimental impulse had been brief. He actually winked, making me wonder if he was revisiting old gossip and scandal or just enjoying the new going the rounds. 'All I'm saying is whatever or whoever killed her, she *ended up* in the sea. Anywhere from here to Splash Point would do it. Old gear catches her, she goes to the bottom— then it'll take an Act of God to get you loose.'

That night I laid out Sara's *stuff* on my swept floor, feeling and probably looking like Tomiko in the kneeling position. But Japanese work best at low level. Fleur's letter answered the obvious query, Why is a valuable manuscript included? It wasn't. The genuine working version of *A First*, decorated with Sara's second and third thoughts was safe in St Clement's library still, in some atmospherically controlled storage, Geoffrey's bequest more valuable now its author was properly dead. I'm not skilled with documents so hadn't recognised this as an excellent copy— sent as therapy by Fleur (and made by her because who else would've had access granted to the original, so quickly and easily?) Renovating Thomasina was meant to be a safe haven for Sara's mind. And this *was* an original in the sense Sara'd attempted to play along as the pen marks proved. Fleur hadn't bothered with the book's frontispiece and title. The Austen quote was dropped in favour of straight into Geoffrey.

Chapter One

'Economic fact cuts through a hill of homilies. In the latter half of the eighteenth century the average male servant was paid £6-5s per annum while the average female received £2-15s.'

Geoffrey Severing, The Money Masters, OUP, 1981

A relaxed old building of local golden stone under a tile roof, the Merman's Tail Inn on the main square of Heystrete Newton once stood about 30 miles out of Bristol along the London road.

At the time we are interested in, its licensee is one Jacob Swift and his wife is Maria and they are enlivened by a small girl child who laughs and chatters throughout a warren of parlours, public rooms, cellars and corridors. Although the structure itself was demolished at the end of the following century, in its history lie events which today would make a preservation order much more probable. For example a young Charles Dickens was a visitor; he stayed a solitary, incident-packed night in February and used some of those recollections for *The Uncommercial Traveller*, changing only the establishment's name:

'Before the waitress had shut the door, I had forgotten how many stage-coaches she said used to change horses in the town every day. But it was of little moment; any high number would do as well as another. It had been a great stage-coaching town in the great stage-coaching times, and the ruthless railways had killed and buried it.

The sign of the house was the Dolphin's Head. Why only head, I don't know; for the Dolphin's effigy at full length, and upside down— as a Dolphin is always bound to be when artistically treated, though I suppose he is sometimes right side upward in his natural condition— graced the sign-board. The sign-board chafed its rusty hooks outside the bow-window of my room, and was a shabby work. No visitor could have denied that the Dolphin was dying by inches...'

With no great stretch of the imagination a peeling but entire merman held by a rusty hook can be conjured up, literally grating upon a sensitive guest's nature. Yet prior to the Great Western's schemes (abetted by a young Isambard Kingdom Brunel), the Merman's Tail had been an example of that most vibrant of enterprises, the English wayside inn, comprising bar, beer garden, restaurant, boarding house, livery stables and several other services less favoured by the local magistrate. And this particular one was the birthplace in 1759 of the child who would come to be known as the Peerless Lady Quarrie.

From other travellers' reports we can be sure a complete merman was the sign under which the Swift's infant daughter played. And it is possible to piece together other visual elements of little Thomasina's early years from William Hogarth's (1697-1764) famous illustration 'Country Inn Yard'. (*Plate 1*). Passengers are being loaded aboard a waiting coach: young bucks already perch on its roof, a matron is assisted by an unceremonious male hand applied to the buttocks, while in both foreground and background a mass of yet more figures compete for our attention. As in much of Hogarth, there is a suggested assault upon the senses with noise, scents, stenches and movement.

At the other extreme of artistic achievement, and a few years further on, we have 'Outside a Country Alehouse' by hack painter George Morland (1763-1804). Here is a chocolate-box scene. The local Master of Foxhounds is being served a much-needed tot of liquor after the finish of 'a good run'; the lounging and exhausted pack around his horse's hooves suggest general contentment. The innkeeper's wife stands in attendance with eyes downcast but, presciently, it is the minute cherub of her little daughter that gazes up, wide-eyed. The glamour of an aristocrat has entered her child's universe and the low ceilinged inn at her back, the grimy interior suggested through leaded lights that obstruct more light than they admit, will not contain her for—

Across the top Sara has scrawled, *where is Dickens' sleepwalking waitress story? Whole point dolt* – a new one on me but I got it. She was heckling herself. A few other single words – such as *unproven, rephrase* and *Starkey?* – also some symbols that didn't appear on any keyboard I'd ever seen (three parallel lines very close together, a circle with two dots in like a button drawing) littered the following pages. Arrows mainly said to me she was thinking of more inserts. I couldn't approve. And Sara seemed to see my point. After Chapter 1 the manuscript was clean. But the backs of *A First* took over from the filled organiser I'd dipped into already which meant while Thomasina's life progressed in good order on one side, Sara's lurched forward in chaos on the other. Only a few entries were dated and these had gaps and additions while whole other sections had been crossed out beyond deciphering, not just rejected— eradicated. The overscoring was so deep it slashed through in places to the Peerless Girl. And was a mess. Beyond deciphering by anybody who didn't work for an antiquities department— for a second I tried to dredge up any contact I might have on the Ashmolean's staff before I had to stand and walk around shamed by my own stupidity. *Dolt!* That boat had sailed. Named *Josh*. He will have been painstaking. After an initial read through, a second, a third, however many it took, his policeman's brain will have made a decision that either:

the journal contained nothing to explain her disappearance, just showed them both in a bad, *really bad*, light or,

it totally explained it and showed them both in a bad, etc, etc.

And since then he'd had years alone, side-by-side with an empty Windsor chair while he went through it methodically, (again and again, Sara's other book) my money was on 2.

I'm no Josh. That sinister woman Sara nearly ran down on the first day snaffles my attention, urging me off on a search for Kim. Tighe. I make a mental note to question Glenn re: Clear Skies Café. Then flick backwards— so how do they recognise each other, hooking up by the railings? Sara knows nobody in the whole of Rhyl apart from her husband. And Eurwen, of course. So—? Back some more to the genie and Sara's three questions— then Meg I warm to as if just introduced, good uncomplicated Meg hasn't changed, a friend to Eurwen when needed, the woman who might bounce if dropped. She was and she did.

The Upton parties didn't need describing. They were happening late enough for me to be dragged along more often than I want to remember, the hot drink always in frozen fingers, smarting eyes desperate to shut. And suddenly there's Kim, again— but she's a small *mouli* compared to one other person I bump into now and recognise. Muscling in at the end of an unsuccessful night documented by Sara, a night of spliffs, juggling, lovers, stars and *Mama Rotti's* ominous lyrics, that's Tomiko there just across from the fire. He's watching a desperate *but good* woman. And he can't be. Because they never met.

Chapter 20

When he said 'a good woman, your grandmother' he implied as a Japanese would because she was your grandmother. It meant what it meant, I thought. Your ancestors are not for criticising. They're for respect. Like I'd ever give you an argument, *otosan*.

The Severings seemed to agree. A gesture to Sara's loss had to be made every year and I was part of it. Fleur and Geoffrey would arrive by train from Oxford and we'd meet them on the platform out of First Class like visiting VIPs, Geoffrey straight as a tree, giving off status like cologne. It was left to Fleur to recognise us and get the first smile in even though she was burdened with The Offering. Our mission was simple— to go straight down to the beach and lay it on the sea. Sara's favourite flowers were violets but who could get violets in November in Rhyl or anywhere? We laid white chrysanthemums – *not* in a wreath – which you could get locally but Geoffrey and Fleur brought with them as though anything Rhylish was tainted. The bunch of flowers, made up by the same North Oxford florist responsible for Sara's wedding bouquet, had usually suffered in transit. Then, once launched, it was in the habit of refusing to follow the absent spirit out to sea— if she'd gone that way. My great-grandfather chipped in words to the effect that Sara, beloved *daughter*, beloved *mother*, was remembered and desperately missed, the pretence being she was held tightly still by this small family of a septuagenarian, his ageing wife, a sulky girl and the boy in her arms with a Japanese father lurking on the edge of things. Who were supervised by a tall policeman, not in uniform though not a member of the cast either. How

233

did Josh bear it? And as the professor aged, the event became increasingly unsafe, top-heavy with his venomous feelings.

I got older and was expected to participate. At eight years and still living with Josh and my mother in Avonside, there was what must've been *the* worst occasion for the adults. To begin with Rhyl sky's cloudless but the wind comes from the north, a true Arctic Circle blow. Fleur is important by her absence through a knee injury, I think, Tomiko is already in Japan— and Eurwen has a cold. Even whiter than usual, her sore nostrils are a match with the unruly hair. Her prominent lower lip's cracked and she gnaws at the damage making me want to beg her to stop, leave the poor lip alone, *please*. She's wearing a scarf of turquoise silk edged with tassels over an ankle-length coat of such intense puce it makes me feel sick. I connect it with the lip and think of bruises, of the way a bruise can hurt especially in the cold. I think cold – flesh – stone – bone. Freezing stone striking cold bone. Now I'm *sure* I'll disgrace myself and be sick. I grit my teeth and anyone that actually sees me says things like Look! the child's shivering, needs muffling up, shouldn't have been brought out on a day like this, is going to cry. Which is true. A quick flashback prior to our expedition— Eurwen and Josh engaged in a rolling boil of an argument during which my mother has stated several times she won't go. Not that she's too ill to go. My mother never admits to illness and never uses it as an alibi. So she *won't go*. Also that it was stupid, the whole horrible thing just stupid— and did nobody any good. She and Josh aren't capable of speaking to each other now. I notice they keep either myself or Geoffrey between them. But Gramps Geoffrey can just about acknowledge his son-in-law to ask a question. Not otherwise. Even then he gives the impression he'd rather look it up.

I'm a conscript in a ritual performed by three people who can only communicate through me. 'Put the flowers in, Yori,' my mother says. 'You're big enough. You do it.'

'You don't want to, do you?' Josh demands.

The tribute looks wider, heavier, and even more battered this year, reaching beyond Geoffrey's black-trousered knees to his black shiny shoes. His reddened fist holds the stems too high up and is crumpling more blooms. They're called white but are green at heart. *Green* flowers, I think as I scan each face for interest in life at my level.

'Be careful,' Gramps Geoffrey says. 'The waves will get you if you're slow.' At least he can be relied on for fair comment. The tide's on its way. (Why I've wondered, since, didn't anyone make sure it was *going out?*) And any second the wind can send a mouthful of sea well beyond what you expect. I push myself back against the soft wool coat. What must the group've looked like from East Parade? Two men almost equal in height, dark-suited, and a dazzling young woman – because any male would see past the sniffles and the scabby mouth – wrapped in imperial purple, the red snakes of her hair meeting the brilliant scarf, both streaming away. And a stray boy they could've just picked up anywhere. 'Well will somebody please *get on with it?*' Eurwen hisses. Josh takes my hand and the lead to where water is encroaching on a line of black rocks. Pebbles caught in the spaces are live, scratching things trying to skitter away, and as he places the flowers I catch at them, let them run through my fingers, a part of the event. Against all odds they not only float but progress along the tideline. My grandfather watches suspiciously but they go on their way in the direction of Prestatyn. I'm tugged back up the shingle and Gramps Geoffrey falls in behind, his arm around my mother who sobs Never doing it again! – which turns out to be true. The swirling wind chooses its moment to throw sand in my face but I don't care. I'm buoyed up by feeling part of things.

I can be there anytime. Still satisfied with my own showing! Though it marked the end of childhood. Born to two parents here, then a young boy with Eurwen but cared for by Josh, I fell in love with the town— and lost it, dropped into a sort of domestic crypt.

Boars Hill, south west of Oxford, used to be the Village of the Dons. On its outskirts Pryorsfield that Eurwen and I got to at dusk, a winter afternoon, shocked the fresh-out-of-Rhyl kid. For a start, it reared up singly out of gravel and gardens without the usual *offices*. And surrounded by thick planting, the curve of the drive was enough to let the building play Surprise! by jumping out at the visitor, me today, in the back of a taxi. Eurwen dragged our bags onto the gravel in front of a house that not only seemed massive, it was. Neck-locking tall. Overwhelming. I wasn't even sure it was a house. The rustic pediment supported three brick storeys and a fourth in the form of a crenellated turret, all hollering about the Science Of Construction to a boy who lacked the concepts but was learning to look. That crenellated bartizan, for instance, burst from *a corner* and I could as easily balance a riding helmet on my nose! To do Pryorsfield real justice there's no point trying to take my ignorance back. Once inside (hanging on Eurwen like Frightened Monkey) the interior was High Gothic maintained over all ten principal rooms. That anyone connected with us owned it was a miracle.

I'd give anything to take the tour again now. Every door at entry level was shot through with enough iron to ward off an axe. Ceilings were coffered, arches pointed, corbels in various locations were monks' heads to rub in the Pryorsfield name, and no two alike. (Favourites? At the end of the kitchen corridor where a comic pair of them had pulled Satisfied versus Queasy expressions for a hundred and fifty years.) But the most eccentric feature is delivered straight away by the newel post of the central staircase. The Pryor himself, life size in oak, in a standing pose. And unbelievably menacing. The carver had gone to town on the robes, cutting so deep you could push a whole child's hand under the fold of cloth that kept his face permanently obscured yet terrifying in the half light—

I can never think of Fleur's kind words, or Eurwen's howling list of complaints without seeing the Pryor's silhouette, his hood drooping forward at me, a macabre fingerpost in the last of the light. It marked the start of an apprenticeship. I put Pryorsfield on to grow up in and it never chafed. I tried to overwrite previous Yori and if I can't remember running mad along the landings or bringing a friend home to build a den in the laurels with, it was because watchful Yori had crept in too. Not unhappy, either of us. And from Geoffrey and Fleur before it was too late I got the idea of Family as a rattle of coins. No need to search your pockets to count them, your entrance fee's covered. These were my great grandparents I was living with, and virtual strangers apart from the yearly pilgrimages. They were towering to my short, grey-white as paper to my putty-coloured, conversational to my tongue-tied. *Aged*. Worth spying on. Opening a window or the letters they still got, all their movements were deliberate and similar. You'd suspect them of knowing they had an audience, were a double act because either they'd grown alike or been the same in lots of basic ways. I look back and it's easy to think brother and sister and forget they were a couple. (I'd seen couples). Creakier than the wooden Pryor, they were at least on my side if he came alive, stamping upstairs and the knife hidden in one baggy sleeve flashed— but long before that happened, I'd learned to disrespect him and pat his head for luck.

Whatever Eurwen told them that first afternoon, we were in.

Straight off, Fleur began on spoken Japanese. She didn't even try Eurwen with joining us— and later, when I got to understand him more, I could imagine Geoffrey's response as something along the lines of 'If you're considering the future, he'd be better off with Chinese.' She just did it, her large (for a woman's) mouth probably aching with the alien shapes it was forced to make. *Konnichiwa!* she greeted me, back from climbing the Jarn Mound* that Pryorsfield backed onto. I was more impressed by a man-made hill than practising tongue-twisters but, Going out again? *Ja mata ne!* She was better at it, tried harder and ignored Eurwen's eye rolling and giggles that made a turncoat of me when I copied her because despite everything no one could resist Eurwen. Any rare time she wanted me, I was hers. But Fleur found Tomiko again— without warning there in Gramps Geoffrey's study, where white walls made the screen a huge iris. Not today though. It contains an upper body in ink-spattered shirt and above, a face with our oldfriend the comet scar. Only blinking gives away Not a picture— really there! 'Your father wishes to speak to you, Yori,' Fleur says and taking her husband's arm walks out of the room. And I can say, 'Hello *otosan*,' and afterwards Fleur explains why it seemed to give him no pleasure. Sorry *chichi* to put you at more distance with wrong word

And Sara lived along side us. In the Turret Room on the south west corner a sample of her belongings lay ready for The Homecoming. Shelf after shelf of books brought over from Tackley Close by Geoffrey. A recorder in its case and an obsolete electric typewriter sat on a kidney-shaped dressing table attracting dust. Her academic gown hung in the cupboard, regularly shaken out and aired. And not the common Bachelor of Arts with its rabbit fur Eurwen hated, but the full scarlet silk, lined with navy. This was, Fleur explained, only for Doctors of the University. I'm allowed to try it on when I get older which

---

*Jarn Mound's a hill that was hand raised by the archaeologist Arthur Evans and his students in 1931 to restore a lost prospect of Oxford. Said to be '50 feet high', slippage means the view isn't clear from the top by I see it. And a blocking development has done for it permanently now.

goes to prove how the creepiness some people might think all this

involved wasn't my experience. Her things were safe to handle even if her name was hardly spoken out loud. Absolutely normal. But the tension that flowed out of the room must've been felt by somebody. Eurwen became scarcer— at meals or for evenings in the sitting room with its huge furniture, brand new screen (bought when we arrived probably) and the piano only Fleur could play. One day when I was ten she didn't come home at all.

Which is why I owe my profession to Fleur and Geoffrey. Eight years at Avonside taught me a lot but not much that passed for education. (I'd arrived on my first day in Rhyl infants knowing how low to bow to my teacher— it could only go downhill after.) So F and G took my schooling in hand and found a tutor (several tutors) when Bradwardine turned its nose up at me. Even then to fill the gaps Fleur had to pitch in, not just with Japanese. Geography, history and music, of course. And Fleur's Music God, Bach. I can't play or sing but thanks to her I'm not immune to people who can. At the age of fifteen (Eurwen's when she ran off) J.S. Bach walked 183 miles from Eisenach to Lüneburg to get his first paid work. Worth finding out, I thought. Maths came via Geoffrey. 'You may not know a hawk from a handsaw,' he began – the one and only time he baffled – 'but the numbers don't care.' He was right and there's not a day I'm ungrateful. *Before we can build first we have to measure it.*

Because I liked to sketch Fleur brought in Mr Dennis— probably quite young but just another grown-up to me. But too scared of children to work in schools any more. First lesson was how to hold the 6B pencil. 'The Relaxed Tripod Grip,' he whispered. Hours went by practising the foreshortening of a white egg at rest on a windowsill. Then a speckled egg. 'Next week, a Conference pear!' He carried on coming, never getting any less scared-looking, always flushed and jittery inside his wool jacket like he'd been chased up Boars Hill by his ex-students. You couldn't not like the man. Though I got ahead of him quickly, I hid it to keep up the sessions. So neither Mr Dennis nor I ever went to school again. Eventually, 'What would you like to do with your life, Yori?' Fleur asked in her bland way. One slow Pryorsfield afternoon it seemed a question like, 'Biscuit or cake?'

'I don't know. What things are there—' You can see I wasn't promising material at this age '—sort of?' Not much in Gramps Geoffrey's bare study can distract. The rest of the house is filled with Fleur's clutter – so clever of her to choose this location with its laquered desktop like a virgin snowfield. His screen is blank— and since me arriving here he's had the stained glass insets in the mullion removed. Professor Severing is observing me under strong natural light. I could be a new set of figures. 'Geoffrey and I were thinking, design maybe— or architecture?'

'Architecture,' I said.

University of Western England took me at eighteen to study Built Environment with Planning. In Bristol. Me at St Clement's or any other Oxford college? No. The night before I left, Fleur called me into the Turret Room. The single bed's blue cover as far as I knew had never been sat on and I chose the rhomboid lid of the window seat now. From the tight squeeze of the book shelves Fleur took down the signed copy of *A First* and gave it me with overflowing eyes. 'It's what Geoffrey wants,' she said and I nodded, Thanks. But once in Bristol, I wasn't in any hurry to start it. Every week I talked to Geoffrey and Fleur. It could've been oftener, me missing Pryorsfield, but they said they didn't expect it, a sort of command. I acquired friends, which was a novelty. Was drunk— once. And had first sex with an Indian girl, Kailash who drew me by the rope of hair bisecting a narrow waist and amazing hips I followed into the student refectory. Her actual features were almost insipid unlike her character I found. (We'd go on to last three point five years in two separate sessions, during which I learned everything about her. We shared a top-floor studio flat in the Montpelier district and cycled to A History of Conservation classes in one of the worst, leakiest new buildings I've ever entered. We travelled by train to inspect many award-winning projects in Southern England, including Slough's Pink Pyramid before it disintegrated and had to be demolished. Kailash addicted me to lists and when she visited Pryorsfield was admired by Geoffrey for her cleverness but not by Fleur. By the end, Yori One was still attracted while Yori Two was ready to set out for the South Pole if it'd shake her off. Anyway, during this period I never thought about Sara, and about Eurwen only when Tomiko mentioned her name. And I looked forward not back. The past was Josh and Eurwen and Tomiko loving and hating each other and my father leaving, which I could see wasn't only because I ate catfood on a Rhyl doorstep. And finally there was Eurwen's flight back to Pryorsfield, with excess baggage, me. Avonside was just an in-betweener, a father and daughter and child trapped by 'a rabbit hutch of a house' and as a structural engineer will tell you, in any explosion it's the containment does the damage.

The Past. Tomiko in his ancient city of Kochi can give the impression he's transmitting from centuries ago. His existence is supported by a complicated mesh of stress deflectors and mental ties and self-imposed guidelines. I went through a teenage phase when my father really got on my nerves – 'Today's *koan* was gardening,' my brat-self told Fleur, 'like it's clearing away nature to make a garden that represents, you know, nature. Rock, pool, light and shadow—'

'Oh and those were his *exact* words?' she asked. You had to love Fleur.

Geoffrey and Fleur also tended to try and leave the past alone but then their choice was taken off them. They became part-of by dying within a few months of each other just after I graduated and there was no going back to Pryorsfield, ever. Unlike Eurwen, I couldn't have sold the house. Slap in the middle of a lavish plot, so afforested we might have been in mid-Wales, it was only seven kilometres from central Oxford— and worth a high-end Casino Pigalle win. Faster than a tropical funeral according to Kailash, the total annihilation of Pryorsfield followed the sale. I didn't go to watch. But now I wonder if it was something Geoffrey and Fleur secretly planned? To lance the Turret Room abscess. Instead my First Class Great Grandparents left me other resources to take back to Bristol or to Kochi or Singapore or the British Antarctic Territory or anywhere that appealed. Or a place I'd dreamt about in every vista, layout and reworking imaginable from the time I was eight years old and was still doing it right up to the last uneasy night I'd ever spend in Josh's cobalt blue house.

In Westport I'd described Rhyl for Josh. 'They'll have to flatten Avonside. Foryd Harbour's a shambles— you've seen?' Of course he had. The flood gave us something to pass the time, a safe topic away from Sara, while the Artell's battery charged. I caught him out relishing mayhem at a distance, something I could almost identify with. But next day the sight of Rhyl was a huge jolt all over again. And the sheer ugliness worsened. Nearly four months gone and areas cleared in the first flush of activity were buried again under mounds of rubbish from other locations. One Monday morning Glenn and I watched skips arranged along the length of the promenade being filled with spoil. Impossible not to try to sort the rubble by eye – sections of original cast-iron were quickly covered with concrete fragments reduced by much handling. I'm about to turn away when there it is, a recognisable Metplas bin (intact-looking from here). I'd sourced them from a small fabricator in Liverpool. Weather-resistant to European Standard EN 840-1-9-7. Impossible to topple, as I boasted to Tess and made her giggle. No sign of her now just when I wanted to tell her, Consider how it was— growing up in sight of the Jarn Mound and a load of trees but hankering to build things yourself. *Finally* back to the place needing it most, in free time you draw, you model, you run simulations— while in working hours? Traffic flow in the Morland Park, Fairfield Ave area needs re-routing. A few doomed trees can go *here*. Bins for the promenade have to be guaranteed bird-proof. In Abbey Street you do a modest drop-in centre which opens a full month before The Wave puts a mailed fist through its glass front. ('Here a smoky quartz atrium suggests a cliché-ridden attempt at openness while at the same time incorporating a pragmatic nod towards client confidentiality.' *Publicnubuildnewsletter.org*) With Gramps and Fleur dead and Pryorsfield flattened, I was twenty-eight and had money I kept quiet about for practical reasons. I thought I had no ties. If Libby Jenkinson's ground floor was intended as a temporary bolthole, when we were hit I was still there.

Now I'm given 1. Miles of the finest sandy beach ever made. 2. A small haven. 3. One cleanish river. 3. The Marine Lake and concrete island. 4. Nineteenth-century terraces of a quality that brings tears to the eyes. 5. A second-hand 87-metre steel pylon minus the ascending cabin. 6. Inland, a handsome church, a stone town hall with an inclination from the vertical and a botanic garden. 7. Twenty-six thousand registered inhabitants plus all the un-logged ones who never expected much out of life and weren't disappointed.

An architect that can't make a town out of this lot deserves throwing off SkyTower.

Chapter 21

Emeritus Professor Geoffrey Severing once explained a financing void as 'more reasons not to do than do.'

So Sara came back. And Rhyl's not-do summer ripened with yeasty smells that couldn't be got rid of by the stiffest breeze. Gulls turned cannibal which I witnessed one afternoon, several adults attacking a drab youngster on the Marine Lake's concrete island. First strike to the breast and it collapsed back onto its tail, stunned, disbelieving. Maybe its own parent was in the mob— anyway the opportunity to fly off was wasted. Then as extra birds joined the frenzy the head was hacked into, blood splattered the mottled feathers and they had it down. There were other walkers and loiterers that had been stopped like me by the ruckus. The lake was drained to a puddle so we could've—

if we'd tried to—

but too far away to save—

interfere and the driven off birds just starve elsewhere—

As it was, only the outstretched wings and flipper-feet were left next day. There's a whole season being lost, I fumed, and our only daytrippers? Ghouls.

That same night Josh hit Sara in the face. *The punch that was never going to be thrown*, seemed a joke suddenly— I'd got into a routine, reading steadily since Westport. Disgusted, I swept everything up, rammed it back into its envelopes and took the lot into my bedroom where Libby has kindly provided a walnut veneer wardrobe c.1950, hanging space to the left and folding to the right. There were too few pairs of dark pants, dark sweatshirts and black loafers to fill five shelves. I slung the parcel onto the vacant top. Now I understand 'Serpent Demon Eats Boy's Ears Off', Tomiko. I should've listened and left well alone.

Should've said, 'Sleep tight, Sara. You're bad luck.'

'What you got there?' Glenn wanted to know.

'It's no sig.'

'*What's* no sig, Yori? D'you want my take on this?'

I didn't.

'The work-hours you're putting in— and you've put in already— they're never gonna be paid for. Since you went on your little holiday, you're a whole bloody team on your own. You're bringing in done stuff that was an idea and three squiggles the day before. Look at you! It's half past seven on a Friday night. That's a brand new elevation, that is, the foot-crossing by the old clock tower. *I think*, me, you've got seven types of sodding sorrow here with all those different levels. And you're just starting on it.'

I moved my arm to try and block his view of PalmWalk.

'Don't bother boy. Seen it. Estimated task time: five point three hours. Task time elapsed: 41 minutes.'

'Maybe.'

'Say again, Why you doing this?'

'You're still here.' My simulation surges forward in time, one year, two years, the gaps close up as soft landscaping matures to give arrow-slit views of a restored Harkers Arcade, then of my all-glass CrystalBox, the shopping mall entrance. Clouds are suddenly scattered. Mid-morning sun ignites the glazing. Seascapes appear in each of its five thousand reflective panes. It's so beautiful it makes my breastbone ache, the ache travelling down across the soft belly parts and into my genitals. It excites me more than Tess. Even Glenn's hypnotised. 'That's quite good,' I suggest.

'Fucking gorgeous! Beside the point.' He leaned over, his face deliberately in mine. 'Tell us.'

Earnest, methodical, dependable and impetuous. These are the qualities of my blood group, Type A, my father's blood group. He's passed the knowledge on only recently. 'But,' I said, 'these are opposite traits.' Through a small window at his back the mountain's showing seasonal colour but the sky above it changes hourly. 'Methodical *and* impetuous?'

'Research was old,' Tomiko said, 'and when new had enemies.'

Glenn had produced nothing useful as long as I'd known him. His Certificate in Urban Studies from a college that doesn't exist any more entitles him to come up with the background of any site I express an interest in, just to thwart me. Tried it there— didn't work. And he's a hooligan as a house guest and still tells you about sex with Alice even once you're rid of him. I have never liked Glenn Hughes, though I put less importance on liking than most people do. (Does the washing water make friends with your skin?)

'Isn't Omar about?' I asked.

'Yeah right. He's working his notice. Gone at four these days.'

Of course. Omar that I'd never bothered getting to know would be leaving for good at the end of next week. Then there'd be just us. Laughable really. To thoroughly humiliate me, the simulation charged on unattended, brushed a gilt illuminated SkyTower and a sparkling series of pools and pavilions opening out into a restored Drift Park. Lusher and tougher. And suddenly unbearable. I got rid. Glenn didn't protest. But – encouragement! – he said, 'It's a small place.'

'It is.'

'And rock bottom now?'

'Yes.'

'Could be fixable?'

'*Can* be.' I should know better. 'Haven't *you* thought This is our chance? How good we could make it if—'

'Only three— no, four times since starting here. First was— 2016, that would be. '

I gave in. I'd been had again. (How old was he?) My killer arguments, 1. that big cities were failing everywhere 2. critical mass suburbs had been outed as more divisive than the caste system 3. but six out of seven social classes live well in SM·Ts— small to medium towns, the Shangri-La of human existence, were all there to be said. I ached to say *This is now orthodoxy even in Beijing*. And I even know how to put Rhyl back and to what— I just can't find the start. Wanting to score points made me change tack and describe Westport to Glenn. But of course I had to go and mention Josh. And carry on to Eurwen— and Sara. (Again *why?* Showing off?) The first two names were small *mouli*. But Sara he'd heard of. 'Fucking hell.' He blew out his cheeks. 'That's the same one that—? And they came and told you? You just went off to Ireland after they came and told—? Fuck me. *You* should've been on everywhere, not that American woman! Why weren't you?'

Gaining and losing respect in equal amounts now, 'Because other people still alive would be—'

He cut me off with, 'Got it.' His embarrassingly huge Adam's apple I can't look at bobbed while he digested the new Yori. Then he went typical Glenn, getting out his other Rhyl vanishings stories. To tarnish mine. One he called The Case of the Rhyl Mummy, a squalid domestic murder everybody's heard of. I tried to make him to stop but no— we're straight into The Kicker. OK, more original and tragic.* Both are out of place here. They were out of place there. It was his personality. Only finally he could circle back to asking questions— and the least welcome? 'And you reckon he killed her?'

*see Appendix B

'No. Who knows? Just being in Rhyl and the alcohol more like. I've got her papers. He wouldn't have handed them over unless he wanted me to— but he might be ill. I'm having trouble reading them.' (Josh had just hit Sara and then walked so the trouble was with him).

'I'd bloody read them.'

'Yes,' I said. The office was quiet with just Glenn and me left and the floors below still unusable. '*You* would. It's her journal and it stops before she died.' I raised my hands for *so no good*. Glenn actually seemed to be thinking, his mouth at rest. The atmosphere was bleak. Our illuminated ceiling had greyed, the workplace nudging us out so its systems could fall into a low-energy trace. Next to my screen Glenn's fingers fiddled with Alice Norman's given ring, too tight to remove – all Alice Norman's fault, this, back from Spain but leaving him spare energy to torment me.

Suddenly he's on his feet. 'Ever been over to Store 20?' he says.

The metal staircase squeaked under us. Nobody was loitering at the back of the building— there'd been a looters warning again in the afternoon— but Glenn was enough to scare away a ghostly army of *onyudos, kashas, satoris*. Then we were onto the Promenade under a night sky like a low ceiling. It was still and cool. East and West Parade were cleared but the replaced street lights only showed up the shambles left between the road and beach. Temporary solid panels filled gaps in the Victorian railings where concrete had crumbled underneath them and jarred loose their old joints— so even the sea's slight phosphorescence, the only beauty, was interrupted. We walked on patched tarmac, hearing the Holyhead train make for its crossing further up the river and once it died away Glenn Hughes grunted, 'I give in! All right you miserable little bugger, aren't you going to ask me? Don't you want to know what's in Store 20?'

'I know what's in it.'

He came to a complete stop. 'You *know?*'

'Something you want me to see.'

'Bollocks to you, Yori. Bloody, hairy, hundred-year-old bollocks! Come on, then.'

He's keen. Soon I'd have to trot at his heels like a dog and at this speed we'd attract the attention of the police vehicle cruising our way. But he took a sudden left into a street I couldn't (how unusual was that?) put a name to. Here the occasional house had been reoccupied and as we passed the first, its lit window showed a stage set— a table, a screen, a sofa, all in a bare room. The next had piled up cartons still unpacked and a woman carrying a child looked out, like she felt she was being watched and I had to turn away, guilty. The interiors should've suggested fresh starts and the human spirit and all that but the reports were of people coming back to uninhabitable dwellings rather than live as refugees. *What's a vestry?* the presenter had asked, trying to get a smile out of his squatter family. I felt ashamed. Even Glenn said, 'This fuckin' place.'

Where the houses stopped someone at the turn of last century had dumped a square industrial building, flat-roofed, at odds with the street and matt black till a security beam caught Glenn in front of its double height doors. The smell of fresh lubricating oil hung in the air.

'Store 20,' Glenn said. 'Guess what? – not an *empty* dried out metal shed as promised by Borough for sole use of Forward Rhyl *but* a half-empty metal shed. The bastards had already nipped in and off-loaded some of their own junk, sorry invaluable records, down here. Including three sealed packs of old hard-drives. They're digitised CCTV footage of the town centre. Several years' worth.'

'Why bother to even look at the inventory?'

'I'm interested in all sorts,' he said vaguely, '—if it's about Rhyl.' (Ungenerously, I had the fake poster flash into my mind. And how many other forgeries?) 'I just did, all right? Lucky for you. I noticed 2008 among others. Even that far back we must've needed watching. Your Sara was in Rhyl? You can see her. You can watch her going round the town. If you want. Enjoy.'

Sarcastic or sincere? Because he was curious about Sara, trying to be helpful *and* running in parallel, insulted I'd told him zero re: myself so far. While there was nothing to tell, this had been tolerated but now I'd rectified the fault, it turned into a crime. 'Yeah, take it all,' he said. 'Long as you need! Told you I'd do you a favour.' I must have looked less than gratified. It was shock. 'So I'll be hearing the full deal if and when, yeah?'

At home Libby Jenkinson was in the hall.

'*Doke!*' (Move, you!)

Actually, 'Hello, Libby— it's not too bad out there!' I said and while she was thinking how to prove me wrong I got past with, 'No shopping! Not cooking!' After slamming the door I put my ear against it for the stairs' creak. It came after an interval— as if Libby knew I was up to something and we had a mental battle going on through the pitch pine. (*Fond of her? I really* needed to be out here.) Avoiding the desk, it was straight to the kitchen now. I dropped an extra 50mg of **A** while standing at the sink— waited. A short delay and here it comes on the tenth or twelfth exhale, a sense of rightness that never lets you down. Not for everyone, I know, but for me. So what if there's a new story every day, **A**lecer's Downside!!!? (Thinning of the skin post seventy, some loss of colour vision, laughably the latest, an overmanufacture of ear-wax!) This injection of CanDo into me is the drug's main upside, being a member of the lucky set it works for. I close my eyes and let the sensation build, watching the streets and groves and roads and crescents and parades splayed out from Gaiman Ave all come to attention. A sort of ripple of reordering goes through them. Pavements shake like rugs. A spotless tide sweeps in and cleans the sand. Trees sprout. That festering lakeside void fills itself with a sleek multi-purpose building— coated in Chromyle tm.*

Why hurry? *Enjoy.* Sara's waited a lifetime.

But I can't wait for—

—*the first time I saw Sara, a sunny afternoon, the last week in September.*

Every sense is on the cusp of alert. My mood soars like it hasn't done for weeks, with or without ▲ as Cruise Control, promises the total footage in which my grandmother features. No great achievement because against the packed background of the first frame, she's unmistakable. My screen's a second-hand Panasony SelfCleaning, and doing the best with what it's got. But even I could identify this character in mid-tone trousers and a pale top, a bag slung over one shoulder. A flash of brickwork and Sara's in motion across it, very upright with a stride that whisks her through the camera's sector. Out again. I've never seen her walk. Lacking none of the grace I allocated her, she still takes me by surprise. Doesn't matter. Stop, refind her, zoom in on a grainy Sara instantly retouched. Hand gestures are the real giveaway in speech. To that passerby she's just accosted, her fingers must seem like they're making a grab. But whether scared by a gull too close for comfort or suggesting 'Avonside?' as though she's asking too much, I can tell the hands are really begging. It's pathetic. Remember I only knew Sara at a desk or in a chair, made up for the camera with her expensive silk shirt, one button undone, and the questions, pre-submitted I'll bet. Here she's somebody else, a stranger. Lost in Rhyl. Following on less positive sightings are on offer from a long list.

*Appendix C

A few seconds' action— a figure appears on the Church Street camera and hurries in the direction of the library. *Probability of nominated subject 86%.* You have to admire CC's understatement because it's definitely her. I order up everything, fifty-nine clips that spread across September, October and November in various conditions. The last *isn't* dated 17.11.08. The Disappearance. But of course. You got this from Glenn, didn't you? Typical— no plot and an incomplete timeline.

So I speed on. Is this how *she* felt, on the trail? All the time thinking, Yes!

OK, everyone may have poked round in this mess but I'm me and this is now and it's going to end well. Hadn't it for Thomasina and her?

There are some scenes almost professionally lit from the east, Sara setting out over Blue Bridge, never very early and only the jacket on or off to mark this start from another. At first she looks determined. Though fine weather always goes with the positive on film, it's what we're used to, still you wouldn't say this is somebody abnormal, not in these early scenes. Anxiety's not wafting after her to the extent people are left staring. She's just busy and not from round here, as Tess says. What *I'm* not prepared for is she's also Eurwen. If I didn't know better, I'd think I was tracking my mother. The profile's Eurwen's, more so than full face which is why photographs haven't caught it, and the way the head sits on the neck. However many single frames you examine, they don't tell you this— she and Eurwen are moving sisters to the eye. A single actress could take on both roles like 'Madeleine' and 'Judy' in *Vertigo*. A change of hairstyle and footwear— you'd never get Eurwen in those cute little heels— and they'd roam the town as each other.

(But Eurwen had to grow into the part and watching that must've driven Josh slowly mad.)

Monochrome Rhyl's more nineteenth century than twenty-first. Back at Sara's Day One, I can confirm nothing's left of Ocean Park Funfair but a giant billboard. The impulse to linger and get a look at the promised development was strong— then comes a shot from a static lens pointed at the main show, the first real Rhyl vista CCs come up with. A hint of harbour, further along the seawall's spattered with tourists while more of them spill out of the camera's remit, dodging each other and the traffic under a white sky.

24.9.08 top right. 12.33 pm comes up bottom left. Sara arrives.

33 becomes 34. No refuge for Sara from virtual pursuit, two or three shots are enough to convince the programme. The woman's possessed in microscopic detail. Even through windscreen glass, her brow ridge and cheekbones are measured, then chin to nose tip, and shoulder width, as her left forearm comes up to fend off the collision about to happen. She's fixed, dissected and reassembled so her grandson can witness at leisure what most people present missed – oh, and I know this next bit! – how she's within millimetres of clipping crazy Kim that crosses busy West Parade like it's public green space. Sara's shaken. Checks the rearview for the pedestrian's fate. (You're not meant to be enjoying yourself, Yori *and* you forgot to do a thorough search for that jaywalker as you promised you would.)

Since you can't see the mother and not think of the daughter, what about her? (My mind slinks off again.) And Tomiko, champion of ignorance. On the subject of family etc, etc, don't ask and never give— so, Father, where exactly are *you* right now? No need to do a search because you'll have kept a low profile. And anyway, ▲ does it better for me, joins all the pieces together, lets me 'see' Eurwen and Tomiko flit in and out of Butterton Road like stowaways, clear of any surveillance Josh had access to. They wouldn't be caught for the simple reason they *hadn't been*— don't lose sight of the story, it's *Eurwen* that's missing just now and they didn't find her. Easy to picture the bossy teenager on Rosemont's path, *her* tone, 'Not that way! It's broad daylight. We'll have to go round by River Street or— d'you know what? Let's not bother. Neil can take us in the van. Later.' And Tomiko retreats, back into hiding. Only in Rhyl would it've worked because, yes, it's a small place with a population the same as Penzance but that's where the similarity ends*. Its residents always came and went— from Liverpool, Manchester, Birmingham, *Japan* and the sort of people they were means Tomiko can be living ten minutes from Avonside, ten minutes to Josh's doorstep— to saying, 'Dr Sara Meredith— *san*, My name is Sato Tomiko from the city of Kochi. I am sorry. Forgive me. Forgive us. Your daughter is well. I am sorry. Come now to be with— ' And your best bad English wouldn't have been laughed at because *she wasn't like that*.

But you didn't. Pleased with yourself, are you *otosan*?

So there's an end to the 2008 season, gone in one night— the crowds thin out and fewer children are in the mix. Heavy rain and winds start regular work. Hours shoot by and then a whole autumn day when it must've turned shockingly winter-like to judge by the miserable looks, all the dashing from cover to cover. Coming up are the last few sightings— so I'm informed at 1.06 a.m. Top right 15.11.08. More importantly, it's two whole days before Sara vanished. But we're into the run-up. *Probability 25%—*

I'm not hoping for much.

Look at the arcades! They're still open but the flicker and dazzle's wasted on just emptiness behind the plate glass as definitely Sara slips inside anyway and I wait politely for her to reappear. What else is there to do? It's the early hours in Sara's nether-world and mine. My flat's heating clicks down into coldness. On the corner of Conwy and East, the one I used for

*'Rhyl and Penzance— A study in failure and success'— Yori Sato, UWE, 2031

sketching, she stands out in the November weather, her hair ruffled by it, catching the glow, close enough to touch. A real Hitchcock heroine tonight.

She's dazed apparently and, though I'm no expert, drunk. Some grim thing is going to happen to her— that's how it works, or why else would we be lingering if not to let the tension build?

She came on stage as a skeleton thrown up by the sea but run her backwards and the horror reverts to my grandmother. I find her really lovely from certain angles which photographs didn't show and she lives, she breathes. For one last time. And she's going to fall. My arms want make a scoop, hold her safe as though I'm the father or the husband.

A freak of a feeling.

Final scene.

EXT. STREET. NIGHT.
MAN appears out of shadow and walks toward car parked half up on the kerb, its driver's door wide open and headlights blazing. He carries the body of a WOMAN in his arms. She is either unconscious or a corpse. MAN stops level with car. He seems to be considering how and where inside the vehicle he is going to place her. Then he gets the passenger side door open. She's small but he has trouble. He lowers her in.

Here's what I was shown. Just this— a man carrying the inert body of a woman up a slope to the big saloon, obviously left by him in a hurry. Nothing's on the road and nobody's to mind he's abandoned the vehicle with its wheels up, its door wide enough open to get ripped off by traffic.

That's basically all it is. But everything is referenced. You can never witness this sort of movie trope even in eerie silence without the hundred other variations you know, Hitchcock's and all the wannabes since, feeding extra info in re: his purpose. The odds are, *bad*. And the result for her? Ditto. I recognise the exact spot it's being played out on and, though his full features aren't caught whether by accident or cunning, who they both are. And with every re-run the component parts read as extra menacing. Her arm drops, solider somehow than it should be. The angle of her head as it sags on his shoulder— and for a split second is perfectly illuminated— is even more wrong. He settles her into the vehicle's front seat and leans in to guarantee the torso's fixed upright and going to stay put. Now he's strapping her down. What's already happened by the lake isn't recorded. So you'd need to be pre-told through flashback, maybe, that she's wringing wet— and so make sense of the dead weight of her and explain the problem he's having.

Chapter 22

Either somebody's shining a torch in my face or it's dawn out there. Libby's house is end terrace so Thorp (if it really was him made us) had given her dining room/ my living room a pair of extra sash windows denied the rest of the row. The wooden chair I'd dozed on was directly in their line of fire. Physically? Only a bit shabby thanks to doubling up on ▲ and because with ▲ it'll always be the dehydration that gets you, and I'd kept the tea going all night. The last half-empty cup was next to my elbow gone cold while the car I was convinced contained Sara was driven off for the nth time. CC sticking to its remit of No Sara, No Interest had chosen that point to freeze.

Replay.

Once he'd tucked her up and joined her inside, the car performed a reckless U turn and exited the scene via the bridge although it was a manoeuvre that had to be completed by your brain. The camera on this side lacked a director's guidance. It stayed trained on Rhyl's distant gleam and by a trick of reflection even the shot you might have banked on straight through the windshield isn't there. Do what you like— zoom, freeze, contrast, reverse— it fails to materialise thanks to that dirty smear of light across the glass. So eventually you let the car proceed on its way. A creepy, deserted Wellington Road is all that's left, the darker strip to its right is land that you know slopes down to the lake. Those scrubby trees (they're taller now) don't offer any obstruction. But this being the wrong angle for Rhyl's signature flash of sea, we could be almost anywhere—

And still I hung on one more time for the closing scene. Held my breath for the dénouement that wasn't going to be provided.

257

When I had to move I stretched, rubbed at my hot eyeballs and yanked Libby's curtains apart, feeling just for a second or two so far out of myself it could be the surface of Mars I'm about to reveal— instead of the good old avenue and an empty sky.

The implication was huge.

I'm not a murderer. I'm descended from a murderer. That's Josh manhandling a female corpse with a lot of effort but not seeming in any hurry. A witness could've turned up any moment, him being stopped on Rhyl's main drag and though it was empty at 1.06 a.m. if a camera was able to record the action, another vehicle from either direction would throw a searchlight on him. But there he was, tucking in. Checking this is OK. Then something else. I actually feel anxious for him as he smoothes the soaked hair away from the face— no the camera couldn't show *that*. But he did. I knew. And he took his time. Love, you'd think, again and again. Tenderness. Also absolute confidence he'd get away with it. Which he had.

Next door my bed's very convincing and I sleep four hours, an unlucky number.

Under the subheading Things We Don't Do Now, Gramps Geoffrey once told me this. Before all our personal messaging systems, to speak to another person you were forced to ring their house. Often they didn't answer. In which case the caller— Geoffrey admitted it was himself— waited a moment and rang again.

'Why would you—?'

'Ah-h,' he said. 'Good question, Yori. Excellent. Because being clever doesn't make you not a silly old fool.'

When I wake around midday as soon as I come to, the Professor's right there. He's solid as that wardrobe. His high-bridged nose, which will always look comic to a Japanese, like something stuck on, is being tapped with one mottled finger. Tap tap tap tap tap. *A silly old fool*. And actually very much not a fool, his expression tells you though he went to his grave afraid he'd acted it over his daughter. I see him and the background is always his white study. He had used Pryorsfield just as the big solid building it was till Sara was taken. His defence against the intolerable? Paint in a shade they could market as SnowBlindness and new glazing. For contrast, matt black gadgets constantly revised. A room with no dark corners and nowhere for dusk to settle. A space he could be master of.

Cruise Control claimed no more sightings of Sara once she'd been dragged from the lakeside but, keeping up family tradition, I ask for one last rerun. Nobody home. No catch— I'm a fisherman reeling in a holed net and feeling just about as sick over it. *And* it was Saturday. No work. I'd slept but felt too leaden to move from the seat.

Tess would have plans or I made up plans for her.

The civil disturbance in East London re: a disrupted water supply is over thanks to Casino Pigalle sending in tankers.

Some ex-friend from Bristol is in hospital in Lima, one leg cast from groin to ankle— he's asking me, and about four hundred others, if we have contacts to help get him to the airport tomorrow?

⌒ ✈ ✗

Tomiko's not in studio but horizontal rain is lashing his window.

Oxford will have 30 degrees plus again today, high for August let alone May.

Kailash has a new man, 'a Malayan billionaire— u'll no name when u hear.'

In a mad impulse, I send *Hurray*! ⛵ ⚓ 🏛 🏛?
Nothing back.

Then there's Josh. But we can't speak. Now. Whoever else saw what I'd seen must have helped him. His colleagues, his friends. How come, otherwise? So never a fool, Geoffrey, you knew the man I thought was Josh was a flicker on a lightboard. Or a shell, maybe, rotted from inside.

I make tea. I wish Libby would come down here and bang on the door and bring her human smell in. (Japanese do not smell and half of me must miss it.) I heat soup. Catch the mug's sulky expression as I choose to drink from a beaker at my desk where I've left Sara's broken necklace lying— Oh and *now* from Kailash a single 🐞. *Yes!* I *feel* like a bit of bug this morning— you'll get no arguments.

There's no difficult call to make. No arguments here, either. I join the ranks of Josh's anonymous accomplices by starting to pack everything up – and the letter from Fleur falls out. Still in its envelope. Opened and put back. Even if I hadn't recognised Fleur's writing there's the postmark across the commemorative stamp (a man in a comedy hat, labelled Henry 1V). Big clue that, the history stamp chosen for Sara. As well as the smudged 'Oxford 15.11.08'.

Pryorsfield,
Monday

Dearest Sara

The time you've been away seems to have flown by. Though perhaps on heavier feet for you? I cannot imagine. I do know the date, and what it will be very soon and how you must dread it. I'd say bear up, darling, if it didn't fix me in a previous century! Geoffrey and I are convinced the more we discuss it (and we discuss little else) that either Eurwen will arrive unheralded or one of Josh's enquiries will come to something. He is a clever, resourceful man don't forget, and a father.

Geoffrey, as you know, was already acquainted with Julien Fortin, which helped. His daughters seem truthful and comment made by Henriette (the cleverer, with the alarming haircut?) has stuck in my mind. It was that she had 'got the idea' Eurwen was wanting to go 'a different way' and made it very plain (before she left) she had no intention of working for her GCSE's, no interest in A levels and would never consider University. So Eurwen has had her own thoughts. When she returns we can encourage her to share them with us.

But it is you who concerns us darling, perhaps as much as Eurwen. You are not answering our calls. Last night I very nearly decided to turn up on Josh's doorstep, weather the storm if there were one (perhaps I'm misjudging?) and to take stock, to find our next move. Would that have been so bad?

One more thing before I leave you in peace. I can say in a letter what I should have but did not when we were face to face (our lunch at La Croix springs to mind). Your problems, your unhappiness can be made better. I am not so vacuous as to say solved. But among people who love you there can be healing. I'm a great believer in the power of love. I send all of mine now.

Yours, as ever,
Fleur

PS Even the work, darling, we can mend.

On Rhyl-sky-blue paper that no one made any more, Fleur's letter was rational and kind. And posted on Nov 15th. Even allowing for a proper postal service operating back then surely it couldn't have arrived in time to be read by the drowned woman? By Josh then? No. Having just proved several times over Josh was responsible for Sara's death, I failed to convince myself he'd open a letter addressed to her. On the reverse side, he was a policeman. By instinct would he turn any information down? No. Yes. I couldn't get over how the letter came from Fleur, a woman he *did* respect, whose intentions he wouldn't go against without— without— ? All this seems trivial to the majority of people. I know. *I know.* But I was right to get hung up on it— just my reasoning was wrong. The organiser/journal still broke off with Sara and Josh in a Rhyl pub joined by Meg who might bounce if dropped. I laid *A First* out all over again in its fat chapters face up. Getting them to this position didn't mean any sort of decision had been made. Turned them over to Sara's side. One good idea was still to burn the lot. Josh had kept his secrets all these years then burst on-screen in the early hours with a body in his arms— nothing put down on paper could blur that. No one but a policeman, my grandfather, could've got away with *that*. He was a violent man at bottom so could've murdered her.

Or, at best, failed to save her.

Did he make the distinction himself? He was letting it kill him either way. But a single action alters your future not who you are. And somewhere deep in the molecules, Josh remained the Josh I'd grown up with. *And* forgetting arguments and counter-arguments, Fleur's letter had been opened and read— and kept. A mistake Josh would never have made.

Chapter 23

16th November, a.m. 2008. *A dream? Perhaps not yet myself, but aware nevertheless, I followed...*

...Thomasina Swift's dash through the fields to meet a lover. At fifteen, slim and supple as bamboo and tall for her age they lock glances, their eyes level. Where could the girl's length of bone have originated? One parent a tradesman, the other a housemaid: so from whence came this patrician height and Renaissance mind? 'The mother Maria, being so tiny her husband could place her on a barrel as a jest, making customers roar to see the doll-like woman beg to be got down. It is probable she never learned more than to sign her own name. Though Jacob Swift was lettered and expert in bills and accounts, before the end of childhood Thomasina could out-compute her father in her head and would do it over and over to win pennies. Turned away by a local clergyman we must assume she taught herself Latin, Greek and some Natural Philosophy since over the course of a single year the innkeeper claimed to have obtained for this prodigy Virgil's Eclogues, some early books of the Iliad (though he was cheated by the seller for it turned out a bastardized, illegible version) in addition to a treatise by Roger Bacon and a tract by Sir Thomas More.'

Of course, in *A First* she was both scrupulous and shy with regards the question of Thomasina's paternity, disproving almost by the way Elizabeth Longford's ridiculous candidature of Samuel Richardson. (The Father of the Novel was otherwise engaged that year getting his eldest daughter well married and writing his will). She, herself, refrained from nominating even when a paucity of evidence made it so tempting, a good story if poor history. It was enough to record one Abram Foley's expression of delight to his brother for 'those tender treats' provided at the Merman's Tail; he is writing in 1757, late June, the month of Thomasina's conception. So it was enough for her purpose to append here: 'Abram Foley, (1709–1778), an intriguing and highly attractive figure of the time, always on the edge of great matters; essayist, revelator, scientist and mystic, friend of Benjamin Franklin, supporter of stricken writer Christopher Smart (even in the poor man's *extremis*, at Mr Potter's Madhouse) and a correspondent of the polymath, Swedenborg.'

Her mind had been flicking through the Thomasina pages of its own volition, scanning ahead as only someone who has given birth to them is able to... *recited Horace's odes by rote, comprehended Pythagoras and Archimedes and yet was blessed with such an exquisite femininity that—* Those opening paragraphs had remained unsatisfactory somehow though the drafts multiplied around her in her shady St Clement's cubbyhole. But who could fully grasp the sheer out-of-time, out-of-gender verve of Thomasina's spirit? It was the very thing whose likeness had been rekindled in women the world over and became their torch.

A pair of crumpled jeans lay draped over a chair next to the bed, a tide mark indicating the level the dirty water had fallen to before evaporation took over. The sight helped bring her to herself, as did the scarf, another stream of blue, dislodged from its position on the chest and seeming to flow down to the carpet. Bought for Eurwen... but she had to bolt for the bathroom and it was there Josh came and found her, slumped on the side of the tub, dry-heaving into the sink. His expression was easy to translate: pity flecked with revulsion at her goose-pimpled nudity. 'I'm all right,' she lied and he backed out.

For penance, when she could stand upright again, it was beneath a barely warm shower. No wonder Josh had fled from mottled flesh the colour of putty, the bones everwhere highlighted. Her feet had the previous night's silt dried into them, a grey fringe to the nails and a gritty line in their hidden valleys, the *tweenies* of Eurwen's giggling joyous babyhood... but she fended off that memory, close to panic. Leaning over to attend to the dirt invited true vomiting so a gentle swish, a toe caress of toe, gave a tinge in the flowing water and had to do. She turned up the heat and washed, one-handed wherever it could reach, the other braced against the tiles until, flushed to a better tone, and very carefully she stepped out, straightened her spine like a good Bradwardine girl, slim not thin! ...and marvelled at the human body's capacity to disguise its internal squalor. Even the face; a candid examination in the swiped mirror showed the jawline firm, skin maybe a touch puffy but unlined: a spatter of Rhyl freckles could almost be taken for good health. Teeth, perfectly maintained since their first erupting, were even and white, only this summer bleached at a very expensive Summertown dentist. Who would ever imagine what the assembled parts hid?

Downstairs, Josh was hardly in the house. He sat on the doorstep, the big muscles along his spine bunched and then relaxed in the familiar (to her) act of shoe-cleaning. *And the smell of it!* An eye-watering essence of turpentine. One and a half pairs were lined up between Josh's trainer-clad feet. His hand made a last for the singleton. Always an obsessive shoe-cleaner, the sight of this doppelganger of a husband was too cruel... he'd sat on the limestone threshold in Tackley Close, calling back over one shoulder, pleading almost *Anything, Sara? Black, brown— I'm on black now. Can do navy next...* the small brush dives into polish, onto a heel of boot, working it forward straight to the instep, roundabout and return. His array of polishes in differing shades suggested an artist's paintbox, every tin and brush and tube lined up, cloths folded neatly as handkerchiefs in bedroom drawers, spare laces coupled with Josh's special knot. At home there had always been a wooden case kept by him, old, steel-banded, also meticulously neat.

With every change of task came the possibility of his suspending what he was doing.

'What time is it?' she asked.

'Where's your watch?' He dismissed his own question. 'Getting on for eleven.'

This boot he was restoring to gloss black had delivered a terrible *click* to a Murcott knee... she could feel its weight, hear again the retort. She squatted down, swivelled and sat, back up against his, experiencing his movements through a thin sweater... and his blessed warmth.

He did not move apart but said, 'It's a wonder you don't have pneumonia. Or dysentery. The Marine Lake? A fuckin' joke, isn't it? It was only saying you could see the reflections did it. Made me think. Otherwise... Probably not even deep enough anyway. I mean if you were serious.'

'Don't! Of course not. I was... I—' She was denied his expression but made a guess at a flinty look in the eyes. Another memory of their married life invaded her peace: the debates that ended only one way: with a slamming door. 'Are you on duty? Are you going out... soon?'

'Later. Tonight.'

'Good.'

'Good?' A long pause. 'Why is it good, Sara? What could be good about being here? You and me, together.' For these few sentences he continued to polish away but something went awry, a lace-hole or boot-tongue catching at the bristles... he began to curse under his breath, annoyance rippling through him and into her like current. He was onto his knees, his feet;

she watched him kick first one boot then its twin across the paving and away... Suddenly he was looming over her. 'Just *stand up!* I can't talk to you down there.'

So not the figure cleaning shoes in Tackley Close after all: the change was more radical than a thickened neck, a network of crinkled flesh below the ears, and what had emerged? Some man he was destined to be. At last. The years in Oxford were not for him; they had been hers and then Eurwen's, with Fleur and Geoffrey sharing in the compound interest. Further out again were the friends and acquaintances, neighbours, dropping in from next door, the well-used jokes, *A pleasant journey, Hugo? You were able to park, Nan?* Drinks carried up to the perfect blue-green sitting room with the perfect daughter already asleep above it: all benefits evenly distributed. Except to Josh. Now his true self had emerged, his proper setting. The pain of her futile, indigestible love seemed fair replevin.

She grasped his forearms to drag herself upright, mentally groping for the framework of what she wanted to say. Last night Eurwen had seemed very close. She was just there, or around the corner after next. And though Sara hadn't found her, it could have ended well... But she had *had* to drink. What better way was there to encourage Rhyl to open up?

'It's awful. I know that. Eurwen—' but a slight shake of his head caused a veering off. 'It's worse for you, I suppose. Having me here, on top of everything else.' Her mood felt sludge-like and Josh's lack of rebuttal a stroke of the stirrer. 'I'm sorry.'

'You were hammered.'

'No. *No.* A couple of drinks, that's all because when you are meeting people and trying to talk...'

A satirical plosive *Huh!*

'—you need to have them on your side, obviously.'

'I thought you were just going with Fortune now. Yeah? Wasn't that the latest? You promise the cards via that Kim Tighe – a

Class A fruitloop by the way – to give up boozing. Eurwen walks back in as reward. Isn't that it? God, Sara, you're a kid yourself. You think I don't know? Master plan! But like I told you, Kim Tighe nuked what passed for brains years ago. And *you're* going the same way. Can't get through a week without—'

'That's unfair! Until last night it was eight—'

'Six days. I counted.'

They argued it out back and forth, tempers rising. And gradually something began to clear… off to one side but definitely there, daring her to look at it, a beckoning ally. The sparkling simplicity of drink.

Chapter 24

Scanning would make it more precise, if it was still available to scan. By rough estimate I started with 40,000 of Sara's words which isn't that many. *A First At Oxford has* 341 pages in my hardback edition and runs with notes, index, bibliography, acknowledgments etc to 101,854. All about Thomasina Swift.

And mine is two people's story.

I am not 'a drunk', she wrote on the morning *after* Josh had dragged her dripping from four feet of water. And she is alive to report this new day, starting with a dream of Thomasina. *Truthfully, until my arrival here I was never less than controlled in a public place or an embarrassment to my daughter, ex-husband, parents nor even the few friends that are left. Much of what is reported on the subject of alcoholism is generic hostility by the fetishistically sober, observations that may be near the mark for <u>some</u> and for them only <u>some</u> of the time.*

Alcohol and history: both confront the present moment. The former by a cushioning effect to life's hurt, though it is self-serving to choose this quality in particular: a commonplace to claim it as an anaesthetic. Also a calumny upon drink. By it we omit drink's positive force, that strong updraft on the spirit otherwise only available, by repute, to practitioners of mystical rites. Of course, in addition it eases embarrassment, instils optimism, smoothes a family's passage through all differences and resentments. It banks down envy, denatures fear, makes boredom bearable and, on your behalf, spits in the face of ageing and death. The second or third brandy of an evening: flames in the grate usurp the dying sun and your own hair gleams at the edge of vision, a robin warbles its possession of the garden... someone you love is about to enter this house. Approbation from your father's lips can arrive in the mind, word for precious word, unbidden, and yet your guilt still contrives to lie easy. A peace so sweet and expansive takes you that it threatens to overflow the skin.

Who would need to live forever?

To me, drink is endlessly beneficent. I have it, that unspoiled evening, the gift of dead stranger, one Hieronymus Brunschwig. Who remembers him now? Where are the statues put up in his honour? Where are the Brunschwig Crescents and Squares? A great man burdened by nationality (he was a Strasburger) and the times (1450-1512) with an unspellable name, even by its possessor, he gave the world a lasting legacy, 'Liber de arte destillandi'. We know it as the Little Book of Distillation. *By its use, Jean Martell would make cognac.*

Then there is that other, higher realm of explicable completeness, The Past. You can take and tease its endless configurations, chose and reject, recalibrating what remains until you have a map for others to navigate by. Our exemplar is Thomasina Swift. Her enigmatic self unravels as a perfect parable for the age, for female power, for the flexibility of Georgian society or for the sexual vulnerability of males. Or any quartet of others... as you will. I pulled the thread that connected her with a highly gifted 'natural' father, a titled, besotted lover and her putative Oxford tutor, the legendary Dr George Buller. Though the scourge of many lesser minds, was he duped by plain Tom Swift out of Heystrete, a second 'marvellous boy'?

Yes. Duped and seduced, I decided: I am a poor but plausible historian so no one suspects I can be false.

All rubbish, to quote my daughter. Confess: how likely is it that Emeritus Professor Geoffrey Severing has no idea his daughter is privately inebriated at every opportunity? Did I mention Fleur in the list of non-combatants? I am inclined to revise the assertion with her also. Too many times I have fielded a look: just wondering. Though I was hardly drunk, no and with nothing vulgar as a slurred sibilant to offend, she is a penetrating woman, my step-mother. A year ago we were two Oxford ladies who lunch though technically employed, I with my next book, she an occasional lecturer at the Taylorian Institute... Small matter, I thought, that her glass remained full, mine empty again. Having gently tested ideas for Eurwen's birthday on me, she moved suavely to The Proposition, the real reason for dragging me out to eat in the middle of the day. Now, with pudding's arrival, Fleur inserted into the conversation the name of someone she had been at school with. Then this woman's protégée... had she ever mentioned she produced radio features and was hoping to pitch The Legacy of Thomasina Swift *to a commissioning editor. Would I take part?*

Absolutely!

A second drop of cream is dribbled unthinkingly over the *poached pear. 'But surely you would wish to talk to her yourself? If only to get a feel for what's being mooted?'

She gave me a chance. Dearest Fleur I see sitting at our window table in La Croix; her attention is strictly focused on the stream of bodies obstructing our view. Every few seconds they became petrified as, inches away, the pavements of The High simmered and seethed to gridlock .

No-o. If it's a young friend of Bea's... of course I remember Bea! Tell her I'm on board.

Fleur literally shied at this. Alarm had taken over her dependable horse's face. Rash, it said. The beginnings of an avalanche— and how ruinous the result? Because the pebbles are shifting. I've seen it before.

...in my mother, Fleur's alter-ego at St Hugh's. 'Beauty and

the beast, darling, though she would never have allowed it in her hearing. I'll wager there was many a pretty Teddy Hall boy called us that.'

Our family legend told how before Fleur loved Daddy, she loved Mummy, her precious friend, the first wife who died suddenly (I was an infant) from 'a reaction to prescription medicine.' Fleur had known all and concealed the details. She, rather than my father, had played gatekeeper to my past. This is where the dead come into their own, with their dates, their solid pair of brackets for the intolerable mess of a life. They can surprise you (the odd outrageous fact is bowled in, adding spice) but still you have them. You have them. Too early to be a part of that particular social upheaval provoked by the Case of X and too late, naturally, to have encountered the notorious Y, they are caught for eternity in the grip of those arms.*

Since she had survived her dip, Josh explained he must work later, the inference, which amused or she pretended it did, being that only her demise would have necessitated taking twenty-four hours' leave. An evening surveillance, he clarified, could prove lengthy. Pointless to wait up. His having to desert her was a comfort in a way: smooth it out or let it fester, it must at least stop. About to leave the room, he changed his mind and leaned back in his chair again, the leather under him complaining. 'Tell you what, come out for a breath of air. I'll be cooped up after. Come on. Do us good.'

Josh and Eurwen both found indoors uncongenial: roofs, walls, safety and comfort, none of it seemed to count with either. Eurwen, a Quaker of a baby, become a toddler lurching from room to room, never able to give an explanation for her movement even when speech became adequate. (She was slow to annunciate, a tormenting time for the Severings). This burning-headed Dervish, bouncing off tables and chairs and child-gates and the legs of adults, was in training for the day she would bolt.

Sara fought the urge to sink further into the cushions, to plead benefit of blistered feet. 'All right.' Her stomach performed a new trick; already a cave, the vacancy expanded into her loins, thighs, and raced down into the floor. For a vertiginous moment, she was a half-creature, floating free. 'Give me a moment.'

Sallow but tidy, she returned and he nodded encouragement. He was in jeans and a fresh olive sweatshirt. Almost they matched. She slipped on sunglasses: *Don't want to frighten the horses!* But he refused to participate, instead grasping her elbow as they stepped out into brightness... and a background bustle reminding her for the umpteenth time of the BBC Radio Drama studios, the eager technician offering his take on Oxford in the seventeen-somethings. An infant yelled. The May Quay's doors stood open and excitement at joining those inside spread to the group heading in its direction. Males talked too loudly, their women shrieked with laughter, merry already, stepping off the pavement to be hooted at by cars, From amongst the caravans they passed, snatches of vintage ditties, The Beatles and Frank Sinatra were being enjoyed by elderly owners... and in odd company, were the church bells which today drifted toward Sara from inland. Only to be outdone as she and Josh crossed the river, by Rhyl's own muezzin, the bingo caller—

—her beautiful night-time mirage had been wiped away, drink being a requirement for generosity towards Rhyl. Very much the Lady Anthropologist this clear noon, cool, disparaging, her metaphorical notebook was at the ready. Take a baby to a pub on a sunny day? Gamble the hours through till dusk in a dark, plasticy den? *These people.* She was answered once they took the first set of steps down to the sand, a vast emptiness in comparison to the town, by a breeze at ankle-level whipping grit across her blistered insteps: extraordinarily unpleasant. Josh chose the route, steering her first out to a shingle bank for the better footing, back in when it petered away to crushed shell. Like Eurwen's, Josh's stride ate up the distance, was uncomfortable to match. Coming up was The Sky Tower and Sara paused to indicate the gondola's slow, nausea-inducing ascent. 'Have you been in it?' she asked.

'Of course. I took Eurwen. First time she came here. Y'know Eurwen— see it, got to try it.'

'Why say that?'

He jerked her onward. But his anger had worn away and a couple more minutes had him offering her, 'Because it's true. Not because it's a bad thing. I think it's a good way to… live.'

'Do you?'

'Can be. Who knows?' He squinted against a stray reflection, a head flick denying her eye contact. 'See you Sara! Daddy's little girl. Little Miss School Swot, working hard to make top of the class. All your life. Where has it got you?'

She should have been immune to an attack so familiar. Around the time of Josh's final defection it was an open subject for one of those vicious half hours a couple can fit in, usually between a school pick-up and an evening with in-laws. Every response is short and neat and careless of the other's feelings as a stage line. If a phrase strikes too deeply, too unforgettably, at the curtain they can take a bow, go back to their real selves, surely? So she should have known better, did know better. 'It got me a good first. And a book from what could have been just a run-of-the-mill dissertation. A television cheque you seemed pleased with once. Eventually a film, which against all the odds, is excellent. Have you even seen it, by the way?'

'*Yes. I've seen it!*'

'Oh.' She had lost track of where they were. An unrecognisable roof loomed over the landward concrete wall with an unwalked part of the beach ahead so velvet smooth it could have been swept. 'Oh, what does it matter?'

Suddenly a striped beach ball came spinning towards her at chest height. The pint-sized players after it froze as Josh punched it back. 'I'm the same,' he said. 'The force had me jumping for jellybeans since I was twenty. For what? I've got D.I. stamped through me like a stick of rock. Came back here on a promise, yeah? You never asked, did you?'

'Once you'd left...'

''Course. Why would you? So I'm back here. Trouble was the promise came from somebody about to get shown the door.'

'I didn't know.'

'You probably think I may as well've stayed.'

(*An hour ago I thought finally I have seen the real Josh, the one that was meant to come about, the personality he could not have attained, burdened with me... a bead of sweat is running down from that well-known hairline to your eyebrow as you polish shoes, a mind already out there at the black comedy of your work. This Josh knows he'll never have to say OK Sara, who have I upset/shocked/disappointed now... is that it? Just tell me, Sara! Look at the state of you! Why? What in Christ's name's wrong?*)

'Yes. You may as well have stayed.' Or come home: find Eurwen and come home, there's still time. But one more word and she would weep.

'No.' *His* self-pity was being shaken off. 'Na. That's the Dad in me talking. I don't mean it... except if I'd stayed in Oxford we wouldn't be here now and Eurwen wouldn't be God knows where. That's all. Ifs, ands and buts don't count. We are and she is. Jesus Fucking Almighty I could wring her bloody little neck!'

'You mustn't say that.'

'Wherever she is, *she's all right*. Believe it. You know, my own

Mam left home at fifteen? Ran off the farm, got to the coast, got a job as a waitress in a posh hotel. Just up there!' His gesture was in the general area they had left but at nowhere particular. 'That was when we had posh hotels. I remember her telling Eurwen about the smart little uniform they gave her, black and white, how it was the best clothes she'd ever had up till then. She and the other girls'd sit outside on the steps of a summer evening watching the *ladies* go by in their frocks. She thought she'd died and gone to heaven and this is a teenager working a twelve-hour day for a few bob a week! You should've seen Eurwen's face. And Mam stayed for the season. Turned up home for Christmas and didn't let on where she'd been. *Eurwen's safe*' He pulled her closer, ran his arm across her back, hugged her to him as they walked.

'Yet when I said that... I knew, I thought I knew she was here somewhere—'

'I was a shit. OK? Come on.'

Gradually they edged outward until the town became nothing. Some strength was left in the sun even as it dipped. With the attractions far behind, more and more beach-users appeared, sea-watchers, dog-walkers and then the static retired, hanging onto the day's dregs behind their striped windbreaks. A waxen old woman, so old her cheeks seemed to be in the process of defecting onto her chest, offered a beautific smile.

'A lovely afternoon,' it drew from Sara.

'Right enough, chuck.'

The vista ahead was unsullied, seeming to stretch on and on under finespun silver cloud. 'That's Prestatyn you can just see on the skyline. There's only the golf links really keep it separate. If you don't like Rhyl, don't go to Prestatyn,' he said.

'I don't *dislike* Rhyl.'

'Yeah.'

'Oh, then it is the Cap Ferret of North Wales.' But with

laughter dizziness threatened to lift the top off her skull. White horses out at sea, the soft umber of sand and ebony of wet posts and their long grey shadows, they were all of them shouting to be noticed… Without any warning the beach came up under both feet and all sense of self began its rise out of her… she was toppling backwards onto the wooden groyn just stepped over.

'You all right?' Josh's grip was fierce to the point of pain.

'Yes. Better— now.' But she hung on while the colours continued to sing. 'Actually, my headache's better. Eased.' She could walk forward and did, like a little girl showing off. 'So where does the town end? If more or less at Avonside and the bridge one way, where at this—?'

'Splash Point. At Beacon Point- not the bridge!- to the west and Splash Point to the east.' And then, almost seeming to arrest her, 'Come on. We've got time.'

Despite Josh's downplaying it as just more of the same, this new area struck her as… she struggled for it, *innocent*. Even the small villas and bungalows that he pointed out across on Marine Drive had charm. He tried to orientate her. 'You probably drove this way in?' but she shrugged. She had no recollection of their tiled roofs fairy-tale red and sharp and turned instead to Rhyl's Golden Sands, a soft, buttery plain: toothsome. 'Did Eurwen come here?' *Poor Josh, you've no idea what's going on, have you? Of course Eurwen was here… comes here… will come here. I can see it though you can't. Through Eurwen's eyes… Poor Josh.*

'Her favourite place to swim,' he said. 'The tide sweeps a heck of way in, hotting up. Makes it great for going in the water. Summertime, anyway.'

'As in clean?'

'I wouldn't know about that. It's warm. Never did me any harm.'

Chapter 25

Under the Coast Protection Act, 28th Sept 1987, profile of stepped concrete revetment to be extended at Splash Point, Rhyl— meaning limestone was dumped and then plastered with tar so the effect is an oil spill come ashore and never cleaned up. They couldn't actually destroy the beach here. But it's bordered by that dirty tide mark and then a three-metre width of pathway, poured in separate sections. Think runway to a processing plant. Back from these outlying defences, the brutalist barrage that reared up over Sara and Josh still exists. So does this part of the town, so who am I to complain?

I would've liked to share an extra feature Splash Point has to offer with my grandmother. On the furthest sand at low water, you can make out the fossil remains of monster trees, stumps of a size that'll never be seen again. And find antler-picks dropped by the Men of Rhyl as they struggled to make a living under the 10,000-year-old oaks.

November 16th 2008

Getting late: it should not be warm enough to sit but it was, side by side, Josh's arm a pressure, the bulk of him between her and Rhyl. The tide had definitely turned.

'It *is* coming in,' Sara said after a silence. *But still a long way out.* 'What happens if someone gets trapped? The water must come right up here and then what? Nobody could climb this wall, not with the overhang.'

'Why would anybody get themselves trapped? Um— steps? There's some every so often.'

'I can't see the next set.'

'Well, they're there.'

'How far?'

'I don't know.'

'Have you ever had to use them?'

'*Had to?* Course not.'

'But you know they're there... within reach?' He stopped bothering to answer. 'Because they seem to have built a sort of canyon. The water could creep up and then suddenly, well I could imagine panicking. If you were a stranger. *You've* been coming here for years and yet—'

'Uh-huh,' Josh said. 'One thing you're right about. We need to move.'

'So the tide comes in very fast?'

'No. I'm on at five.'

'You said six.'

'Did I?'

Neither moved. This wall could certainly hold the heat, a huge source of pleasure where the spine moulded to it, as were the brush strokes of sunshine twisting with each wave, pretty as tinsel... as the Christmas decorations that Nora Meredith came home for— 'Josh! There's someone out there. I can see a head in the water.' She pointed at the small darker object. Waves threatened to break over it, but it did not disappear. Round... shiny... a bathing cap! And eyes in a human face that presumably had a human form submerged beneath. He, she, was staring inland from fifty yards off, staring at them.

Josh followed her direction. 'A buoy?'

'A buoy wouldn't move. Wouldn't blink either. That... person has come *along* parallel to us.' She jumped to her feet but the swimmer was so far out, a new position offered no better information. 'Buoys are fixed.'

Grudgingly, a hand above furrowed brows, he said, 'Just seems to be treading water— if it's a swimmer.'

'Perhaps in trouble?' She could make out an erratic motion of both head and neck now. This was not someone at ease, this was distress. They were witnessing a desperate bid to stay afloat. And how cold would it be today, out there, every wave threatening to fill the mouth, the arms and legs of ice and near useless, the beach never getting any closer? Some other perverse current was taking this person out, keeping him or her back from where she and Josh stood safely deliberating. And then Josh laughed and he stooped to slip an arm around her shoulders with a reflex he would surely have quelled if stronger feelings were not in charge. 'You know what that is?' he said, grinning. 'That's a seal!'

The 'swimmer' seemed to raise an elongated face to the sky, in despair, it could almost be despair as though the battle was too much... he, she was about to surrender. And then the gleaming dome of the skull slid under and was gone. 'Are you *absolutely* certain? Someone could be drowning—'

'It's a seal,' he said.

'A seal. Are they common?'

'No.'

'So why—?'

'Wait.' He refused to take his eyes from the piece of sea he had set watch on.

'But there aren't any! You said so. It's more likely to be a—'

'There!'

For a second she failed to locate it, the distance moved coming as a shock: eastwards, very markedly.

'It's moving away from the town.'

'Yes... *yes*.'

'But when it gets to a quiet stretch, it'll follow the tide right in... after fish.'

Just a seal, then. The arched cranium became inhuman and recognisable. 'But have you seen one before? Here, I mean.' she persisted.

'Only once. I'd be six or seven. She— Mam, brought me and our Rosie down after school. There was a seal fishing off the Point that day. We watched it half an hour... or it seemed that long to a kid.'

'And you remember.'

His arm still encircled her shoulders, but she was forgotten. Childhood lit up his face. 'Christ— that's getting on for forty years back.' And then he seemed to recognise the woman he held. When he detached himself it was to brush the backs of jacket and jeans and to initiate their return. 'I'll probably be dead before I see another,' he said.

Josh was easy. Cruise Control offered a hundred sightings of him through the second half of 2008, a dozen for November. One afternoon he can be seen hammering on the door of a house not far from the Westminster Hotel which gives me a stupid thrill for no reason. Anyway the lack of response from inside makes him saunter out of shot talking into his phone. Late one night he carries off a drunk, dripping, *living* wife. And on 16th – an afternoon Sara described – he took some exercise on the beach. Or I assume he did. The camera has just a slim chance and almost misses him. Obstacles are everywhere, too many people and vehicles, a massive kite with a child's legs from under it. Like an idiot you expand the image and get madder still when the van or the clot of broad bodies expands with it. But Josh's face and shoulders are just visible as the rest of him follows 'the first set of steps down'. I try to hang on to him. Fail. And again.

For a second, no, more like a fraction. Maybe it's for those three frames the old

movie makers found the eye likes to run on. Enough to persuade me Josh is speaking. To *her*. It has to be. He's let Sara go ahead of him as she would expect, putting her first but too low down on the steps. For me. And they're intending now to have a walk and talk. They're going to mistake a seal for a drowning swimmer and be easy with each other for the last time.

I ought to leave. Apart from on that first occasion, shocked by my appearing from nowhere, Josh has told me no such thing though he wishes it. He's more charitable than I deserve. I should go home; in what seems another age, Nora Meredith will have wrestled with the same conclusion and thought, back to the farm for me… She disapproved of Josh's choice as vehemently as Daddy ever did, old snobs both. Hence my failure to research her teenage spree while the opportunity existed.

But Eurwen has accomplished it for us both, it seems.

The longing for Eurwen intensifies in a way I could never have imagined. Deliberate hurt is its theme… and these are the incidents memory keeps choosing to convey her with. The view I take: a fellow student at Eurwen's school used to cut herself and one day, waiting outside for my dilatory daughter, here comes the self-victim, small, trembling, a faun in school colours being hustled into a car by a stricken parent. The blood that taints the girl's white shirt also runs freely across the back of one little hand but it's Eurwen's expression that is the more vivid now: disgust. 'Is she a friend?' I ask.

'Her? No, of course she isn't!'

'Poor creature.'

'Don't think so.'

Other, skilfully selected scenes round her out, this semi-stranger, this changeling: they pave the way for June and the day of her history exam. 'You're not dressed, Eurwen.'

'Neither are you.'

'But Mrs Fortun won't be picking me up in fifteen minutes.'

Her lazy expression was turned, very slowly, in my direction. That slight push of the full lower lip preceded, 'Nor me.'

'I beg your pardon?'

'No point, Mum. May as well go in for the afternoon. Or not bother.'

'What?'

'Haven't done the work. Not even the course work. You know I can't stand it. A total snooze.' And she giggled, inviting me to join in.

'Get dressed! However badly you do, you must go and try.'

'No.'

'Eurwen! I won't have you give up school and... and all the opportunities that go with it. I want you out of this house. By the time I come down. Out.'

Did we explore other possibilities, the results of one course of action as opposed to another? I seem to remember we did. I am almost certain I stayed calm in the face of unreason, pettishness, rudeness of a type only a mother feels she must accept.

I experience again the breathlessness that overtook me when she called me a particular word.

'You have five minutes to make yourself presentable. We'll talk when you come home,' I said.

'Fine.'

On the stairs, my heart is pounding well before I reach the top and I sit on the huge French bed I once shared and drink just a single, out of a tooth-mug. The door below has banged. I shower, have another drink, still modestly sized. I seek out clothes but find I am sitting again. Time passes. The final drink provides three things to juggle with, an empty bottle, the mug, the top off the bottle which falls and rolls under the bed never to be recovered... Mrs Ali is so slipshod these days. At six the phone rings. Eurwen has arrived in Rhyl. This begins, whatever this is. I have a word for it: the interregnum.

*Of course wanting Eurwen home is the main requirement…
but Fleur, Fleur I need you desperately. Unruffled Fleur, no one
ever looked less flower-like. Eurwen, now, she brings on a mood
that deepens from frustration, to agony to… why not admit it?
A sort of ferocity. I want her this moment, safe, so I can scream
'I love you more than anything, more than Josh even because I
lost him and I had you and I was still alive!' Then my anger
fizzles out as though already enacted and exorcised and I say,
'It was a history exam. The world doesn't end with a history
exam.' And I hold her and shake her until finally something
comes into those eyes that I can recognise. I would be content
with that. But 'Books, books, books,' as the poet says and,
'Your life's all shattered into smithereens' takes over somehow,
repeating itself until I think I'll go insane.*

*Monday's child is fair of face. I often think fair of face and full
of grace, Eurwen. She is both. Not even certain I wanted a
child, I let Josh's unquestioning, simplistic (I have said it)
enthusiasm sweep me along and for a time the future was as
promised. The husband, my work at its pinnacle, the child. She
never cried, this genial self-sufficient baby… but no, even
further back, was an easy, cycle-riding, proof-reading pregnancy
that culminated in… Fair and Grace.*

*Once (she was walking now) I attempted to chivvy her along
St Giles to where Fleur waited. Eurwen refused my chosen
direction. Her fragile legs sped her away without a trace of
wobble or indecision and, being in a hurry, I swept her up. And
a woman who had that moment stepped out of Balliol, I think,
a rather aggressive-looking woman, a positive Madame Defarge
in full sub fusc, paused and said, 'She is ridiculously beautiful.'
We stared at each for the briefest instant in our separate
progress, I realising that this woman was the more surprised by
an observation ripped from her.*

I should never have had a child.

Instead of grown Eurwen, all my mind fastens on today is the lovely girl who played young Thomasina in the Tom Swift film. Her slight asymmetry of features was captured by the camera but never punished; just out of RADA when she landed the part, she passed easily for sixteen. We had tea at the Randolph. She was very shy of me and strange, surrounded by all the hotel stuffiness, ordering cake which she cancelled immediately as though caught out in some way by her choice... disappointingly not quite tall enough but then film is the least truthful medium. Virginia Madsen, was it? ...no, not her. She was the Hollywood actress, already famous, stunning, who played the mature Thomasina. Having had absolutely no hand in the writing of the screenplay, my annoyance was uncontained. 'An American! How on earth can it work?' I asked my editor and old friend from Pythian.

'Don't rush to judge. The film needs a name. Look at all those Austens, full of Americans. They train them with voice coaching. You'd never guess.'

'I would, I think.'

'Don't decide to hate it, Sara. Anyway, the rights are sold. You may as well just lie back and enjoy.'

Excellent advice since Virginia Madsen proved ideal: poised, quick, elegant and with just a tinge of Wiltshire about the vowels... which reminds me of Virginia Woolf and how welcome those slips of diphthongs would have been to her. How vindicating upon the Nawabess of Bloomsbury's ear.

No image of Thomasina has ever been authenticated; the pastel sketch that once hung in Heystrete's Yellow Room long discredited. So, in visualising the face of the actress who played the young Thomasina, I'm not capable of recalling a name. Virginia Madsen's is available but not her image. Smithereens. And I have lost the sight, the sound and almost the touch of my real daughter so I run my fingers over the silk scarf again and again as though it comes warm from her throat. I prick my finger on a sharp detail of broken jewellery before it drops into the envelope. And I raise a glass to her. Today is your birthday, darling Eurwen!

Chapter 26

Seen it all and read it all— I thought. Like a fool I re-checked Glenn's gift but the phone rang in an empty house at every search of the Parades, Blue Bridge to Splash Point, doubling back to the town centre. What happened to Sara at the last wasn't there to be found and I came out of my lost weekend unrelieved. From her own hand, Sara was clear-headed and more or less sober (she does say *a* glass) on the day she went missing and there's no sign of my grandfather after he drives away at eight a.m. He returned to Avondale late evening according to the reports— Charity Weiksner repeated them as verified— to no Sara. Of course Josh had kept *the stuff*, moved it with him from home to home and passed it on to his grandson, knowing the small part he was playing that day, just a couple of mentions while Eurwen runs riot through the end pages. Thomasina Swift gets twice his allocation. Josh was an innocent man or at least not a guilty one, a good result resting on fact. A good man. Once the chase is over and I'm not in pursuit mode, I come to my senses. Every vestige of Sara in my possession has been someone else's first and examined, taken apart and put together by Josh. Or by Geoffrey or agents of Geoffrey which meant time and resources on free issue and an unslackening will. No one who'd met Emeritus Professor Severing could escape the power of *that*. Yet Sara had slipped away from the two huge male figures that overshadowed my life and on Eurwen's sixteenth birthday she'd abandoned her father's indulgence of a car outside her husband's house. And walked off along her own path.

Back in my office on a filthy soaking Monday, Glenn Hughes

is wearing a polychrome sweatshirt so harsh on the eyes the pattern actually strobed. But my quick nod is well below his due. He followed me to my workstation, he leaned in front of my screen looking super alert— and intimidating with the bobbing apple throat and that ask-me-anything expression. Why, when I'd first been put in post, didn't I established the proper relationship with Glenn?

'Right then. What you reckon, eh?'

My muscles weren't enjoying use this morning, probably from being only half Japanese. 'Ye-s-s.' Translated, 'still considering so too soon therefore shut up.'

'What you wanted?'

We're the only ones in. No Tess, when a chat with her would act like an upper. No official visitors— there's a feeling in the Borough that Forward Rhyl's doomed which might be catching. It's the start of Omar's final week— but arrive on time, why wou

ld he? On my screen a dynamic picture, a present from Tomiko, keeps drawing attention to itself. It shows him crouched on his studio floor in a house I've never visited, in the process of finishing an ink wash study of *Kawaguchiko Threatened by Storm, Number 12*. The images are set on cycle. 'What I *wanted?*' At the point I've begun to take notice, my father's body is in knots as the largest of his brushes – *Big Cloud* – delivers a shower of grey water onto unsuspecting paper. 'Well, yes.' This is the moment he's been striving for. After more versions than he bothers to count, this is the day he captures the event in less than ten strokes of bamboo and wolf bristle over an existing wash. The downpour is about to obscure an entire mountainside and lake, birch branches in the foreground are stretched to breaking point by the rush of the squall and a hat from an unseen pilgrim flies skyward, spinning. Somehow you can see it spinning. 'And no.' Tomiko falls back onto his heels. Having presented me with this gift (A Glimpse of the Artist at his Moment of Triumph) he's recently turned against the triumph, *Number 12*. Is on the brink of disowning it. *Not near quite good outcome.* He's always trying to force English into finer distinctions. Soon he'll make another attempt only this time, he *will eat no food*. Should I take the image down? Though exactly the same as when given, it ought to go.

Glenn's keenness shows by the way he licks round his mouth. 'So did he do it? Did he ice'n'dice your granny?'

'My grandfather wouldn't harm his own wife.'

The chair sighs under Glenn's weight. He frowns. *Not near quite good.*

Tomiko creates a rock-strewn gully with minute expenditure of ink.

'I'm gonna need more than that,' Glenn said.

'Other people'd worry about the tone being wrong— you know, annoying or rude. Not you.' Tomiko's completed work makes up the final seconds of the display cycle. I realise I don't admire it any more. This mountainside lacks substance, the birches are thin— and unbalanced. And what is going on with that hat we're meant to believe has been ripped from an offstage actor? Was it a blemish, a false line somehow incorporated into the whole so it fooled most people, including me, but not the artist? Because *you* wouldn't hide, Tomiko. Sara saw you. Across from the fire she must've been instantly recognisable as Eurwen's mother and you gave yourself up. You were offering to be the victim. She notices you even on this totally bizarre night, and of course your excellent balance. Also how you can't meet her eyes. If she'd spoken you'd have spilled the story. Gone back to drag Eurwen for her out of Jay and Neil's van—

Glenn looked where I was looking and said, 'Bollocks to that. You've got to talk to somebody. Yeah?' He head-gestured at

Tomiko, back to recharging *Big Cloud*. 'Family? Till this I didn't even know you had one.'

'Everybody's got one.' Watching Josh carry a corpse to his car had stirred up stupid responses. Childish responses when I should know better. I'd pretended to myself he could've killed her or been in on her death, let her die— whatever, just greedy for reprieve. As though the puzzle mattered. That was also a crime, downgrading Josh into an excuse of a man when he'd saved her once and would've kept on trying, given the opportunity. Geoffrey and Tomiko, I'd always respected— but I'd managed to lose sight of *the courage and professionalism of Officer Meredith* that used to make my eyes sting when said aloud. 'She was a sad woman with— her problems, a lot of problems.' I told Glenn. 'She wasn't caring for herself. She thought her husband and child didn't want her, either. Then she seems to have gone out one day and decided— all too much. Nobody else involved. You let me see. ' Glenn deserved the bit of flattery but as I was saying it, it turned into truth. I'd never have sorted out Sara's journals without *something to watch*. We all live in pictures in the end. So worth it, Glenn and as promised you've done me a favour. 'It gets worse. Now she's really dead I bet there'll be her life story coming out. There's plenty about her doing the rounds. The *Tom Swift* film's getting hyped, have you noticed? Like making more money is some sort of homage while it'll actually be torture for the people left. Josh especially.' I should've added Eurwen but Glenn came back with a list of the mentions he'd noticed himself, snippets of Sara, 'That Charity woman looks a bit of—' he made a vile sign. Then The Vanished muscled in. We knocked around the ideas you'll find at the start of this section, a lot of them Glenn's. I'd never heard of Ambrose Bierce or Lord Lucan, for instance.

At least Tomiko's safe, I didn't say, protected by distance and rusty English. 'There's no answer. The day she went missing I can't find her in town. She doesn't show. And the rest of the time— she's just this sad woman looking for her daughter, wandering round, in and out the Clear Skies— gets mixed up with some scammer from there! D'you want to see?' I show him Kim Tighe or at least the billboard Kim Tighe claimed was her. I know her story's end at least.*

He breathed out. Said, 'Sod it, eh?' but he continued to lurk, staring now at my white seashell of building under blue sky, another secret he was going to be prying into soon. By bringing on PalmWalk, hunching over the next section, doing concentration about as subtly as a Kabuki artist, the shirt was encouraged to fade away as I had reached an untried route that could be absorbing – in fact, a real skill-bender – and probably was going to turn out more therapeutic than all the talk. Rhyl's a small place but complicated. There are numerous other possibilities, twice as many as you first think. I make a new beginning hovering over the flat Apollo cinema now and finally I find it, the desire line everybody wants to follow—

November 17th 2008

The sun is a weak colourless disc and Sara has it behind her— means she's shivering in SkyTower's shadow. Then swamped by the school-party outside the lost Seaquarium. All the time she's making for the quickest way out of town, using the edge of the land.

Nobody notices her. Not the massive workman stumping from a construction site in bulky overalls, though some instinct makes him glance over his shoulder. Two lovers are clinched in the middle of the path causing a pedestrian snarl-up she'll need to skirt round but at the last moment they drift to one side as though half-aware, clearing the way. That cart-pushing oldie with cleansing implements pauses. He's enough to obscure the

*See Appendix D

slight figure he maybe recognises as the one who smiled— he was litter picking in Market Street the afternoon she shopped for Eurwen's scarf. But even the camera has missed today's chance to give her up.

Like AH is telling us she's really 'Judy', she's really 'Rebecca'. She's a ghost already.

III

Stone

Viewed from Rhyl, Sara's life well justified the advice Tomiko gave me as a child. Re: family, wealth, occupation, place of origin— say nothing. *Mizu ni nagusu.** Write her story, Yori? That weight tied to your foot's finally flown off, has it? And hit you on the head? – which is exactly what I asked myself hour after hour, knee-caps to the polished parquet of Libby's floor, trying to piece together her final days.

But another vantage point you can see Sara from is Oxford's. *Yare yare!* (means *Wow!*) My grandmother – *my grandmother* – was an idol here. I learned that while growing up at Pryorsfield, heard it all the time, even out in a city overdosed on its own brainpower. Even my tutor Mr Dennis with the shakes so bad they could stop him drawing a straight line relied on her grandson having some facts (whether about Ruskin or Rembrandt) 'because of your, er, impressive background.' The academic take on Sara stayed positive and it was buttressed by hundreds of thousands of non-combatants, history-dabblers, television-viewers and movie-buffs who bought her just to read and while the first group never admitted the second mattered, it did. And to date you'd still have trouble finding much from either team that damages her reputation. The meanest? Maybe she couldn't have pulled it off a second time. She'd found *the* subject to make any researcher look good. Lucky Sara. But never out of print right back to when most books never made

*'Let it flow away with the water' – fitting for Sara. Perfect for Rhyl.

it into print, when publishing was the last cartel, that says a lot.

Sara's vanishing trick may've left holes in our family roof but for maintaining a profile it was one brilliant stroke.

And *I* got given her confessional. OK, it has already been sifted through by Josh, then his fellow officers. It has been shared with his superiors— interviews that result with him sunk in everybody's estimation including his own and ended in *his* life being picked over. Never painless. I can imagine Kailash describing me. 'Of course he was more or less dumped by his mother – so a real problem with women. Hardly went to school! He did what? No, it does *not* surprise me.' As for Josh, Careless, huh? was probably passed around behind his back. You've heard the daughter's turned up again, boyfriend in tow? – now the wife's done a runner! Like a fuckin' comedy.

The partner always heads the suspects and it was going to be worse for one of their own. 'Officers investigating a missing person case will require access to the home address for a search with your consent' is still part of the protocol. (Had the journal already been surrendered? Yes to that. Since Josh didn't destroy it, he'll have come clean straight away.) Then there's the Last Seen Wearing report Charity reproduced on her site. Light brown chinos. Cream shirt retrieved from dry cleaners in Marsh Road. (Query when?) A man's hooded jacket, gunmetal, bearing an H for Haglöfs logo, property of the husband. Heeled sandals. (Query why not the Orla Keily sling-backs recently purchased as proved by the receipt from Clarks Shoes, High Street, Rhyl? Style: Milly, Colour: Mint, Price: £89.99— cheap she'd called them, probably the most expensive pair of shoes she could find in the entire town!)

It could be accurate. Or invented by Josh. At least the journal, copied and returned to him to pass to me, proved she'd come through some dark times in that final week and survived or how else had damaging CCTV pictures of a boozy wife dragged home in the early hours been suppressed? Unless they were never in the public domain— unless fellow detectives totally believed Sara in silk shirt, chinos and borrowed coat was still out there, a Misper who left no note. But even back then a man in Josh's fix, policeman or not, wouldn't get an easy ride. His career is wrecked. Especially as the hunt goes on and on – and was stumbling along right up till child Yori watched a bunch of white flowers set sail off Splash Point.

Charity Weiksner's recent post on her brand new ☧ HeresSara ☧ is tagged Women Funds University Virgin Isles Thomasina Swift Disempowered Refugee Abuse Access Memorial Scholarship. She's lived up to her name by endowing one. Still she can't leave it alone. 'Sara's husband and only child have always refused to discuss my wonderful sister,' she has to go and remind strangers. 'So unless there's an amazing turnaround of events, the mystery of her death is going to stay just that.'

Wrong.

Chapter 27

By mid-May an inquest had been opened and adjourned, Rhyl-style in a pre-formed structure on the corner of Wellington and Westbourne. Just-thrown-up clubhouse had the drop on public building. The burnt-out shell of Corbett the Bookmaker that Glenn said had stood on the site showed more gravitas. Not long after I returned from Ireland, the coroner issued to Sara's next of kin – neither Eurwen nor me but Josh still – an 'interim certificate of the fact of death', freeing her from the half-life she'd lived for thirty years. That she'd died wasn't provisional now, only unexplained.

Round this time, when my New Rhyl of the mind kept getting intercut with days generating nothing, I tried to stay in contact with Josh because A. He was Nearest Male Relative in every way that counted. B. Nobody could judge him hard as he judged himself which meant my grandfather was due a respect rebate and c. Neither of those was a real reason. Something close to panic would grab me several times a day and it was always connected with thoughts of him. A message arrives about tenders for salvage from demolitions in Avonside— and my mouth dries, my pulse races. A detective inspector announces a crackdown on thefts from the Royal Alex Hospital— I have to freeze what I'm doing and lose track of the task. Keeping him informed is the spin I tried to put on our conversations— he usually already knew as much as me. ''Course *you* won't be called when the real inquest's held. Why would—? It'll be me they want. Unless they'll accept my statement because the coroner's still got all the original case notes available. There's a number of possibles for the verdict—

accident, suicide, unlawful killing or open. Take your pick.'
These were reeled off without a stumble over *killing*. 'Or there's
one called a narrative. But they mightn't want to bring that in
because they don't have enough facts.' *Do they?* 'Accident's
most likely. Open is the last thing anyone wants.' The
background to Josh's head was a vertical field of broken rock
that fixed his whereabouts. Croagh Patrick's Pilgrim Path was
about to enter a testing stretch by the looks of it.

'Because?'

'Leaves a forever stink. That's what they used to say, the
bosses.' He shrugged. 'People like things tidied up. Open is,
well, like admitting it's bad and just how bad who the hell
knows?'

'You'll be coming back for it—?' but I'd misunderstood.

'Not if they don't force me.' That set face again. 'I've nothing
to give them. Not new.' At a distance over one of his shoulders
a figure was making poor progress from boulder to boulder,
slipping back, spine bent, head tucked in. Reminded me of a
subject by Tomiko. No one was sketched out enjoying a sunlit
stroll, he concentrated on wretched humans struggling through
hostile landscapes and this looked pretty hostile. I'd never set
foot on Ireland's holy mountain and according to Josh every
July fewer pilgrims bothered with the mass ascent. While also
according to Josh – he, a non-Catholic – walked there once a
week.

'Are you going up or down?'

He laughed as if I'd made my second mistake. 'Just sitting.
See that!' The terrain lurched. He showed me out to flat grey
cloud cover blending into flat grey sea full of leaden lumps, no
birds or vessels to attract the eye and no competition for the
perfect vision of Clew Bay we'd shared only a short while ago.
It gave a moment for us both to think. Then, 'Yori—'

'What?'

A hiss of breath then, 'Take care of yourself.' His voice had thickened. After 👁 U, Westport At Night came up, colourful, busy, The Jester's doors swinging behind an elderly couple holding hands. I thought, How can he stand that? Yet from our few minutes' chat you'd assess him as in the top ten per centile of OK. As though he was signing off on the past. Or was it relief he could put his name to a document saying nothing in his possession (now) had any connection to Sara's disappearance that November 17th, their daughter's birthday?

Result? *I* was never going to know what happened to her. If I leaned towards letting Josh off all charges, it left one familiar culprit. Nothing you *did* Yori, I told young Archie Kao in the wardrobe mirror. He was in black pants, charcoal T-shirt, up on his toes, fighter-style.

But it's looking like it killed her anyway.

There wasn't a date set for the proper inquest 'pending police enquires' and the legal process kept pace with life at Forward Rhyl. I won't wander far off-message. I know the town doesn't count for anything with the inhabitants, never mind you but Rhyl was the last one to see Sara alive. It figured somehow if only as her enemy. September came in. If Sara was shocked when she arrived in this month in 2008, she'd be horrified now. *How can you live here?* I imagined her Oxford diction like a scalpel used on Josh. All major refurbishment has stopped. Not been completed. Stopped. Some days in the office— these were the busy ones— what we did was handle sinister requests from other agencies for information. So the population template could be declared inaccurate while the design code for the delivery of quality outcomes in respect of Massing, Density and Height was too detailed. To maintain our keenness, backing for this or that project was *really* a goer – was about to be drawn from a pot that had recently materialised – and had been reallocated – was never intended for us anyway because sealed by criteria that we'd failed to meet at the outset. Then we were put to work on a new Magic Formula. The brainchild of muscular planning superstar D. P. Cutler from *Melbourne**, it takes weather pattern forecasts, familial resilience scores, changes in 'personal downtime usage', current central government/private enterprise health campaigns plus all the usual retail/commercial/service industry demands – there's no column for architectural merit – and predicts what you should do with a dead beat area. Less than a week and D.B. Cutler was a hate figure at Forward Rhyl. Neither Glenn nor I could find a single UK instance of predictions based on Cutler's formula being A. practical or B. just not mad.

But that didn't stop his rise to first planning dollar-billionaire, did it? So our 'robustness of benchmarks' needed to be improved for Rhyl to get even to base camp on the Cutler GoodGradient. As a matter of urgency. Just to *start*. Rhondda Jones, ex-leisure services and now Recovery Czar had said it. Glenn's fake poster business must be beckoning again. He predicted unemployment on the hour.

On the positive side, I stole time to fiddle about with the PalmWalk projection. A twisted cable of retrofitting and modern engineering, its aim was to tighten the fractured sea front and hold it in place for others to make something of. This strip of real estate is responsible for Rhyl's existence. Starting in the 1820s and for a hundred plus years men on-the-make jostled for frontage, pouring in time, effort and hope like gold prospectors. Where land meets water is the thing – it is everywhere – and along this edge they'd strung their buildings and successful attractions, Morfa Hall and Lodge, the Italianate Baths Hotel, the Grand Pavilion, Victoria Pier, Queen's Palace

*That's Melbourne! – as in 'How Not To Do Docklands— A Lesson,' the first text I ever paid for.

and as late as 1930, Goodall's heated saltwater pool that a quarter of a million people entered in its first season. And – from the middle of the 20th century – some so hideous the brief might've been 'Kill Rhyl!'

Here's another not-so-magic formula. Knock out the signature pieces that make This Place not That Place. Infill using for a guide a blind man's take on beauty. Then couple it with the tunnel vision of a mugger. Result? A seafront that demands, 'You! Yes, you! Give us what bit of money you've got now. All of it NOW! Then fuck off home.' But stripped bald by The Wave and redrawn by me, what I could offer was exactly what the site provided to start with. The ultimate desire line, the route people chose to follow when developers, civil engineers, local authorities, private landlords – and architects – let them. You can find tracks trampled across grass verges, running through broken down gates or holes in fences, cow paths they used to be called and it was a rule of planning once that you didn't pave them. Like it was giving in.

I began modelling my Rhyl cow path, enjoyed the making and, creepily, Sara kept me going. She'd walked it or tried to. Starting on West Parade, jostled by a coach party. She nearly tripped and fell opposite Harkers— or was that Clear Skies? Come along, I invited her. It'll give you the lowdown on the town that stole your daughter, from Splash Point in to the Blue Bridge out. All through your journey up here, crazy as a go on the Dodgems, you stayed fixed on Eurwen at the fair, leaning too far out, asking for disaster. You wanted to be at the Ferris Wheel, waiting for the finish – it's rubbish and you don't get long, the story of Rhyl – ready to pounce the moment she steps off. Instead you found no Eurwen and no rides. And plenty of freed-up space. But the practise of architecture takes nothing and clothes it in metal, glass, brick, concrete and a dozen other new materials. For pleasure and use. (*You should've stayed around if only to witness what I could do!)* Getting her involved through October was automatic— see my Walk wrapping itself round the base of SkyTower. You knew it when it actually worked! I envy you that. Allow me to impress with its refurbishment in Rhyl colours, my audioplaque to Princess Diana that it made sick, my removal of four physical barriers over the next one hundred metres, my tough little buckthorns employed for greening and, bringing you here to this exact spot, my hard landscaping in slate, a substance manufactured 400 million years ago. In Wales. Wasn't that what *A First* was about, collecting your history together then knocking against its limitations to break out of the groove?

The month used itself up. I wore away my new pair of Adidas Felons going up and down, worrying about Josh, actually working, making *mochi daifuki* for Tess who told me when I said flavoured with green tea, well you'd never guess!

But she sounded a bit less convincing? Having to spend extra on her now looked likely— I must price up how much a new improved affection quotient would cost.

And November was on its way with an anniversary.

Chapter 28

You'll remember autumn 2040 as brilliant. In the Botanic Garden that The Wave never reached all the snakebark maples were like flares— but the cold snap gave our surviving trees everywhere great early colour. Then a warm, still, sunny week stretched and stretched now it couldn't do us any good and the colour stayed on. At home, between cruising clips from Sara In Rhyl, I cleansed the flat like a maniac, right down to the filters. Everything inside went out and at least it entertained Libby— 'You're gonna make some'dy a brilliant little househusband and what happened to that girl, why's she not giving you a hand?'

Not Tess, obviously. Tess would never come looking for me of her own accord. It was a sad confession to myself as the vacuum nozzle probed the sofa. Thanks for that Libby. Instead of outlining the whole point of *higan* for her I acted deaf.

'Yeah— you *know*, that one came here the time you were on holiday. Bit snobby and thin. Your sort of build—'

'It wasn't a holiday.'

'If you say so.' Libby was dressed for— something or other, all in pink, with pink shoes her feet were trying to climb out over the top of. Waiting for a taxi.

'I never managed to find out—'

'Well you should of. Or I'm gonna be stuck with you forever. He's here! Bye!'

She waved as she went. A grudging bow in return. Not only was her reminder of the visitor unwelcome – who was it? I'm not superstitious but seriously *who?* – so was Libby's life-coaching that managed to turn normal hygiene into displacement activity. I hoisted the sofa up the front steps, acknowledging Mrs Yilmaz, the Turkish doctor's wife who'd stopped to watch Libby off. Probably feeling superior. Mrs Yilmaz is a jowly, sour-faced woman with patches of moss for eyebrows so Libby's still well ahead on points, on my planet. I threaded the sofa back through my front door where it slid into place equidistant from an architectural model taking up most of the desk, and a small pedestal table. I went into the bedroom and came back with Sara's personal possessions, took down *A First At Oxford* and laid the lot on the tabletop. According to Tomiko what you do now is fill a drinking glass under the tap and add that. You've got Sara's shrine.

Her broken necklace often made me want to touch it. Of *the stuff* this seemed most hers and most bittersweet, pretty and fragile, made of cheap nickel silver and moonstones, which are only feldspar anyway and what she seemed to feel she deserved. After failing to fix it I'd let the links run out onto Josh's floor but it'd survived and back home with me, a touch of style developed. Each droplet was cleverly positioned to give a shiny ripple to any throat it was round. Then I reread Sara's description of buying herself this treat and even the gems improved. Opalescence was good under bright light with no surface flash— a giveaway of exposure to heat, I read, and fakery. Authentic then. Like the journal writer. What I am is here. Feldspar instead of diamond. Not durable. A broken link. All flaws as seen. It drove me crazy. Crazy enough to come to a decision. Natural moonstones deserved to be worn.

'While I'm gone, will you do something for me?' I tried Glenn with. He was in my kitchen next to the suspect vintage poster. I'd been interrupted finishing a salt pickle roll with curd cheese. He wasn't expected and in the wrong. Therefore I could ask another favour. I added, 'I've more if you could eat one of these?' because he wouldn't.

'What do you think?' It was black enough outside for Glenn to slick down his wiry hair in the window. The big ears bunched it out again. 'So— you want?'

'William Jones.' (Glenn's grunt says a bit of a minor character. He'd been down to the harbour with me to see WJ at work but Glenn's main interest right now is a bottle of Hope & Glory lager I don't have. He lived here nineteen days and still isn't capable of believing I don't drink.) 'When he's ready to launch, will you make sure you get it for me? I won't be gone long but could be any day now.' I was feeling better all the time about the request. He was used to me wanting Rhyl oddities, being a source himself. Places and things usually. William Jones was a hostile old man which made no difference to the grace of the craft he'd restored— nor would stop me using its rebirth in my pitch sequence *Harbour and Riverside*, the mark in time and space for where PalmWalk started. 'And I'll need her name, a close-up of that.'

'What's he calling it?'

'I don't know. I gave him materials and he still wouldn't tell me.'

'I'll find out,' Glenn said, winking at the challenge— then casually, 'Just a short trip, then?' He just couldn't seem to give up admiring his own forgery skills. Or was it really another of his gifts he was checking on? He'd be disappointed. The mug's obsessive gaze had turned out to be unbearable, so banished now to under-sink. Glenn wandered next door and sprawled, feet up and chewing my cashews, much the same as on every night he'd been my guest, looking for anything else to poke into. Sara's watch caught and then lost his attention. But not her necklace— that had been collected from the repairers coming home from FR and was already stowed away. The heap of withered orange leaves were just rubbish to Glenn – I wanted him out or Sara's glass of water would get drunk next, once the cashews were finished. 'Your screen's off,' he told me. 'Bust? You're coming back, are you?'

'No. And yes, I'm coming back.'

'Yeah right.' He chomped some more, mouth ajar, mulling. 'That time after it hit, and us up there and seeing just acres of crap, I thought he's off! Omar *maybe* but him for sure now it's all gone.'

'Not all. I made a list—'

'Aw-w and there's you with your Abbey Street job just finished! Whack!' His arm was The Wave again smashing through the smoked glass clinic window and he laughed till his face bloated and his big nose ran.

I sat it out. 'But a wider site's left with multiple uses. Thirty metres at lea—'

'Fuck it, I'd hate to be cheerful as you.'

'No danger.'

'And I was thinking Chrr-rist, this time it might *have* to be Spain. Me'n Alice, we'll be at each other's throats *muy rápido!*' He winced. 'Then you go off on your schemes.' He switched to a higher register. 'Oh we'll have this Glenn, we'll have that. Along here we'll put the Crystal Palace—'

'Box.'

'And shops people with money might wanna go in and an apartment complex, a weird shape— and weirder than that even, we'll have a new funfair. Every day the mammoth runs amok!'

'Not a real one. A simulant.'

'You got that right! Couple of years from now they say they'll be doing real mammoths again— d'you believe that? Na, me neither. But anyway, it'd be more Llandudno, eh? Classier by miles. A fake mammoth's for us— yeah let's order a whole herd of fucking dinosaurs, that'll bring 'em in. I was almost on board, you know?' Getting excited, he'd broken through to different feelings. They'd been there all along. I saw it, Glenn finally turning serious over our current state. 'But it'll never happen. You can't buck a slide like ours. So a short trip, then back here?' He had a yawn and a scratch of something inside the formal black pants he'd turned up in. I had no warning what was coming next. 'Only it's not like you need the job, is it?'

Another advantage of being half-Japanese. You blush in secret.

With no answer, 'Rhondda—' he followed it up, '—controls your budget these days.'

'Therefore?'

'Our Rhondda noticed, after the changeover, how for three months on the trot you don't get paid. Which was more than you did. Three months and not a murmur. Me, I'd have been at 'em every day. Where's the loot? What d'you think I am, eh, a fuckin' seagull can live out the bins? She sorted it and you still never said a word.'

My resources. I smiled only because it was safer than showing anger at my stupidity— and the First Grade unfairness of it. So I'd failed to notice I should be getting into debt. Why would I? Libby was sorted months in advance. I didn't gamble or drink and hadn't travelled since Westport. Tess cost but it was modest, (actually with the little extras she was going up all the time) but nothing like Kailash had (Kailash had *really cost.*) And I'd never been one of Rhondda's customers. As for everything else, clothes, food, possessions, obviously they weren't flashy. They needed to fit in.

What I ought to say is, I've got money. But that led straight to me smirking every time Glenn complained about tax on lager and meat and sugar or shared his fantasies about a Casino Pigalle jackpot. I saw that. He'd see it. (*And* at Omar's lookatme tailoring – and how might it work with Tess, her going *Gorgeous house, Yori. All of Rhyl out that big window! Wouldn't you just love to be able to—?*)

And at the cheap Nepalese banquets we'd shared at !Terai!

'I've got money enough to live on,' I said, stalling. So he was insulted. What about *Tess?* I mapped out the roleplay. She took it well, not resentful, not too many questions, and then we went on better than before. Couldn't quite get it. 'Fleur, she was Geoffrey's—'

'Brought you up, *yeah.*'

'She left me her own things.'

This made him stop chewing and sit up. He even wiped his fingers on his pants. 'Worth a load?'

'She liked clutter.'

'And some of it was worth a load? What, for fuckssake?'

'Well, you know—' I tried to sound apologetic. It *was* shameful. A child from Rosemont— father a penniless Japanese student and an unemployed, unqualified mother— had managed to scoop up everything I reeled off. 'I got her Meissen collection and the Early Delft which was just coming back up after the dip. Sold them. A Steinway piano. Loads of furniture. Also now got rid of. There was a painting or twenty.' Now he had a handle on me is what his face said. But decision made, no thought – dolt! – I had to go and give him, 'Favourite was always a drawing. Quite small and spare, graphite with touches of oil pigments on tinted paper.'

'Who by?'

'Not signed. Used to be in the kitchen corridor nearly in the dark. At Pryorsfield. When I lived there. The subject's—'

'How much?' he said over me.

'—a shingled house front up to the eaves. In the foreground, branches. You look at it and you think yes, *very* good. The artist's showing you how the building holds together. I guess it would've been worth a lot more if the subject was a woman.'

He tried staring me out. I hung on till he nodded. He believed he'd find how *muy costoso* my list added up to. But I didn't tell him I'd sold *Façade and Bald Tree*, did I? So he couldn't.

'Sounds a nice tidy stash. Lucky prick.' Confidence in being able to price up my art work was putting him in a better mood. A power thing. He reverted to, 'Splash the cash and you could be fighting them off! Lucky, lucky prick. But there's only me'n Rhondda knows.' (A lie, Glenn or soon will be— your mouth's bigger than the old Ghost Train's). 'Good for you though! Never bloody me, huh? Not even close on Casino these days. Fuck, I've gotta dash— You're a tight one! Me, I'd just sod off.'

'You wouldn't.'

He shrugged. 'Anyroad, it's our full rehearsal.' Without warning and very loud, he sang *Bring them in sweetly/ Gut them completely/ Pack them up neatly/ Sell them discretely/ Oh, haul a-way!* The rich, accurate, accentless tenor/baritone from Glenn was always a shock— actually it was embarrassing, *him* performing well. I'd have been happier if he'd cracked on a difficult note, though they all sounded difficult in this work. 'You've heard 'bout the Stop the Opera group now? Supposed to be against it because of that kid went off the bridge. We're only doing Selections for Chorus for fuckssake then it's straight into Cole Porter and then the *Mama Rotti* tribute band from Colwyn Bay headlining.'

'I hope not with *You're the Girl.*'

'What? Dunno. Whatever. But some bastard has to go blabbing how Peter Grimes' cabin boy dies, doesn't he? And his *next* cabin boy. Two in a row! Then Grimes ups and drowns himself to finish.'

'No surprise happy ending then?'

He ignored this. 'Oh and it's not Christmassy. We had three performances planned for December. Fucking typical of this fucking place. Fuck 'em!'

'Don't worry. There'll be a Keep the Opera group in twenty-four hours. Massive support from um— Mexico. Or anyplace with floods this year. They'll pile in.'

Not convinced he squinted, started checking. 'Look! 14,973 against now. That's half Rhyl if it was all votes from here which it might fuckin' be. Even Alice isn't coming! Not back till the 23rd. You're away down south—?'

'Tomorrow. There's a person I need to see.'

He could read my mind. 'You're still at that. Thought your granddad didn't do it.' OK, he made references to my family and I'd have to accept them because of the Sara images. But I seem to keep giving him more ammunition. Why? See now, I'm tempted to describe the mystery woman visitor, it was the sort of story he loved— but he was reaching for his coat, thank-you *Benzaiten!* (music deity), part of him already being off with the difficult tenor parts. My windfall carried on bothering him though. 'Train, yeah? You certainly know how to live it up,' he skitted, a joker not a buffoon. I admired his battle with the multi-fastening parka – teenagers were wearing similar along the Rhyl front right this minute – and the way he pulled it straight over his chorus uniform that wouldn't be needed, probably. On his way to rehearse an opera. Subject? Deaths of cabin boys whatever they were. No wonder the show was as doomed as an accident-prone fisherman.

'They'd be wrong to cancel,' I said. More's needed— even Alice isn't coming. 'I'll buy tickets.' He just hunched his shoulders. Debt-wise I still wasn't clear.

Once I'd seen him out the door and checked the avenue – only Ram and Musa Yilmaz on a wall keeping out from under the eye of their mother – I made tea, got as comfortable as you can on a chesterfield and called for 'Peter Grimes, synopsis and best bits.' Apart from *Sunday Morning By the Beach* everybody knows from the coffee dramads, my knowledge was entry level—

—a full orchestra fills the room with a string section that cuts through you like a wire. Even after the theme fades your scalp zings with needle sticks. It was a brilliant choice. My blood pressure must've fought the last dose of ▲ I'd just swallowed to rocket skywards. It was also a terrible choice. As the rich female commentary (by the mezzo-soprano Wendy Silvester of MidOpera) explains Peter Grimes is poverty-stricken and isolated and freaky and his cabin boy has just died at sea— how exactly? An inquest! He's given the benefit of the doubt— a narrative verdict, then. Grimes finds himself a replacement from the workhouse, another spare kid, not wanted. This one's beaten. Slips off a cliff. They point the finger— that'll be Glenn in the Chorus doing that— but he gets away with it. Doesn't! Scuttles his boat for the finale.

No— it was a terrible *and* brilliant choice. Ambition, violence, loss of respect, misery, shame, suicide. Glenn never mentioned this story was Japanese—

—probably not his doing though. And he only sang because he could and wanted attention but then anyone with a shred of talent does that. Look at me. Look at that architectural model (an architectural model, *these days?*) that had taken chunks of time. Look at the sketches of PalmWalk filling the walls where a hundred takes on Rhyl had been pinned up.

With just journey fodder left to pack I let Peter Grimes, the best bits, go again as I tidied Sara's shrine then put *Facade and Bald Tree* up on screen to enjoy *By Egon Schiele, believed lost.* It was actually safe in an Oxford vault. Schiele's carbon marks, his continuous output direct from eyes never leaving the subject, were down in the dark like the mug. And still making a house. In the foreground branches strain at the sky— a net full of nothing, Josh's old tree. Your own mind fills it with the early greenish light. Extraordinary. And so was Fleur as a student buying or being given it, because Vienna was her area of study, she'd visited often, but still, a chance find? Schiele and Fleur— one of the few images he ever made that she'd be attracted to.

(See for yourself, the contorted lovers, the hags, the portraits of the artist as the devil or a madman, the body parts.) Even then Fleur condemned him to the half-light. But noted my admiration. *Convergence*, people say like it explains anything, like my mother and father, or Josh and Sara. Only together because some thief looked at moonstones and silver, thought *trash* and left it for PC Meredith to bring back in person.

Eurwen said, This was meant for you. (We stood sizing each other up, gunfighters either end of a passage, an empty Pryorsfield echoing round us to). Take it, Yori!

The Egon Schiele is worth— enough to free me for life. Or build one great building. I'm tracing chestnut stems grown through an actual spring in 1913, when a rush of future-zest comes over me so powerful I have to grimace. Things might be about to change, after all wasn't I off in the painting's direction tomorrow? That wasn't it, though. 'It' escaped me, left me with OK, exposing the family secrets was a poor strategy but not as bad as putting money on Casino Pigalle— and when you mention *those* odds to regular players they say, yes, *yes* but in any town that gets seven sevens up the player gets a billion dollars. (Seven sevens in a row on a forty nine square grid— the odds on Caesar's last breath are better). *A billion dollars* they repeat *and the Cassie P girl off the lightboards will go naked through the streets.* Like she was real.

Because if the whole of Rhyl didn't kid itself blind where would we be?

I'd won the Sara footage on the strength of a small stake, a few confidences, and it had got me back to the diaries. Seeing is everything and I'd needed an Alfred Hitchcock to stalk her and he had. She might be a problem to people she knew, to herself, but to the camera she was Marion Crane, she was Judy Barton, she was the first Mrs de Winter, she was Dead Woman Walking and however many times you watch, if you're human you get angry at the waste. Why doesn't somebody stop her? you keep thinking. Every step. Why not stop her, AH?

He answers. Says it's what he wants you to ask – before, like any good storyteller, he explains.

Chapter 29

A train journey's a kind of movie. It bottles characters up. I try to keep off boats and planes— and out of cars as we're told to. But I'd choose trains anyway. They're the future if we've got any sense which we won't have.

After not enough sleep (Peter Grimes, you deserved to die) I snoozed out of Rhyl on the ten-thirty. Twenty minutes later I'm off again at its first stop in England, handsome Chester. Doesn't matter it's sham and sincere in about equal parts so you're walking along a street going 1530, 1830 or 2030? Doesn't matter it's greedier for your money than Rhyl is. I like— and if you're travelling you need to suck the experience dry. At The Grosvenor in the heart of Eastgate I have tea and a plate of sculptured savouries that cost more than a meal for two back at Rhyl's little Nepalese café because The Grosvenor's where the Severings always stayed. Multiple guilty Yoris watch me from the Brasserie's mirrors savouring slivers of Kobe beef on the tongue while a pair of very thin older (maybe) women sip watermelon juice and consider a young Archie Kao as their post lunch entertainment. Another time, maybe.

The afternoon connection came as a reality lesson. I had to stand all the way to Wolverhampton, the model in my arms— it's like travelling with a baby except I'd attract sympathy if it was a baby. And then into a seat and downing my fizzy water, the halt at Oxford arrives in what seems like five minutes. I haven't been *here* since Fleur died. No time to get off. Rain will be blotching its signature limestone all the way from Fleur's workplace at the Taylorian Institute – into Magdalen Street – along The Broad – darkening the leaded dome on Gibbs'

313

Radcliffe Camera, more perfect than St Paul's Cathedral – kissing the pavement for the geniuses of All Souls (Eurwen's joke) – until, coming down like stair-rods over The Plain, it closes on St Clement's College. An unimprovable route *and it's nobody's scheme*. Who'd be in my business? Stop planning and you get Rhyl. Plan hard and you can still get Basildon—

—our carriage is steaming up. So am I at the woman opposite. She's had *A First* loaded since getting on at Warwick and every so often needs to pull at her neckline for air so the jacket gapes on flesh that I don't want to get noticed staring at. She's twentyish, has long blue/black hair braided with those tiny cubebeads that've gathered between her breasts. Student. Oxford, not— London, maybe? Meaning even less chance, every weekend who's coming to who, where's half-way? Doesn't matter, I'll pay, must remember to offer, making the beads swing as she nods. The halt turns into a long one so I rough out our conversation, *really well-written I think but then I would*— I rifle that Camille woman for a quote, 'Meredith's Thomasina, the girl from the bayou, is a righteous icon for females of every age and race, pushed to the front of the "talkers-back"' and then all the way to authentic personhood.' No help there. And *A First* is keeping Reading Woman hypnotised, speaking straight to who she would've been if a Thomasina hadn't come along. No surprise that since Sara's bones stranded, Lady Quarrie is more of a brand than ever, ninth place today (up three) in the list of Most Famous UK Hers, behind Jane Austen and Princess Diana but miles ahead of Virginia Woolf. The Severings would be proud. I'm proud.

Didcot's Parkway Station is filthy but then 59,975 people pack the town (doubled since Sara's day) and try to use it. Most of them are at this now, clumping along the train's length, young, old, exhausted-looking, coats thrown on top of overalls or admin-types in sub-Omar suits. I've only ever been through before, not off. Why would I? Once a nineteenth century railway junction, Didcot's other name is Oxford's Servant Quarters, fifteen kilometres down the line from the City of Learning and a light year economically. Lo-cost and lo-care. In the lo-en gloom around the exit, I have to squint to make out a battered Sustrans bikerack through the press of bodies. In the open air for the first time in hours, I can predict we've barely outrun the rain without checking. My ears itch. Japanese ears are useful that way. And Reading Woman is hurtling towards London without me. And ahead there's a ride in the dark and then the real climax of the opera. Hope takes a dive.

Shape up Yori. At least your pre-ordered transport's ready for release— the kiosk says *Thank-you-you-have-paid-for one premium cycle forecast-in-this-area-is- fine- with showers later.* I try to catch the tailend of maybe thirty other cyclists off the train. The first section of Sustrans Way is a gloomy gully to keep us off a B-road edged with apartment blocks, thick with traffic. Flat South Oxfordshire's a pushover though, to a man on two wheels. I'm soon away, almost high after being cooped up and this county seems like another home, even its unloved corners. Yori's husk is back there in the carriage and real me is whizzing along like a *tengu*, now trying to overtake, now diving through a better-lit tunnel that takes us *under* the railway— clumped together, a race but the tunnel makes us a string now. Cyclists start to peel off, shouting out to each. The last one calls, 'See you, sluggy!' and that's Didcot done with. I'm on a flat, glowing surface run through open country. Except what I make out as undeveloped scrub either side has a condemned feel, with the town close enough to take it with one flick of the tongue.

A crosswind's coming at me out of an invisible landscape of rattling stems. *Ahead forty metres* the machine says— and thunder like a demolition drowned out the rest. Then came rain.

On the plus side the lane I'd got into was traffic-free (I've had a morbid fear of the bike/car/rural dark combo since three fellow students were killed on the Bath to Bristol overnighter in my final year)— a minute or two more peddling and *You have reached end point*, the bike said.

I dismounted.

At first it seemed there was nothing— then tall bushes trying to link hands across a narrow side turn started to make sense to my eyes and I pushed through, one arm shielding my face. Got a soaking anyway. When I looked up ANIMAL FARM in big luminous letters hung in space, about level with my chin. I blink but they persist, free-floating against matt black. End point, Yori! Apart from Didcot's distant mechanical hum it was quiet, or nearly quiet. A bit of dripping. The bloodswish in my ears is from nerves that have rattled like those stems along the entire journey.

Animal Farm. Never welcoming or sounding like any place you'd want to visit. To disturb me it doesn't need to do what it does now— open up that yellow rectangle about ten metres beyond the sign. And have Sara Meredith step out.

'Where have you been?' she said. What a question from her! She actually shouted it because the exact moment the doorway appeared dogs started up from behind the building. She tries to pull me across the threshold while I am still getting my bike balanced and baggage de-secured. 'So what's wrong with taxis?' The sound of her is enough to do it, the challenge in a light soprano – that pure Oxford 'wheah?' instead of 'where?' as taught by Bradwardine School among others – all working together to inflict the same old insides-pulled-apart pain. Then there's the thin white hand on my arm, the brush of her hair across my eyes, the scent of it. It was Eurwen, of course. My mother. About time she re-entered the story, the person I'd been waiting to see again, maybe the last few hours or the last five years depending on how the next couple of seconds go— and the daughter Sara's ghost will always search Rhyl for unless I—

—and she's an instant frustration, moving or dipping her face into shadow when I need to look at it full on.

'I still prefer bikes.'

'You're soaked.'

'Spare clothes in the bag. This is worse than Ireland!'

'You must have brought it, then,' meaning the storm, 'because it's been fine for days,' she accused me and we were inside and she closed it out. And here comes the awkward bit. We stalled. Somehow there's rain in her hair too that glitters under the bare bulb. As though she wasn't bright enough.

'Sorry.' No good – everything depended on the moment and it was slipping past – always like this, looking forward, the warm up, the rehearsal or the lack of rehearsal, both useless, and then the meeting itself, spiked by a random thing. Being soaked this time. With the model wedged under one arm, I could just about open my other one in half-love but don't bank on her coming close again. She doesn't. I admire how she's slim as ever inside the dark trousers and fitted fleece, and is only about my height though seeming taller-because-narrower and her red hair's still worn spilling over her shoulders, lustrous and untrimmed down to the waist. The heavy-lidded eyes have maybe a touch extra shadow round them. The smile's like someone else's. *She's here, this is her, straight in front of you, dolt.*

She didn't help me off with my rucksack and waterproof but my sodden trainers were almost snatched from the floor and she was gone leaving me to follow. I'm inside a tiny, totally empty hallway. Not a rack, not a peg. Up a tiled step, resisting the urge to duck because the hall ceiling's not much higher than the door lintel I've entered under, then a ninety degree turn, another step— I don't know what I was expecting. Nothing, probably. Eurwen and I had shared various houses, none of them hers and during that time she never gave any hint of how she liked things. Hit by the rise in temperature, I loosened another layer of clothing while I stood in an archway and took in her latest home.

The living space was maybe seven metres long but too narrow and said non-domestic by its fibreboard panelling and overhead lights. In the exact centre, bizarrely, a pair of claret leather sofas from Geoffrey's study (but they'd seen life since) faced each other while Fleur's Edwardian vitrine bought to display the Early Delft bridged a gap between thick-curtained windows. Hence the blankness as I'd pedalled up. The only other object was a white Kofod Larsen reclining chair, also my great-grandfather's, and a present from the Royal Danish Academy of Science and Letters the year I went off to university. It pretty well completed the effect of a few Pryorsfield pieces being stored in a vacant unit while they waited for auction, unappreciated. My ex-dining room at Libby's was homely in comparison. I walked forward. Now all the through routes for pedestrians showed, giving a hotel reception air – aided by the music that started to filter in, synthesised, using a female voice as the instrument in this track, Tess's sort of taste, *Mama Rotti*— the real thing too. They were on the cusp of a revival. No pictures hung up or were projected (just like Josh) and no screen visible— so in fact an *unfinished* hotel lobby.

The exception being the hand-painted floor.

Take away Reading Women immersed in Sara, take away Eurwen herself, suddenly and out of the dark, and this is the weirdest thing yet. Instantly recognisable as Glenn's 'before' image from the Butterton Road House Collapse, here it was again, intact under my stocking feet.

'Go and get warm,' Eurwen ordered.

At the room's far end the log-burner she indicated was throwing too much heat at the poor cabinet's walnut veneer. Although I could never have housed the thing, this was actually *my* walnut veneer. On show inside instead of blue and white plates and chargers were pottery mugs with the logos of various charities my mother and Henri Fortun have been involved in, FOURWAYS being just one of the biggest and crudest. As a job lot they brought back no happy memories and cumulatively looked too heavy for the shelves. If only I'd sold the thing along with the rest. *Bou-ah, bou-ah, ah, ah* suddenly livened up and turned jazzy and the *Rotti* lead threw a few near words into the mix. *Hurt* might be one and *bou-ah* turned into *you-back* very plainly.

'Like it?'

For a moment I thought she meant either the mug library or the song. Masses of red hair swung as she passed through without stopping and out of another door then she was back offering me a big striped towel. 'The bathroom's through there.'

'Thank-you. Um, it's different.' I gestured around. 'From Thame,' meaning the cottage in Oxfordshire's capital of quaint she once rented. With Henriette Fortun. Details of its many lop-sided charms had been sent me in Bristol. Here's the spare room— if wanted? I'd graduated, was working but between projects— no, wrong, was drifting and had just been dropped for the first time by Kailash. Maybe Eurwen expected *We'll all fit!* would tempt me. Or maybe expected my no thanks?

'What was it?'

'Ah-h!' She was impressed. Her smile offered a part in a conspiracy. 'Good question. Just like you. Well, it was an office when the gravel extraction was going on,' she head-gestured to mean close-by. 'That's finished now. I bought the two flooded pits, one of them very big— with swans! Imagine it, covered in swans the first time we came here. Plus sixty acres. Some of it's ruined land but improvable. *And* this redundant storage facility, as was termed.'

319

Near the mark, then. 'Change of use?' I'd no idea why I was asking. Or why we were talking about it, except it felt safe, i.e. not what I'd come for.

'Of course not. But we were frantic to find some grazing. The situation with the equines is heart-breaking, Yori. Racing never changes its ways. Nor the breeders. Nor the meat-men. I thought I'd need to buy somewhere else close for us to live, Appleford village say, rather than Didcot— obviously.' Us— her and Henri. She must have seen a reaction though I tried to keep my face blank. 'Come by the fire and I'll tell you.'

'I'm damp still.'

'That's hide you'll be sitting on. It's been out in all weathers before it was furniture. Not my choice,' she shrugged, 'but there you are.'

I thought Geoffrey's chair was terrific, in fact I'd forgotten just how terrific, elongated and moulded to the sitter's body. I came over but chose the fire surround instead. 'Are you legal then?'

'Absolutely. When we were mucking the whole place out we found a box under a pile of rubbish— up there.' She pointed to the ceiling hatch. 'Full of old photographs of a family that lived here in the nineteen sixties! The transport foreman with a wife and child. Nobody had registered this as their home at the time but the precedent meant it could be lived in again— well, you'll understand. To me and Henri it was a miracle, being able to be on site. So— we were only near to not-quite habitable in the spring when it all happened. Your flood. The rest.' Leaning closer remade her, from the Sara I'd been watching just lately in turn-of-the-century Rhyl back into herself. And superb. Particularly sparking with enthusiasm, like this, so the huge turquoise eyes looked almost warm. 'I'm using the rest of the Pryorsfield money to buy every bit of land I can. Even blighted, it's still really expensive! I know, I know— that's because they're not making any more.' She knelt next to me smiling in triumph. 'I've just completed on a new patch along the lane. Everything is— working out!'

'Yes.' Only my mother could inherit the Severing fortune and delight in a brick shed and ex-gravel workings. 'I'm pleased to see it.' I swivelled and with a bit of cooperation, got both arms this time round her, if awkwardly. Her face fitted into a space I formed between my neck and shoulder and suddenly I felt her very bones all through my chest. She was so thin. *Breakable.* But also crackling with purpose and only settled on me the way a moth settles. Through my shirt flowers of grass, snagged in her fleece, prickled. Hay-scent filled my nostrils. Her heat was the main thing, though, Eurwen Burning, never a wife not that Tomiko would say it, or a mother. A fiery sister maybe. I always intended one day to look after her, I know that, and would never be allowed to. 'If it's what you want, well done you.'

She breathed, 'I know!' onto my skin.

Was I paying her off for Henri by saying, 'I'm sorry about Sara,' and waited for a response and held her tight while I thought she might be going to cry?

She didn't. It got us closer, anyway. We had a normal for us chat – neutral topics. She asked chocolate or coffee? had to be reminded, and went to make tea. I tried to keep my mind from filling with past scenes because I wanted no distractions from the buzz of *me,* in her home – not exactly *at home*, but hearing her make tea. Smelling hay on the towel. I was grilled down the front from her fire but cold down my back and it was a thousand per cent better than comfort.

I counted colours in the floor. Grey, coral, black and white stripes, a cinnamon shade— quite amateurish and with not enough over-patterning. A puzzling copy. 'Henri did it,' she said making me jump. 'While I was out. I saw someone else's a long time ago. That was by a real artist and properly done, therefore— and I remember thinking I *like* that! I must have shown the image to Henri and last month I came back from Benson— mm, the Campbells had called us about a cat stuck on the weir. It took the three of us all day to get him. Then there was finding a vet on duty, bringing the cat back here. Fallen in!' The irises glinted. 'Thrown in, I'd say, wouldn't you?'

'I don't know.'

'Don't you? You must be walking around in a dream then. Anyway after all that there's Henri, painting away like mad.' She dropped onto one of the sofas and folded her legs up as part of the same graceful action. 'Yori, stop perching and sit down!'

I joined her about to say, *I know about the floor. It was Neil Rix, the artist, Tomiko's friend. I must've seen it when I was baby! Before*— but as always, she was too quick. 'Where are you going to sleep?'

Fair question. I was here at my own request— Could I come and see you, talk to you? 'On this.'

'Too short. Not you! The sofa.'

'In Gramps Geoffrey's chair then.'

'Are you hungry?'

'Uh-uh.' My last food had been a slimy hummus baguette, eaten somewhere south of Leamington Spa. I was starving my stomach said but I wanted to stay like this, me turned to her, Eurwen not— just right for studying her profile, the high forehead and the very fine upper nasal arch and then that slight scoop toward the nosetip. The shading beneath a cheekbone. And when her hand went up to cup the point of her chin, I surprised us both by taking hold. Tomiko's jade ring was loose and mobile beyond the index knuckle and none from Henri. I smoothed her fingers out on my palm as you would a sheet of paper. All the nails were clean but untended and a purple brand at the heel of her thumb could've been a bitemark. I took a deep breath and said, 'Sara being found was a shock. But you seem to've taken it pretty calmly. I'm only going by Josh who—'

But she mimed *No!* and then choked and this time she did cry, going from perfectly normal to caved in— the speed of change was a stunner in itself. Suddenly the fingers were trembling but she pulled them away, a signal she wasn't wanting anything from me. Then a shock wave ran through her and her voice when it came back was hoarse. *I always— knew that she'd gone— that we'd never— ever— see her again— that everything was going to be different from now on— Dad couldn't make his mind up— and Gramps Geoffrey— and Fleur— wore themselves— out with worry— at it— but— but not me— because—* Deep breath— *I knew. I'd killed her.* The look was somebody running on their sword.

I haven't done her justice. I've fallen into Sara's trap, describing things she says and does, the Western way, as if it made her. A betrayal— Sara realised that. Eurwen's like nobody. She's not my mother or only technically, not my sister, certainly not my friend and we have nothing in common. But I'm the ugly little boy who lived for the goddess and I worship her. Sometimes it's a feeling makes you think you've swallowed a hot coal but there it is. Remember though, we hadn't talked for five years and we still probably couldn't be alone together for long – because what *can* you do when a tiger's sharing the cave? and wearing stripes doesn't work and begging to know what uniform she wants you in gets no answer? She wasn't Japanese— but she'd still managed to beat my father into a two-dimensional on-screen extra. She had power. *She* would never kill herself. Actually, seeing her like this, I couldn't believe she'd ever die. Sitting in her don't-care room I had a vision of myself grown old and keeling over one day still at work and they'd bury my ashes under a building I hope I wasn't too ashamed of— and there unchanged Eurwen would be, telling whoever turned up, *Just to-oo morbid! Under his own creation? I'm glad I don't have to live here.* She said, 'The number of times I must have heard "famous Oxford historian's last day in Rhyl!" It's the only thing I'm an expert on. Your grandmother walked out around ten in the morning, she took the clothes she wore and no money apart from any coins there may have been in her pockets and no keys. But one book by somebody she'd been at college with – she took a bloody useless history book *but no money* – what does that suggest? Oh and Dad's coat. She wore Dad's oldest, grubby coat. You don't need to be a genius, do you, to decode it— what she was telling us? So I *should* be able to stay calm by now.' She rubbed her dry cheeks in a way that was meant to say Over it, you see? 'Not as if—' she shrugged.

'I didn't mean to upset you.'

'No?' The switch to hostile was instant. I had radar set for this mood. 'Well, let's take it as read shall we?' A long pause though. She didn't take it as read. 'If Dad has become a wreck, and we have spoken by the way, that only shows he kept hoping. And I never did. Not possible, you see. We were linked, her and me. When I was small she'd describe knowing when I was ill, odd incidents like that. And then, on *the day,* my birthday, I was in Jay's kitchen, late afternoon. I can describe it exactly—' was that a tremor? – 'Jay's scraping carrots to make a cake, there I am crouched on the floor, trying to feed a bird with an eyedropper, and suddenly I thought, My mother has died. It was as clear and evident as Jay at the sink and Tomiko across the room sketching— and the starling in my hands with its heart going crazy.'

'But how?' Before she could explain, if she could, I followed through with, 'and who did you tell?'

'Nobody. *Nobody!* I carried on trying to get the bird's beak to stay apart without hurting it, to get the sugar water down. You have to use a fingernail in the corner, very gently.' She sighed. Maybe it hadn't worked. 'Then I stood up and put the starling back in the cage. I said to Tomiko, I'll write to my father and you'll have to take it.'

I can recite what you wrote, I wanted to boast.

'*But* then there was composing the thing! We had a lot of tries, between us. Not that he was much help. The afternoon dragged on and then he said No writing! Not needed.' She smiled at her own impression of him. "I will go to your mother and father." That's what he thought.'

'You didn't let Tomiko in on this?' (Who would probably have believed you though I'm having trouble. With Sara there was always the drink to fall back on, but *Eurwen?* Though I'd reassess her story later, for the moment it changed her and I resented the slightest change. I liked my mother inside her sharp black outline.)

'We had a huge row which was a relief— a distraction, at least. Then we made up and Tomiko said things would get better, now I'd decided. We could write down— well, whatever was necessary in the morning. Jay gave me something to take, Jay always had something, and we slept on it. But things were blunted, next day. And I started having doubts.'

'You knew Sara was in Rhyl?'

'We did.' She shook the red hair and swept it back from her face till the skin stretched. 'It's a long story. Tomiko actually *saw* her. As did Jay and then Neil but with Tomiko it made everything worse afterwards. So— I could have texted, I could have phoned but for some stupid reason, I stayed fixated on writing— and the *next* day there was Mum's picture on the news. Missing. Dad had got it up straight away, policeman you know. And so I'd put things in the letter Tomiko took that were already lies by then. Pretending. Because, honestly, I'd felt her die.'

Anyone would pity Eurwen for what was to come next. Constant reruns of 'Oxford historian's last, etc' activated even

Renate Desmond, her old headteacher, among the other sympathisers. But for the daughter of a dead mother it was already a case of the words crossed out, the calls not made. That text. She'd calculated less than ten characters could've turned Sara aside from her walk. Then six. Am OK – E

'I never managed fewer.'

'But nobody saw what happened! She *could've* been alive all this time. There's not a single recorded sighting of her on November 17th —'

Like Josh, even stricken she was alert. 'Where did you get that from?'

'I've been reading up.'

She pursed her lips, dismissive, as always, of every POV not her own. 'Then don't. *They* told themselves she'll be back, it will mend.' She expanded on the damaging consequences of Josh never quite getting going again with Meg– keeping Sara's spot open? Gramps Geoffrey hanging on to Tackley Close like a limpet, finally letting only to single women. No children, no pets. 'It had to stay pristine!' Fleur's way of mourning had been to search the faces in Sara's Oxford on a regular march that started at the Taylorian Institute, skirted the Radcliffe Camera, kissed the pavement outside All Souls, then took a sharp left and over Magdalen Bridge and so down to St Clement's College. Where she'd eat her sandwich under the Thomasina Mulberry Tree. I knew it well. I must've gone with her dozens of times, unaware we were on a mission. And it was Fleur's grief brought Eurwen to a stop.

I said, 'You mustn't feel guilty because—' Convincing her was my feeble aim. But she was disagreeing before I could finish. My intentions may be exactly as my name promised— Proper, Dutiful, Well-Motivated or whatever— but the strategy? Impractical. I didn't have the materials and they weren't making any more.

'Why mustn't I? She killed herself thanks to me. People always say, oh it was years ago— you were somebody else then. Henri says that. *I* wasn't, not in the essentials. I feel the same person I am now, went away with Tomiko because he'd do anything for me. And I was wanting— such *a lot*. Instead of wanting others. It's no more complicated than that. Dad tried. Talk to your mother, he said. I can't do it but she loves *you*. She'll come round. Then home you go and back to school for her sake if not your own. Give it another year. As if! He couldn't cope. I couldn't have coped in his position. I was so—' another lost ending. 'Then he started saying we would have to invite her up and sort things out. But I told him if she comes here I'll run— again. He was *furious*.'

Yet he hadn't invited her. She'd arrived. By which time Eurwen was pregnant and fled with my father. 'Did Josh ever hit you?'

'What? *Of course not!* Where did that come from?'

'No idea. Sorry.'

'I remember his telling me it was time to grow up. And I did— just too late. I loved her back, though.' She searched inwards, shaking her head. 'She was— I see now she was as good as she was able to be. No one knew what was going wrong for her. But it was *bad* and it started before Dad left and it wasn't getting better. No one could help. You think they didn't try? And yet she was a sort of celebrity.'

'She still is.'

'Yes. But you had to experience it in real time. Do you know, even Henri and her sister, they were followers? If Mum had questioned them herself instead of sending Fleur I— mm-m, they'd have given me up. And as for all the rest—' More past movies were playing behind her eyes. 'Usually they'd be older than me, undergrads. They'd make their first approach, awestruck, in the Marks and Spencer's queue or Blackwell's.

Once I remember I'd been to her talk at her old college and we went afterwards and ate cherries in Headington Hill Park, throwing cherries to the squirrels. And this man came and just sat down by us. Almost touching, you know? There was vacant bench too, but no, which made it— disturbing. His manner was off-key, she could see I didn't like it. Very casually she got up and gave me a tug and the instant we were out of earshot she said— you'll have heard this, 'I do not love thee Doctor Fell/ Why I don't I cannot tell.' It was brilliant. Spot on! Then we got the giggles just as three girls, really pretty girls, recognised *Sara Meredith*. Oh, they were *majorly* into the book, into Thomasina, into *her*. She listened to them and then, 'Thank-you for that,' she said. 'And your timing. My daughter and I were just sharing a joke at male expense.' She could always say the right thing to the Thomasina groupies. Even when a nuisance.'

'She didn't like being respected for her book?'

Eurwen gave the question more thought than it seemed to merit. 'It's odd but now if you press me I'd say she *didn't* care for it— totally not. And she became more uncomfortable as time went on. '

'Why? Why would she?'

'I don't know! She hadn't written anything else for years by then. Maybe that was—' but the wasted attempt was soon over. '*I don't know*. We never talked about *history*. She was very guarded – I realise now – and she gave less and less away. Of course she had to be quite clever about the drinking so only Gramps and Dad and I suspected.'

'And Fleur.'

That made her pause. 'And Fleur told you?' *Not exactly.* 'That's a surprise— you see, Sara Meredith was special. It was as if you had to use other standards for her— another reason why my running off wouldn't matter, I thought. I couldn't take the books and Oxford and history and reading and the people next door popping round to tell us about more bloody books they'd been reading. Hated the lot. And poor Fleur— 'Darling, when you're older you'll appreciate all this.' Wasn't happening for me Fleur! And still it's not. I'm more Dad. And there's *more* terrible luck. He and she, they *fell* in love, literally. They had to let themselves go— for each other.'

'I think so.'

'When I was small she used to describe how they'd met, how it happened because I liked hearing. But it was a sick joke played on them. Love? They hardly spoke the same language. Nature never meant them to be together. Then there was the drink! Don't ask me about that. No one seemed know why, not Geoffrey, not even that therapist he came up with to treat her 'depression'. Dad jumped ship— to Rhyl. She was never going there.' (Saying But she did! would put me on the wrong side.) 'And I was *odious*— if I really wanted to hurt her I'd let fly at Thomasina. How nobody could be that wonderful. Always seemed to work, my telling Mum her precious Thomasina was a fairy story, that I'd like to dig the Peerless Girl up and give her a kicking. Henri reminds me of it now and then, if required.' No wavering— she was steely again which was something to be grateful for.

It sounded a warning though. The Henri-and-Me chat might be overdue and whatever I'd come down here for it wasn't that. As an adult I could see how Henri Fortun had cultivated a part of Eurwen's character, her one strip of weakness based on guilt, for her own gain. Of course my existence isn't appreciated. Not just because the first Sunday she was invited to tea on Pryorsfield's terrace, I kicked a football straight at her head and our relationship has gone downhill since. 'You're alike, you and Sara,' I said quickly. 'Though you're actually more—' I never got to tell her what.

'I looked too much like my mother!' she almost spat. 'That was our problem. She kept seeing herself as everyone did and it was so far from the truth. The Rhyl me was much closer.'

I couldn't win this. 'And when did you find out about—?' I tapped my own chest.

'Mm-m. Well, I met Tomiko at the start of the summer. We'd go to Jay and Neil's and one night we stayed on. My decision. That would've been a few days before she arrived. Everyone assumed I must have known I was pregnant by then because it made a great alibi. Tragic but understandable— yes? Even *Tomiko!* He wanted to be completely responsible.'

'So— you weren't?'

She laughed as if it was nothing. 'No! You're as bad as he is. I mean look at his *art*—' she made it sound like a vice, '—mania more like. For years, nothing but pictures of the water. Because of her. Sato Tomiko has to take it all on himself!'

Thinking of anything but what I was saying, I told her, 'He's given that name away. It's somebody else now. So I'm not sure what we're meant to call him.'*

'Oh-h for God's sake!'

Mama Rotti had finally shut up. I was aware of the crackle from inside the woodburner and some appliance humming in the next room. Eurwen seemed to have run down as well— she'd put all the available information she thought she had out for me. And unless you bring it up, I realised, she won't add anything. Less tired, Yori,

less in thrall to the goddess, you'd have picked her up on the one new thing you'd learned tonight. Instead— Time for you to clear the air and do her some good, I decided.

—so Sara came to find her daughter or wait for her return. But Josh's house proved too much. She cooked food for him to come home to— she mentions that, though never any cleaning.

*See Appendix D

Meantime, he almost convinced her you were safe and they'd get you back. In her imagination— when she drank— she could see a new life stretched out. When she didn't, it disappeared again. Meanwhile they went for walks like the old days. They talked. Not allowed when only one of you thinks they love. He might've murdered her by giving her hope and then seeming to take it away. But she was in the wrong too. If he's what she wanted she should have tried harder. There's never nothing to do— instead of going out to kill yourself, I mean. Can't we agree on that? I've come to get her story straight and let us both off. Josh too—

'Do you still have the scarf?' I asked. I'm reporting my idiotic change of subject because it turned out Smart Bet. I had been about to make another mistake.

She was into her own thoughts, like me. 'Mm? What? What scarf?'

'Blue-green, a big silk square. With a decoration at the edges. You used to wear it when I was small.'

She frowned. 'Dad must have bought it for me, I think? That was years ago.' Irritation now. '*No*, not any more. It's long gone. Yori, you really should come back to Oxford.' But the mood had lightened. 'All that *past* blowing in the streets!'

Being mocked was a thrill when it hinged on her knowledge of me— and I might still have told her I was putting together 'Sara in Rhyl.' But she hadn't read the journals, or the scarf would mean something. Of course she hadn't read them, *dolt!* Josh, having sense and being a father, would see them as not suitable for a teenage girl struggling with sex, loss, birth. For Eurwen all the courses of adult life had come along on one platter. And by she was old enough and due some re-education— I thought of the bitter morning on the beach, the chrysanthemums successfully launched but the electricity still discharging over my head— Eurwen was about to take off. She and Josh had had less contact than Tomiko and me ever since. 'Rhyl's got a past,' I defended it.

But she brooded on about Oxford as if I hadn't spoken, how she'd never want to live in the city again, how it changes but it doesn't, not really, because it thinks it shouldn't have to. Her words were hypnotic, reminding me of sleep. I had to keep blinking and then the floor's colours crept and overshot the joints, off-white curdled into adjacent indigo. Next thing, the plaster walls started to pulsate, as did Eurwen herself with that hair rippling at every movement. Her voice seemed to fill a room stretched corridor-thin and getting thinner and the only fixed point was the cabinet I'd rejected in a lifeless Pryorsfield— *Decide what you're keeping Yori. I know! But it's all yours. There's a mountain of furniture and the ceramics— and I can't count how many pictures. Fleur said you had a favourite. You must have that, if nothing else—* She'd known it was more valuable than everything else put together, of course she had. But to show gratitude now was an admission of the lack before. Pleading thirst I heaved myself up and out into what I assumed was a kitchen. It was and vast. Bigger than the living room— a former canteen? Never meant to be part of dwelling, its refit with composites and steel appliances wasn't at war with a gravel-pit pedigree. And it was where she actually lived, you could see by the chaos. The tops were crammed with packets and cartons and it wouldn't be for human consumption, in fact I recognised the catfood – still loyal to her usual brand – and the net of misshapen horse carrots spilling from a cupboard reminded me of cake and Jay. There was a refectory table long enough to seat an entire workforce at but catering seemed to have given way to her office. Against the far wall a workstation held every gadget, old and new and even then there was room for more chairs around the Pryorsfield elm coffer, a pony bridle thrown down on lid. And other-than-Eurwen's possessions were all over. Two raincoats for instance on the back of the outside door. A waxed fedora you could easily imagine topping red hair. Its companion bucket hat had Henri's blunt face hovering in space under it, an illusion convincing as the Animal Farm sign. And Sara Meredith stepping out.

I popped three **A**'s at a go under the running tap, feeling both exhausted and an intruder and checked messages to bring me back to myself. The first four, no five stacked up were all from Glenn— all ending 𝄞 ?

　𝄞 ? 𝄞 ?
　𝄞 ? 𝄞 ? 𝄞 ?

I don't need to hear. The opera's cancelled. I don't need to hear. Your parents killed Sara, Yori. Leave it at that. Don't need to—

Chapter 30

It has to be perfect.

The construction must be practical, the meaning open and readable by anyone who uses it. Material is crucial. Not just in itself. Consider its provenance, the connections. With each element immaculate, the whole can be transformed, cut free from the act of making.

He's reading from an old report, recently obtained, on his chosen quarry: *Welsh slate, for hardness, is unsurpassed... The Ancients sometimes roofed with Marble... the expense of the material... cost of labour... of no account. The use of Tiles for Roofing purposes may be based upon the fact that they are more artistic than Slates, but those who have built with Tiles, in search of the Artistic, have often found that they have grasped at the shadow and lost the substance.* Extraordinary. An auditor's report that included this sort of language. *Before iron, probably before antler and tusk, by the virtues of stone animals were killed and butchered, bellies filled. Flint, shale, slate all had their uses. They named an age.*

I sat up. Opened my eyes trying to think what day it is and what was this contraption I'm in and where am I? And *butchered?* How had that got there? *The virtues of stone* — well, OK, but *butchery?*

'Yori! Are you awake? I'm coming through.'

'Huh? Er-m-' The tartan rug turned traitor. Having covered my entire body it was not up to being pulled round the waist. A fringe caught in the chair's handle became a hitch and the reclining mechanism reversed, shot me upright. On my feet now, with the rug sarong-like, the garment undid its own knot. My mother entered the living room, palmed the switch and was treated to the sight of bare buttocks as I groped around my own ankles. 'Hang on. I'm—'

'Don't worry,' she said. On her way to the kitchen, dressed, she was wearing much the same as last night. Unless it was the same. 'You fell asleep with the light on. I had to come and do it. And that's nothing I haven't seen before.'

But perhaps she was embarrassed— it was *very* clipped North Oxford this morning. I heard the tap running, cupboards banging, speculated about whether I could get into my stiff-looking pants before she thought of returning. Just made it. My undershirt lay with spread arms raised across one sofa— shot and lifeless. No sign of trainers or jacket, though, or a belt. I was her prisoner.

'So,' she said as we sat in the kitchen, the table between us, the tea pot between us, a five year separation back between us that had smoothed over last night and turned jagged again, 'you were going to tell me what you've been up to. I guess that's why you've come.' Her hair hadn't been properly brushed out and tangled at the ends but her attitude said fully awake. 'Town Architect?'

'A joke. Senior Design Consultant, Project Forward Rhyl. I'm planning things.'

'Such as?'

'Well—' *uh, the brightness of those eyes* '—before I came away, I started a new project. *Just* got the go ahead. Yesterday. For a path.'

Thanks to Glenn's persistence last night, the subject of PalmWalk was a pleasure now and I felt like selling it. But her mouth – an unimprovable mouth, peach and open slightly, Sara had described it, and still a girl's mouth though fifty would be here in a few years— lifted at each corner. 'Oh, a *path*.' I was glad to see that mouth screened by her RSPCA hedgehog cup.

'Not just a path. Obviously. It'll be part of the regeneration scheme.' *Come on! You could manage a nod. It was your town for eight years.* 'Connecting key elements along the Promenade— from the bridge, up West Parade, then East,' I prompted. *You walked me along there. To play on the sand, to the shop— later on for my short career at school.* 'The path's important.' *That's one reason why it's important.* 'Also it's the line everybody wants to take. But things got muddled and Rhyl forgot why it was there. The beach.'

She was considering. For one heady moment I thought she was going to turn inquisitive, *These links,* say, *are they your next project?* I framed a reply. But the far side of the window it was getting naturally light. A dog barked and was joined by another and then another in a rousing dogs' chorus. She jumped to her feet almost upending my tea.

'Their breakfast's imminent.'

'I'm thinking of slate for the Walk,' I said. 'For lots of reasons. It cleaves beautifully, wafer thin if you need. But can take immense pressure. It's *formed* under pressure and it's local. Six good sources in North Wales alone, still. I've found a really special one over in Pantdreiniog.' All my correct pronunciation got me was an *oh-h!* She had her boots on now, was looking around for something to pull over her grey T and leggings, the eyes still showing amusement as she searched at this half-Japanese that could do Welsh. She could've passed for sixteen. 'There's two seams of it, one purple, one blue. I like that, two shades from the same quarry. I thought mix them, you can get the feel of their layers, their nature, from something like that. Mix them, cut them absolutely exactly, of course, then—' she pounced on some fallen object behind the industrial-size waste bin. '—there's the other aspect of it, the one where you're thinking slate, yes, protective,' my gesture was a steeple, up in the air, 'but *whoa!*' Now a halt signal.

'Look. It's being used for something under your feet. A foundation.'

A sweater, old and very shaggy, was what she straightened up with. 'Sounds very, um, good. Your shoes and things are down here by the way. Are you coming to help? In the yard?'

'Of course. I'll get something else on.'

I sacrificed stretches and lunges (again) but not showering and a shave in the newly-installed bathroom, the tiling not grouted and the shower the latest Watermiser model. When I emerged it was to stop-dead facing the room directly opposite with a door just open a crack— into the only part of the bungalow I hadn't entered. So far. Hers and Henri's. I reached out to give it a push but didn't. Why Henri of all people? Apart from her being smart and patient and optimistic and even-tempered and funny, I mean. Who could smile when hit full in the face by a football. *Eurwen, forget it – it was an accident – and anyway, time we were off!*

And an achiever. Henri Fortun, activist, zoologist, journalist, spokesperson, a professional 'talker back', as that Camille woman would have it, who'd loved my mother since forever in the only way she'd been able to be loved, with no interest on your investment expected. Or paid a lot of the time, knowing Eurwen. Yeah, Yori, who could explain the attraction?

I let go the door and went and found Eurwen out under a no-colour sky smudged with white. The yard was wide enough to accommodate a truck's turning circle but tree seedlings and weeds showed up crack-lines in the hard standing and she'd need to decide soon how much to resurface and how much to green. Some planting would improve the aspect from her living quarters which at the moment was flat, dull and worn out whereas she'd been able to view Jarn Mound above a sea of tree tops and once the Irish Sea itself from an attic. But not a bit bothered at having her environment degraded, she was cheerfully going about her dog-feeding. It was almost done in fact. While she gathered empty bowls from the crazed concrete, dogs of every size and sort milled around her. Nothing pale, though, and nothing long-coated. She sighed when I drew attention to this – told me these sleeker, dark ones were hardest to rehome. Lighter and fluffy were prized. There were a dozen at least I estimated and no identifiable breeds among the pack, just thickset or leggy, square-headed or tapering. One tragic-eyed monster stood high as her hip bones, another low tubular thing skittered around on two hind limbs and a single front, like a trick it kept on performing and you kept on expecting it to fail.

It shrank from me touching. 'How many have you got?'

That earned me a glare. 'They come and go. Now Bilbo here – the lab cross – he's down the road on Monday. We've found him a home. He's for Henley-on-Thames and going up in the world. Good adopters are like gold dust.'

'Hard to believe. I guess you're after a dependable maybe older couple—?'

'Mm, yes.'

'With a big country house and, oh, the income to support—a dog, say?'

'Ideally.'

The dogginess intensified, a corn chip and motel bed combo with a hint of nettles. They weaved their way around behind me which I resented, hitting the backs of my knees, circling and jostling for Eurwen's notice, nosing her. Three-legs showed its teeth. The monster whimpered. Otherwise the canine tension became sub-vocal and almost worse than their racket. Something seemed about to happen. 'What next?'

She smiled properly, fully, this time, obviously content and in no hurry and sensing it, the animals dispersed in two and threes. A wrestling game started with some shoulder charges. I dodged away. 'I don't know,' she said, enjoying it, enjoying herself. 'Whatever you like. I do the chickens, usually.'

Out in the dull morning her face was a pale oval above her dark sweater, with every ingredient familiar, the slight freckling, the perfect symmetry prevented by that small mole contained in one eyebrow nine out of ten people wouldn't notice. The best-known features in the world, mine included. In step, we walked from the modern timber kennels and the wired dog runs, left agape – I resisted suggesting we round the dogs up and call a halt to playtime – to our next appointment in an older, brick outhouse. Set at right angles it formed a third boundary to the yard and had been a store for some useful commodity in the gravel business. There weren't any other structures showing above the shaggy privet that hemmed in the fourth side of the enclosure and cut off further views. 'So do you like living here?'

'Oh, yes.'

What did I expect— no? In fact, what did I want? Never mind all that about passing for sixteen. She'd had me at sixteen, a child-project she probably never tendered for but found herself pulled into anyway— and managed to complete. She'd produced me when she didn't need to, at sixteen, half my own age, well nearly— now I was bending the numbers her way. But who'd have ever put money on Eurwen seeing it through?

Not me. Not someone who'd stayed away for five years— because I hadn't allowed things to lapse or been sidetracked. I'd been keeping apart. So you're here now under cover of a tidying up job, Yori? Or to get a response, even if it means opening an old wound?

I was Bad Son.

Shame. Like a ton of gravel. I took her image in from a few metres off, bent over the doorlock, childlike in the way she braced her whole body as she fought it— I could hear her hard-breathing anger from this distance. Just as all those times as a child, now it kept me from going forward. Doing the obvious by saying let me have a go. Instead while she fiddled with a rusted finger-latch I surveyed where I'd come to after dark. The bungalow's pretty much as expected, gaunt, nineteen-thirties buff brickwork, every course of which needed raking out and repointing as part of a complete refurb. New lights would have to be made to order to fit five identical punctuations of glazing— make that new frames. The list wrote itself. Three replacement downspouts. A fan-shaped stain unfurled beneath a length of soffit added of its own accord, 'and guttering'.

'That's a good slate roof you've up there, anyway. Uncommon for this area—'

'If you say so.' She was really labouring with the latch but when I leaned over and did it then grabbed the bottom part of a stable door, she snapped, 'Don't open it any further! What d'you think you're doing, Yori? If they get out this way, the dogs will have them.'

'Really?'

'*Really.*'

We ducked into the poultry fustiness, poorly illuminated and made unbearable by the mismatched hens' frantic dashes through sawdust. Their noise wasn't up to the dogs' level but – higher-pitched and madder – it was as horrible. Eurwen of course clucked soothingly. My eyes prickled and then a violent sneeze threatened to knock me backwards.

'Try not to scare the feathers off them, will you? It's winter next week.'

'I was thinking—'

'Open that far hatch. They'll go out themselves.'

'I could come down here again for—'

'Well you've found your way once.'

'—a couple of weeks, maybe—'

'*Fully open!* Let them see the outside. Now get further away. You're scaring them. Further!'

'—and do repairs.' The chickens formed up into a squad and made a break for the outside. Slamming the hatch down with force enough to threaten the hinges repaid me with a finale of squawks. I made for fresh air myself, holding my breath, desperate for the yard.

She was waiting, her expression dry. 'There's no cockerel now.'

'What happened?'

'The fox! Probably the vixen that was in the lane last night, just before you got here— when I was looking out.'

'You were looking out?'

We swished back though a drift of fallen leaves, litter from a shrub well-established up against the kitchen wall, an elder whose roots I could feel strangling the drains beneath each tread. She put an arm through mine. Any minute now, she reminded me the *girls* would be dropped off. It was my turn to smile – *Of course* – being one of the things we'd talked about till the early hours. *No never lonely. Henri's here.* Pleased that it was only *most of the time*, I hadn't paid attention to her next sentence. *I'm so busy and there are the girls.* She'd gone on to name them, Zadie or Dodie or whatever she was called, the one who just loved ponies and donkeys— the other was mad keen to walk dogs. My imagination, or was that a vehicle now jolting along the track I'd cycled in blackness, losing faith in Eurwen's welcome?

Why had it taken me so long? Why become addicted to missing her instead of just seeing her? Why never sugar and always salt?

Forget everything. Forget Sara even because for now Eurwen was as much of her as I wanted. Again and under her roof. 'That's good Welsh slate up there,' I repeated. 'A thirty-degree pitch, probably copper-nailed. At least that's all right.'

She left to do messaging. I lurked outside. It was definitely clearing. Though the temperature would linger at seven or eight degrees till the sun got stronger, it was absolutely still, a rarity back home. The fine day was forecast in one corner of the screen, but I was looking at Glenn's big ruddy face. 'Amazing huh?' he smirked. 'Did I tell you last night? Casino Pigalle made more per person in Rhyl than *anywhere else* in UK last year. We're top at something! Us! That's how we got the grant. So how fuckin' long are you slackin' down there?'

Lovely Linda Darnell or Cassie Pigalle or Tess or whoever, had come across after all. The only condition being a pair of mega Casino lightboards had to stand either end of PalmWalk. I could live with that— one of my best girls to start and finish, I could certainly live with that. And it opened up a complete new plotline for me and Tess. 'Not sure.' She'd just need to be incorporated, another design challenge. 'Not long.'

'So that mug? You worked it out yet? Na— 'course not! What they do is—'.

'I've nearly got it. But can't talk now.'

'Hey! Yori. Don't you wanna know what that boat's called? William Jones's?'

'Has he launched? Send it. Yes— of course I do. *What?*'

'Tell you when I see you,' he said.

See you later Eurwen was promising somebody at her workstation, still in her heavy woollen and boots. I didn't want to spy and risk identifying Henri, —*and don't worry!* she said, full of sympathy for somebody, *We'll fit them in. We will! And we can always—*

I darted through into the hall and came back with the gift. Her fingers still worked but she glanced up. 'All done.'

Did she see the box, me waiting with the box, my hands lining the box up along the edge of the table? 'I've brought you this.'

'Which is?'

'Just something.'

I'd already stripped away sheets of shred-wrap. She decided to play. Now she was looking at the box I'd made specially from rag-board and lacquered to an egg-shell finish. Long and deep, not wide, it could contain a musical instrument or a weapon. What she had to do was touch the button which said OPEN! But she drummed her finger-tips. No wonder she wound animals up just by being next to them. 'Is it going to leap out at me now?'

'No way would I—'

'All right.'

Finally she pressed the button. Four sides fell back each taking a segment of the top with it. A 1:2000 scale model of PalmWalk sat there, the thick band of ultramarine I'd used for water standing out instantly, then gold for sand, and last the emerald way itself. Tiny resin structures along it, all pastel shades and deep ochre, showed a level of detail way past the skill of a Sato Tomiko, aka Soon To Be Decided, sorry *otosan*. It was the sort of detail you couldn't have produced even a couple of years ago and I'd bought myself the new ruinously expensive printer especially for this. Yet in among miniature planting my buildings were what the eye worked hardest to pick out – exactly how it would be in years to come. 'That's West Parade—' she said, 'ah, it's your path!'

'The first half. Toughest part.' I was all prepared to conduct her from Blue Bridge to Old Woolworths—

'Very good!' The tip of one finger hovered over shrubs the size of lavender sprigs across from a pygmy hotel, now restored in all its lemon and terracotta glory. It had reminded Sara of Keble College once, or a Keble in some parallel, blasted Oxford. The trees I could've told Eurwen were native sea buckthorn, *Hippophae rhamnoides*, and a lot cheaper than palms. Which was why nearly three hundred would be needed to fill out the exotics along the route. (Oh and tougher. If we ever did have another frost in Rhyl *they* wouldn't need replacing.) 'Thank-you. For the model. It's very— seducing.' *Yes*. I was ecstatic with the word. That was exactly what it should be. 'You were always making them when you were little.'

'Not like this—' but the vile dogs restarted and she jumped up to go look and, catching one edge of the table, sent a seismic tremble down West Parade and a mini typhoon sweeping through the buckthorns. An omen. I steadied the base and pushed it further into the middle for safety.

'I haven't hurt it,' she said.

'No.'

'It's not alive.'

We never got things right. 'Come on,' she was at the open door. 'Can I look later? Here's—' the rest was drowned out by the worst din so far. I tried to make myself heard and failed. The teenage girl leading a donkey around the corner of the henhouse thought it hilarious. She nodded and mouthed *Hiya* to Eurwen, ignored me, and tethered the animal to a ring in the wall just as it let out another ear-splitting two-syllable bellow.

Crook, the old enemy.

'Yori, he remembers you!' To the girl she said, 'This is my son. Can you believe it, he learnt to ride on Crook?' She went forward to start the petting. 'You loved him, didn't you?'

Crook. His withers bone protruded as if threatening to burst out of the skin and the stick legs now housed knees swollen by arthritis like bulges in lead pipe. The hooves that had been prone to deliver sharp kicks to my shins were ridged and flaking away. The chocolate muzzle was grizzled. He stared fixedly at Eurwen while the girl gently ran a soft brush over his ribbyness. Clouds of hair and scurf from each stroke danced in the sudden patch of sunshine and my mother stepped into it with a morsel of something to be slipped under his hideous smoker's teeth. They ground together while she ran each of the ridiculous ears through her fingers. The whole creature was rank. 'We adore him don't we, Zade? He's a great age— we're not really sure what— but even for a donkey he's veteran-class. Isn't he clever, Yori? He *knows* you.'

'I know him.'

How was he here? But of course Eurwen had kept track of him. Crook, the undeserving old devil, got a tickle from his attendant who was dressed almost identically to Eurwen and was as slim. A dark girl, she was a prettier Kailash, but unlike Kailash would've been, wasn't scowling at the donkey, scurf laid down on her clothes, nor the way he turned his big head and used her body as a scratching post. In fact it looked like a sensual exchange.

'Everybody dotes on Crook. Jay was asking about him only—'

'When?'

Eurwen rolled her eyes. 'When I saw her in Rhyl of course.' She went ahead, away from the house to a solid galvanised gate that let out of the yard. It swung easily on oiled hinges and she was through. 'Come and see! Feel how warm it's getting. A pity to be in. I've not forgotten your model— as soon as we get back, I promise. It'll be soft underfoot but the grass is short—'

'Wait!' My sharpness made Crook snort. 'Just tell me, will you? You came to Rhyl?' But she would *never* stop— off now onto stony pasture that widened to the size of a football pitch. The hedge surround here had been recently 'laid', raw wounds from the blade standing out, flayed bark hanging in ribbons. Then the sun broke through a swipe of cloud again and dewdrops glittered like gemstones on the back of Eurwen's head and I had no choice but follow if Zade wasn't to be part of the conversation. 'When did you?'

That exaggerated raised-hands *oh please!* thing she did before relenting. 'Jay still lives there. Neil's long gone. May be dead, I think.' *Why would I care?* 'She married somebody very different afterwards and went to work for the coroner's office. Janine Preece? In fact she must be retiring soon. But she's still selling her mushrooms!' Getting no response – ur-rgh, my face! nothing I could do about it— she tried to pass all this off as trivial. 'Oh there's *llym* as Jay would say. Don't be hard on me Yori, when for once I did the right thing. No, no— listen first. Keep walking. It's good for us. I always get on better walking, not sitting. Dad's the same. Watch there—' I let her steer me away from a deep mud-filled rut. 'I heard about Mum being found, probably when you did. Jay called. I didn't get in touch because believe it or not, I couldn't. I just couldn't. I had no idea what I'd say. Give me some credit, Yori. Everything I told you last night was true. It wasn't news that her *body* had been found— rather than her, you know? But it still hurt. A physical pain.'

'That's what Tomiko thought.'

'Yes, he would. We were quite close at one time, believe it or not.'

I ignored the sarcasm. 'Right. But *Rhyl?*'

'The next day, after I'd heard, as soon as I could arrange things for the animals, I travelled up there. As luck wouldn't have it, Henri was away with the vehicle, so Jay met me at the station and— but it wasn't a good visit. Jay's still Jay. She asked about you. But *the town!*' Did she have any clue as to how she was mirroring Sara, in tone, gesture, the tilt of the chin? 'And then, by the time I came to see you—'

'I'd gone to Ireland.'

Yet another bigger field through another industrial gate— in contrast to the area round the bungalow the grazing here was well-maintained. Aggregate floored the entrances and any thinner runs of hedge were lined with post and rail. A pair of almost white draught horses cropped the turf in here. As they mowed their hooves came off the floor unwillingly and thumped back down like foundry hammers so you expected to feel the shock. From this distance they were quite picturesque against the green background— if you liked that sort of thing.

'That's Ant and Dec,' Eurwen said at my shoulder. 'It's a joke! Ant and Dec were two very little men on the television when I was small who— never mind. Don't look so serious.'

We followed the progress of the horses that, even I had to admit, had great dignity and presence despite coats dull with damp and stained with earth. I found it hard to picture them heaving their great weight back up having once lain down. Following each tear/crunch they'd step forward almost in unison into a mist of their own making and great dark eyes checked us out— we were no more than dogs to them, puny, possibly dangerous. 'You were in Rhyl,' I accused her.

'To touch the bones. I had to. Surely you can understand?' She shivered. 'I did come to see you but—'

'I was with Josh.'

'Which was probably for the best.' The Eurwen that swept in and out like a squall was back and I couldn't trust myself even to agree with her. 'I don't do lamentation. You were very kind on the phone and we said it all then, didn't we? *So—* everything you can see between where we stand and the river is mine. There's been a lot of machinery on in the past and we're still trying to sort the drainage out— Oh Yori, your face! What's the matter? Worried about the inheritance?'

'Hardly,' I reminded her. But things were edgy and I wasn't sure why. Or she was right and I did resent her squandering— not money but time and energy and attention on *this*. Difficult, inconvenient, uncooperative, anarchic animals. It had puzzled Sara as well, Eurwen's championing their cause. Not with sentimentality, either, but more like the ferocity of a guerrilla leader. Nothing in the family gene-pool had prepared them for that.

'We may as well do the circuit.' She chattered on. Across and along— I was offered a look through the hedge of a wired-in, steep-sided hole, half-filled with last night's milky runoff. 'Ah— nothing on there today,' she said balanced on top of the wooden stile. When she made way, I saw the nature of the land changed radically here. The industrial agriculture that's taken over the county isn't picturesque but what we stepped into now was a Marscape, a plateau more extensive than the sum of all we'd walked through so far, a rough bowl of maybe ten hectares— and literally Martian from the prevailing ferrous oxide tint. The crater bottom was scattered with metal piping in lengths and various lumps of complex metallic objects that I couldn't classify but had been parts of either a single huge machine or a medium-sized processing plant. There were also what must be hundreds of corrugated iron sheets in the process of crumbling to rust. It was virtually stripped of vegetation and the odd tuft of bile-yellow grass explained why. At the extent of vision a chainlink fence seemed to mark out my mother's kingdom but the closest concrete posts were rotten and her security non-existent. Three kilometres away, Didcot Power Park, having cheered up my last night's ride, now poked into a sky wide as Rhyl's. The only other vertical was the falling-down sectional barn that – if he'd lived – Egon Schiele might've been tempted to sketch and colour. It was his palate and his mood. 'Well this is the awful bit,' she said, trying to speed me up. A handful of crows flapped from their posts at our intrusion, complaining. Nothing else lived here.

I stopped and toed a corrugated sheet. 'What did the environmental report say? More importantly, what was their estimate? For clean-up and de-tox?'

'Space is space.'

I'd landed a hit. 'You mean you just went ahead and *bought it?*'

'There was very little else around. And I wanted it. We'd found nothing too terrible.'

'Well that's lucky.'

Don't tease the bear. 'Yes! We'll get it back. Henri's convinced.'

Good for Henri. Once through Scrapmetal Meadow, it was a relief to be onto a pure sloping gravel bed that ended in a flooded pit, a real lake this time. Eurwen stopped to stare, biting her lower lip. The stark edge showed gouges down to a grey subsoil where the last huge machine had left off. She said, 'The water's incredibly deep.'

I picked up a rock and lobbed it in and got the muted splat of a wet mop hitting a floor before the surface recongealed.

'This is where Henri's hoping we can start in the spring. Next door will take a massive effort,' she conceded, 'but around the pit area we'll buy new topsoil for it from the next Reading expansion.'

Good thinking. But, 'That's nearly finished,' I said.

'I mean the *next* next Reading expansion they haven't announced yet. Ten thousand apartments. Henri can tell you herself— we did oppose. She may be back from London tomorrow. She been on the Species March— it's the last chance for so many things, Yori! And the rescue side of the work here is brimming over and we've only just opened officially. Henri knew how it would be. She's the practical one. Can turn her hand to most things.'

Such as lying well enough to scam Fleur. That's what she did for you. No, I don't know where Eurwen is! 'I've got a present for Henri,' I said. 'A mug. A special mug. She collects them, I remembered.'

'Have you? Anyway, come and see what you get for a quarter of a million these days.'

Even after what we'd just seen it was less than impressive—

and I thought I knew the price of land. We'd wandered in a long curve, a clear sky brightening all the time over our heads. The bungalow must be getting close judging from the girls' voices, calling to each other in the yard. Our shadows had switched sides though and, getting my bearings, I found my brain automatically charting Animal Farm as an island of workable ground with a diseased interior. Now Eurwen showed me it petered out in a tongue of coarse grass dipping into a morass. This brought us to a stop. The new field was smaller than the rust crater, still several football pitches in size though and more carpark post rained-off event than sportsground. To gain us perspective, a high-sided van appeared now and followed my last night's approach and after that dead maize stubble stood waiting for the plough right to the horizon. And this was the healthy land. 'We can get into the lane from here,' she suggested, sensing my disengagement. 'The feedman cometh.' She chose the oblique route for firmer footing, me trailing, my ankles getting a thorough workout. 'Come on!' she encouraged and grasping the top of a post she was over the fence in a single, smooth movement. Eurwen's vault – my mother never bothered looking for a way round anything when long arms and legs could get her across twice as quick. She turned, her eyes ablaze, her lips forming, 'Oh-h! That was only just!'

'Don't think so— well clear, in fact. You're keeping up with your A?'

'Do I look as if I am?'

'You look fantastic,' I said.

I was about to straddle the rickety top rail when it caught my eye as any movement will, a clay shape that was detaching from the sodden depression where it had lurked. Too low for horse— a bloated, near legless pony, maybe, struggling and stuck? Eurwen had mentioned the depth of mud here, the ruined drainage— but no pony was ever— surely?— and the hide!

Folds of hairless rind, or no— this wasn't organic, make that armour plate..

What was it?

Properly on its feet now the thing let out a long low note to celebrate.

'Hello Marvin,' Eurwen called. 'I'd forgotten you were there.'

'What's that?'

'He's a Gloucester Old Spot.'

Two metres long. At least a metre and a half at the shoulders. More if it ever got out of the swamp. 'Yes?'

'*A pig*. What did you think he was?'

The *boar* was thirty metres away but pointing straight at us. I could see a snout the size of a dinner plate pierced by twin black holes, expanding and contracting as they sucked in our scent. A pair of tiny eyes down in the canyons of its face were insignificant in comparison.

'We've just walked through there! With it. It looks like a rhino.'

'Rubbish. He's *heavy*,' she conceded. 'They're not so big normally. But only because they're never allowed to live long enough,' Eurwen's tone was severe, suddenly. Towards me. 'He came from one of those so-called farms outside Newbury. The woman running it had saved him as a piglet. He was sickly so she got him well and I don't think even she knew why. And then— this is the unusual part— she couldn't send him to slaughter.' Leaning forward enticingly, not caring that the rail under her hands was wormy enough to collapse with a breath, she called, 'Mar-r-vin,' in a sing-song voice.

The pig swivelled a fan-shaped ear to rival one of Crook's at us and began to amble forward. The effect was odd, with the rolls of flesh in motion but behind the main action like an afterthought. Gloop and solids dropped from the underside. Everything in slowtime. Then it began to trot— comically. And then to run. Each stride seemed so great an effort it was impossible to follow up but it came on at increasing speed, leaving me in no doubt. This was a charge. The thing must weigh over 300 kilos with a stopping distance somewhere out in Berkshire and it was heading in our direction. My direction. And the barrier between us was a line on a map rather than a hindrance, was made of matchwood, old as the gravel workings. A malevolent beast was going to trample me to death and above the thunder of it Eurwen was laughing her head off.

Chapter 31

'Marvin,' I said later while I was at the MultiCook rustling us up *Oyakodon*, (it translates as 'Mother and Child'), 'is pretty light on his feet.'

'*I know*. Don't worry. Your clothes will clean— if you've put them to soak.'

As the pig swerved to a stop I'd got a full frontal stuccoing of mud and worse. 'Why did you have to go and call him?'

'You see? One day and we argue. He was coming over anyway. Pigs are innately curious beings, much cleverer than dogs.'

'More get eaten.'

But Eurwen was preoccupied— at the other end of the kitchen she was sending 'material' to Henri. Needed urgently. Across her screen the pictures flickered, selected or rejected, all apparently involved animals but it was hard to tell. Human bodies mainly obscured the violent activities. 'What did you say?' barely caught over Mama *Rotti*— again. Singing *I Want to be a Celebrity* this time, that I actually liked enough to join in, falsetto, 'And I want to be famous for just being me! No time to learn a new skill that needs discerning/ My only concern is that I will be earning.' She and Sara were like timetwins, disappearing then three decades later, a revival. 'Nothing can stop me with my self belief/ with my new hair cut and bleached white tee-th!' Except *Mama Rotti's* lead still lived. To prove it her shout of triumph overlaid the final eight-bar alto sax riff. 'Be it,' she shouts, 'Is! Am! Life!'

The air was dense with starch from rice steaming and sharp with the dregs of soy-sauce I'd just emptied onto hot red peppers in my pan. Cooked onions, put aside, added their note. (Also cat smell from the streaky-grey tom that had come through a dip in the Thames and was under my feet.) And frying eggs. I eased them gently away from the sides, folding inwards, cosseting the yolks, losing myself in the perfection of their change. I was less than satisfied – with life not the eggs – but not unhappy. Sara was all boiled off somehow. I hadn't even remembered to ask if Eurwen had ever met Kim Tighe, for instance. If Neil Rix *had* been the fairground artist and painted the portrait of Kim on a billboard for Sara to recognise, then it was likely they all knew each other. It was a small place— and Sara wasn't stupid. Researcher's intuition had told her she was onto something, that Kim could lead her to her daughter. I liked that, her not being wrong about everything. And that if she'd carried on or held on and Kim hadn't fried her own brains, it could have worked out. Sara's journals and the rest of *the stuff* lay safe in my rucksack. But why, Yori? Just say nothing for another night. You'll be here tomorrow. And what does it matter if you never know more than you do now? It doesn't. (I tried to convince myself anyway, nearly succeeded).

'That's the liquid gone onto the onions.' I said. 'Very soon, now.'

'You couldn't wait to learn to cook!'

'I probably knew I'd need to.'

'Ouch!' She stopped what she was doing and came down the length of the kitchen and stood looking into the pan. 'Was I a dreadful mother?'

'No.'

'You were a nice baby. I don't think I've liked another since. Never bad-tempered. You watched everything. We knew you were mulling it over.'

'I was. This is near ready.'

Obediently she took the place I'd laid for her with Fleur's second-best crockery and Arts and Crafts flatware, a satisfaction to handle. 'Ah!' Finally, she'd noticed Sara's necklace coiled next to her glass. 'I haven't seen this in *years*. Mum gave it me. Where on earth—?'

'Josh has been keeping it for you. There was nothing else I thought you'd be interested in. Only this.'

Nodding, she held it up to the light and the moonstones shimmered. 'It's been mended!' In putting it on, her fingers showed they knew how, with no fumbles, and the clean fleece she wore was opened at the neck making the fall into its V perfect.

I'd known it would. 'Happy birthday!'

'Thank-you!' As she half-rose to kiss me she flushed through her white cheeks and all the way down into her throat, hardly looking, IMO, any older than when it had first been given. Did the makers of **A** ever predict this when they were passing out their tickets to happiness and good skin and not-thinning bones, how parents and children ended up siblings with all the problems of *that?* My only loss was I'd never see her in peacock silk wanting to please everybody round Fleur's table—

—also that the PalmWalk model was shifted to the furthest shelf to gather dust. It had not, despite her promise, been looked at since this morning. At least the necklace was a success. Then she took it off and handed it back. 'There's no point— I won't wear it. Too sad. Anyway, Henri and me we don't do that sort of thing. I can't remember the last time I needed to get dressed up. It was a kind thought, Yori, but really, take it home with you. Give it to— I don't know, whoever.'

Josh had told me, 'Don't be disappointed with her,' as we'd stood, side-by-side, and looked into his apple tree. 'If you let yourself, it won't drive her down— she's not Sara and thank Christ for that— it'll just drive her away. See me.'

I brought the rice over, then the 'child', fried eggs. Then into another warmed dish I heaped the 'mother'. It was all vegetables though it ought to have included stewed chicken—unmentionable in *my* mother's kitchen. I sat opposite. And couldn't stop myself saying, 'Why animals?'

She didn't pretend. And at least considered it seriously. 'You know I can't properly tell you. It's what I do. Or perhaps all I'm able to do. Sometimes it makes no sense but that doesn't stop me. And it's a burden, caring about them so much which I always have. I can't let them suffer. It would— it would *belittle* me to let them suffer.' I was reminded of someone else, another attempt to reason out an attachment that wouldn't stand up— Tomiko's. When I'd told him my plan was to come here and I said *Eurwen* out loud, he'd tried to talk and failed. Stared at his feet. Anyway she seemed to have mystified even herself because she flipped it to a joke, 'and of course the whole point about donkeys and starlings and dogs is *they never read books!*'

'There's that.'

'Yes! And why the question? In fact why do you keep staring like that?'

'I can't believe I'm here. I can't believe I'm looking at real you.'

'Huh! Too real, probably.'

Silence, apart from her messages announcing themselves and the cat's long, regular tongue-rasps across its own belly fur which was unpleasant. I do not like cats almost as much as donkeys. I filled both our glasses from the water jug noting she'd gone for the same utilitarian design I'd chosen equipping my flat at Libby's. 'Don't let your supper cool.'

'I won't. What happened to Kailash?'

I held up my spread fingers, looking straight at Eurwen. 'Daddy's company. Pick of projects. Success. Money. One boy, Hari. ' But as I said it, I knew another reason. Even salt is never salty enough.

Eurwen nodded anyway. 'Families!' and seemed about to start then put her fork down. 'Oh, I've just thought! You used to do pretend meals for a little girl— you'd made her up. My friend would like food. Here is noodles. Here is aubergine. My friend has no dinner at home. Her brothers steal it. She is very poor. Very hungry. Here is rice. What was her name? I always blamed it on Tomiko or whatever we're meant to call him now. Him and his stories. What *was* her name?'

'Tess.'

At the first mouthful she said, '*Tess-ss*. Mm— very nice!' but then leaned back away from her plate and took stock. Her kitchen was orderly now, the surfaces gleaming, canisters lined up and dry goods stowed away in shut cupboards. Stone floor flags were damp at the corners still. It had taken me hours. The scrubbed deal table sat in its own pool of light while the rest of the room remained dim. I was pleased at the result and as part of the same thought, I realised the necklace mattered less than it would've done once. It was mended. She'd worn it. She was going to eat her *oyakodon*, winding strips of pepper onto her fork, still not putting it to her mouth though, smiling— more mockery on the way? But it was only a hint she would squeeze my arm with her free hand and giggle at herself. And then Eurwen said something made me want to shout out loud with love. 'I'm amazed you found anything to cook.'

IV

Lantern

When I wake up in Geoffrey's chair, it's at the middle of a wrinkle-free sleeve of a building stretching as far as the residents need. Animal Farm's a lot fitter for humans. Windows open, drains drain and though those good Welsh slates weren't as sound as they looked, they *are* now I've been on the roof. I try to coincide my stay under it with Henri's raids on London or Brussels— H, I'm meant to call her if I have to call her anything. When poor planning puts us together we turn into a pair of those not-wanted dogs jostling for Eurwen's attention. And H still hasn't seen the funny side of what happened with the mug. How could I've known? I never figured out the mechanism that made the mug obsess over one person, never mind how it hated another. Or what would happen. So much for the smile I thought nothing could wipe off H's face. But things can *just* work if none of us speaks the name Sara.

2041 marked the thirty-third year since her disappearance and death, the reason for which *was* left open by the coroner when he reconvened. It made all Josh's fears valid because the verdict spawned a Sarafest of mentions and clips and theories. CyberSara really is a work in progress which I can't help getting a charge from. *My grandmother.* Eurwen's livid, of course, over Charity's collaboration with an up-and-coming documaker though I think what's threatened shows Charity as just somebody else with a weight tied to one foot. Only my opinion. You decide.

Chapter 32

Josh isn't bothered by any of this. Not many weeks after the inquest, which they didn't force him to attend, he was found on the slopes of Croagh Patrick. He'd got himself a comfortable position to sea-gaze from, spine supported by a boulder, his belt pouch of coffee uncapped ready to drink. So Macy Kennedy from Gisborne, NZ assumed till he saw frost on the eyebrows and the white horseshoe moustache that turned out to be icicles. ('He was obviously an oldie sort of guy so I thought it was, like, a lot of facial hair, eh?') Sometime during the previous night Josh's body had given up. He'd been willing it to since my delivery of the Sara thunderbolt. Now that he knew for certain she was dead, he must've decided *why wait?* Lack of ▲ plus untreated inflammation of the lungs will overwhelm the system but takes effort— and even then some extra final push. He'd made an efficient job of it, getting the height and exposure needed to finally achieve what all that clambering up the Pilgrim Path had been in aid of.

So another return to Westport. Eurwen and Henri would fly in together and separate from me. I made sure I outdid them to be able to play the host in the cobalt blue house, to have a fire lit and the stale air replaced— though when it came to the sense of desertion, there wasn't much to be done. It'd been noticeable when Josh was still alive and rehearsing his moves with all the courage and professionalism of Officer Meredith. For a natural exit. This knowledge meant the blaze of cut gorse stems (all dried and stacked ready in the hearth), and the Windsor chairs pushed back as if Josh and I had just stood up, and the two books on the shelf where there'd been three, all failed to get to me. But with everything sorted and only the tea to set out, it was his kitchen reduced me to tears. The chipped enamelled sink I'd once disturbed a live spider crab in, ('Fisherman I natter to down the quay gave it me but it can go back tonight—') still had a chalky deposit from its final scour. The counter-tops were cleared apart from A Present from Somewhere that held no fruit left to rot. Cupboards emptied as well, which sort of fitted with his request for 'burial, no fuss or service of any type'. That's Josh for you. Actually cremation would have been no or least fuss. Only Meg with her local connections had enabled me to wheedle and grease my way to getting him a grave – not simple or cheap in modern County Mayo – while she'd picked the simpler job of organising the hearse to ferry him to it.

She also brought the two women from Shannon. They were late and rushed, Meg apologising though it wasn't her fault. 'No wonder flying's the new smoking,' Henri said. She was, as ever, very bright, busy and irritating, her look jumping around Josh's home which she'd never entered before. My mother on the other hand was gypsum pale, almost trancelike in her movements, didn't join in the chat but still succeeded in giving off impatience. All wore casual clothes. Meg, who'd put on weight over the years, was padded out further in one of those past-the-knees, thermal cylinders Libby took to in winter. Henri seemed to be dressed for messy maintenance work of some sort in a navy onepiece with matching skull-cap that turned out to be her new dye-job on a severe buzz cut. Eurwen's signature charcoal shade was at least lifted by acid green wool gloves and snood that made loose coils of her hair even hotter by contrast. They didn't stay to warm themselves at my fire, late as we were, but formed a line in the hall ready for the undertakers' knock. I felt stupid in my special purchase, a black Crombie coat.

It was an afternoon burial in the cemetery at Aughavale (the locals say it *Urr-vul*) where Protestants and Catholics can go in alike. Space not sectarianism had been the problem trying to gain entry for Josh. A couple of kilometres from Westport by funeral car, our route was mainly rural but along the fast coastal road. So unwalkable. But I'd have preferred even a dangerous walk to follow my grandfather under a January sky with the white sun up there somewhere. Now you see it; now it's gone. Even if the fields on either side were desiccated to khaki and salt-lashed, anything would've been better than cooped up in the artificial warmth of the funeral wagon across from an Eurwen who'd erected a cordon around herself neither Meg nor Henri, let alone me, dared cross. When our eyes met accidentally— a tortuous journey, continually being overtaken by every sort of vehicle including farm machinery— my mother didn't blink. *Just the four of us*, Meg has whispered to the driver, dark-suited like a film extra. Now her words seem to clear up any late curiosity over Josh's life here. Or so I assumed. But there was a minor surprise in store for us, and very welcome it was. Creating confusion, it helped break the journey's spell. We found our arrival at the bleak, walled cemetery being watched by a dozen strangers in a tight group, ready assembled on site, muffled up in layers of clothes and still having to huddle together against the chill. Henri, always needing to know what was going on before it went, asked Meg, 'What's this? What's happening?' Meg shook her head. It took a moment for any of us to understand why they were here. They marked the spot the coffin-pushers were leading us to, the lines of sight being obstructed. Aughavale, very old and Irish was exactly as I'd researched, packed full of crumbling pillars, simple crosses on plinths, Celtic crosses of man-height but leaning, and massive wedgestones and heavy, raised structures that had also tilted. And fancy ironwork fences topped by vicious finials, half-rusted away. Images that had seemed picturesque in reality suggested they had trouble keeping the dead down.

The reserve mourners took advantage of being home side. Mostly short, quite old-looking, more males than females, they were pre-installed and ready. I wasn't. I'd only ever witnessed cremations and on-screen burials, so for a start I was expecting a decorous green-swathed, putting-the-corpse-to-bed type of thing. Not this hand dug hole with the severed roots on show down the sides and moisture blackening the bottom. You had to stare down at it, at its simple wicked utility. My mother did. Eurwen was probably also getting an education re: burials but kept herself well in check. The Irish observed the lowering of the plain wooden coffin as if they'd only come to ensure everything was done right, and then they paid really close attention to Eurwen and me dropping handfuls of earth on top. Which I'm glad to say we managed without making a sound. No one was officiating and neither of us spoke. Then I was aware the locals had started glancing over their shoulders. Expecting what? Gatecrashers? A band? Apart from Meg's sobbing, it was soon obvious nothing else would happen and the undertakers/drivers, both women, had stood well back, heads bowed and stayed that way. No help there. A humiliating interval (for the family) ended with the oldest man among the strangers coming around and whispering a few words to Eurwen in that soft Connemara way with them. There was a quick pat for her acid-green glove. There was nothing for me. But with my façade who could take offence? He nodded once into the hole and this was the signal for them to leave, all together, exactly like the quiz team or hobby club they probably were. Car doors slammed beyond the cemetery wall with some calling out and what could've been a snort, a choke or a laugh. We, the official party lurked till they'd gone and during the wait I realised that on the subject of façades and what was behind, I'd have given anything, I'd have ripped the Egon Schiele out of its vault and out of its frame to trade for an afternoon in Clew

Bay again with Josh. Me and him, counting its islands. A good man, my grandfather. Someone should say that out loud. But Henri's eyes were darting from Eurwen to grave to Eurwen again, her only concern. Meg had aged extra years with cold and was shivering inside her padded coat. Eurwen stood straight, stylus-thin and quiet, her lips slightly apart tasting the sea on the breeze, like me. Her fine-textured skin had been pinked up and was flawless and *harmfully beautiful*, came into my mind also how the wild west of Ireland was just the perfect setting for her— you could see how in the past women like this started fierce tribal wars and I couldn't help wondering what difference it would've made if her personality had been slotted into a snub-nosed Henri, say. *She* wouldn't have stopped Tomiko in his tracks that day by the Lake— so end of Yori because end of story before it begins. So not harmful. Life giving. (Or Meg, say, only ever pretty and quite plain now, not looking as if she'd bounce when dropped.)

Henri fidgeted, Meg snuffled into her tissues, Eurwen seemed petrified. I'd got no real insight into what anybody was experiencing except my own self-disgust at the months spent puzzling over Sara when Josh that I respected, had taken pride in and still loved, was killing himself. That's you, Yori. And now here's you, the Primary Male Relative present and not even speaking when—

'I ought to have thanked those people,' came from Eurwen suddenly but she was already dismissing them. She seemed drawn to the next field where a mass of small twittering birds rose and came low over our heads, buffeted by the wind. Finding us beneath, they struggled to gain height and Eurwen saw the flock safely on its way till just a foxing of the eastern sky. 'We can go as well.'

'Absolutely!' Henri said.

There weren't any wreaths to lay or bunches of flowers

because for obvious reasons he could never stand either but as we left, the diggers were starting to backfill so we had the damp clay smell clinging in our nostrils instead. Among the Durkins, the Gills, the Stauntons and even, bizarrely, a smattering of Murcotts, Joshua Meredith, who died January 22nd 2041, Aged 76, would have Croagh Patrick in his sights for the foreseeable future, the best finish Meg and I had been able to give him.

Back at Josh's pub, The Jester, we sat in outdoor clothes, waiting for our order, needing to thaw out. My new coat had been a specially bad choice, absorbing damp. It was obvious Henri was now more anxious than ever about Eurwen, which I resented. She kept worrying with her fingers at a piece of hair behind her own ears. Then she had to push the sugar forward for Eurwen's immediate use after almost snatching it from the waitress. 'I think I'll get you a brandy,' she said.

Eurwen wouldn't even glance up. 'No.'

'It might do you good.'

'In what way, exactly?'

Meg shared a warning expression with me, then an attempt at a smile. 'I bet you came in here, Yori, him and you, when you were over?'

'Once or twice.'

'He'll have loved that. He was— I mean he had people he knew, they were there, weren't they? That was nice, I thought. But, well, you know—' Poor Meg.

Scented with cinnamon and coffee and chocolate, the vapours coming up from cups and pots and jugs still threatened to freeze. Henri had the good sense to leave me and my mother as soon as it was decent to. She took Meg off to help her 'forage for tomorrow's breakfast' as she put it since Meg's offer of a room had been refused by Eurwen. Before the keys were returned to Josh's landlord we'd sleep over at the cottage which would be a first for his daughter. In no mood to spare herself or the rest of us, she and Henri would share Josh's bed. 'Goodbye Megs,' she said now. There was an awkward moment. Did Eurwen intend standing up to be hugged by her ex-father's ex-partner? She didn't and I realised they'd barely exchanged a couple of sentences all afternoon. What had Meg really known all those years ago that made her and Eurwen behave like partners in crime today? 'And thank you, Megs.' It was properly done but I thought she sounded shakier than at the graveside, as though inside her, things had worked loose. After watching Meg and Henri out the door – Henri's backward look and, 'OK?' weren't answered – she said, 'Damon Williams sent me a nice message. You won't remember the name, even— So that's the end, isn't it? First Mum, then Geoffrey, Fleur. Now Dad. The world goes on.'

'Yes.'

'And it's a *much worse* world. You would think I'd be used to being robbed.' Was the reference to her parents' history deliberate? No way of telling. 'But *him*.' She exhaled, shut her eyes and threw both long arms out, clasping her own wrist, somehow missing the dirty crockery and plate of uneaten biscuits. It seemed she might be going to let her head fall down there with them and let the hair spread over, not caring. The Jester is one of those narrow Westport bars that seem to go back forever from the street and we'd chosen the near empty mid-section between noisy drinkers in the window and the rear screens and pool table. It was four-ish by now and the few customers in had probably been drinking since midday. So who'd notice a redheaded woman crying into a pub tabletop? But at the last second she straightened up, scraping her wooden chair over the floorboards. They noticed *that* and winced. 'Sorry. It's not— I can't quite—' Mystifying herself, she tried again. 'You don't believe in anything I suppose? Do you? It is late to be asking, I know. I was watching the coffin and I said to it, So Dad, you in there, what now? Or am I talking to nothing? Just because I can say So Dad, it doesn't mean any communication's going on. I'm fooling myself is more likely. When you stare at the light and then the bulb bursts, you can see it still. Even through closed lids. But the bulb's shattered and you *are* in the dark. Does that about sum things up?'

Thankfully, the background hubbub and glasses clinking and the stutter of the games feedback seemed to relegate this to small talk. 'Probably.'

She wasn't satisfied. 'Tomiko wouldn't agree. He was into the lingering dead. He used to tell you stories. We had massive fallings out over the stories. I didn't want it to take in you, all that wackiness.'

There went two thousand years of Shinto! I could've told her there was never any danger of it 'taking'. But I didn't. I could've said the only ghost I had reply to me was Gramps Geoffrey's and it said, There's no such thing as ghosts, Yori. It's the living you have to watch out for! But I didn't. Henri and Meg had been an annoyance to have around— that's what she was demonstrating now, *being with me* and talking, whatever this was about. And I wanted to come up to standard and not displease even though I couldn't help thinking Have you forgotten those Pryorsfield Christmases and Easters we joined in with Fleur? You helped with the flowers at St Peter's then went to evening carols. We had to sing *Little Donkey* at home, your favourite, but not included in the service. Why single out Tomiko?

'I suppose I'm forced to think about it because I've got nothing. Completely nothing. I didn't have any warning— as to what was going on with Dad, I mean, up there on that foul Crow's Patrick, if that's how you say it. No messages via the *paranormal*. And yet I felt Mum die. I told you.'

'Yes.'

'Yet he and I *were* alike. So I believe in nothing and at the same time I was asking myself, at the grave I mean, is this silence by choice? Well Dad? Mute of malice, it's called in legal terms. He told me that years ago when I moved out of Pryorsfield and he phoned. I'd been arrested— not for the first time but he wasn't playing the heavy father, just doing that policeman thing of his, yes? Is there anything you's like to say? Did I need any help? What was my current address? *Ah, thank-you miss, and who else occupies the property?* He could be funny, couldn't he? I said, It's off the Cowley Road, DI Meredith. I'm sharing with Henri. You do remember Henri? One of the Fortuns? I told him about what we were hoping to achieve— we'd only just started on Species Alert and he was interested. He was! That's fine, he said. You're grown up enough and smart enough to do anything you want now. Your mother would be proud of you, by the way—' Her eyes shone and reddened and overflowed as they hadn't for Sara. 'And this is the last time we have to talk about it— or her if you want. And all the things we got wrong, the three of us. That's what he said. And oh-h, *thank God, Yori!* we kept to it.' Suddenly a face already deathly white was transparent and the veins, a near-match in shade for her irises, stood out across her temples. 'Proud of me? As if!' She's going to faint, to fall— I panicked and made a mis-timed catching-lurch that got shrugged off. 'I'm proud of *her*. We all can be. Order another pot of whatever this is. I'm cold again. *Funerals!* Remember Gramps Geoffrey's and hail in April as we came out of the college chapel? And suddenly it was a Christmas card, white over the lawns and the paths and the— those carved thingies? It took your breath away. *He* certainly didn't believe— and yet we still had to go through the full ordeal, the parade of the worthies. And today I keep remembering Julien Fortun reading, 'There is nothing covered that shall not be revealed, neither hid that shall not be known.' It's from The Bible.

Therefore complete and utter garbage to Geoffrey. Rot as he would say. He could be *scathing* behind Fleur's back. We all go to fairy land and the naughty children get found out and spanked and the nice ones are given prizes? No. I don't think! But he left his instructions. Insisted on— well you were there. So Dad would have to listen. Nor did it occur to him how, if it were true, I'd be the one sitting and saying to herself *I'm for it, then*. Not Josh. Me! He couldn't see past Dad though. Preserve us from intelligent people, huh?'

'You're intelligent.'

'No-o. Never have been. All that petered out with Mum, which was a relief— I've no complaints there. And it was for nothing, Geoffrey's last swipe at Dad, because we won't ever be sure, will we? The husband's fault? The daughter's? I—' From nowhere a couple of teenagers came level with our table, locals, making for the Casino Pigalle board, discussing strategies until they saw Eurwen. She returned their stares. 'It was white over,' she repeated, making them invisible. They shuffled off but it had been a well-timed intrusion, judging by the new hard smile she turned on me. 'These events would be worse in high summer, don't you think?'

No. I went to the bar to order actually thinking if Josh had set out for The Other Shore with Sara and Geoffrey and Fleur, then a less functional travel group's never been put together. Imagine the disputes, the snubbings, the demands for affection. I pitied Fleur. A more comfortable spin would be Sara had stolen a march on them all and an early start meant they'd never catch her.

Chapter 33

You should let her go as well, Yori. Because? For one, I was pained beyond pain over losing Josh. Unlike Geoffrey, who'd gone straight from Great Man to Perfect Ancestor, Josh left this life as Tomiko's 'Wolf With Wounded Throat'— its message? *Good acts will be ignored— you're a wolf!* Looking to the future, I'll miss the cobalt blue house and him in it for a long time, the pared-back interior of hard Windsor chairs, scrubbed things, jelly jars along a shelf, driftwood polished by handling, the smell of smoke— gone. Sara's work again. *And* the minor tasks we'd never get round to like pruning a tree, painting a gate. 'Take care of Eurwen,' I told Henri. (Unnecessary, her pretend smile said.) Yet another argument in favour of doing nothing was Charity Weiksner, seasoned Sara follower and now with a professional narrator in tow. Something has happened to Charity lately, some fix up has made her not so Geoffrey-like about the chin area as she gives her interviews, dropping lures everywhere for *Toys of Desperation*. The title alone tells you where it's going. A dead husband is just fuel for more shabby hints.

I'm at that husband's door for the last time. Asking along the lines of why not speak to Charity— it might shut her up? gets me from Eurwen, 'Because it's more complex than you want things to be. How many times do I need to say this, Yori? She wouldn't be content, people like that never are. And I've been informed through a third party—'

'Who?'

'That she only ever liked Fleur.'

'Everybody liked Fleur.'

'Exactly. '

'Fine.'

'Which is what I used to say to *my* parents.' Was that Eurwen sounding *resentful*? No— she took the sting out by pointing where on her cheek I ought to kiss her. The colour was properly back in her complexion since yesterday, but my lips touched chilly flesh and her eyes glittered like ice-crystals. Strands of hair I'd had to watch Henri teasing out with the brush half an hour ago caught the light as they reknotted themselves, whipping into my mouth. It wouldn't surprise me if this was the time her physical beauty reached its peak— *Ka chou fuu getsu*, Flower, bird, wind, moon. So what's that about, father? And Tomiko had floundered, Um, all have beauty getting bigger— maybe as they extra time of?

Bigger? OK, bigger, higher, deeper— Eurwen's effect went too deep for hooking out by word. Now it delivered another dose of the Animal Farm pleasure with a tinge of dissatisfaction, the old warning of heartburn. I really didn't want to leave like this, undecided if we were entering a new phase or not. In future would we always be pleased to see each other, even during bad patches, and be able to build on that?

'Bye Yori. Go, *go!*'

She meant nothing by it, I'm sure, apart from get out of the cold, get on your way.

But you can always look on the reverse. Tomiko asked in the summer, I think it was— I know work on PalmWalk was creeping ahead by then and I'd been showing him the progress with my sea buckthorn saplings gone in— *Is she well? Is loss of father still hurt her?* And I admitted I hadn't visited Eurwen since.

Thirty-Three Years On. In the Eastern world this is a sort of graduation for the dead— or if that's too remote, try thinking of it as the Next Life equivalent of up-and-down Croagh Patrick in bare feet. Except ghosts don't have feet. I could pretend what comes next is 'from Tomiko' again but here's Fleur instead. A face Sara once called horsy is lost in a borrowed volume by Kunio Yanagita, the king of Japanese folklore, while her frizzy hair's held back by some sort of cruel metal clip. Fleur, the stereotype Educated Elderly Englishwoman right down to her cashmere cardigan, could dress an Alfred Hitchcock set without a single line of establishing dialogue. The expression I can't make out will be fixed in concentration. Pryorsfield still stands around us. The satisfied and the sickly monks still lock eyes across the kitchen corridor. '*Now* the writer comes to how and when death must be dealt with,' she says. 'Mmm. After thirty-three years, the dead are literally *gone*. Very specific, isn't it? Every culture has its coping mechanism but I do admire the Japanese way— it's taking a ruler to life and drawing a line. Thirty-three. And so rational— ye-s-s. If the loss were suffered when you were a child, then you've reached adulthood before the final goodbye. If the person died when you were an adult, then you're mature enough for acceptance. It's quite humane. As far as I can determine, this next section we come to is on the subject of purification. Tomur-ai-i-age. *Tomuraiage*,' she corrects herself and glances straight at me over rimless glasses slid to the end of her nose. I'm just into my teens but as always she addresses me on equal terms, so lets me see she's confused. 'It's some sort of ritual you have to perform for the *shirei*. Ah-h, the afterlife and the whole question of good and bad and blame— well they're virtually side issues by comparison. By this time. This is what you have *to do*. Yes. I think so.'

Josh's funeral made the idea of signing off on the past seem like sense. As my father demonstrates in every act— loving my mother from a safe distance, say— the Japanese are practical people. They take a ruler to life. Who knows what they *believe*?

After thirty-three years, a day arrives when you can stop bothering the *shirei*, and tell him or her, OK, we've done our bit. We've been respectful and remembered your good qualities. We've apologised oftener than we've drunk tea. Your turn now. Being a stiff's no barrier to a new career – so go get busy on our behalf. Watch over the family. Bring us lots of wealth and dutiful children and success and good opinion and luck, especially luck.

I like it! To be able to say, Hit the highway, ancestor. Or in this case, Sara—

—because every ripple of applause for her bones was something to hold against her when grief for *him* smashed into me like a train. There were moments of, So what if he did cause her death somehow—? Losing Geoffrey and Fleur was nothing in comparison and even back at work, there were days I wallowed like Marvin the pig in mud. The Westport house I could only picture now as emptied, items left on the doorstep for neighbours to take away, the local custom. And the casual Croagh Patrick ramblers would soon stop expecting to see him, also the fishermen on Roman Island and that Maltese couple who keep the store we bought our wood, nails and glue from. Yet on two separate continents people were working on Sara. The First Definitive Oxford Biography hasn't even got a title yet but that doesn't save it from being openly trashed by Charity. 'With this Apolline Reith you're getting a professional historian, OK, and yeah, she knew Sara— briefly. Half a century ago! She doesn't have the insight a family member could provide.'

It was enough to make you do Ray Milland's* smile from *Dial M for Murder*, the close up that finally lets the audience in on the secret. He intends to kill his wife.

---

*Who is Welsh not many people remember. His real name was Alfred Reginald Jones. Born in Neath, a coal-mining area of South Wales, so he named himself after the town's Milland Road— not vice versa as I've seen claimed. Jones/Milland was the first Welsh actor to win an Oscar. His fan base will tell you his greatest achievement was *The Lost Weekend*. But it's Dial M for me.

Thanks for that AH. I'm glad I kept you. Let Tess go but kept *you*.

My pleasure.

Nov 17th 2041
7.09 am

It's a Saturday and eight months on. Something has happened. If you don't mind, I'll explain as I go along—

—*so* my entire floor of Gaiman Ave including the step-outside shower room has been swept and cleansed and on the bed there's new linen. Consider this as *higan* plus. No food has been cooked or eaten for twenty-four hours. Nor **A** taken for same period. I'm noticeably light-headed. Other effects? Too soon to tell— maybe the dry mouth I've just rinsed, having even denied myself a cup of tea. And because after returning from Animal Farm that first time, I cancelled Tess, I've nothing to give up in that category. My biggest luxury, she being time consuming, an interactive instant learner. Substatial too, holographic quality state-of-the-art. She was *good*, too good, over engineered I often thought. But a spot-on question from Eurwen burst her like a bubble. Sorry Tess. I could've let her down gently or received heartbroken messages over a six-month period, tailed her off. Decided against. If I ever needed a top-up of personalised abuse, Kailash showed no sign of running out of steam any day soon. But new development! Regular weekday appointments with Rhondda Jones, formerly Leisure Services now Renewal Czar, for a light supper at 8 Gaiman Ave (me to provide) plus basic sex. She isn't slim and definitely not delicate. You need to think Romanesque not Regency. And all of a sudden she can't get enough of me. Thanks Glenn.

The usual practice of *tomuraiage*, a last anniversary for the departed, should start with tidying up the tomb that's probably got a bit unkempt after three decades. Just the word tomb calls up weathered Aughavale gravestones and one under— anyway, since Sara's remains have been cremated and her ashes are to go in with G and F's on the south side of St Peter's church at Boarshill, (when Eurwen gets round to it) my yard will have to do for the ritual. At 7:13 it's almost dawn, breezy and less than four degrees. A fine day's being promised, meaning trippers and footfalls on PalmWalk. Excellent omen. Now I carry the shrine I've kept in the corner of my living room outside— and place it on a brick plinth specially constructed in the angle of next door's wall and Mr Jenkinson's workshop. 7:16. As I go in and out I'm desperately praying to any god that'll listen for Libby not to break with habit and get up early. The fleecy sleep suit smelling of her bed, the daisy tattoos, the new-dyed hair and the Rhyl accent in which she shouts *whatyoucookingonthebarbecueinthebloodydarkfor?* would scare away my guest.

7:19. Overhead is still the no-colour of a switched-off screen that you hardly ever see. Since The Wave, the big difference about out here is my neighbour's missing birch tree, now back on his side as a log pile I helped make. The sky's wider and the moon's at the half (actually 48%) and, having risen just post midnight, it's balanced on the rooftop but without branches for support. Glenn's hibachi has at least agreed to stay lit (second attempt) and better still I didn't have to invent a story for the lend. Alice is home— insatiable. And I've got my white chrysanthemums and other necessaries, the lamp being the most important, a cheap rechargeable model you give to children scared of the dark. Just enough to guide her back. I'd like a real Kongming lantern as mentioned by my illustrious grandmother in her journal but they were banned years ago for fire raising. So I add my Raku wide-lipped tea bowl with freshly made tea – like me she hated coffee – and slices of blood orange and grapefruit, sugared and also personal to her. She shared them with Josh. (I'm so hungry just the smell makes my mouth water.) The photo taken at St Clement's College, chosen for *A First's* dust jacket in what seems like a past aeon from here and now, is propped up and I've printed her name in white on a black card that keeps falling over. I've bought a silver-metal bell from the GiftPlanet that's been allowed to set up. *There*'s something to connect anyone to the real world, ersatz rubbish sneaking back into Rhyl— but just in case, and because my hollow insides are complaining, I ring the bell anyway. And wait.

7:20.

And wait. 7:21. Not that I'm expecting anything. I'd be worried about Yori

otherwise.

7:23. A shiny streak in the east. As the breeze drops the yard fills with smoke. It takes an effort not to cough – 7:25 – or ring again because that tea and blood orange are pretty tempting and even if I'm half Japanese, what I'm doing makes less than half sense – *Hello Yori!* – even if it wasn't for the drug withdrawal and a growling stomach and being out early always reminding me of Josh—

Did somebody say *Hello Yori?*

Like everyone my age, I haven't been off ▲ since I was eleven. If ▲ is The Great Smoother, then *Hello Yori!* might be the sound of me hitting a bump. Hard. You'll find wilder symptoms reported by people who just stop.

I said Hello Yori.

It seems cold but was cold before. And the 48% moon is incredibly zapped up but thin cloud will have cleared from in front, as promised, is all. A minute ago the gulls' usual abuse was loud from the beach direction— no squawking now but there has to be a last, doesn't there? Always. Yet something's changed. Smoke thickens into shapes—

—and I don't want to give a false impression here. I'm not registering anything uncanny. I can't see her. Well of course you can't, dolt!

Where are your manners?

But she's arrived. It's not like she walks through me. I remember another time, her on the corner of Conwy Street and me, watching the footage felt her suddenly there and not there— a moving *shirei*. No. This is more how the essence of somebody I recognise is now present and, by coincidence, it's in the exact space I'm using. I've made room. *Welcome Grandmother*— is what you're meant say. Bit late, Yori, considering she's already in, all the thoughts, experiences, instincts, feelings and desires, especially *them*. She was real once. Solider than Rhondda and a thousand per cent more substantial than Tess. I'd imagined Sara fragile *and* sharp like a good blade used too often on the wrong material— jagged but it can still cut. Which she did. Ruthless and greedy, though, they came as a shock. She's ravenous for a daughter who never existed except as Sara's invention and couldn't be revised but that won't stop her trying. And something else, something gone dormant before it erupted here in Rhyl of all places— she's ravenous for Josh.

Hi Sara! Glad you made it. And so what d'you reckon on us? I mean me, of course. I'd like to hear. Think I've pretty well got it sorted re: the rest of the gang. Big pity about Josh— or maybe not from your POV? Attraction, regret, low expectations, anger and fake indifference at the end— I totally understand. Douse them in drink! Stop caring! Respect is an echo according to Tomiko— well fuck that, eh? Why can't Love be? That would really make a difference to the world. To be loved back the way we want, when we want, from the person we want. For as long as we want. That would be worth the game. We've masses in common, you and me, a pair of brackets round Eurwen— because I know exactly how she makes you feel. Same as on my planet!

That lovely woman and the brave man coming fresh from a School Nativity, riding on his broad shoulders the child dressed as a shepherd, were ALL players once! Then two of them only got to watch the show—

The rule is, I'm told, Get Tough On The Departed. For example the sun'll be up any moment. After crossing the sand, the ultimate tracking shot, it'll pimp the town. My new paint on SkyTower is almost luminescent in itself and the gold beacon in the shape of a flame— whose idea?— is masterly. No one cares there's a missing gondola Princess Diana rode in and felt sick. A good digestion and a short memory was Ingrid Bergman's recipe for happiness, as given to Alfred Hitchcock – and it's always worked for Rhyl. Putting Rhyl back doesn't mean 'like it was', Sara. Streets I'm intending to transform have their gaps ready cleared. It'll happen and it'll be good. A really great new building by the Lake. Better. Whereas *Nothing for you ever again, that's the only offer anyone can make to the dead. Sorry, Sara. Your choice.*

7:26 I have the evidence. I flap her confession at the fire. She can't argue with that. Citrus leaves saved up over the months are well alight so I tear out and feed in *It was my good fortune that tree-lined Polstead Road was devoid of other vehicles now, placable and familiar as ever, otherwise I may not have begun my journey at all or at least with something less spirited than,* 'Look, Eurwen! Lawrence of Arabia lived here!' *spoken aloud and* 'Here's where J.R.R. Tolkien grew tired of marking exam scripts one day and wrote "In a hole in the ground there lived a hobbit ".' And from then on it's easy.

7:29 My messages to her on rice paper which strictly speaking

I should've burnt first— I got carried away— come next. Six of them.

I'd like to have known you goes in before I can take it back.

I build things here because of you which is probably nearer the truth.

Time to give up wandering.

Be a good kami, huh?

You can get properly lost in Rhyl now I know your secret.

Deal? Or do you need it spelling out?

7:37. It's light! Still freezing though. I'm here dithering over the notebook's (recyclable) cover before poking it in with the late Mr Jenkinson's screwdriver, willing the thing to catch. Stubborn— wouldn't you know it? First shrivelling then the fumes given off are eyestinging before it seeps down to tar. Her scribbles, doodles and every bit of correspondence that started *Dearest Fleur* and either not progressing or going on page after page and still never sent are handy to encourage total combustion. The Thomasina manuscript, the main bulk, comes after, squared up and put out next to the hibachi on the yard. Turned over, it would be Sara hopeful, Sara useless, Sara self-harming, Sara down in Slot-Machine Hell meeting a native fellow boozer before she staggers out onto the Parade and sensory overload—

—I find I'm Josh. I'm frustrated and impatient with the process, experimenting with how thick a wad of paper will burn through at once. Try to fan the next lot, Yori, get the oxygen in there. In fact the temptation is to shred a sample, that'll get you some heat. Who credits *tomuraiage* anyway? And wouldn't fragments of Sara blowing over town be just as right— or wrong? But the idea of some visitor stooping into the gutter along Grange Road, which is where the breeze is making for, to pick up *I realised I had been unconsciously expectant, catlike,*

willing and waiting to respond. Now the force of the delivered
blow was enough to snap my head around and send my body
sprawling after it in one ungainly arc. My wrist gave way, of
course, as I struck the floor with a secondary pain that was
almost wel—

No! Burn is best. Sara loving us, Sara hating us, Sara sneering
When is Rhyl's season exactly? Burn the lot and leave less
written in aqua fortis (her words). Damage limitation is the
whole point of *tomuraiage*, the denouement, fade and closing
credits as the individual is finally washed away. The clothes she
chose were the ones she'd arrived in and a husband's borrowed
old coat to keep the chill out and no money for this (technical)
millionairess and an ex-friend's book to distain on the journey,
they all shriek of an occasion, of her own ritual. She should
understand.

Singeing my fingers twice, I reach the end with a blaze so
respectable it'll need watching for stray sparks. But from the
kitchen window. Hardy but no masochist, I retreat, safe from
the threat of Libby now being ready armed with What am I up
to? I'm just starting an early breakfast, Your Landlordship. See,
marinaded tofu and burdock strips, prepped to go. Delicious.
You want? Be plenty! More than enough for two. Flames dying
down— all ready! You sure?

Sara is thin grey smoke and glowing ash if she was ever here.
She won't mind being cooked on. Now I've one last duty— and
the toughest. Back in the kitchen is an item I've saved so far. I
pounce on it. I'm holding— my first impulse is just to describe
what I wish you could see, the yellowed paper fragment, thin
as the *gashenshi* gauge Tomiko uses only for important work.
But this is spotted with mildew and snowing bits of itself at the
corners and fold and showing way too much age to be abused,
left lying around. She should've known better, I thought. Had
it 'conserved', not tucked away in a piece of her own gash A4

as poor protection to be found by— wrong word. Never lost. Always been there. For some reason at the nth time of looking, the last, probably because it *was* the last, I laid flat an ancient, well pretty ancient, document and nothing to get excited about if you're me. Hidden in this dump of drafts never sent and random replies and her worst thoughts and to be honest a lot of senseless, wandering wackcrap from her drunk days, is just— something. To Dr George Buller, it starts off, Master's Lodgings, St Clement's College, Oxford. The author is Sir Louis Quarrie. Actual writing by Thomasina's husband when only his name on deeds or bills is thought to exist. When made? Who knows? Except reading between the lines, Sir Louis, has got lucky by now, mopped up his inheritance and married The Peerless Girl.

And it's a time bomb, he made. You won't get the significance first off, of material that if come across by Josh, (I've no way of knowing he did) was 'more bloody Thomasina— just what the world needs!' And for me, realness was as important as contents— to begin with. The script's near illegible so try and decipher a whole sentence and your eyes do their normal flick round the screen for the translation. Except it's not on screen and there isn't one, so you don't bother. You turn over. No reverse side. And yet Sara had this in her possession when she died and the sheet of A4 used as wrapping for a priceless item, a bit of padding—

—is her note. A responsible suicide, she'd left one. It just wasn't what we were looking for and not in the place everybody looked.

How did it happen? It is vivid as a day picked from childhood... more so, since mine seemed to slip by on a current of sunlit Alice Liddell afternoons. But for now spring had only just arrived and along rural dual-carriageways was putting on a festival of catkins, sloe blossom and, lesser blooms whose names

*would not have eluded Fleur. She and a doll-like Eurwen had
shrunk in my rear view mirror and were far behind me, while
ahead, I thought, lay joy of another order. To Heystrete Hall,
to echo Pepys who in June 1668, had fewer words to say about
it than the highly relished 'Bristol Milk,' later responsible for
his insensibility. I'd taken this road once as a new graduate
student: a ninety-mile jaunt from Oxford into Wiltshire that
changed my life. This is what I set down then, a modest scene-
setting that my editor at Pythian took against and excised.
('So-o History sweetie! Could we have just <u>you</u> arrived— <u>your</u>
impressions that first time?')*

   'The Quarrie name, its roots in the Old French word 'quarre'
meaning squarely-built and possibly implying stoutness, was
synonymous with Heystrete for four hundred years. (Although
in an earlier reference, Matilda Relicta atte Quarrie is recorded
carrying on her late husband's glove trade at Chippenham
during the fifteenth century.) The Hall on its present site began
as a plain, timber-framed yeoman's house of the 1600s but
during the next century was embellished with so much local,
curd-coloured limestone, so many loggias, bays and broken
pediments that…'*

   *And so on. Today the door is opened by a teenager in a soiled
dress; the fleshy, fussy little man she summons to meet me is
new and from no aristocratic stock either. All around us the
familiar old Hall is being dragged from its winter dream. In a
month the first visitors' eager push will be accompanied by
injurious light… Curtain rods are being tested, carpets
groomed, ormolu tables unclothed and glass in numerous
cabinets must sparkle for the Easter arrivals… and is why a
space has to been found for me elsewhere. Cramped and low,
in contrast to the Long Gallery, Rose Saloon and Card Room
along our route, the Comptroller's den is surprisingly frigid,
even after out-of-doors. I shiver as though in the grip of*

premonition. Yet before me lies, in all likelihood, hours of frustration as a fan heater wafts away anything not anchored down and I dip my bucket into a dry well. Littered with broken pens, embellished with likenesses of a wife and children, it is to here the reeking hoard of paper, jottings and missives, newly ripped from beside a water tank, is delivered... and fills the desktop. In the distance a volunteer workforce prattles while a dozen vacuum cleaners drone like bagpipes. I yearn to begin. Yet the little man lingers to assure me of Thomasina's enormous value to them, the strengthening stream of fee-paying admirers she lures in... that she personally has eradicated fungi the size of dinner plates sprung from oak timber, banished much worm and even relined in their original ecru silk the hangings of the Chinoiserie Bedroom. And though politeness requires, 'Ah-h! I'm so glad,' I think this: as my revision of A First *is nearing completion, has another rich vein of Thomasina been broken into? An accident of maintenance...*

He departs. And it is only a short interval, before I seize upon:

Heystrete Tues Jany 26

My Dear Sir

Thank you for yours I Rec'd yesterday & am much obliged for yo amiable service and advice. I was please'd to return the mare to Ruben Smith & say it is not want'd. The fellow is drunk most times & this afor noon. I have spoke to him but he does not recall. John Jenks came t'day at about three oClock to say the old man John Jenks his father dyed who hd the Life Lease at Benger by whose death the property there descends to me. I am very sory for it. It is a fine property worth 1000l. You must soon wish me good fortune of it.

Our friend Lady Nairne is to come to us tomorrow. The house is all in uproar as there is a vile smoke from the chimneys *but I do not think Lady Nairne will be fobb'd off with soot.*

The hound Faithful has dyed. My Lady Quarrie sends her love to you & my Ant.

I am Your affectinate nephew etc

L. Q.

Of course, it's a fake, Yori. He's read it through once, twice— or maybe not? Again. Realises what it says but also what it means. And even then, taken in before by the products of Glenn Hughes' invention— simmering at how often— he's still got doubts.

Honestly? I've got no doubt – and I'm back there with Sara, sitting through another rerun of a rancid memory. Hoovers drone on and volunteer oldies try to spike their boredom with jokes. Muffled giggles follow sudden crashes or banging doors. Endless offers of tea are made. Of course she's gone over all this before in her journal. No mention of the *objet trouve* though. She turned that into a poem or song or other ornament to hold up and distract the audience with. And her description was a lie. (Like I'm the young Archie Kao that I'm not, but much better for you to be imagining handsome him than plain me as we went along, yeah?) Now here's the original scene. I admire how she cuts it— just at the frame where one mouldy sheet of paper is set aside and her good work, her whole future, *shattered into smithereens*. Because the well wasn't dry, was it Sara? More like poisoned. Sir Louis Quarrie's wandering scrawl re: horses, chimneys, dead dogs and peasants had, on second thoughts or no thought, been left to stick in Heystrete like a sting. And was real. She knew. I know. Read it and learn how a modern Sir Louis' fortune would've stayed safe from Casino Pigalle and any number of Linda Darnell lookalikes. Never a gambler, the 'wager' he'd won with— who? John Cane and the Honourable Somebody (I could look them up only their page is already burnt) wasn't so much a bet as a racing certainty. Thomasina hadn't needed to shine keeping her term at the University. A great brain didn't need dazzling. Because 'duped' Dr Buller had always been Family, a poor relation like Yori, OK, and along a weak branch that history'd lost sight of, yet Family. And the proof was stolen by Sara Meredith, teaser-out of the Thomasina legend, architect of The Peerless Girl and project manager to a million bettered lives from Manchester to Manila to Mombasa to— wherever. Which made the entire Thomasina story and each testament to her suspect, a jumping-on the bandwagon of a bright child that revelled in Star Attraction billing in a country pub. A celebrity. And smart enough, behind her pretty façade, to take everybody's measure, including the ale-drinkers, and parrot back all she picked up in her father's tap room till she managed to break out and become *famous for just being me.*

Even Fleur couldn't have guessed the size of the question mark hanging over 'Tom Swift'. Nobody knew except Sara— and now Yori— that she'd removed the evidence but not destroyed it. She'd come clean to the future but never told. Only one quarter of suicides ever do tell because I've checked, (*Kuso* – what are those, mammoth's footsteps pounding on my ceiling joists?) and so Sara had spared The Peerless Girl. Not herself, though. Like the honourable Japanese she turned out to be she walked her desire line on blistered feet. Thumpthumpthump is getting louder. Outside, dolt, now! – that *is* Libby you can hear on the stairs – and use what you've got in your hand to feed the fire.

Appendices

A

The Murderer At The Fair

In 1961 it was a Londoner called James Hanratty who came to Rhyl after shooting a man dead and raping his girlfriend. Hanratty like many a drifter before him got work at the fair, on the Dodgems, no questions asked. Dodgems would have been his choice— the cars with the trapped inside girls, having to be unjammed back into circulation, Hanratty perched on the flanges, a ready stream of dirty jokes. First day, Hanratty met up with some 'like minded individual'. A vicious loner straight off the bus, where else could he meet up with a 'like-minded individual' but in good old Rhyl, already on its way to being the sink-hole of north Wales? His new friend was Terry Evans who let him sleep on his sofa that night and gave him a pair of shoes. Well that was one story. Another is that at the time of the murders, Hanratty was already tucked up in a Rhyl guest house, Ingledene a grim sounding bolt-hole. A dozen assorted Rhyl residents could vouch for him. If you're charged with murder this is definitely a better story than a stint on the Dodgems and a night on a couch. Which makes it all the odder that Hanratty didn't try it out on the police in the first place. But he didn't. Perhaps there's something about witnesses from Rhyl. They weren't called to testify. None of them. So Hanratty – though he must have been innocent, mustn't he? – was hanged, as they were just about to stop doing back then. He was the sort that bad luck followed around like a stink— which is why he became the eighth last person to get the death penalty. But wait a bit. Once DNA was discovered, surely that could settle the score? So there's an appeal goes in on Hanratty's behalf. It failed. How? DNA at the scene of the crime was— James Hanratty's. So Hanratty may or may not have worked at Ocean Beach. And a man called Terry might have given him a new pair of shoes, while in London, 200 miles away, someone else, that one in a billion match with his DNA was committing murder. Or not.

B

The Kicker

The history of Rhyl's riddled with plans and schemes that went pear-shaped. From attractions that bankrupted everybody involved to the small-scale shaggy dog stories. Or shaggy bird.

Reginald Cobb was a comedian, singer and acrobat. You could find him at the bottom of the bill in music halls up and down Britain. He surfaces in Rhyl in 1902, one half of Reggie and Roma, a musical duo. 1903 has him back, solo, at The Pier Amphitheatre, as The H'archbishop of Humour. By 1904, Cobb's living alone minus his Roma at an address in Butterton Road. It's here, according to local legend, he somehow got hold of and started to train a young ostrich. It was called The Kicker.

At first a backyard was big enough to keep the bird in. Training on the beach often drew a small crowd and Cobb could take round the hat for pennies. There would be a bit of added knockabout when The Kicker tried to eat the coins. Cobb was always short of money and ran up bills at a local corn-merchant as The Kicker's appetite grew. But the act seemed like a real prospect. The bird could soon 'do a simple dance with wings outstretched in elegant fashion'. It also dribbled a football. The Kicker became a local celebrity and Reggie Cobb had hopes of a spot at the newly opened Queens Palace. He told people it had been promised him.

On a Sunday morning in June, 1904, Cobb and The Kicker were on their pitch and by ten o'clock were into their act. Then it all went wrong. Perhaps it was the church bells. Maybe someone brought along a dog that The Kicker hated.

The ostrich stopped listening to Cobb's instructions and started making dives into the crowd. A big man in a straw boater (another of The Kicker's pet hates) shouted he'd been pecked. Women screamed, children yelled and in trying to control the bird, Cobb got a blow to the head. Some thought The Kicker had done it. Others said the man in boater hat had punched him. It must've taken a superhuman effort for poor Cobb to get the ostrich back to its pen, a good two hundred metres from the beach. But he did. And he fed and watered it and then seems to have sat down in the corner of the yard. He spent long hours here anyway, keeping The Kicker company so if any of his neighbours looked over they wouldn't have thought it out of the ordinary. Only when it was going dark did somebody check and discover poor Reggie Cobb stone dead.

People always want to know what happened to The Kicker. That's the funny thing about the story— you can't find out. They say in Rhyl that the owner of the house just opened the yard gate and let the bird walk off. Rhyl was even smaller then and the countryside a lot nearer. Perhaps it made for the hills.

But it was a six-foot-high black and white ostrich.

You'll find Reggie Cobb's overgrown grave in the churchyard at St George, a village 6.5 kilometres 'backaways' from the coast. His brother-in-law and sister Anne Foulkes are listed as poultry dealers there.

C

How Sato Tomiko Lost His Name

My father's never married. He returned to Japan to the small property his parents left, and is a poorly-paid teacher of calligraphy for his living. His own art lies in smallness and obscurity, designed to duck even the possibility of reward. For instance, when he learned a painter from the ancient city of Kochi (Sato Tomiko) was being mentioned as a notable practitioner in ink, he took immediate action. To his most promising pupil he gave away his name. This isn't quite as weird as it sounds, not for a Japanese. The great Hokusai himself did the same and then faced with the commercial success of 'The Floating World', was tempted to barter it back. Search for my father, any method, and you'll come up with a smug-faced *young* man from Osaka, but recently moved to San Francisco and becoming collectable— it says. You'll also find an image of him. Prominent ears and unchipped teeth. No scar.

D

No Such Thing As Good Luck

I did find her.

As I told Tess, some things shouldn't connect. Sara, for example, shouldn't have trusted in Kim Tighe's 'talent' or let her latch on in the first place. Where was the scholar in her? You only had to look at this shell of a person to ask yourself how likely is it? Tomiko's sayings make more sense. No wonder I wanted to forget the woman last seen running from Avonside with money in her pocket, fear in her wake, wearing black and totally right too.

Here's my Kim Tighe file:

1. A photograph taken at an outdoor party. In the crowd is Eurwen next to a dog-suited person, identity unknown, and someone blonde and familiar. Stare at it for long enough and you're left in no doubt. The red-haired girl and the blonde know each other.

2. The newspaper story of a female body found in an empty building off the Parade. (It turned out to be one of Clive Upton's properties). Her age was put at 'around sixty'. An appeal was made for next of kin or anyone else with information to contact the police without delay. Date? Well the body had been there for some time. A spree with Sara's money would be my guess.

3. Two more snippets from the following week reporting the body as Kim Tighe's, aged, it is believed, 35. Cause of death? Drug toxicity.

4. A crude painting of a young bikini-clad girl, the caption is 'This little smasher once gave passersby the come-on above an

391

arcade near the corner of Sydenham Avenue, the edge of the funfair—' More text beneath carries over from a previous page and reads 'and nobody's sure what the name Rhyl actually means. Tourists, when there were any, must have thought it was just one more Welsh word they were unable to say because of lacking vowels.' The book-plate had been so faded it was a wonder Kim Tighe's still recognisable as the face of Old Rhyl.

Painted Kim Tighe is disturbing— too pitiful, too scabby, too real. But when I finally did ask, Eurwen claimed they'd never met.

Acknowledgments

The lines from *Book Ends* are quoted with the generous permission of Tony Harrison.

Celebrity is quoted with the generosity of lyricist Shane Renton Mellor.

Extracts from the libretto of *Peter Grimes* (Benjamin Britten/Montagu Slater) appear with the permission of Boosey & Hawkes Music Publishers Ltd.

My agent at MBA, Laura Longrigg, has been an unfailing support while this novel was in the making. Susie Wild, my editor at Parthian, took over and brought a clear, fresh look to the product. I'm grateful to both and all at Parthian.

THE MISSING WOMAN and other stories

Carole Burns

ALIX NATHAN

THE FLIGHT OF SARAH BATTLE

PARTH

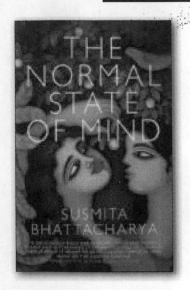

THE NORMAL STATE OF MIND

SUSMITA BHATTACHARYA

CARLY HOLMES

www.parthianbooks.com